'Twas the Fright Before Christmas in Deathlehem

An Anthology of Holiday Horrors for Charity

'Twas the Fright Before Christmas in Deathlehem

An Anthology of Holiday Horrors for Charity

Edited by
Michael J. Evans
and
Harrison Graves

A
Grinning Skull Press
Publication

Bridgewater, MA

'Twas the Fright Before Christmas in Deathlehem
Compilation Copyright © 2022 Grinning Skull Press

"The Fine Print" copyright ©2022 Janet Alcorn
"Black Solstice" copyright ©2022 Dane Cobain
"The Chimney" copyright ©2022 R.A. Clarke
"Convicted" copyright ©2022 Mike Marcus
"Last Supper" copyright © 2020 Liam Hogan. Originally published *Death Throes Webzine: Horrific Holiday Edition*, December 9, 2020. Reprinted here with permission from the author.
"Part and Parcel" copyright ©2022 Nathan D. Ludwig
"Pond Person" copyright ©2022 Evan Baughfman
"Not a Creature was Stirring" copyright © 2022 D.J. Kozlowski
"Silent Scream" copyright ©2022 C.L. Hart
"Christmas in Four Parts" copyright ©2021 Lisa H. Owens. Original published in *Journeys*, the Writer's Journal Blog, Elaine Marie Carnegie-Padgett & Kerri Jesmer, eds., October 23, 2021. Reprinted here with permission from the author.
"End of the Line" copyright ©2022 James Jenkins
"The Yule Lads are Coming" copyright ©2022 Villimey Mist
"Spirit of the Season" copyright ©2022 Paul O'Neill.
"A Christmas Snuff Story" copyright ©2022 Dino Parenti
"Little Helpers" copyright ©2022 Matt Starr
"That Christmas Feeling" copyright © 2022 D.S. Ullery
"Mad Shadow" copyright ©2022 Bam Barrow

The Skull logo with stylized lettering and the interior graphic was created for Grinning Skull Press by Dan Moran, http://dan-moran-art.com/.
Cover designed by Jeffrey Kosh, http://jeffreykosh.wix.com/jeffreykoshgraphics.
Interior graphic by The Creative Factory, Romania.

ISBN-13: 978-1-947227-83-5 (paperback)
ISBN: 978-1-947227-84-2 (e-book)

DEDICATION

As always, to the Staff of
The Elizabeth Glaser Pediatric AIDS Foundation,
who are working toward a world where
no mother, child, or family is devastated
by HIV and AIDS.

ACKNOWLEDGMENTS

We would like to thank the authors who, year after year, join us through their contributions to help fund research to battle a virus that has affected the lives of so many.

TABLE OF CONTENTS

GHOULTIDE GREETINGS

Well, another year has come and gone, and we're still here. I mean that collectively, in like we haven't been wiped off the face of the earth. Yet. And even though outwardly it seems like the world has returned to some semblance of normal, it really hasn't. COVID is still a shadow that hangs over us, and while we may have vaccinations against it, and boosters, is there still a chance that some variant will come along that is able to bypass all the protections our bodies have in place? The fact that there are still folks masking up in public seems to indicate that fear is present. Is it that ever-present shadow that continues to dampen the holiday spirit? I mean, around here, a majority of yards that, pre-pandemic, used to deck the halls, so to speak, are still as barren as a post-apocalyptic landscape. Or are folks still reeling from the loss endured during the past few year? Has it scarred the soul so deeply that it's taking people longer to recover?

I'm of the school that believes folks are still adapting to all that was lost. And that's something I can relate to as well. Not that I lost anybody as a result of the pandemic, but I have lost loved ones, as most people have, to other causes. If you've been with us since the beginning, back in 2013, when we published the very first Deathlehem anthology, you'll know that this anthol-

1

ogy series was start out of a sense of loss. I lost my oldest brother just before Thanksgiving, my sister New Year's Eve, and my mother and father shortly after New Year's Eve. And while I miss them all, it is the loss of my mother and sister that is still as painful today as the day I lost them, and I know that folks handle grief differently, but it wouldn't surprise me to find that's a big reason for the lack of Merry, Happy, Ho-ho this year. That, and the current economic situation, but I'm not getting into that.

And it's because of that sense of loss that I can totally relate to our opening story, Janet Alcorn's "The Fine Print," which deals with a grieving father mourning the loss of his daughter on Christmas Day. It's a moving story, and you might be inclined to think that this one will have a happy ending, but you need to remember that this is Deathlehem, and there are no happy endings ever. Unless it's for the monster.

And let's see… What other horrors will you encounter when you turn the page? Hmmmm… Let's see….

In Dane Cobain's "Black Solstice," you'll meet a family preparing for the holiday and a possible visit from… But wait… That can't happen because he doesn't exist. He only exists in stories parents tell their children so they'll behave. But little do they know…

There are a couple of lowlifes hanging around, up to now good, as usual. It's a case of the bag guys getting their just desserts, but in Mike Marcus's "Convicted," Ray isn't really bad. Just desperate. And in C.L. Hart's "Silent Scream," the guy… Yeah, he's a bad apple, but does he really deserve what happens to him? And speaking of lowlifes… What do you do with a man who kills one of Santa's reindeers? In Matt Starr's "Little Helpers," you'll meet a very non-Hallmark Santa and his elves, who want justice for justice for Dasher.

And what's a holiday without food? In Liam Hogan's "Last Supper," we'll see that an act of charity was not done out of the goodness of the host's heart. In "Part and Parcel," Nathan D. Ludwig serves up a smorgasbord of treats to ring in the holiday season.

We'll even take you behind the scenes of a holiday movie shoot in Dino Parenti's "A Christmas Snuff Story." Who knew elves were into such things?

Well, I guess I've rambled on long enough, so I'll let you get to it. We hope you enjoy your visit to our humble little town.

Ghoultide Greetings from
us to you,
Michael J. Evans and the staff
at Grinning Skull Press

T̶HE F̶INE P̶RINT
Janet Alcorn

O̶n a foggy Christmas Eve in Stockton, California, Josh Fogarty fell to his knees on his daughter's grave and howled. It'd been nearly a year since Hannah had found Emmie dead in her bed on Christmas morning, but the wound felt as raw as if his heart had been gouged out of his chest five minutes ago.

Josh—Pastor Josh to the youth of Brookside Community Church and to, well, pretty much everybody—dropped back on his haunches, covered his face with clammy hands, and sobbed. "God must've needed another angel," Nikki Kurwood told him one Sunday morning after church as she handed her own angel a juice box. "Everything happens for a reason," Nikki's husband, Tyler, had said as he put an arm around Josh and patted his shoulder. His boss, Pastor Gabe, had spent hours trying to comfort and counsel him. Unlike the Kurwoods, Gabe knew a thing or two about suffering. His daughter, his miracle baby, had spent months in a coma from encephalitis, and then his wife had dropped dead on Christmas morning. Gabe told him, "It'll get easier with time."

It hadn't.

Josh still led the youth group at Brookside. Still preached sermons and hosted lock-ins and led mission trips to feed the homeless in downtown Stockton. Still read the Bible every day and prayed every day and carried on every day because the kids were counting on him, and he was their role model, and he was called to lead them to Christ.

But Emmie would never giggle with her friends at a lock-in or ladle soup in a shelter. She would never walk down the aisle. Never hold a baby of her own. He imagined her doing all those things and sobbed harder.

"Dude, are you okay?"

The voice, a man's, came from behind him. He straightened, newly aware of the tears and snot on his face and the damp grass soaking through the knees of his sweatpants. He clambered to his feet, mopped his face with a soggy tissue, and turned toward the voice.

The man looked a few years older than Josh, maybe early 30s, with short, dark brown hair in a side part, a goatee, and thick eyebrows. He wore skinny jeans, a plaid flannel shirt, and a fleece Patagonia vest with a red and white Santa hat perched on his head. Tech bro chic except for the hat, but there weren't a lot of tech bros in Stockton. Stockton was the Pittsburg of Northern California—gritty and industrial but with better weather and more crime. A lot more crime. Without meaning to, Josh let his hand stray to his wallet.

The man laughed, flashing perfect white teeth. "I'm not going to mug you. I was just out for a walk and heard you crying. I'm Nick, Nick Deville." He held out his hand.

Fear not, for I am with you. Besides, did it matter anyway? *So what if I get mugged?* The forbidden thought followed right behind. *So what if I get killed?*

Josh wiped his hands on his sweatpants and shook Nick's hand. "Josh."

The man nodded toward the grave and its shiny head-stone. "She was your daughter?"

Daughter. The word twisted in the raw wound in his chest, digging flesh, scraping bone. He swallowed another howl of misery and choked out, "Yeah."

"I'm sorry. Children shouldn't go before their parents. It's not right."

It's not right. No one at church had ever said that to him. A few had said it at the funeral—his brother, two of his un-churched friends—but at church, the rule was: God doesn't make mistakes. Everything happens according to His perfect will, and apparently, He had needed another angel.

"No, it's not right." A tiny sliver of Josh's pain eased with those words. He pulled out another tissue—he kept his pockets full of them—and blew his nose.

An awkward silence fell between the two men and hung there like the tule fog that settled over the Central Valley this time of year. It might burn off today. The branches of the old oak above Emmie's grave had sharpened, no longer blurred by mist.

"Do you come here often?"

Nick's words jolted Josh back to attention. The sentence sounded like a pick-up line from an old movie.

"Every Saturday." Sometimes other days, too. Sometimes every day.

"Man, that's rough." Nick took a few steps closer and studied the headstone. "She died on Christmas? That's even rougher."

"Tell me about it." Josh was startled by the almost-snarky response. It sounded like something he would have said to a friend before... Before those friends had stopped calling or inviting Josh out for coffee or a hike. Before they'd looked away from him at the men's group meetings. Before they'd left the seats next to him empty.

"Why don't you tell me about it? Come walk with me. You look like you could use someone to talk to."

He *could* use someone to talk to. Was desperate for it, even. Not for the grief counselor his church had sent him to, a middle-aged guy lobbing scripture and platitudes across a polished desk littered with pictures of his kids. He was desperate for honest conversation where he didn't have to be Pastor Josh, the Lord's earthly representative, the shepherd of teenage souls. Where he could just be Josh, bereaved father.

Broken man.

Suddenly he wanted to hug this stranger, to grip him tight around the shoulders and sob out his pain on that Patagonia vest. But hugging some random guy who showed up at his daughter's grave would be...weird. Maybe the guy was weird. Maybe he was gay and trolled cemeteries to pick up vulnerable, grief-stricken men.

"Dude, I'm not hitting on you."

Josh blinked. Did everything he thought show on his face, or was this guy just really good at reading people? "Sorry. I'm not used to spilling my guts to strangers."

"Most guys aren't. Do you have a friend you can spill your guts to?"

His lips started to form Hannah's name. He pressed them together to hold it back.

"Your wife was your best friend, huh? A lot of marriages break up after a child dies."

Josh's pressed-together lips fell open. How did—?

"Oh, come on. If she's not here at the grave with you, you must've split."

"Yeah, we did."

"Sorry, man. That sucks."

"Yeah, it does."

"Tell you what. How about we walk over to Denny's and you let old Nick buy you breakfast." He pointed across the street and down two blocks to where the yellow Denny's sign provided the only pop of color amid the gray fog and rundown neighborhood. "You look like you're freezing."

As Nick said the words, Josh felt the cold for the first

9

time. He'd come to the cemetery straight from the gym, his workout pants and *Not of This World* t-shirt soaked with sweat and now damp from the fog. He shivered and followed Nick out of the cemetery.

"Sit anywhere you want," a middle-aged waitress called from behind the counter. She waved a hand at the nearly-empty dining room. "We're not very busy this morning."

Of course not. Most people would be home with their families on Christmas Eve. The restaurant was quiet, no clatter of plates or buzz of conversation. Just Mariah Carey singing, "All I Want for Christmas is You," over tinny speakers in the ceiling. Josh's eyes burned. All he wanted for Christmas was Emmie.

The breakfast rush consisted of two elderly men sitting at opposite ends of the counter and two middle-aged couples at booths near the door. Josh followed Nick past an artificial Christmas tree and a sign advertising the Denny's holiday menu to a round booth in the corner furthest from the door. He pulled his cell phone out of the pocket of his sweatpants, set it on the table, and sat.

The waitress brought them coffee and menus. Josh scanned the breakfast options without interest. The restaurant smelled like bacon and eggs, which would have made his mouth water before… Now it reminded him of weekend mornings with his family. His former family.

When the waitress returned, Nick ordered pumpkin pancakes off the holiday menu. Josh pointed to his mug. "Just coffee, thanks."

After she left, Nick said, "Bro, you're a mess."

"Yeah." Josh cradled his mug, concentrating on the warmth seeping into his cold fingers as he put on his game face. "It's my first Christmas without her, and she died on Christmas. It's hard, but I can handle it with the Lord's—"

"Doesn't look like you're handling it." Nick regarded him with an unblinking stare. His eyes were bright blue, an odd contrast with his almost-black hair and eyebrows. His eyes looked unnatural, like a Hollywood actor wearing colored contact lenses.

"I just need time."

"You need more than time. You need a friend, someone you can be real with. I bet you've been faking it with everybody, haven't you?"

"Yeah." Another sliver of pain eased with the admission. "How'd you know?"

Nick chuckled. "You're sitting here in a Christian t-shirt and no jacket when it's forty-five degrees outside, talking to me about God after I found you bawling your eyes out on your daughter's grave."

"So?"

Nick gave an exaggerated sigh. "I don't have to be Sherlock Holmes to deduce a few things from that state of affairs. One..." He raised one long finger. "...you're trying to maintain appearances with the shirt and the fitness routine and the God talk." He raised another finger. "Two, you're too wrecked to dress for, or probably even to notice, the weather." He raised a third finger. "And three, you're alone on what's probably gonna be the second- or third-worst day of your life. Christmas Eve and the anniversary of your kid's death. That, my friend, is fucked up."

Josh winced. He didn't spend much time with unbelievers, and, at least in his church, believers didn't drop f-bombs. He should take advantage of this time with Nick to show him God's love, maybe plant a seed...

The waitress appeared with a plate of food for Nick and a coffee refill for Josh. After she left, Nick picked up his fork along with the previous thread of conversation.

"If you were honest with people about how you're doing, they'd be there for you." He popped a forkful of pancake in his mouth and regarded Josh with that blue-eyed stare.

Josh's church was full of good people, caring people. Any one of them would pray with him or invite him to Christmas dinner. Wouldn't they? Or would they pelt him with platitudes and flee if he showed them the hideousness, the obscenity of his pain? He thought of Job, abandoned by his friends, alone with nothing but his pain. "They shouldn't have to comfort me. I'm a pastor. It's my job to lead them, to be an example of—"

"Of what? Surrendering to the Lord in suffering like Job did?" Nick straightened, and his blue eyes glowed from under the fluffy, white brim of his Santa hat. He spoke in a parody of a preacher's voice. "'The Lord gave, and the Lord has taken away; blessed be the name of the Lord.'"

The hairs on Josh's arms rose. *How many times has he read my mind?*

"It's okay to have needs. It's okay to have wants. Desires

even. You're allowed to be human."

"I know that, but—"

"Tell me what you really feel, Joshua. I'm a stranger. You don't owe me anything, and I won't judge you." His eyes, those x-ray eyes, never left Josh's face as he forked up another bite of pancake, chewed, and swallowed.

And the wound Josh had been patching over for the last year split open and words gushed out like blood. Words he'd never said to anyone, not even himself. "It hurts. It hurts so bad, and nothing helps. The pain never stops. Never. And I pray all the time. All. The. Time. One time I prayed all day. I sat on my living room floor and prayed literally all day. And you know what I felt? Nothing. Nothing but pain."

Josh wrapped his hands tight around his mug. It shook in his hands until coffee splashed over the rim and onto his t-shirt and burned his belly.

"What did your wife do when you did that?"

"We'd separated by then."

"How long did you stay together after your daughter died?"

Josh flinched. No one ever said his daughter *died*. She *passed away* or *went to be with the Lord* or some other euphemism that minimized his loss. Minimized his pain. "Six months. It wasn't her fault. She tried to get me to open up just like you're doing, but I shut her out."

"You blamed her, didn't you?"

"No, of course not." Josh looked up from his mug and into those eyes, those unblinking eyes that looked inside him and made lying seem pointless. "Yes. Yes, I did. She was her mother, she was home with her all day every day. How could something be so terribly wrong and she didn't see it?"

"Did you tell her that?"

"Of course not. I never told anyone that."

"Not even God?"

"Not even God."

"Did you really believe it was her fault?"

Josh watched the old man at the far end of the counter drink his coffee and chat with the waitress. Some country version of "Silver Bells" played from the ceiling speakers. He forced himself to meet Nick's eyes. "No."

Nick didn't respond. He scraped up the last of his pancakes, set his fork on his plate, and regarded Josh with his piercing blue stare. Waiting. Knowing.

More words spilled out. "It was my fault. It was my job to protect my family, to keep them safe. It's a man's most important job, and I...failed."

Nick patted his hand, just a brief pat, nothing creepy. "No, you didn't. The coroner said your daughter died in her sleep from an undiagnosed heart defect. How is that your fault?"

Josh froze. He hadn't told Nick how his daughter had died. Was he a counselor sent by someone in his church who knew the story? "How do you know—"

The waitress appeared then. She swept away Nick's empty plate, refilled their coffees, and deposited the check in the middle of the table. Nick took it without looking at it. "You aren't responsible for your daughter's death. Sometimes things just happen. Sure, there's a reason, like a bad heart, but it isn't anyone's fault. You didn't make her that way."

Again the hairs on Josh's arms rose, and for the first time in who-knew-how-long, he felt something besides pain. He was afraid of this weird man with his creepy eyes and Santa hat and uncanny ability to know things. Josh pushed his chair back and made to stand.

"Wait." Nick didn't raise his voice, but the word was a command nonetheless. "One more question, and I'll let you go."

Let me go? Did he mean that figuratively—or literally?

"What do you want more than anything else?"

Josh's fear was swamped by a fresh wave of familiar pain. "I want my daughter back, but that's not poss—"

"Doesn't Luke, chapter one, verse thirty-seven say, 'For with God nothing shall be impossible?'"

"Yeah, but that's—"

"Figurative? Doesn't your church believes the Bible is the literal Word of God?"

"We do, but—"

"But… ?"

Josh sagged in his seat as he spoke the words he'd never let himself acknowledge before. "Sometimes God says no."

No. No no no no no no no.

The coldest, emptiest syllable in the English language.

No.

"But I say yes."

Josh straightened and regarded Nick. Same piercing eyes. Steady. Confident.

"What are you talking about? She's dead."

"Oh, ye of little faith. Don't you believe your own holy book? The widow of Nain's son? Jairus's daughter? Lazarus?

And don't you teach your parishioners that God works miracles every day?"

"Who are you?"

Nick gave him a smug smile and touched the white pom-pom dangling from his hat. "Call me Santa. You know, St. Nick. It's close enough. I can grant Christmas wishes. And I can make people live again. Or not."

"Oh, for—" Josh mastered himself. He'd thought this guy actually cared, but he was just some nut job. He stood, snatched at his phone on the table, and knocked it onto the tile floor. He picked it up and stuffed it in his pocket. "Thanks for the coffee."

He made it a few steps from the booth before Nick's voice stopped him. "I'll prove it."

Josh turned. What stunt would this nutball pull? Would he whip out a pack of tarot cards or a Ouija board or some other occult prop?

"See that guy at the end of the counter?" Nick jerked his chin toward the old man. From where they sat, Josh could see half the guy's face as he sipped his coffee. He looked about seventy, with grizzled stubble and a reddish nose. *He looks more like Santa than you do.*

"Yeah."

"It's time for him to meet his maker." Nick held his hand out, palm up, then snapped it into a fist. The mug fell from the man's hand and shattered on the floor, the sound clearly audible over the Christmas music. He toppled sideways out of his seat, and his head landed in the pool of spilled coffee with a wet smack.

The waitress screamed, "Call nine-one-one," to no one in particular and ran to the man.

Josh started to yank his phone from his pocket, but the other man at the counter was already dialing.

Nick spoke into his ear. "I can make your daughter live just as easily as I made that man die."

Josh skittered back several steps, but he didn't leave. Instead, he stared at Nick's hand, now open and resting at his side. Limp. Harmless. "You... You killed that man. How...?"

"Does it matter?"

I can make your daughter live. He could have Emmie back. Hold her, hear her laugh, watch her open presents. He still had her presents, the ones she should have opened last year, stacked in his closet beside a new pink tricycle with streamers and a shiny silver bell. "What's the catch? She comes back, but I die like that guy? Or she's all messed up, like—"

"No, none of that *Pet Sematary* shit. She'll be healthy and whole. She'll live a normal life, and you won't die like that guy."

"Then what's the catch?"

Nick regarded him with those creepy blue eyes, and this time they glowed like the flame of a gas burner. "Another child has to die in her place."

Josh didn't remember the drive home. He didn't remember climbing the stairs to his second-floor apartment or stripping off his clothes or showering or crawling under his secondhand comforter and falling asleep. He woke, disoriented, in his cold, dark bedroom, with the foul taste of sleep and stale coffee in his mouth. He checked his phone. 7:48 p.m. He'd slept all day.

A crack sliced across his phone's screen protector. When had that happened?

And then Josh remembered. The phone falling off the table. The old man toppling off his stool. The ambulance careening into the Denny's parking lot, siren wailing, lights flashing off the fog.

Nick's parting words as they left the restaurant. *I'll contact you tonight in case you change your mind.*

And before that: *Another child has to die in her place.*

Josh had backed away from Nick, shaking his head like a wet dog, then turned and ran the three blocks to his car.

Now he tried to pull himself together. Maybe Nick was a doctor and he recognized the signs of a heart attack in the old man and timed his demonstration to match his collapse. Josh had been watching Nick's fist. Nick could have waited 'til the old man started to fall, then pulled his little stunt.

But why?

Why would a total stranger play such a cruel trick? Josh had no enemies as far as he knew, definitely none who hated him enough to hire someone to follow him to the cemetery and pretend to have supernatural powers.

Maybe he was cracking up, finally losing it after a year of trying so hard to keep going, keep doing the Lord's work. Had his mind finally snapped from the strain of… What had Nick called it?

Faking it with everyone.

He got out of bed and rinsed his mouth. He pulled on a

clean pair of jeans and a polo shirt with "Brookside CC" embroidered on the pocket, then slipped his feet into a pair of canvas loafers. He stuffed his jeans pocket with a wad of fresh tissues and picked his sweatpants off the top of a pile of dirty laundry. He examined the grass stains on the knees, green smears against the gray fabric. He picked up the *Not of This World* t-shirt and touched the coffee stain. Still damp. Still real.

He hadn't imagined the morning. He hadn't imagined Nick. Which left only one possibility.

But he couldn't go there. No human could kill someone by clenching his fist. Hadn't he taught his youth group kids that people who trafficked in the supernatural—fortune tellers, tarot card readers, Wiccans—were at best deluded and at worst mocking God?

No, the supernatural wasn't real.

Don't you believe your own holy book?

Don't you teach your parishioners that God works miracles every day?

That was different. That was God, and He didn't strike down old men in the middle of their Grand Slam breakfasts.

Josh's phone buzzed. He yelped out loud and snatched it from the nightstand. He had a text from a number he didn't recognize.

> Have you changed your mind? If you want your daughter back, click this link.

Had he given Nick his cell number? No, but he didn't think much about that.

If you want your daughter back

If you want your daughter back

If you want your daughter back

And he could see her, as clearly as he could see the pile of week-old laundry under his bedroom window: Emmie sitting under a twelve-foot Christmas tree trimmed in silver and gold, wearing the red velvet dress Hannah had bought her to wear to church on Christmas morning. The dress she was buried in.

The dress, crusted with mud and hanging in tatters from her pale, decaying body...

No, Nick had promised, none of that *Pet Sematary* stuff. She'd be healthy and whole. Her face would light with joy as she unwrapped her presents, the book of Bible stories and the doll and the toy kitchen set. Her eyes would bug out when she saw the pink tricycle hidden behind the tree. Then, after presents, they'd go to church—Christmas fell on a Sunday this year, how perfect was that?—and he'd tell everyone about the miracle God had wrought. His daughter was lost and now is found. Was dead and now lives. What a witness that would be, especially for the lukewarm believers who only came to church on Christmas and Easter. They wouldn't be lukewarm anymore. They'd be saved, just like Emmie.

Josh swiped right on the message, catching the pad of his index finger on the crack in the screen protector. He tapped the link.

A document opened. It looked like a typical click-through license for online software or a website. An opening paragraph in all caps instructing him to read the agreement carefully before accepting, followed by a list of definitions for words like "agreement" and "license" and "comparable," and several more blocks of legalese with headings like "RIGHTS & RESTRICTIONS, CONFIDENTIALITY, WARRANTY AND INDEMNITY, LIMITATION OF LIABILITY, and TERMINATION. Josh swiped past those, leaving a bloody smear on his phone screen. His index finger stung. He examined it and found a cut running the length of the pad. He pulled a tissue from the box on his nightstand and wiped the blood off his finger, then peeled the cracked—and apparently sharp—screen protector off his phone. He tossed it and the bloody tissue in a nearby wastebasket and resumed skimming the agreement.

Several screens in, it got to the point:

"I, Nicholas DeVille ('Vendor'), agree to re store the life of Emma Louise Fogarty for the consideration of the life of a compara ble child to be selected by Joshua David Fogarty ('Customer')."

For the life of a comparable child.

Another child would die in Emmie's place. To take a child's life, even indirectly, would be an abomination. He couldn't justify it, not to himself, and definitely not to God.

Or could he? What if the child in question were already dying? What if the child lived a life of constant pain from an incurable disease? Mercy killing was wrong, but was it forgivable? Maybe.

He flicked through more legalese—"ENTIRE AGREE-

MENT," "FORCE MAJEURE," "SEVERABILITY," "JURISDIC-TION." He skimmed faster.

Another bloody smear. Josh glanced at his finger. Blood still seeped from the cut. This time he didn't bother to wipe it off.

The document ended—finally—with a bland, gray button with white letters that read, "I Agree." Immediately above it was a box for his signature and the date, and immediately above that was a checkbox next to the text, "I have read this agreement in its entirety and agree to all terms of service." Josh tapped the checkbox, scrawled his signature with his bloody finger, and added the date. He hesitated, finger poised over the "I Agree" button.

Thou shalt not kill.

Emmie opening presents. Emmie wobbling down the sidewalk on her new trike, ringing that shiny silver bell. Emmie laughing, hugging him, smiling up at him.

He tapped the "I Agree" button, leaving a bloody fingerprint on the screen.

The screen went blank. No acknowledgment message, no further instructions, nothing. Had it worked? Was the agreement even real, or had he been taken in by a cruel, elaborate hoax?

He pictured the old man toppling off the stool.

His doorbell rang.

"Hello, Joshua. Have you chosen a child?"

Nick stood on the front porch of Josh's apartment in the same skinny jeans, flannel shirt, and Patagonia vest he'd been wearing at the cemetery that morning. Same Santa hat, too, only now it was perched just off-center, giving him a jaunty air that didn't match the reason he was here.

Chosen a child. Like they were going car shopping. Or to an orphanage to adopt. Pastor Gabe and Sara had done that when Sara couldn't get pregnant. They'd gone to an orphanage in Siberia and chosen a child. Then Sara had gotten pregnant with Ana right afterward. She was the same age as—

Nick snapped his fingers in Josh's face. "Anybody home in there?"

"Uh, sorry. No, I haven't chosen a..." He hesitated. "Child. Not yet. But I know where I want to go to find one. Do you want to come in for a minute, or...?"

"No, thank you. We need to get moving if you haven't chosen a child yet. That process can take some time, and you only have 'til dawn per our agreement." He sounded more business-like than he had earlier. "Get your coat and come out here, and I'll tell you how this works."

Josh left the front door open—it seemed rude to close it in Nick's face—and rummaged in the laundry pile for a hoodie. He pulled it on and stepped onto the porch with Nick. The fog had thickened as it usually did at night, making the mini-mart across the street nearly invisible. He closed the door behind him and deadbolted it. The next time he unlocked it, he'd be a dad again.

He turned to Nick. "So, how do we do this?" He was shocked at the eagerness in his voice.

23

"You tell me where you want to go, and I'll take you there. Most people need to look at a few children before they make their choice."

A few children.

Most people?

"How many times have you—?"

"I do this every year. Now, where do you want to go first?"

The skin on Josh's neck rippled. This… man killed a child every Christmas. He looked from Nick to the locked front door and fingered the keys in his jeans pocket. If he noped out and tried to go back inside, would Nick stop him? But no, he had a plan. It wasn't right, but it was forgivable. "Please take me to Stockton Children's Hospital."

Nick raised one thick eyebrow but didn't comment. He rested a hand on Josh's arm. The world around Josh went dark, like he'd dozed off for a second, and then they were standing in the hospital lobby in front of a two-story-tall Christmas tree covered in white twinkling lights and blue and silver ornaments. Gene Autry crooned, "Rudolph the Red-Nosed Reindeer," from overhead speakers. A woman carried a crying toddler over her shoulder toward a set of automatic doors under the word *EMERGENCY* in glowing red letters.

Should Josh follow them? The kid didn't look seriously ill, but maybe there was another child in the ER, maybe about to die from a car wreck. The fog was thick, and lots of people got drunk on Christmas Eve. If he timed it right… but no, a critically-injured accident victim would be surrounded by doctors and nurses. There'd be no chance for Nick to…

He walked toward a bank of elevators to the left of the

welcome desk, scanned a sign beside it labeled *Directory,* and found what he was looking for.

Nick appeared beside him, and Josh pointed to the words *Intensive Care.* "Let's go there."

Nick took his arm, the world went dark again, and then they were in a brightly lit hallway outside a set of glass doors etched with the letters, PICU.

Josh turned to Nick and whispered, "How can we do this without being seen?" He'd been there once before when a kid from his youth group, now grown and married, had a baby with a serious birth defect. It'd been hard to snatch a few moments of prayer with all the medical people responding to alarms and administering meds.

"That won't be a problem." Nick gave him a smug smile. "Trust me."

Trust him.

Again he saw the old man toppling off the stool, face-planting in a puddle of coffee.

Right.

Josh slapped the automatic door opener, and the sharp smell of antiseptic burned in his nose as he followed Nick into the PICU. Medical personnel and hollow-eyed family members passed them in the hall as though they didn't exist.

Trust me.

They passed a nurse's station tricked out with red and white wrapping paper on the front of the counter, an artificial tree beside it, and oversized ornament balls hanging from the ceiling. A nurse in green scrubs spattered with red and white Santas typed on a computer. She, too, didn't react to their presence.

Just past the nurse's station, Josh peered into a room on his left. The lights had been dimmed for the night, and the room was quiet except for the hums and whooshes and clicks of medical equipment. The room held four small beds, each containing a child and a web of tubes and wires.

He walked to each bed and considered each child. Two looked like they were recovering from surgeries but were otherwise healthy. A third was flanked on either side of her bed by a man and woman Josh assumed were the parents. The woman stroked the child's forehead, then kissed it.

The fourth bed held a child nearly invisible under a tangle of tubes, including two the size of small pipes snaking from the mask on her face to the ventilator beside her bed. It hissed and clicked in a steady rhythm as it pushed air into her fragile body.

Josh closed his eyes, offered a prayer for the child's soul, and said, "This one." Then he turned away, unable to bear looking at her.

Nick regarded him with an expression Josh couldn't interpret. "How do you want to do it?"

It took Josh a beat to process what Nick had said. *How do you want to do it?*

You. Do it.

You.

"The contract said I'm supposed to select the child. The rest is up to you."

"Actually, it isn't. Apparently, you didn't read the fine print."

Josh's chest tightened, and his next words came out half an octave higher than normal. "What do you mean?"

Nick pulled a cell phone from the pocket of his skinny jeans, tapped the screen a few times, and held it out to Josh. "Here. Read it for yourself. Which you should have done before you signed it."

Josh squinted at the screen. Under a section headed CONSIDERATION, just below the bit about providing a comparable child, was the text, "Customer shall sacrifice the comparable child using a method of his choosing."

"See?" He put on an exaggerated, pompous attorney voice. "The contract clearly states that you, Joshua David Fogarty, must sacrifice the child."

Sacrifice the child.

Child sacrifice.

Josh hadn't put the situation in those terms before. The tightening in his chest became a fist that squeezed 'til he could barely breathe. Maybe he'd keel over like the man at Denny's. Maybe it would be better for him if he did.

Child sacrifice.

"Now that that's settled, how do you want to do it?"

Do it.

Josh squinched his eyes shut, like a toddler who thinks she can hide by covering her face.

Do it.

The ventilator hissed and clicked.

Do it.

Whispered conversations with his buddies at church camp. "Are you and your girlfriend gonna do it?" "I heard Brandon and Rachel did it."

Hiss.

Do it.

Click.

How.

Hiss.

How, how.

Click.

His head swam, and he stumbled. Nick's hand closed around his arm, steadying him. He sucked in a breath in time with the ventilator's hiss and focused on the reason he was here.

Emmie.

He could unplug the child's ventilator. Simple. Easy. No more hiss. No more click.

But she'd suffocate, maybe slowly. She might suffer.

He forced himself to open his eyes and face Nick. "What's the most painless way to kill someone?"

"Dude, your contract doesn't include consulting services."

Josh's body tensed, and he imagined blacking one of those unnaturally blue eyes. He breathed out slowly.

Hiss.

Click.

"Please."

Nick appeared to consider, then sighed theatrically. "All right. The most painless way to kill in these circumstances would be with an overdose of insulin."

Insulin should be easy enough to find in a hospital, especially if he and Nick were as invisible to the staff as they seemed to be. "Okay, I'll do that. I'll have to find the hospital pharmacy." Josh nearly bolted for the door.

"No need." Nick produced a capped syringe from his vest pocket.

Josh took it and fumbled the cap off. The needle flashed silver in the dim light as his hand shook.

An alarm shrieked from the child's ventilator. He jumped and almost dropped the syringe.

He gave Nick a pleading look. "I know the contract doesn't include consulting services, but where… Where should I…?"

"In the abdomen." Nick gave that smug smile again. "But a better question would be, Why?"

To get this done. Duh. "I don't understand."

"Why do you want to kill this child?"

The terror crushing Josh's chest eased. Was Nick just testing him, like the Lord tested Abraham, staying his hand before he could slay his son? "I'm following the terms of the contract."

"Well, actually, you aren't. Once again, you didn't read the fine print. The agreement said, *comparable* child. Your daughter was healthy, so—"

"She had a heart defect."

"No, she didn't." Calm, matter-of-fact.

Certain.

The nurse with the Santa scrubs strode in and flipped a switch on the ventilator. The alarm stopped shrieking. She fiddled with one of the tubes, then left with no sign she'd seen either Nick or Josh, though she'd passed within inches of them.

"You said she had a heart defect. Back at Denny's, when

we—"

"No, I said the *coroner said* she died from an undiagnosed heart defect. You need to pay attention to details, Joshua. Especially when signing documents in blood."

"Okay, then, the coroner said so."

"The coroner was wrong."

"She had to have died of something. Healthy children don't just…"

Nick stared at him with unblinking eyes and an expressionless face.

Oh, Lord, no. Oh dear Lord, no. "You mean someone chose her to…?"

"Exactly."

He shoved the needle in Nick's direction. He took it and held his other hand out. "The cap, please."

Josh dropped the cap in Nick's hand. His stomach twisted, and he was glad it was empty. He'd almost killed a child. For nothing.

He whirled and started for the door. "I have to get out of here."

Nick seized his arm. An instant of darkness, and they were in the lobby. Josh's knees shook. He sank into a wood-framed chair, pulled the whole wad of tissues from his pocket, and buried his face in his hands. Someone had chosen his child, his beautiful Emmie, to die. Had whoever it was stood over her pink princess bed, pointed to her angelic face, and said, "This one?"

He pounded his fists on his thighs and stifled the howl of rage that threatened to tear out of his throat.

A hand rested on his shoulder. He wiped his eyes with the already-soggy tissues and looked up, expecting to see Nick, but Nick was standing a few feet away.

"Sir, I'm Reuben Torres. I'm one of the chaplains here. Would you like to go somewhere where we can talk?"

The chaplain looked to be in his 40s, with brown skin and a thick but receding head of close-cropped black hair. His eyes were round, brown, and kind.

Josh almost said yes. This man would pray with him and comfort him, not lecture him about fine print and tell him to kill a child.

Like someone killed Emmie. My Emmie.

This man would assure him his daughter's death was part of God's plan, that she was happy and at peace and he'd see her again someday and all those other clichés he'd heard over and over until he wanted to hit every last one of those sanctimonious jackwagons with a bat 'til their brains spattered across the neutral beige walls of Brookside Community Church.

This man could do nothing for him.

He clenched his jaws tight to hold back a year's worth of unsaid words. A few forced their way out anyway. "Will talking to you bring my daughter back?"

The man removed his hand from Josh's shoulder. "No, no, of course not, but—"

"But what? Talking about it will help?"

"It might."

"Or praying? Praying about it will help?"

"It might."

Josh closed his eyes. Breathed slowly.

In.

Out.

Opened his eyes. Looked at Chaplain Reuben Torres. At his kind eyes that radiated compassion.

Looked at Nick, whose glowing eyes radiated power. The power to take a life. Emmie's life.

And the power to give it back.

"No, thanks," Josh said to the chaplain.

The man reached into the pocket of his sport coat and produced a business card. "Here's my card. Call me if you change your mind."

Josh took the card and put it in his own pocket without looking at it. The man left, and Nick sat in his place.

Josh asked, "Who chose my daughter?"

"I can't tell you that, Joshua. Didn't you read the confidentiality clause in the contract you signed? You really should read documents before you sign them, you know. Sometimes there's important stuff in that fine print."

"I don't need a lecture right now."

"True. You need to get moving right now. It's after midnight, and—"

"Yeah, yeah, the fine print says we have to be done by dawn."

"Correct."

"Let me think for a minute."

A comparable child. He closed his eyes and folded his hands in his lap like he was praying. Who had a child Emmie's age? His sister Julia's best friend Amy and her husband had a son who'd been born a few weeks before Emmie. They were over six hours away, but if Nick could teleport to Stockton Children's, he could teleport to Orange County. But Amy and Robert were unsaved, so they'd never see their child in heaven. And losing a child might drive them further from God, and he couldn't be responsible for damning their souls.

He'd have to choose someone from his church. Someone faithful whose salvation was assured. Pastor Gabe was the most godly man he'd ever known, and his daughter Ana was just a few months younger than Emmie. But how could he choose her after all Pastor Gabe's family had been through? Infertility, sickness, death. They'd suffered enough.

The Kurwoods. Nikki "God must have needed another angel" and her husband Tyler "Everything happens for a reason" Kurwood. They should have been on the cover of a Christian marriage manual, always holding hands and making gooey eyes at each other. They led every marriage retreat Brookside CC offered. And Kayla Kurwood had just turned four. Surely their marriage—their perfect marriage—could withstand the pain of losing a child. They'd see her again in heaven, and in the meantime, he'd comfort them as best he could. Better than they'd comforted him.

Josh raised his head and opened his eyes to find Nick watching him, the light in his eyes faint enough that the families coming and going with balloons and Christmas presents wouldn't notice anything off about him. "Kayla Kurwood. Take me to Kayla Kurwood."

The Kurwoods' Christmas tree loomed in the corner of their living room, visible as little more than a greenish shadow in the porch light filtering through their closed blinds. The Kurwoods only had the one child, but based on the size of the pile of presents under that tree, you'd think they had five.

Josh didn't want to look. He wanted to get this done—carefully not thinking about the specifics of *this*—but he couldn't tear his gaze from that tree. So many packages, so like the stack still in his closet for Emmie. He stepped closer, picked up a rectangular box, and angled it toward the faint light.

Green paper with Winnie the Pooh and Tigger wearing Santa hats like Nick's. The same paper on Emmie's presents from last year. He dropped the package back on the pile and peered behind the tree. He squinted and saw, or maybe imagined, the outline of a tricycle.

He could leave. Unbolt the Kurwoods' front door and walk out into the fog. Call an Uber to take him home. Learn to live without Emmie.

"Kids wake up early on Christmas morning," Nick whispered, and Josh's whole body jerked. "She'll be easier to kill if she's asleep."

Ice-cold dread rolled like a drop of mercury down Josh's spine. He just had to get this done, and then his daughter would open presents and laugh and weave around his tiny living room on her new tricycle.

He turned away from the tree and walked to Nick's side. Nick took his arm, and the world went black.

A night light lit Kayla Kurwood's bedroom, glowing yellow-white from the wall next to her bed. It cast just enough light for Josh to see her as she slept. She lay curled on her side in a twin bed, her head resting on her folded hands like the children in old Christmas prints with their artificially red cheeks and angelic smiles. Her breath came in little not-quite snores. Emmie had sounded like that when she slept. Sometimes he and Hannah had watched her sleep, arms wrapped around each other, saturated with love for the tiny being God had given them.

And someone had taken away.

"Here." Nick held out the hypo of insulin between two long fingers like a cigarette, cap off. Josh took it and squinted at the clear liquid in the barrel. "This is enough?"

"She'll lose consciousness almost instantly.

"Won't she feel the shot and wake up and scream?"

"Not if you do it right."

"How should I do it?"

Nick gave another theatrical sigh. "Was there a training class mentioned in the contract you signed?"

"Please. I don't want to hurt her."

"You're okay with killing her, but you don't want to hurt her."

"No, I'm not okay with killing her." He could still leave. Walk out the door, down the stairs, out into the night. Call the Uber, learn how to live without... "But I signed a contract."

"In blood."

"Right. So what choice do I have?"

Nick didn't answer that. Instead, he pointed at Kayla's

stomach. "Inject her here. If you do it fast, it'll be over before she feels it."

Josh knelt beside the girl's bed and gripped the edge of the mattress to steady himself. Then he raised her t-shirt, slipped the needle in where Nick had pointed, and pushed the plunger down.

The child stopped snoring. Her eyes opened wide. She sat up, opened her mouth as if to scream, and fell back on her pillow.

Josh stood. "Take me to my daughter."

Josh stood beside Nick on the porch of what had been his family home. The suburban cul-de-sac was silent except for the hum of central heating units. Josh barely felt the damp cold.

The porch light formed a yellow-white halo in the fog, but the house was still dark. It wouldn't be for long. Emmie never let them sleep in even a little bit on Christmas morning. She'd bound into their room, launch herself between them, and demand they get up to see what Santa brought. They'd stagger out of bed and stumble downstairs behind her, wishing for another hour of sleep.

Not this morning. This morning Josh stared at the front window, willing the lights inside to come on. Imagining the sound of Emmie's feet clomping down the stairs. Her squeals of delight when she sees the pile of presents around the tree. "It'll be like she'd never died, right?" he asked Nick for at least the third time since they'd arrived. "The tree, the presents, everything?"

Before Nick could answer, faint light appeared in the window. The upstairs landing light. Josh's mouth spread into a wide smile. The sensation felt strange, his skin stretching like old, cold taffy. He hadn't smiled like that in a year.

Thudding footsteps, then the window lit up. A squeal. *Emmie.*

Warmth spread through his chest, another strange sensation. He peered through the curtains again, just in time to see her run to the tree and grab a present. She tore off the paper—the same Winnie the Pooh paper he'd saved in his closet—and squealed again at the doll inside.

It'll be like she'd never died.

Josh seized the doorknob and started to turn it.

Nick's hand clamped down on his, rough and warm. "No, Joshua."

Josh jerked his hand off the knob and whirled to face Nick. "Let me see my daughter."

"You've already seen her. You've even heard her, though your contract doesn't say anything about seeing or hearing."

"You said I'd have her back. It'd be like she never died. Now let me go."

"Well, actually, the contract says I'll restore her to life. It doesn't say anything about you getting her back." He made air quotes around the last three words.

"After all you made me do, and you won't let me—"

"Well, see, what you did is the issue."

"What you made me do."

"No, Joshua. What you chose to do."

"I signed a contract. In blood. After all your talk about the fine print, are you seriously telling me you would've let me walk away?"

"Dude, you chose to sign that contract. You even checked a box affirming you'd read the contract in its entirety. If you had read the contract in its entirety, you would be familiar with the Termination Clause. It clearly states you could have terminated our agreement anytime cardiac activity was detectable in the replacement child." He gave one of his theatrical sighs. "You really should have read the fine print, Joshua."

"Would you shut up about the fu—" He clapped his mouth shut, then opened it again. "The fine print? Okay, I didn't read that part. But I did read the part that said you agreed to restore my daughter's life for the… what was the word? *Consideration* of the life of a comparable child. You got your comparable child. Now let go of me so I can see my daughter."

"You've already seen her, but you can see her again. She's right there." Nick let go of Josh's hand and seized his upper arm instead. With his other hand, he pointed at the gap in the curtains on the front window. Emmie rolled a pink tricycle out from behind the Christmas tree, her squeals now shrieks that could probably be heard from across the street.

Josh tried to tug his arm out of Nick's grip. "Let go of me! I did what you wanted."

"We've been over this. You did what *you* wanted. And now you have to pay the price. Your soul is forfeit." He spoke the last four words in a deep voice that was almost a growl. His hand tightened around Josh's arm.

Only it wasn't a hand anymore. It was a claw. A red, leathery claw.

Josh's pulse pounded in his ears, loud enough to drown out Emmie's joyful squeals. "Who... what are you?"

Nick gave him a shake. "Are you serious? Damn, you really are the King of Denial. My name is Nick Deville. Deville, Joshua. De. Vil. I even referred to myself as Old Nick once. You talk about me all the time in your sermons to those church kids, you know, when you tell them I'll take their souls if they wank or bang their girlfriends. And you didn't recognize me when I was right in front of you."

Josh sucked in a breath, then let it out in a moan. "Oh, God."

"Bzzzt. Wrong answer. He can't help you now. You—"

"Yeah, I know; I signed a contract—"

"In blood."

"But it didn't say anything about giving up my soul." *Did it? Oh, God, did it?*

"No, it did not."

"Then what's the issue? I'm a sinner, we're all sinners, but God will forgive me. I just wanted my girl back." His voice rose to a whine. "I'm not evil."

"You murdered a child, my dude. You don't get more evil than that."

"But... but—"

"You've always been evil. Everyone is, or they can be under the right circumstances." He grinned, and his face turned red and leathery to match the claw still digging into Josh's arm. His glowing blue eyes turned flat black, and the tips of his teeth narrowed to sharp points. "And it's my job to create those circumstances."

Horns sprouted from under his Santa hat, curving up past its white fur brim.

Josh's whole body shook, and his teeth clattered like dry bones in a windstorm.

"Church people like you are the easiest to tempt. You have an image to maintain, so you aren't honest about your feelings. Look at you. You were furious at God for—"

"No, I wasn't. His will is perf—"

"Yes, you were. Don't lie. It's too late for lies. You were furious at God for taking your girl, but you couldn't admit it, even to yourself. You couldn't be honest, and you still can't. Not with yourself, and sure as hell not with any of those church people who are supposed to love you so much. So all that anger and pain festered in your soul."

"And then you showed up and took advantage of my weakness and tempted me."

Nick shrugged with the shoulder not attached to the arm holding Josh. "Well, yeah. Tempting the weak is kind of my thing."

"Wh—Why? Why m-m—"

"Why you? Why not you?" Nick hiked an eyebrow, now thin and black and sharply arched, and regarded Josh with an expression that might have been pity. "I know, you did everything right. Went to church your whole life, didn't curse, virgin on your wedding night, never looked at another woman. You checked every box."

"Then why?"

Another theatrical sigh. "Sinners are such whiners when they're held to account. But okay, fine, I'll tell you the truth. Whatever you and your brethren say about me, I never lie. It's not your fault I chose you. I mean, you did sign a con-tract—in blood—with someone who murdered a guy in front of you. Then you murdered a child. Those things are totally your fault."

"But—"

"No buts, Joshua. We've been over that. Now, where was I? Oh, yeah, why I chose you. You see, it's this little game I play every Christmas. All the Merry Christmas, peace on earth, goodwill toward men crap gets annoying, you know? So I decided to create my own Christmas tradition. It's kind of like those paper chains little kids like Emmie make, only I don't use paper. I use souls."

"Wh—What are you talking about?"

"You haven't figured it out? Really?" Nick rolled his flat black eyes. "I suppose the confidentiality clause doesn't really matter now." He leaned in close to Josh like a middle school girl about to spill a secret. "Remember Ana, your pastor's kid? She wasn't really in a coma all last year."

Ana. Pastor Gabe's daughter. *She wasn't in a coma all year.*

A coma.

All year.

"Oh, G—"

"Figured it out, did you? Good job. But have you figured out the rest?"

Josh shook his head.

"Come on, Joshua. It's not that hard. Your girl is alive

41

and well because you sacrificed another kid in her place."

Another kid.

In her place.

Another kid.

And the horrible truth hit Josh with the force of a fist to the solar plexus. He sagged and would have fallen to his knees if Nick's grip on his arm hadn't held him upright.

"Sarah didn't have a stroke on Christmas morning. She…" Josh struggled to finish the sentence, as if forming the words would make them true. "She… chose Emmie."

"She did." Again Nick's look was almost pitying.

"And now she's—"

"In Hell, where child killers belong." The last three words came out in a deep, resonant growl. Nick's body swelled, and his clothes split with a series of audible rips. His thighs grew to the size of tree trunks, their red skin striped with the tattered remains of his skinny jeans. His chest expanded, shredding the flannel shirt and Patagonia vest.

Nick's body stretched taller, taller, 'til his horns brushed the eaves above Emmie's second-floor window. Josh's feet left the ground, and he dangled by his arm from Nick's claw.

Nick lifted him 'til their faces were level, and his teeth— now three-inch fangs—were inches from Josh's nose. With his other claw, Nick adjusted his Santa hat so it sat at its usual jaunty angle.

Josh's body went limp. His bladder and bowels released, their contents sliding warm and slick down his legs.

Nick wrinkled his red, leathery nose and held Josh further from his face. "I'll give you one more freebie." He lowered Josh to the level of the front window so he could catch one last glimpse of his daughter. She was riding the pink tricycle in a wobbly figure eight around his ex-wife's living room, ringing the shiny silver bell.

B*lack S*olstice
Dane Cobain

"I'm dreaming of a black solstice."

– Bling Crowley

"Tell us again, Daddy."

"Oh, no, it's far too late for that."

"Please?"

"Well...okay."

John Reid was sitting on an uncomfortably small chair at the foot of his daughters' bunk bed. It was late, it was cold outside, and he had an important meeting in the morning. He stroked his powerful hand through his beard and glanced automatically at his wristwatch, which was illuminated by a *My Little Pony* lava lamp. Tupac, the family cat, was nestled in the lower bunk, curled around Jessie's feet like a black spot in the pages of a Bible.

He sighed.

"What story do you want to hear?" he asked, though he already knew the answer. There was only one story that the two of them could possibly want to hear at this time of year, and he was the only one who'd tell it. His wife, Mildred, believed the old superstitions and said it was bad luck.

"Daddy, Daddy," little Jessie said, her eyes staring out from the darkness like two bright beacons of hope and innocence. "Tell us the story of Satan Claws!"

"Satan Claws?" he replied, raising an eyebrow. "Aren't you a bit old for that?"

"No, Daddy, no," Jude said. "Go on, tell us the story."

"Okay," John said, shrugging his shoulders and shifting uncomfortably in the chair. "Well, the story goes like this. Back in the olden days, a long, long time ago—"

"Before you were born?"

"Yes," John chuckled softly, feeling his age, along with an ache in his back from where the cold weather and the storm front had taken its toll. "Long, long before I was born."

"So what happened?"

"I'm getting there," John replied. "It goes back to the Bible. Adam's first wife, Lilith, flew into a tremendous rage after God created Eve, and God punished her for her jealousy by making her mortal. But then, as she wandered the Earth alone and in the depths of her despair, Satan went to her in the form of a goat and asked her to drink his blood."

"And did she?"

"Yes," John said. "The unholy blood was too much for her, and it killed her. But though her body died, her spirit lived on, and she was doomed to spend the rest of eternity at his side, feasting on the blood of children, just like you two."

The two girls shuddered in their beds, and John Reid felt the beginnings of a smile despite himself. Scaring children during solstice season was a tradition as old as time itself, and if the legends were true, it served a purpose.

"Lilith is the mother of them all," John continued. "The she-devil, Missus Claws. They say she still sleeps beside him in their double coffin, hiding from the deadly sunlight as they wait for the winter solstice, the longest night. They add others to their cause when they can, corrupting their victims with a bite and creating creatures of the night. Your grandad—"

"Grandad Woodynge?"

"No, Jessie," John replied. "Granddad Byegrave. He used to be what they called a staker. It was his job to search the cemetery for little air holes or disturbances amongst the graves at Saint Editha's. When he found something, he had to dig up the grave and put a stake through the heart of the poor unfortunate that was buried beneath the soil."

"Eww!"

"That's nothing," John said. "In some other places, very far away from here, they decapitate their dead to make sure that they don't come back."

"What does depapitate mean?"

"Never you mind," John said. "In Italy, the doctors wash their hands with communion wine. When their patients die, they break people's legs and bury them upside down."

"That's gross, Daddy," Jude scolded, pouting at him as she put her little hands over her ears.

"Well, it's a small price to pay," John said. "It's better for you to know these things. The vampyres are dangerous, with superhuman strength and speed. They're also immortal."

"What does that mean, Daddy?"

"It means they don't die," John replied grimly.

He thought once again about whether he was telling them too much, but then he reminded himself that, like the birds and the bees, it was just one of the facts of life that they needed to know.

"According to the legends," John continued, "if someone died and their body was left unguarded, they'd turn into a creature of the night. Your other granddad, Granddad Woodynge, used to work as a watcher."

"A watcher?"

"Yes, Jude," John said. "He'd stand guard over the dead with a lit candle, watching day and night until it was time to bury them. He used to hold a loaded shotgun and keep watch for animals."

"Like rabbits?"

"Uh-huh," John replied. "And cats and dogs, too. The old-timers say that if an animal jumps over a body before it's buried, it'll turn into a vampyre by the following night."

"They say a lot," Jude said.

John paused for a second and smiled in the darkness,

struck again by just how smart his kids were. They were little prodigies, clever clogs who'd been raised on classical music since their time in the womb, even though he knew the Mozart effect was a steaming pile of bullshit. But they'd played Mozart to the girls anyway, just in case the scientists were wrong.

"Is it true that only bad people become vampyres, Daddy?"

"No, Jessie," John said. "They used to say that only those who'd led evil lives or who'd refused religion could become vampyres. They suspected witches of being vampyres, too. But we know better, don't we, girls?"

"Yuh-huh," Jude said, sticking a thumb in her mouth and looking out at her dad from the top bunk. "Grandma Wood-ynge is a witch, and she keeps us safe from Satan Claws."

"Exactly, girls," John said. "So there's nothing to worry about, is there?"

"Nuh-uh."

"Good," John said, yawning slightly and stretching out his arms. "Now, I think that's enough for one night, isn't it? Besides, we can't let your mother know we've been talking about Satan Claws again or she'll have my guts for garters."

"What does that mean, Daddy?"

"Never you mind," John repeated, his mustache twitching as he suppressed a laugh. "Now go on, you two. It's time for you to go to sleep. Sweet dreams."

"Simply having a terrible solstice time."
– Paul McStakeInTheHeartney

On Solstice Eve, the two Reid girls were running around in the garden and playing in the snow when they saw a magpie in the trees. It was soon joined by another, and then another. The birds lined up like black-gowned judges, waiting to pass sentence on the children.

Jude nodded at her sister, and the two turned and saluted to the birds. Then they started to sing together in cherubic harmony, their time in the church choir shining through as they worked their way through the rhyme.

"One for sorrow," they chorused. "Two for joy, three for a girl, four for a boy. Five for silver, six for gold, seven for a secret never to be told. Eight for a wish, nine for a kiss, ten a surprise you should be careful not to miss. Eleven for health, twelve for wealth, thirteen beware, it's the devil himself."

"Magpies are always bad luck," Jessie grumbled.

"Like breaking a mirror?" Jude replied.

"Exactly."

There was a sharp gust of wind and the magpies took off, their departure leaving a heavy silence that settled over the garden like a fog. Both girls were wrapped up warm, but they shivered in tandem as the sun sauntered behind a cloud and cast the garden into shadow.

They looked to the snowman they'd built for comfort, but there was no warmth to the coal he had for eyes, and the twigs they'd used for his arms looked brittle and uninviting.

"Let's go inside," Jessie said.

The inside of the house looked like an explosion at a jumble sale with all sorts of weird and wonderful items scattered throughout it. The decorations were mostly red, green, and gold, symbolizing the blood of Christ, the eternal life of the evergreen tree, and the gifts of the three magi. The initials VM for "Virgin Mary" had been carved repeatedly into the wooden door and window frames.

The banister, which crawled lazily down a steep and narrow Edwardian staircase, was carved with obscene phalli, stiff and floppy dicks saluting the girls every time they ran upstairs. Mildred didn't like them and had begged her husband to get rid of them, but he'd always overruled her because of the old apotropaic superstitions.

That was why he had also agreed to bury an old boot outside the back door.

"What's the difference between an amulet and a talisman?" Jude asked as the girls raced up the stairs toward their playroom.

"One's got an 'n' in it?"

"Well, that, too," Jude replied. "But that wasn't what I meant, silly."

"So, what's the difference?"

"A talisman brings good luck," Jude said, "and an amulet wards off evil."

"So, which one do we need?" Jessie asked.

Jude shook her head grimly and said, "Both."

"'Twas the night before solstice,
when all through the shack,
not a creature was stirring,

not even a bat."

– Clement Van Helsing

The house smelled like garlic.

A silver chalice sat on a silver tray on a table in the kitchen. It was filled with a clear liquid, holy water from the healing springs of Lourdes, and two communion wafers sat on a silver plate beside them. A wooden crucifix lay between the two of them.

It was midnight on the morning of December 21st.

The house was one of several dozen nestled beneath the blanket of snow over Greyfriars Close and the rest of Mile End. Upstairs, in their bedrooms, the Reid family slumbered on. John Reid was fast asleep, his mustache-net holding his precious curls out of his nose and mouth. His wife, Mildred, was sleeping beside him, though she was twitching.

In the other bedroom, the twins were still awake.

And they were terrified.

Jessie and Jude were seven years old and just about old enough to still believe in Satan Claws. Some of the children at school had said that Satan was made up by capitalists to sell more products, but Jessie and Jude kept to themselves and didn't give a hoot what the other kids said. Perhaps Satan Claws was just their father in a silly suit... But then again, perhaps not. And they didn't want to take the risk and then find out they were wrong.

John Reid had told them they were taking Pascal up on his wager. They hadn't known what he'd meant at the time, but then they'd asked Mister Griffin at the school, and he'd told them all about it.

It made a lot of sense after that. Perhaps Satan Claws didn't exist, but then again, perhaps he did. If they took the proper precautions and he did exist, they had a shot at surviving. If he didn't… Well, they'd just look a little silly. And Jessie and Jude didn't care if they looked silly as long as they survived.

And so they'd stayed up late on Solstice Eve, roaming around the house and performing the final touches, scattering salt circles around their beds and polishing all the mirrors. A couple of weeks earlier, they'd found some sticks while they were walking by the river, and they'd spent the days between sharpening the sticks with their daddy's penknife. Luckily for them, he hadn't caught them.

They'd hung a silver horseshoe above their bedroom door, polished every shiny surface until they could see their faces, and placed mirrors by the doors and windows. In the back garden, tear-shaped nazars hung from trees, channeling the old magick to protect the house from the glare of the evil eye.

The house was festooned with images of Christ, and they'd woven St. Brigid's crosses out of rush to hang in each room. In their bedroom, a homemade dreamcatcher made of yarn hung above their bunk bed, occasionally bopping Jude on the head if she sat up in the night. Blown-glass witch balls hung in every room, and so did bunches of wildflowers, including branches of ash, oak, wild rose, white heather, and hawthorn. Jessie had even asked her daddy to bring her some clippings from the aspen tree at the bottom of the garden.

"Does it have to be aspen?" he'd asked.

"Of course," she'd replied matter-of-factly. "That's the same kind of tree they used to make Jesus's cross, Daddy."

They'd scattered mustard seeds on the floors and even convinced their parents to leave the taps on, thanks to the old story that vampyres couldn't cross running water. They'd also asked their mother if they could hang some mistletoe, but she'd refused.

"Mistletoe is a patriarchal tradition designed to apply social pressure to young women until they agree to kiss old men," she'd insisted. "I mean, the juice in the berries represents jizz, for goodness' sake."

"What's jizz, Mummy?"

"Never you mind."

But the girls were hopeful that they'd be able to wear her down eventually, just like they'd done with the gun and the silver bullets. The two girls had been making zero headway until they'd presented their mother with charts and graphs showing the prevalence of home invasions. She'd relented after that, and she'd been their key weapon when it came to convincing their father.

John Reid would have done anything for his daughters, and so he'd purchased an illegal firearm from a guy called Silky at the local boozer. He kept the gun and the holy bullets inside a shoebox in the drawer of his bedside table.

That afternoon, Mildred cut her hand while helping her daughters to bake communion wafers. She'd tried to hide it from them, to cover the wound with a plaster before they noticed, but the twins' eyes were as sharp as their intellects, and before she'd even removed the first aid kit from the kitchen cupboards, they'd told her what she needed to do.

"You did an oopsie, Mummy," Jude said. "You know the rules."

And she *did* know the rules, too. It was said that any wound left untreated with boiling water was enough to let the evil in, so traditionalists poured boiling water over graves during funerals. In the Reid household, that meant she had to pop the kettle on and take a couple of aspirin.

That night, she was sleeping with a bandage around her hand.

"He's making a list, he's checking it twice."
– Satan Claws is Coming to Town

John Reid woke up with a start as something primal took over him.

He was a full-grown adult with thirty-one winters behind him, but there was something about the old traditions that still held sway over him. He could remember a time in his own childhood when John Sr. had taken the boy on his knee and given him "the talk."

"Son," he'd said, "I think you're old enough now to know what's what. We maintain the old traditions because there's often a grain of truth to them. They say it's better to be safe than sorry, you see. Now, the winter is a dark and unpleasant time, a time that's full of dangers and where the elements themselves turn against us. Might be that there *is* a Satan Claws and that the legends are true. Might be that there isn't. But if what they say is true and he's the Antichrist, the Prince of Darkness... Well, maybe it's better to take the superstitions seriously just in case, eh?"

That was the solstice when John Reid had stayed up all night, his eyes darting frantically from shadow to shadow, convinced that Satan Claws would sweep in at any moment and rip him apart. Once the sun had finally crept over the horizon, he'd passed out and caught an hour or two of sleep before being woken back up for the celebrations. He'd spent most of Solstice Day dozing off at the dinner table and waking back up every time his chin dipped into the gravy.

Satan Claws hadn't come to visit that year, nor had he come the year after. In fact, Satan Claws never came for John Reid, but the name alone was still enough to send shivers down his spine.

He heard a creak on the landing, but the house was old and had a habit of singing to itself. He extricated himself from his wife's arms and rolled over onto his side, then folded his pillow in half and rested his head on the cool fabric. His ears twitched as he listened to the darkness, but there was nothing but a sleepy silence, a treacle-like emptiness that filled his ears like a spoonful of honey.

Then he closed his eyes again and tried to catch some sleep.

"Does he ride a red-nosed hellhound?
Are there weapons on his slay?"

– Slayed

The two girls were still awake, and still terrified.

Jessie was the older of the two by an hour, so she was the de-facto leader of the Reid twins. She was the first out of bed, and she used the nightlight's glow to climb down from her bunk and onto the hardwood floor. The snow outside was still falling, piling up against the concrete walls and chilling the house beneath a wintery blanket. It had seeped through into the floor and chilled her feet as she navigated to the dresser and picked up the rosaries, which lay incongruously amongst a pile of stuffed toys and collectibles.

She placed one around her own neck and one around her sister's. They worked in silence, their ears tensed as they listened for sounds from elsewhere in the house. Next, the two girls scattered seeds and rice across the floor, upending jars and wrenching open plastic packaging until the wood was covered with kernels and grains. Anne Welsh from their maths class had told them that vampyres were obsessed with numbers and that once he saw the scattered seeds, Satan Claws would have to stop and count them. If they kept him busy for long enough, the sun would rise and the light would kill him.

They didn't know whether they believed that, but they'd done it anyway.

Suzie Reid (no relation) from the year below had told them that Satan Claws had a legion of minions made up of some of the vilest people from history. Vlad the Impaler was the obvious one, the fierce Walachian who'd earned his nickname by impaling his enemies on wooden stakes and leaving them to die. According to Suzie, Vlad used to eat bread that had been dipped in his victims' blood while he watched them die.

Then there was Mike Austin, Lucy Austin's older brother. He'd told his sister—who'd told the rest of her class—about Countess Elizabeth Bathory, a Hungarian heiress with the blood of dozens of enemies on her hands, as well as her lips and tongue. According to the Austins, Bathory had her victims brought to her so she could bite them. After they died, she'd have her servants drain their blood before pouring it into a bathtub.

Mike Austin said that was because bath bombs hadn't been invented yet.

Stavros said they were called *vrykolakas*, but Besnik called them *shtriga*, and Anca said they were *strigoi*. Mr. Ricard, the substitute teacher presiding over the class at the time, said it was all just a matter of semantics.

"Do you know how to stop a strigoi?" Mr. Ricard had asked. He'd looked out at the sea of interested little faces and sighed. When no one answered, he'd continued, "They used to bury corpses upside down and put scythes and sickles in the grave. It was said that if the body bloated before becoming a full-fledged vampyre, the sickle would prick them and put them back down again. As for vyrkolakas, the best option is to leave a coin in their mouths so that they can pay the ferryman at the River Styx. If they can't cross the river, they come back to feast on flesh."

Then he'd remembered he was supposed to be teaching geography and had moved on to talking about continental drift.

But all that had been during a happier time, during the summer months when the coming of the vampyre was a distant shadow over the future and not an immediate threat to their survival. That had been then, and this was now, on Solstice Eve, the hunting night of the vampyres.

The two Reid girls were as ready as they'd ever be. They just didn't know if they were ready enough. They closed their eyes and bowed their heads, and then Jude led them in a prayer.

"Dear Baby Jesus," Jude intoned solemnly. "Please keep us safe from Satan Claws, or better still, send us a sign that he doesn't exist."

But no such sign was forthcoming.

"I'm keeping my distance, I've got my gun drawn,
if he comes any closer, I won't shoot to warn."
– John Lemon (and Yoko Ohnothevampyreiscoming)

But Satan Claws did exist, and he was having a bad day. His flying hellhounds had got lost over Marseilles, and it had taken Adolf's red nose to sniff out the English Channel. It had been raining in Transylvania, but the rain had turned to snow as they flew west in his slay.

He drew back his fiery whip, a solstice gift from his friend the Balrog, and swung it through the air. It broke the sound barrier with a sonic boom that echoed out over the English countryside.

"Now, Slasher!" he cried. "Now, Stabber! Now, Brawler and Basher! On, Killer! On, Screamer! On, Pouncer and Crasher!"

And his hellhounds flew on into the darkness.

"You scumbag, you friar, no match for vampyres."
— The Rogues feat. Kirsty MacBarlow

Just as John Reid was about to doze off for good, he heard a noise from above that sent a chill of fear through his soul. It was the sound of slay bells, the horrible, funereal gongs that echoed through the sky like a thunderclap. He sat bolt upright in his bed, then shook Mildred into life and put a finger to his lips.

"'S'appenin'?" she murmured, still drunk on sleep.

"Are you awake?" John asked.

"What do you think?"

"Yeah," John whispered. "I couldn't sleep, either. Did you hear something?"

"Like what?"

"I thought I heard something on the roof," John said. "I thought it might be... I don't know..."

"The vampyre?" Mildred asked. She'd woken up a little and had pulled herself up so that she was sitting upright, too. John reached over to the bedside lamp and clicked it to life. "John, aren't you too old for children's stories? There's no such thing as vampyres, husband. There are just people who *believe* in vampyres, and sometimes that's just as bad."

"Ah, *those guys*," John replied. "The ones who get professional fang fittings and who carry out rituals and shit. Those guys are idiots. But just because a few fools like to play fancy dress, it doesn't mean that the real things aren't out there."

"But vampyres, John," Mildred argued. "You're talking about bad guys from the depth of the night, created in the twilight hours before God rested. Lilith, the demon wife of Adam, and her dark lord husband drinking the blood of children. You can't believe everything you read in the Bible."

"I read it on Wikipedia," her husband said. "Did you know that you can find a vampyre's grave by leading a virgin boy through a graveyard on the back of a black stallion? Sounds fishy to me, considering vampyres can't walk on consecrated ground. They used to bury corpses with lemons in their mouths to stop them from coming back."

"Do you know what I read on Wikipedia?" Mildred asked. "In two thousand-six, a physics professor wrote a paper proving that it's mathematically impossible for vampyres to exist thanks to geometric progression. If the first vampyre had appeared in January sixteen hundred and fed once per month, turning each of its victims into a vampyre, the entire world would have been vampyres within two and a half years."

"That's not the point."

"Then what *is* the point?"

"I think Satan Claws is here," John replied. "And I think he might be coming down the chimney."

"Bullshit."

"Come on, Millie," John insisted. "We might as well go and take a look, just to be sure."

"Fine."

"Should I take the gun?"

"No," Mildred replied. "If you do, you'll end up shooting someone."

"Yes," John said absently. "That's kind of the point."

"Last solstice, I gave you my neck,
but the very next day, you went back to heck.
This year, to save me from fear,
I'm going to hide in heaven."

– Splat

Satan Claws *was* coming down the chimney.

The front door would have been easier, but that was protected by old magick, a power greater even than he was. He was the Antichrist, the first vampyre, and vampyres had to be invited over the threshold.

He was thirsty, so thirsty, and it was time for his annual feast. Blood was the thing, the delicious nectar of life that sustained him. The blood of virgins was better. The blood of the young was best, for they were free and innocent. They hadn't yet been touched by evil.

He worked at night by the light of the moon, chasing it across the sky and returning to his crypt before the first rays of the morning sun filtered over the horizon. The sunlight, along with the warmth that it brought, was deadly. That was why he worked at night. Solstice Eve—and Solstice Morning, until the dawn at least—was the one night of the year he worked.

Every year, his evil elves delivered a list of who'd been naughty and who'd been nice. He'd work through the list, taking care not to touch the paper against his flaming beard in case it caught fire. Then he'd shortlist a dozen names from the top of the "good" list and carry out basic reconnaissance on the run-up to solstice. It was the good little boys and girls who tasted the best. The bad boys and girls tasted like rotten apples and gave him the bloody equivalent of a hangover.

And that was how he'd settled on Jessie and Jude Reid.

He'd been watching the girls for several months, documenting every decision they made in his diabolical notebook. He tracked their searches on their smart speakers and digitally snooped on them as they plowed their crops in *FarmVille* or popped bubbles in *Candy Crush Saga*. He knew more about them than anyone, including their parents.

He'd been preparing for this moment for some time. And now he was finally ready.

He hit the fire at the bottom of the chimney feet first, but the flames simply fed his desire and regenerated him, leaving him stronger and more determined than ever. He could smell the two girls, and they were ready for him.

Satan Claws smiled grimly and climbed out of the fireplace, unfolding himself to his full height in the middle of the Reids' suburban living room. He was bloated, his stomach distended like a starving child in a charity campaign. Lesser vampyres resorted to draining the blood from cattle and sheep, but Satan Claws was a purist. Only the freshest human blood could pass his palette.

And he was thirsty.

He walked out of the living room and into the hallway, his footsteps falling silently with soft *thup-thup-thups* that didn't make an echo. The hallway was dark, but that wasn't a problem for Satan Claws, who could hunt by smell just as easily as by sight.

The floorboards creaked as he placed his weight on them, but the darkness swallowed up the sound. From above him, he could discern the subtle thumping of four heartbeats, two in each of the upstairs bedrooms. He drew his tongue across his lips, sending filthy, dead blood dribbling down his chin. He gnashed subconsciously at the air, just like his thralls when they chewed through the shrouds in their graves.

The house was an unwelcoming place, packed to the rafters with the symbols of white magick. But Satan Claws was a hunter, and like all hunters, he reveled in the thrill of the chase.

It would make his meal all the better.

"I'll have a black solstice without you."

– Elvis Deathly

The door to their bedroom seemed to open of its own accord. Then the darkness changed texture, and a figure stepped silently through the doorway.

Satan Claws was dressed in black robes, though they were trimmed with crimson. To the two girls, who were still learning their relative scale, he looked ten feet tall. But that was impossible because it would have pushed his head through the ceiling and up toward the roof, where his slay was still perched precariously, his hellhounds scrabbling their claws across the tiles and sending them crashing down to the floor.

"Oh, oh, oh," Satan Claws growled, his voice sounding like the rattle of a corpse as it swung in the breeze at a medieval crossroads. "Merry Solstice."

He held his dark hand up and tensed it into a fist, sending a ripple of evil washing over the room like the fog from a smoke machine. The candles in the window, which symbolized that Christ was the light of the world, were extinguished by a wave of black wind. The vampyre's psychokinetic energy erupted outward like a sonic boom, except it was visible as it passed through the darkness. A fierce wind blew through the building, detonating the girls' nativity scene and sending the baby Jesus flying through the air to shatter against the wall. The china models had been valuable family heirlooms passed down from generation to generation, but within a couple of seconds, they'd been turned into nothing more than a pile of brightly painted broken pottery.

Outside, in the garden, the snowman's head exploded, its coal eyes firing through the night and into the windows of the girls' bedroom, sending shards of glass scattering across their stuffed toys and all over the floor.

And in the bedroom, the two girls looked out imperiously from their bunks. The vampyre had protruding teeth and an aquiline nose, as well as the hungry look of a man who hadn't eaten for a year. As he looked at the girls, his gaze alone was enough to freeze them to their beds, as though they were trapped between wakefulness and unconsciousness in a satanic sleep paralysis.

He took a step toward the girls, and then another.

"Get away from my kids, you make-believe bastard!"

The vampyre's head turned in a full semi-circle, taking in Mildred Reid in her nightdress and her husband a step and a half behind her. She had a wooden stake in one hand and a hammer in the other, and she was rushing toward him like a woman possessed. The sharpened wood was closing in on him, but the vampyre was too fast for it, clicking his fingers and dissolving into a whirling cloud of bats, which dodged the woman's jabs and batted against her, their little legs getting tangled up in her hair. John swatted ineffectively at them while Mildred continued to swing the stake through the air at a target that no longer existed.

In their beds, the girls came back to life again, their innocent bodies no longer pinned in place by the vampyre's evil eye. They moved toward their stockings.

There was a growl from the darkness in the hallway, and then Tupac was in the room, too, a black cat batting black bats, but the bats were fighting back, and the cat was howling. Its unnatural yowl seemed to break the spell, and the room flooded with volume as everyone tried to move at once. Satan Claws reformed, the bats disappearing beneath his robes, while John and Mildred made a rush for him. The girls were at the foot of their beds, rummaging through their stockings for the gifts within. Jude was the quickest, and she tore the wrapping from what looked like a bottle of perfume before raising it in both arms.

Satan Claws took the hit of holy water straight in the face.

"Well, tonight, thank God, it's them instead of you."
                                    – Band Aids Over Puncture Holes

"Oh, oh, oh," Satan Claws growled. "Is that the best you can do?"

Time stood still around him. Jude was still holding the bottle in front of her face, visible mostly as a pair of bright green eyes in the darkness. Jessie was in the bunk below, her hands still buried deep within her stocking. Satan Claws was in the middle of the room with his back to the door; Tupac had bolted beneath the bed and was watching proceedings unfold with the disinterested wariness of the common housecat. John and Mildred were to either side of the vampyre, their hammers raised in the air as they fumbled with their stakes.

And Lilith was standing in the doorway.

She was like Satan Claws but with style, a biblical beauty who'd added flavor over time, like a fine wine. Her husband was unkempt for a vampyre, with flowing white hair, a bushy beard, and a big belly. Lilith looked like she took care of herself, like she worked out every night lifting the lids off crypts or doing gothic lunges. She was dressed mostly in velvet, with a few hints of leather, and her lips and fingernails were painted the deep scarlet of an aged bottle of O negative.

"Enough of this, husband," Lilith said, clapping her hands together. When her palms touched, the two adults were thrown to opposite sides of the bedroom, where they smacked against the walls and then slid to the floor in a broken symmetry. "Let's feed."

"Like hell," John growled, pushing himself up on one knee

before slumping back down again. Blood flowed freely from somewhere on his scalp, and his wife was unconscious but breathing.

"My good man," Satan Claws said, "I have no desire to hurt you or your wife. I remember you as a child. You used to write me letters every solstice, begging me not to take you or your brothers."

His mouth fell open.

"All we want is to feed," Lilith said, her voice floating eerily on the supernatural wind that was still blowing through the house, sending ornaments tumbling to the floor and rotating crucifixes where they hung above the doorways.

"But they're my daughters!"

"So?" Satan Claws replied, leering evilly at him. "You planned a solstice dinner tomorrow, did you not?"

John Reid said nothing.

"Yes, husband," Lilith added. "They have a turkey defrosting in the refrigerator."

"But that's different!" John protested.

"Is it?" Satan Claws growled. "It died so you could live. How is this any different?"

"It just—"

"Mister Reid, I grow tired of talking to you," Satan Claws said. "Don't make me kill you. After all, alive, you can make new children. Dead, you're no good to anyone."

"You bastard, I'll—"

"It's okay, Daddy," Jude said, her voice sounding eerily calm amidst the chaos. "I know what we have to do."

"Yes," Jessie agreed. "It's the only way."

"Girls, I don't—"

"Yes," Lilith said. "It's as it should be."

She clicked her fingers, and the girls' leather-bound Bible flew off their bookcase and toward their father's head. It knocked him clean out, and he snoozed on in silence like his wife while the vampyres moved in on the two girls.

They offered no resistance.

"I'll be eligible for parole come Valentine's Day."
– Tom Waits for No Man, Solstice Card from
a Vampyre in Minneapolis

John Reid awoke to a bloodbath, though his pale-faced, angelic daughters had been drained of the stuff. They were both still in their bunks, their glassy eyes staring up at the ceiling, the puncture marks in their necks looking like recharge sockets for androids. Their skin had turned a papery white, matching their pristine bedsheets and giving them the look of department store mannequins wearing old-fashioned wedding dresses.

Tupac, the cat, was dead, too. His head had been torn off and thrown at the girls' stuffed animals like a bowling ball. The rest of the cat was poking out of their Jesus-themed litter bin, making a mockery of the savior's own suffering. Christ, who was hanging from a cross on its façade, had blood on his forehead and was looking out at the scene with an expression of beatific resignation.

Mildred was unconscious still, though she was coming around. She had a bloody nose that had dripped onto her chest, and John supposed she was lucky not to have landed differently or she might have drowned in the stuff. He himself had bled heavily from the wound to the back of his skull, and he had a splitting headache that reminded him of his hangover days, before he'd given up the bottle after the kids were born.

"Mildred?" John said. "Millie, are you okay?"

"*Nghh...*"

"He killed them," John murmured.

"Nghhhh?"

"The girls," John said. "He killed them. Drained them of blood. They're gone, Millie."

"They're whuh?"

"They're gone," John repeated, pulling himself unsteadily to his feet. He looked around the room again. There was blood on all four walls and the ceiling, presumably from the cat, and the girls' normally tidy bedroom looked like the aftermath of a bomb blast in Beirut. Even their dreamcatchers had been torn down, and on the far wall of the room, their portrait of Christ stood watch beneath his crown of thorns. Someone had drawn a goatee, horns, and glasses on him in the cat's blood.

John picked up one of the stakes and his hammer.

"No," Mildred said. "Not that, John. Anything but that."

"We have to."

"I can't."

"Then I'll do it."

Mildred tried to pull herself to her feet, but all her strength had been taken away and she stumbled and fell again. John flashed a glance of concern at her, but then he returned to the task at hand.

He dealt with Jessie first because she was on the bottom bunk and she was easier for him to reach. When he placed the stake above her heart and smacked it with the hammer, the wood pierced her flesh and an unearthly hiss filled the air. She crumbled before his eyes, turning to dust and bone.

Jude came next, with the same result.

Once the job was done, John Reid glanced resignedly at his wife and then walked silently out of the room. He returned several minutes later with a shoebox in his hands.

"What are you doing?" Mildred asked as he removed the gun from the box and started loading bullets into the chamber.

"What do you think I'm doing?"

"It's too late," Mildred said. "They're gone. Your silver bullets are useless, just like the rest of these trinkets."

"It's not for the vampyres," John said sadly as he loaded the cartridges into the revolver. "It's for us."

"For us?"

"It's our fault that the girls are dead," John said. "We didn't believe. We *couldn't* believe. But we were wrong, Millie. *I* was wrong. If we'd just believed, if we'd just been a little faster, we could have fought them off. The girls might still be alive. But now there's nothing. Nothing to live for."

Mildred seemed to think about it for a moment.

Then she said, "Okay. But as long as you shoot me first."

"You'd better watch out, you'd better not cry."
— Satan Claws is Coming to Town

The family was found in the morning when the three Jenkins kids from number 17 stopped by to sing some solstice carols. When they went to knock at the door, it was already hanging open, so they'd let themselves inside for a break from the cold.

They'd found John and Mildred in the smaller of the two upstairs bedrooms. They were slumped, arm in arm, with their backs against the wall, their glassy eyes staring vacantly toward their daughters' bunkbed. They weren't moving, but that was no surprise. Most of their heads were missing. Little Jessica Jenkins screamed and bolted downstairs towards the front door, her two older brothers hot on her heels. They called their parents first and the emergency services second, and both of them arrived at the same time. The Reids were carried out an hour or two later, their destination the city morgue and, eventually, its crematorium. Sergeant Gary Mogford of the Homicide Division had theorized that it was a murder-suicide, though if pressed to ask what had happened to the girls, he could only have given a guess.

They were still awaiting results on the strange gray ashes that had been found in the girls' beds, as well as the sharpened lumps of wood that had been lying beside them.

As for Satan Claws, he'd flown on back to hell, his hellhounds baying in the wind, his thirst slaked for another year as his wife slumbered in her seat beside him.

"Oh, oh, oh," he'd bellowed, his deathly voice echoing like

a thunderclap as he flew over the Chilterns. "Merry Solstice. And until next year…"

THE CHIMNEY

R.A. Clarke

Flakes whip and whirl. A whiteout surrounds me. The temperature's dropping and nobody's found me. What should I do? I can't last the night. With no heat to speak of; no shelter in sight.

I should've been feasting, tipping back beer. I could've been singing songs of good cheer. But the boss man gave out a last-minute mission. Which thrust me into this precarious position. See, we needed more samples from our latest find. A routine procedure; so, the rest stayed behind to cherish a relaxing *warm* Christmas Eve. I cursed my short straw, then packed up to leave.

But I ventured too far from my research base. Next the GPS failed; screen frozen in place. Then I saw someone stumbling in the distance alone. I tried to go help, when in swept the snow. Now my tracks disappear as fast as they're made, and that person has vanished—I'm baffled, dismayed. With no way-points to guide me, I've lost my home trail.

I feel panic rising... "Breathe deeply. Inhale."

But breathing won't help—the air's laced with blown ice. I need to get warmer in order to fight. For frost creeps so slowly, permeating the skin. Cold seeps into bones, icy fingers dig in.

The radio's still static. I've run out of luck. My ski-doo's gas is waning. Yep, I'm truly fucked. Though I've never been lucky, I wouldn't have guessed. I'd get lost in the wild and then freeze to death.

Yet there's one silver lining that's helping me cope. Since I haven't checked in, they'll come looking, I hope. So, I just need to last—survive this white storm. But my engine just died. Now I'm stranded. Forlorn.

There's no time to waste. I grab all my gear. A flint and a flare gun, in case help comes near. Plus, a blanket and a water bottle that froze. Then I get my legs moving to warm up my toes. Up ahead I spy trees. I break into a run. My cheeks burn like fire. I can't feel my thumbs. A huge sagging tree, like a spruce or a pine, will offer the most shelter. That's what I must find. But the trees are all spindly—there'll be no reprieve. I'm too frozen to build. Useless, shelterless me.

Wait, what do I smell...is that cookies and cream? And there! Up ahead... Could that really be steam? No, it's smoke from a stack sticking out of the ground. Looking closer, it's bricks with ice all around. A chimney! But why, and who, what, and how? It's the top of the world, with nothing around. The smoke plumes and curls, blown away by the wind. I step warily closer, can't help but lean in. I take a quick look. A curious peek. Down below, there's a glow. And a glorious heat.

I warm up my hands, inhale the sweet smell. But the rest of me's frozen—brain foggy as well. I need to get in, though there's no door in sight. What choice do I have? I must last the night. I climb to the ledge five feet off the ground. It'll be a tight squeeze for me to slide down. Then an echo of laughter comes from below. A hearty guffaw. A bold "Ho, Ho, Ho!"

What the hell? Are you kidding? That can't be the man! The one with the reindeer and world gifting plan? *No, I've lost it.* My mind's gone numb from the cold. It's a freezing mirage of a toasty north pole.

I dangle my feet and get blanketed up. If I stay sitting here, it might be enough. I must last until morning—'til my partners to come. Else hallucinate warmth as I slowly succumb. But then something grabs me and yanks on my feet. I slip off the ledge and down my form streaks. Like a blur, I am falling at terminal speed. Hitting bottom will hurt. Yes, I'll burn or I'll bleed. As I brace for impact, savage fear takes control. It grows hotter and hotter, far worse than the cold. Is this real? I can't tell! Am I already dead? Was I judged and found wanting—sent to hell instead?

"No, it's not hell, and you're certainly not dead," a voice says below me. My gut aches with dread.

Did he just read my mind? How else could he know? My

body starts tingling, then sideways I go. Whipping out of the chimney, I fly through the flames. As I land on my butt—my eyes see a face. I gasp at the likeness, those twinkling eyes. That blazing white beard ain't no damn disguise.

Fuck me, that is Santa! The Claus man himself. Rosy cheeks and round belly, red coat, and black belt. "Is this really real? Are you really you?" I whisper in shock, with no clue what to do.

He hands me a cookie, then stirs a big pot. His smile curls with amusement. "And what if I'm not?" With a booming "Ho ho," the beard melts off his chin. "Best trick in the book. Boy, you'll wish I had been!" He cackles and shivers, his form changing shape. Soon, dark matted hair and pale skin take his place. Cloaked in dark rags; with two missing front teeth. A woman appears while I scramble to flee.

With a flick of the wrist, she locks me in place. Then comes to inspect me; my hands, feet and face. She gives me a sniff and licks my left ear.

"W-who are you?" I sputter in pants-wetting fear.

"My name is Gruthelda, the *true* Christmas witch. Not wretched old Gryla. That troll's just a bitch. When I sensed your dire troubles, quickly I came. Tis the season of giving— the north my domain. Had I not intervened, I'd feel such re- morse. For I find desperate souls…and save them, of course. But my help isn't free. You must pay a price. If you wish to live, you must risk your life."

"W-what must I do? Just let me go home," I plead, weak and helpless. But her face is a stone. Devoid of all kindness, no em- pathy there. She wants what she wants without a spare care.

Gruthelda whispers, "Give a limb for my stew. If you last the whole night, then it's home-bound for you." She smiles as she waits for me to decide. "So, what will it be? I don't have all night."

All I can do is stare without words. I cannot believe what I have just heard. With a whimper, I ask, "What will happen to me if I do not accept—if I do not agree?"

Her answer is sharp, rolling quick off her tongue. "To take such a stance would be dumber than dumb. Your death is assured if you dare to refuse. One way or another, I'll flavor my stew."

Sobbing, I nod. "You can have my left hand. I won't give you a leg, 'cause I need both to stand."

While patting my head, her eyes flicker like fire. "Just hold out your hand, boy. This needn't be dire."

Once more, I am locked in place by her charm. Then her axe swiftly drops and off goes my whole arm! The hot blade does its work—even cauterizes some. Wailing, I tremble; hold my bloody stump. I watch the witch dicing my sacrificed limb. She gives me a tourniquet; wipes blood from my skin. I throw up from the shock and the smell of her brew. But the worst part of all is seeing her chew.

Feeling weak and bereft, the night ambles along. Then finally, *finally,* it comes time for dawn. Trembling and nauseous, I make my appeal. "I lasted the night—fulfilled your dark deal." It grows harder to focus, to remain awake. And strangely, I no longer feel any ache. "Gruthelda, I beg you; I really must go. I must find a doctor. I need to get home."

She snickers and thanks me for doing my part. "But it's

not morning yet. My home is still dark."

I shake with sheer rage and show her my watch. "No, we made a deal. You've taken your chop!"

Gruthelda's cold irises shatter my soul. "Then prove that it's morning, and I'll let you go." Up the chimney she points. "There, that is the way. See the light, and I promise you'll be home today." Tossing logs on the fire, she beams with smug glee.

I cry, beaten and helpless. *I'll never be free.*

She'd been toying with me right from the start. A desperate traveler with ripe body parts. My memories flash slowly — stuck on replay. Gruthelda hums softly while I fade away. She pulls out a bowl and spice for her brew and then preps for more pots of lost traveler stew.

✹Convicted

Mike Marcus

Ray crumpled the casino wager slip in disgust and dropped it in his half-eaten bowl of cold, greasy gumbo. Another New Orleans Saints fourth-quarter collapse, and for Ray, a C-note down the drain. He rattled the ice in his nearly empty whiskey glass and glared at Sylvia behind the bar.

"Tough night for the boys. Couldn't even get lucky playing at home two days before Christmas," Sylvia said, turning from the television to Ray. The cheap Christmas lights strung overhead cast red and white splotches across Ray's face and t-shirt. The lights appeared festive to anyone who didn't know

Sylvia left them up year-round, just as the dust-covered cobwebs in the corners weren't leftover Halloween decorations.
The bar owner nodded to the empty glass. "You sure you want
another?"

Ray nodded, staring at the television as the game clock
counted down the final minute.

"Got money for it?"

Ray sighed and dropped two twenties on the bar. Sylvia
poured the whiskey and took the money before shuffling to
another customer.

Ray pushed the gumbo away, brushing yellow cornbread
crumbs off the sticky bar. Sylvia's Place had mediocre gumbo
and worse service. But the food was cheap, and the cornbread
was good. Sylvia also poured full drinks, not that watered-
down stuff they serve three blocks away on Bourbon Street.

Ray's cell phone vibrated on the bar, the screen lighting up
with his daughter's face before a text from Danielle appeared.
He thumbed open the message and fought the urge to throw
the phone into the mirrored bar back.

> Pick Kaley up at 3 pm tomorrow. Please
> don't forget and disappoint her. Again.

Ray sipped his whiskey, took several deep breaths, and pictured his happy place. A big boat out on the Gulf, seagulls
floating overhead, a dozen fishing rods with bait in the water,
and a cooler full of ice-cold beer next to his chair. He could almost hear the seagulls and smell the diesel from the outboard
motors. The visualization was a trick his parole officer recom-

mended when dealing with his ex.

Ray swiped through photos of his daughter, his anger fading to a low simmer. Kaley, a few days after she was born, her face red and squished like an overripe tomato. At six months old, just before he was sent upstate to Dixon Correctional. Danielle didn't send him any pictures of Kaley while he was locked up. He didn't expect she would, with how things ended between them. She knew that little girl was the only happiness in his life, the only reason he had to try to be better than his old man was to him, and Danielle lorded that over him every chance she got.

Five years in the dankest hole in the state because of a stupid bar fight. How was he supposed to know the guy couldn't take a punch and would end up in the ICU? At trial, Ray learned the smug LSU bastard who started the fight was Judge Halloran's nephew. The public defender warned Ray to expect two years, but that was before the prosecutor brought up Ray's record. He tried to make Ray sound like a violent man on the verge of homicide. The public defender wanted Ray to be quiet, but he insisted on speaking, on trying to get the judge to understand that the first two strikes—domestic battery convictions— were bullshit. Ray only succeeded in digger a deeper hole. It didn't matter that Danielle gave as good as she got when things got physical. All the police and judges saw was a cute little blonde girl in a crop top and shorts with a black eye and busted lip.

Strike one—thirty days in county.

Strike two—ninety days.

Strikes, three, four, and five—five years in the state pen

with five years' probation tacked on for good measure.

Another text popped up, blocking the photo of Kaley from a month ago, now a seven-year-old, blonde-haired little girl with missing front teeth riding the carousel at the zoo.

> Did you get the doll? She keeps asking about it. If you didn't, Scott can still get it.

His PO's voice rang in his ears. You don't have custody rights. You need to play nice if you want to see your daughter. She didn't ask for child support because you were locked up. Don't give her anything else to use against you if you want to see Kaley.

Ray tapped out his response.

> Yes, 3 pm. I'm getting the doll for her.

He put the phone face down. The damn doll was almost two hundred dollars. What kind of doll costs half his rent? For the past two months, Kaley wouldn't shut up about it. It was all she wanted. If the Saints hadn't shit the bed, the money wouldn't be a problem. His gig working part-time at the Bienville Street minimart or under the table doing drywall wouldn't cover it, but his little side hustle was a sure thing.

Six months ago, when he realized he would be short on rent that first time, Ray started hanging out on Bourbon Street, lifting fat wallets off drunk tourists. Women juggling oversized drinks and unzipped purses were the easiest lifts. He and his buddies perfected the bump lift in high school, stalking tourists flashing too much cash for their own good and "accidentally" colliding with them on the crowded sidewalks. The out-of-towners usually apologized and walked away, not realizing they'd lost their wallet.

Sylvia worked her way back down the bar and topped off his drink. "That's it for the night, Ray," she said, putting the bottle back. "You should go home and get some sleep. You look like shit."

Ray nodded, knocking back the last drink. But he couldn't go home. He had work to do if he was going to give Kaley anything for Christmas.

Ray floated down Bourbon Street, carried by the crowd in one direction before crossing the street and bobbing back in the other. He admired the twinkling Christmas lights wrapped around the light posts and clinging to the front of every res-taurant and bar along one of the world's best-known tourist destinations. People packed the French Quarter, though not as full as at Mardi Gras. Ray picked out accents from across the country as he strolled the sidewalks. Boston. Minnesota. Cali-fornia. Maine. Pittsburgh. Baltimore. And all of them oblivious.

A young woman wearing a tight halter top with a lobster-red sunburn stepped out of a bar drinking a large Hurricane in a plastic cup, obviously not her first of the night. She bumped into Ray as she joined the throng on the sidewalk. "I'm sorry," he said, steadying her by the arm. She gave him a drunken smile and turned, disappearing into the crowd with two similarly drunk twenty-somethings. Ray tucked her wallet into his jacket pocket with the others. He'd picked six wallets in the hour since leaving Sylvia's. Tourists were easy marks, flashing money and credit cards with abandon, especially when drunk. Nobody came to Bourbon Street to stay sober, especially not pretty girls in their twenties.

Ray started north toward his parked van, clearing the heavier trafficked—and policed—tourist areas. He'd check the wallets when he got home. From other nights on Bourbon Street, he guessed he had close to four hundred dollars in cash, plus what he could get selling the credit cards to a fence who also lived in the Breakwater Motel. It would be enough to cover rent, the doll for Kaley, and Christmas dinner for them.

A block from Saint Louis Cemetery, he saw the woman. He wasn't looking for another target, but her arms were full of packages as she struggled to lock the back door of the shop. A heavy, expensive-looking woven purse dangled from one arm. Ray paused at the alley entrance, trying to appear casual. It was almost midnight, and the street was empty. The purse shimmied and bobbed in the moonlight as though it knew he was watching, urging him to take it.

Ray stepped into the alley, disappearing into the shadow behind a dumpster. The woman was maybe thirty. The harsh white light over the door distorted her features, but she wore long braids and a short black skirt with cherry-red high heels. A party girl, probably. Her type had money to burn and frequented the high-roller nightclubs around town. Ray didn't like stealing from locals, but sometimes they were easier than tourists.

She glanced up just as Ray arrived at the door, big brown eyes catching his face as he put a shoulder against her and grabbed her purse. She yelled as she tumbled to the pavement, the packages falling around her as the strap fell from her wrist. Ray didn't slow until he was on the far side of the cemetery.

She didn't chase him, and there was no indication she called out for help. Ray stepped into a doorway and looked back. No one was following. He rifled through the bag, searching for a cell phone. Cell phones were trackable, but he was surprised. No phone. Only a wallet, five or six smaller bags, and four small bundles wrapped in brown paper and string, like the larger packages she'd been holding.

The morning light streamed white-hot through the dirty motel window, burning Ray's closed eyelids like an arc welder. He flopped over on the worn couch, pressing his face against the rough woven pillow. His cell phone chirped with a text message.

Ray took a deep breath and sat up. His mouth tasted like an ashtray, and everything ached. He hadn't hurt like that since his first beatdown at Dixon Correctional, when he smart-mouthed Bubba Hanson before he knew the old man ran the cellblock. Ray looked around the apartment, shielding his eyes with one hand, and picked up his cell phone. More texts from Danielle, reminding him yet again of Kaley's pick-up time. It was almost ten o'clock already, but fortunately the toy store was on his way.

A flash of silver caught Ray's eye, and he squinted, remembering the ring. It wasn't his. He'd never owned a silver ring with a polished black stone. Ray's head swam and his stomach flip-flopped as he stood, and he sat back down before he fell over. On the coffee table, an empty fifth of whiskey lay next to a plastic ashtray holding the remains of the two joints he bought off the guy down the hall. At the far end of the scarred coffee table sat the purse and a pile of now-empty wallets. Through the hangover haze he remembered finding the ring in a small black velvet bag at the bottom of the purse.

The cash was folded and wrapped with a rubber band. He must have counted it last night, as it was sorted and in order, sitting next to the ashtray. Ray focused his swimming eyes on the cash and recounted the money, stopping to vomit twice in the small plastic trashcan next to the couch. From the acrid stink and the soiled toilet paper in the trashcan, he was glad he'd brought it out of the bathroom last night.

Despite the hangover, last night was one of the best he'd had in a long time. Almost $600.00 in cash and nearly two dozen credit cards. He could sell the credit cards and IDs for forty bucks a piece.

The purse was a bust, though, and he kicked himself for taking the risk. According to the expired driver's license in the wallet, the woman's name was Marie, and she lived in the Ninth Ward. No credit cards and only twenty-two dollars. The little bags inside the purse weren't worth anything, either. Make-up. An old wooden rosary. A worn tarot deck, a handful of dice, and random dominoes.

The paper-wrapped packages weren't any better. Candles. A box of white sidewalk chalk. A small bottle of cheap whiskey. A baggie of mixed bird feathers. Incense. Dried rose petals. Ray swept the packages and their contents off the coffee table and back into the woven bag. At least he got the ring, though he doubted it would be worth much if he tried to hock it. Maybe he'd just keep it. A little gift to himself.

Ray slid into his usual booth at the Silver Dollar Diner. The twenty-four-hour greasy spoon catered to down-on-their-luck gamblers from the nearby casino, employees at the pawn shops and bail bonds offices lining the highway, and the ex-cons using the motel across the street as a way station. His PO had set him up with a room at the Breakwater Motel when Ray got out two years ago, and he'd never bothered to find somewhere else to live.

The booth, halfway down the front of the diner, was close enough to the doors to keep an eye on who was entering, but distant enough for a quick exit out the backdoor in case of trouble. It was a prison habit, like deciding where to sit for chow. Plus, the booth was in Valerie's section.

"Hey, Ray, how you doin'?" Valerie chirped as she rounded the counter, order pad in one hand, a mug of steaming coffee in the other.

"Hi, darlin'," he said, turning in the booth to face her. "You're a sight for sore eyes." The petite bottled-blonde turned down his advances in the past, but he wasn't giving up. Flirty little things like Valerie didn't always know what was good for them. She'd go out with him eventually, and one way or another, he'd find out what she was hiding beneath that frumpy waitress uniform. He'd bet one of the other ex-cons at the motel twenty dollars that he'd seal the deal over the holidays.

Valerie stopped short, the hot coffee sloshing over the rim of the mug, burning her fingers. She stared at Ray, keeping her distance. "You okay?"

"Yeah, why?" Ray asked, dropping the menu onto the table and looking up at the waitress. His eyes were drawn to her breasts, as they always were when he was talking to Valerie. More than once, she reminded him where her eyes were located. "What's wrong?"

Valerie gingerly stepped forward, like a rabbit prepared to sprint if the dog looked in its direction. She put the coffee cup down in front of Ray and stepped back, not sitting across from him for the usual chit-chat, not reminding him to stop staring at her breasts. "How are you feeling?"

"I'm tired but no more than usual. Why are you looking at me like that?"

Valerie pulled out her order pad and clicked her pen nervously, her eyes avoiding Ray's face. "Nothing. Never mind."

"What the hell are you talking about?" Ray asked, snatching the aluminum napkin holder from the end of the table and holding it up to see his reflection in the polished metal.

He almost fumbled it as his gaze focused on his reflected face. He was gaunt and pale, beads of sweat growing on his forehead. His right eye was a pool of blood, the white obliterated by broken veins. His shaggy black hair was thin, with new hints of gray at his temples.

"What the hell?" Ray repeated, pushing up from the booth. Valerie stepped back as he rushed past and into the bathroom at the far end of the restaurant.

Ray stared confusedly into the mirror. Last night he went to sleep a healthy 38-year-old. Now, dark circles ringed his eyes as though he hadn't slept in days, and the stubble covering his chin and cheeks had turned salt-and-pepper. Most concerning was his eye. What did he do overnight to obliterate the veins and leave it a bloody mess? Ray splashed cold water on his face. He was tired, but none the worse for wear despite how he looked. Maybe he needed to lay off the booze and pot. He closed his eyes and splashed more water on his face, taking several deep breaths. He almost screamed when he opened his eyes, startled by a woman standing behind him in the mirror.

He spun around, but he was alone. Ray looked back into the old steel mirror. She was still there, just behind him, light brown eyes staring. Twice he turned and looked, almost hoping to find the woman had accidentally wandered into the men's room.

Ray took a deep breath, clenched his eyes, and silently counted to ten. It was a trick a cellmate taught him when things were bad on the block. Merle was a squirrely little guy with anxiety doing a ten-year bid for arson and insurance fraud. He talked incessantly but wasn't bad compared to some of Ray's other cellmates over the years.

"You stole from me."

Ray's eyes flashed open. The woman was still there, standing so close Ray was certain he felt her breath on his neck.

"You stole from me. No one steals from me," she repeated calmly, like a Sunday school teacher with a classroom full of kindergarten students listening. "Return my things by sundown and I might undo what has been done."

Ray closed his eyes, bit the inside of his cheek, and took two more deep breaths. He gripped the sides of the cool porcelain sink. "I'm alone. I'm imagining this. There is no one in here with me," he said, trying to calm his nerves and reassure himself. He repeated the mantra three times, as Merle used to do, and opened his eyes. He was alone.

Ray's hands shook as he wiped his face with a paper towel and tossed it toward the trashcan. *Get ahold of yourself,* he thought. *There was no one in here. You were alone and imagining things. It's probably because you haven't eaten since that shitty bowl of gumbo yesterday.*

Ray returned to his booth and slipped into the seat, his hands jittery on the table.

A minute later, Valerie approached tentatively. "You okay?" she asked.

Ray nodded. "Yeah. I haven't been sleeping well. I guess it's just wearing me down more than I realized," he said, stirring sugar into his coffee, the spoon rattling against the side of the worn ceramic mug. "I don't know what I did to my eye. I guess I need to get it looked at."

She gave him a small smile, one he'd seen her use before, usually when a customer finished their meal and realized they didn't have the money to pay. There was a sadness behind the smile, as though she came from the same hardscrabble existence they did, though Valerie never talked about her life beyond excuses why she wouldn't go out with Ray. "You want your usual?"

Ray nodded, and Valerie disappeared into the kitchen. He gave a start and nearly spilled his coffee when his phone buzzed on the worn Formica table with another text from Danielle.

> Can you pick up Kaley at 1 instead of 3? Scott made surprise Christmas plans I didn't know about.

Fucking Scott. Somehow, Danielle climbed out of that trailer park where they'd lived together and landed herself a secretary job at a law firm. Then she bagged herself a lawyer. Ray wanted to punch him in the mouth every time their paths crossed. Perfect Scott, with his perfect job and his perfect hair giving Danielle the perfect life she'd always wanted while he struggled to get by. The phone buzzed again in his hand.

> Are you awake? Sober?

Ray ignored the jab, ran a hand over his stubble-covered cheek, and checked the time. He could still make it to the toy store at Canal Place to get the doll, but only if he moved quickly and didn't run into any delays. Valerie slid the platter in front of him as he responded,

> No problem. Will be there at 1.

"Here you go. The Bayou Breakfast Special, eggs over-easy," she said, adding a smaller plate with buttered whole wheat toast, almost burnt. Valerie might not go out with him, but she was a damn good waitress. Not only did she know his usual order, she remembered he liked his toast dark.

"Thanks, hon," Ray responded, setting his phone aside and unrolling the silverware from the paper napkin as Valerie tended to a couple at another booth.

Ray dug in, cutting the sausages with the edge of his fork, sopping up the runny yellow egg yolk with the toast before shoveling it into his mouth. Three bites in he winced, salty copper flooding his mouth. He spat the food into a napkin, the saliva tinged with blood. A bit of partially chewed sausage had two teeth stuck in it. His tongue probed the new gap in his teeth, slipping into three holes in his gum. *What the hell is happening to me*, he thought. *And where is the third tooth? Did I swallow it?* Ray dropped his fork and took a swig of coffee, the heat scorching the raw, empty sockets. He ran his tongue around his mouth, feeling each of his teeth. At least four others wobbled in their sockets, including his two front upper teeth.

Ray's stomach turned from the taste of his own blood and he gave up on breakfast, dropping a ten-dollar bill on the table. Valerie stepped out of the kitchen as he left and called after him, but Ray didn't stop.

He sat in his van, his tongue wiggling loose teeth as though it had a mind of its own and was trying to break them free. Should he drive across town to the free clinic? A clinic visit was six hours in the waiting room for a five-minute visit with a nurse. But it also meant missing Christmas with Kaley. If he messed this up now, he might not get another chance. Not if Danielle had anything to say about it. Ray started the van and turned toward the highway to the mall to pick up the doll.

The brake lights came out of nowhere. One minute, traffic was flowing along Route 90. The next, Ray was standing on his brakes, watching the back of the stopped tractor-trailer creep closer to the front of his car as he screeched to a stop.

Ray punched the steering wheel, watching the minutes pass as he sat in gridlock. Lynyrd Skynyrd was on the radio, singing about being free as a bird, though free was the last thing Ray felt. He was trapped. In traffic. In New Orleans. In dealing with his ex-girlfriend so he could see his daughter. In a shitty job and an even shittier apartment. All this after being sprung from the pen. "What I'd give to be free of all of it," he said, glancing in the rear-view mirror.

"If you don't bring me my things, you're gonna be free from all of it soon enough," she said, staring at him in the rear-view mirror.

Startled, Ray spun around, fighting the seatbelt holding him in place. The back seat was empty except for his toolbox and some fast-food trash. He looked up, and she was still in the mirror, just as she had been in the bathroom.

"Look, bitch, I don't know who you are or if you're even real, but I'm getting really tired of this shit," Ray said, more to bolster his own nerves than to scare her. "Go away."

"I want my things, the things you took from me last night. You return them, and maybe, perchance, I'll let you be," she said, swinging her long braids back over her shoulder.

Ray thought back. He'd had a lot to drink last night after

getting home. He had dinner at the bar, then worked Bourbon Street for a couple of hours. Then he snatched the bag from that woman coming out of the shop near the cemetery.

"I'm losing my fucking mind," he muttered, running his hands through his thinning hair. Strands of white hair clung to his fingers like loose threads. "This isn't real. It's a hallucination. I either have a fever, or that bastard down the hall laced his marijuana with something and I'm still feeling it."

The woman in the backseat laughed in the mirror, a full-throated, open-mouthed laugh that echoed in the car. "You think I'm a figment of your imagination. That may be the funniest thing I've heard in a long time," she said. "*Mon cher*, you don't know what you're dealing with. You took things from me, things that I want back. Until you return them…"

Ray grabbed the rear-view mirror and wrenched it from the windshield. She was still there, talking to him. "…you are dying. Bring me back my things and you will live. It's that simple. You have until sundown."

Ray threw the mirror out the window. The brake lights on the truck in front of him flashed, and traffic started to move. Ray rubbed his eyes, still hearing her voice even as the mirror was crushed beneath the traffic.

Ray couldn't help but notice the people staring as he entered the mall, riding the escalator to the Canal Place's second floor. Blightman's Toys was across from the food court and down from the kiddie play area. Ray hurried inside, and the kid behind the counter stepped back as he approached.

"I have a doll on hold. The name is Ray Landry," Ray said, leaning on the counter. His chest hurt, like after running in gym class in high school after he'd started smoking.

The teenager stared at him and backed up against the display of cards and toys behind the counter as though a monster had walked into the store. The color washed from his face.

"Well?" Ray growled, pulling the folded bills from his pocket.

The clerk with the bad complexion hesitated, then turned and found the bag with the "Hold" sheet on it bearing Ray's name. "Uh, yes, sir, sorry. It's two hundred and twenty dollars."

Ray took a deep breath, a pain shooting down his side and around his back. It felt like someone punched him in the ribs, rebreaking bones he'd broken in a car accident years ago. The pain throbbed and ached with every breath. He glanced at the digital clock behind the counter. The drive to the mall took longer than he'd anticipated. Parents shot him strange looks as they entered the store, giving him a wide berth and steering their children away from the counter. Whatever was happening to him was getting worse, and he could only imagine what he looked like.

"Fine. Whatever," Ray croaked, counting off the bills and dropping them on the counter. He snatched the bag from the clerk.

Ray stepped outside the store and a wave of nausea washed over him, worse than the hangover puke from earlier that morning. The restrooms were nearby, but as he crossed the mall, he saw her again. The woman with the braids was staring at him from the large mirror in the Piercing Pagoda. Then she was in the polished metal signs outside Abercrombie. Ray pushed through the Christmas Eve crowd to the men's room.

The handful of men and boys cleared out of the restroom when he entered, and one boy said loudly to his father that Ray smelled. The boy's father hustled him out of the restroom, whispering that Ray was probably homeless and telling the kid to hush up. Ray stepped in front of the row of mirrors over the sinks, the fluorescent lights overhead casting a pale white light that only worsened his appearance.

He looked minutes from death. His cheeks were sunken, his lips thin and bloody from the lost teeth. Most of his hair was white. Liver spots dotted the backs of his hands and his face.

Ray grabbed the "Closed for Cleaning" sign from behind the trashcan and put it in the bathroom entrance. He needed privacy, if only for a few minutes, until a janitor or mall security came by on their rounds. Ray stepped into one of the stalls, sat on the toilet, and tried to catch his breath. Shooting pain radiated up and down his back. His knees hurt sitting there, aching like he'd run a marathon.

He sat staring at his cell phone, not wanting to send the message but knowing he had to.

> I'm sorry. I'm sick and can't take Kaley. Please tell her I'm sorry. I have her doll. It will be at the apartment for her.

Her response was almost immediate.

> Fine.

Ray shoved the phone in his pocket and stepped out of

the stall, thankful everyone took the cleaning sign seriously and stayed out.

"You're looking rough, cher," she said from the mirrors. The woman was in every mirror in the bathroom, even the round security mirror high in the corner. "You must have done some real bad stuff in your time for you to be dying this quickly. That's the rub, you know. You do something bad, and it comes back to bite you, don't it. When you do lots of bad things, well, that all adds up."

Ray nodded his acknowledgment, too worn out to protest.

"You know what you gotta do," she said, her voice softer than before, as though she were talking to a child. "Bring my things, and all of this will end. You'll take a nap, and it will be like none of this happened. You'll remember it, but you'll be your old self again."

Ray stopped in front of the full-length mirror attached to the wall just inside the restroom doorway. "Just make it stop."

For the first time, Ray saw her full length in the mirror as well. He'd only gotten a glance of her in the alley, but in the full light of day, she was stunning. Mocha-colored skin with bright brown eyes that radiated health and power. Full lips and dark braids reached halfway down her back. Her dress was long, flowing cotton that brushed the tops of her bare feet; her toenails were painted blood red. She was young and healthy, the exact opposite of his present condition.

"Don't take your time. Get here before sundown," she said. She had a lilt to her voice and smiled ever so slightly, as though she enjoyed watching him die over some cheap trash wrapped in brown paper. No, he shouldn't have taken her bag last night, but nothing he took warranted what was happening to him.

"I'll be there," Ray snapped.

Ray struggled up the steps to his second-floor motel room. If the aging slowed, he hadn't noticed. He stopped counting how many teeth fell out as he drove, spitting the teeth and bloody drool into an old McDonald's coffee cup. His hair turned thready and white, revealing the thin pink skin covering his skull. He looked like his grandfather the last time he saw him. Pop had been lying on a nursing home hospital bed, cancer ravaging his once-strong body.

Ray noticed the smell as he bent to pick up the purse from the coffee table. At some point, he'd lost control of his bladder and bowels, soiling himself. He went into the bathroom, trashed the ruined pants and underwear, and cleaned himself up the best he could. There wasn't time for a shower. Time seemed to play games with him, speeding up and slowing down to make him rush but knowing he couldn't move any faster as the pain spread through his body.

Ray waddled into the bedroom and pulled on a clean pair of underwear and jeans. They were baggy on his emaciated frame. He tightened his belt and dropped his cell phone in his pocket. He didn't recognize himself in the bedroom mirror. The reflection was that of a concentration camp survivor, not a generally healthy 38-year-old. At least he was alone in the reflection. Hopefully, there was still time to undo this, and if the bitch refused, he had something else planned for her.

Ray parked in the alley he'd run down the night before, flinching as the overhead security lights flashed on one at a time as the sun set behind the buildings to the west. He'd circled the block three times, trying to remember exactly where he'd taken the bag. He stopped once on the facing street, staring at the large plate glass window.

Madame Marie Guidry

Spiritual Readings

Religious Supplies and Talismans for Every Need

As Ray waited for the traffic light to change, he saw her cleaning glass display cases with an old-style feather duster. The shop was dark, with only a few tabletop lamps glowing yellow through the windows.

The purse lay open on the passenger seat next to him as the car's engine cooled, ticking in the quiet alley. Ray looked again at the bag filled with the cheap items, all rewrapped the best he could. The aging slowed on his way to the shop, but his back and knees ached, and his hands shook. Stabbing pain ran through his arms, and his shoulders throbbed, the pain spreading down his hands and into each finger. Bright blood and green pus leaked from around his fingernails, dripping down over the steering wheel. He picked at his hand, and his fingernails peeled off, exposing infected, bloody flesh. By the time he arrived at the alley, bloody fingernails littered the car floor, and blood and pus stained his pants.

Ray opened the glove box and pushed aside a stack of fast-food napkins, removing a piece of heavy waxed canvas. He unfolded the fabric covering the revolver, wincing with each sharp pain through his fingers. Getting caught with the gun meant another trip to the lock-up, but he didn't care. If this woman wouldn't undo what she'd done to him, then he wouldn't die alone.

The last vestiges of daylight receded over New Orleans as Ray hauled himself from the driver's seat and crossed in front of the car, leaning on the hood, a trail of bloody fingerprints on the gray metal. He didn't knock at the door but pulled it open, the purse in one hand, the gun bulging in his pants pocket.

The shop's back room was dark; a chandelier of dripping candles glowed dimly in the middle of the room. A broad wooden table filled the center of the room, the top scarred with knife marks and stained purple and red in places, like a cutting board. Candles on bookshelves and stands glowed around the room, melting white wax pooling around strange glass containers with yellowed labels peeling at the edges, the fine handwriting on each label faded with time.

Ray groaned in pain as he lifted the bag onto the table, something popping in his shoulder. A tall, gilded mirror leaned against the far wall. Ray barely recognized himself. He looked like a corpse dug up from its grave weeks after being buried, skin tight and paper-thin stretched over his skull. He fell atop the table, fighting to stay on his feet.

"Look what the cat dragged in," Marie cooed as she swept

through the strands of beads hanging in the doorway separating the front of the shop from the back room. "I was worried you weren't going to make it before sundown, though you are cutting it pretty close."

Ray wheezed, struggling to breathe, his lungs burning with the effort as though he were trying to breathe underwater. "There's your bag. Undo whatever the hell you've done to me," he gasped.

"All in due time," Marie replied, pouring herself a glass of rum from a bottle on a nearby table. "Drink?"

Ray shook his head. "Please, just help me."

Marie smiled broadly, bright white teeth gleaming in the dim light. "Come now, mon cher, a little rum makes everything better," she said, stepping into the pool of light cast by the candles overhead. Ray gasped as her appearance changed in the light.

When she entered the back room, she was the beautiful, mocha-skinned young woman he saw in the mirrors. But in the candlelight, she morphed into something Ray could only think of as a bayou witch, the kind he'd heard stories about as a boy. She was short and squat, with thick, dirty dreads. Bleeding sores and strangely colored splotches covered her brown skin. The white cotton dress was replaced by dirty, blood-stained burlap. Fat, black flies buzzed around her head, settling on her hair before alighting and returning to their circling. The hand holding the rum glass was missing its pinky, the other fingers scarred, and the remaining fingernails jagged and dirty.

Marie cackled, spittle spattering across the table. "The

right light changes everything, doesn't it, boy?" she asked, sipping her rum.

"Please. I brought your stuff. I'm sorry. I didn't know," Ray mumbled, two more teeth falling from his mouth and skittering across the table. "Please. I'm dying. Undo this curse."

"Why should I? You're a miserable little rat of a man, I can see that from here," she said, circling the table like a buzzard. "Maybe I'll just let things run their course."

Ray wheezed and winced, pain shooting across his chest and down his arm. "Lying...bitch...." With the last of his strength, Ray pulled the pistol from his pocket, aiming the .38 Special at Marie, his hand shaking as he struggled to hold the gun.

Marie chortled, the laugh growing until she was cackling again. "You go ahead, boy. Pull that trigger. I wanna see you do it."

Ray grimaced, leaning on the table, gripping the pistol in both hands. He struggled against the trigger, the muzzle wavering around his target as he tried to fire.

Marie stepped closer, ignoring the gun aimed at her chest, and tapped his finger bearing the silver ring with the black stone. "I gave that ring to my Edward in eighteen thirty-four for our first anniversary," Marie said. "It was for luck, I told him. My Edward liked the dice."

Marie took the gun from Ray's outstretched hands as easily as plucking an apple from a tree. Ray collapsed to the floor, staring up at her with wide, frightened eyes. He struggled to get back to his feet and wobbled like a turtle stuck on its back.

"My Edward, he was so handsome," Marie said, opening a cabinet drawer and dropping the pistol in amongst several others. "I loved him with all my heart, even if he was a cheating bastard. Every Saturday night, he was at the riverboats, gambling away our money and visiting the cathouses. I let it go for a long time, until we couldn't pay our rent. I said something to him. That was the first night he hit me."

Ray's eyes danced around the room, looking for anything he could use against the witch. An iron fire poker leaning against a cabinet. A heavy wooden broom propped in the corner. A length of braided ship's rope beneath the table. He couldn't get to his feet, let alone fight her. His eyes settled on a thick rope hanging from a nearby cabinet, dried gourds attached every few feet. He wasn't listening to Marie anymore; his attention focused on his breathing and the rope.

"The beatings got worse the more he drank. One night, he almost killed me. Auntie Delphine—she lived out in the swamps—found me bloodied and broken. She wanted to feed him to the gators, but I wouldn't allow it. I still loved him. One night when he was asleep, she took his favorite ring, the one that was supposed to bring him luck. That's it you're wearing," she said, nudging Ray's hand with her bare foot. "She took a drop of my blood and mixed it with a bottle of rainwater, then dropped in thirteen shiny pennies. She wrapped it in pig skin and buried it in the cemetery. The next morning, the ring was right back where Edward had left it when he went to bed. He put it on his finger and didn't realize it had been changed.

"That Saturday, he went whoring and came home drunk, but when he raised his hand to me, he couldn't do it. The curse wouldn't let him, but it made him old and weak. He never tried to hurt me again, at least not like that. I guess that old spell has gotten stronger over the years if it's done this much to you since last night. It was just your bad luck that ring was in my bag when you took it. Then again, it always finds its way to those who deserve it."

Ray stared wide-eyed at his hand, his knuckles swollen knobs on thin, sticklike fingers. The ring swung loose on his finger, stuck behind a bony knuckle. His eyes shifted from his hand back to the rope. He squinted at the gourds hanging from it and gasped. They weren't gourds, but a half-dozen shrunken heads, the skins dried dark brown, the features shriveled, some with their mouths sewn shut. As he flailed on the floor, struggling to turn over, the eyes in the heads watched.

"Oh, you've noticed my boys," Marie said with a broad smile, revealing only two remaining teeth. "Edward was my first. That's him on the end, with the silver earring and his mouth sewn closed. Then there was Henry, Philip, and Walter. All boys who couldn't stay out of trouble."

A voice croaked from one of the shrunken heads. "Let him be, witch. You were the only trouble we found, and look at us now. You don't need any more prizes. Just let him go."

Marie walked over to the heads and poked the one who had been talking with a stubby finger, her jagged nail marking its forehead. "You shut your mouth, Philip, or I'll shut it for you with the needle and thread."

The grotesque shrunken face sneered at her but remained quiet.

Ray's head dropped to the stone floor, bloody drool trickling from his mouth and pooling on the floor. He wheezed again as Marie knelt next to him, humming along with the Christmas carols playing on the radio in the front of the store. She pulled a dark knife from beneath her rough fabric dress and ran it across his throat. Three cuts later, Ray's head was freed from his body, but he was still acutely aware of everything happening.

Marie carried him to the sink in the corner and jammed Ray's head down onto a wooden peg. She used the same knife to slice off his earlobe, tossing it into her mouth and gumming it like a piece of jerky.

"What are you doing to me?" Ray croaked, surprised he could still speak. Despite the separation from his body, he still felt the cold stone floor beneath him and the old woman's tongue on his ear as she chewed and sucked on his severed earlobe.

Marie washed her hands in the sink, ignoring his question and chuckling as the water splashed Ray's head. "You best enjoy that water while you can. You ain't gonna have anything else to drink ever again," she laughed. "You should have taken that rum when you could've."

She turned, and as she crossed the pool of light from the overhead bulb, she morphed back into the beautiful young woman in her white cotton dress. She stopped just before the beads and looked back at Ray's head in the sink. His eyes were panicked and stared back at her.

"You just take it easy now," she said with a smile. "I'm going away for a few days for the holidays, but when I get back, we'll get you all dried out like a nice little raisin, then you can join the others on the chain. You best keep quiet, too. If I hear you been making noise, I'll be back with my needle and thread to keep you quiet like Edward over there."

Ray's eyes circled and examined the shop's back room as Marie flitted through the room, blowing out candles and turning off lights. "Have yourself a merry little Christmas," she sang, taking Ray's car keys from his pocket. She picked up the bag from the table, glanced at its contents that Ray had rewrapped, nodded, and turned toward the back door.

"Thanks for rewrapping everything, Ray. I can make my Christmas deliveries to my best customers after all. See you boys after the holidays," she said, locking the shop's back door behind her. A moment later, Ray's car started in the alley, the tires squealing on the wet pavement before catching, the car engine fading in the distance.

Last Supper

Liam Hogan

Gabriel Venkworth trembled as he eyed his empty plate. From a sideboard, wafts of cooked meat made him itch to twist around, to see again the piled-high platters that had been marched into the dining room.

But it would mean glancing, however briefly, at those seated to either side of him, and he wasn't quite ready for *that*.

There were an unlucky thirteen at the table, arranged not in alternating man–woman, but by rich–poor, rich–poor, rich–poor. He and his six fellow destitutes had been plucked from doorways and from beneath bridges barely an hour ago; as dusk descended and temperatures dropped, the doors of the sleek, black carriage flung wide in wordless invitation, refusing to move on until that invitation had been accepted.

An act of seasonal charity, the cadaverous butler who greeted them explained when the carriage pulled up on the grounds of the mansion. His Lordship and his honored guests always catered for far too many, and it seemed only natural at this time of year to share that bounty with those most needy rather than let it go to waste.

But there were no gilt-edged plates in front of the wealthy, only in front of the poor. Crystal goblets, yes, though also currently empty, in front of both. Venkworth, seated at one end of the table, was horribly aware of the vacant chair at the other as the hour edged toward midnight, the day toward Christmas.

He fidgeted, scratching dirt from beneath ragged nails, desperate to avoid the humiliation that *must* be coming. Equally desperate to accept it, if that meant being fed, even if only the scraps from this opulent table.

From the shadows beside the hearth stepped a tall man, dressed in somber black, and the table seemed to exhale.

Their host then, Lord of the manor. Somehow, the fact their number was no longer such an ill-fated one did nothing to calm Venkworth's nerves.

The nameless Lord stood behind his seat, gazing down the table, staring straight at Venkworth. Venkworth found himself unable to tear his eyes away, fascinated and appalled. The man's face was as deeply crinkled as a screwed-up page. Not merely *lined* by age, and in no other way did he appear old, but rather as though the skin had never been smooth to begin with, the corrugations deepening with the passing of innumerable years.

"Dear friends, and welcome strangers," the Lord said, his thin hands encompassing all. "On this day, we who are privileged with wealth, and status, and with long lives, serve those we find in the gutters. Please, attend our guests."

Instantly, there were only the seven from the streets at the table, empty seats yawning between them, as behind Venkworth there came the clink of serving spoons. This was what so spooked him. It wasn't the *appearance* of the wealthy, the woman with the mirrored spectacles, the fat man whose teeth gleamed gold in the candlelight; it wasn't the way they gazed upon the poor with small smiles at the corners of their cruel lips. It was the way the rich *moved*. As if unconstrained by gravity, by the limitations of mere mortals. Limbs repositioned in the blink of an eye, flickering like black smoke.

Venkworth and the others stared at each other across the table. An old woman gave a toothy, malodorous grin, then shook her dirt-smeared head and made the grin vanish. A boy, no older than ten or eleven, sat wide-eyed, snot bubbling from beneath one nostril. To Venkworth's left, a pock-faced man slipped a silver knife beneath the torn sleeve of his thin coat.

Then the wealthy were back, and the plates were full. Glasses, too, a deep red wine, though only in front of the poor.

"Now, please, *eat!*"

Venkworth stared at his plate, at the pink slices of goose, the potatoes, the vegetables, and the gravy. His fingers edged uncertainly toward the fine cutlery before snatching up a piece of the tender meat. Oh *gods*, it was delicious.

He took a gulp of the wine, rich and complex, heavy with tannins, almost obscuring the bitter edge of... Laudanum?

Around him, the rich attended the needs of the poor, re-filling emptied goblets, encouraging them to feast, making light conversation met only with eager nods and full-mouthed grunts as grease and wine dribbled down chins. He alone was left to his own devices.

Slowly, he lowered his fingers, smearing the gravy on his trousers. From the far end of the table, he felt the gaze of the Lord and realized, that he, Venkworth, at one end, was paired with their host at the other.

"Is the meal good? I'm sure it is. Tell me, do you know the rhyme that begins, 'Christmas is coming?'"

"The goose is getting fat?" Venkworth couldn't prevent himself from continuing the verse, having swallowed a mouthful of the same fowl.

"Ah! You *do*. Delightful. And then?"

"Um, please put a penny in the old man's hat?"

"Yes, yes, do go on."

"If you haven't got a penny, a ha'penny will do, If you haven't got a ha'penny, then God bless you!"

The Lord tapped his fingers together in silent applause. "Curious, is it not, how the childish doggerel leaps from fattening a goose to the terrors of extreme poverty? As if the two were intricately connected?

"We, too, fatten the beasts." The Lord waved his hands, and Venkworth looked once again around the table. The rich held glasses full to the brim with a crimson liquid as if in anticipation of a toast, and the poor...

The poor were slumped over their plates. Every last one of them, except him. Asleep? Or...

He almost rose. Almost fled.

Almost.

A firm hand pressed down on his shoulder. A hand adorned by a gleaming metal spur, sharp and curved like that from a fighting cock. The hour began to chime midnight as the Lord bent to whisper in his ear:

"Christmas is coming..."

Part and Parcel
Nathan D. Ludwig

"Fuck Christmas in its stupid ass," Miles Ford mumbled as he exhaled in utter defeat.

The fickle cold weather of December in Central Virginia had decided to rear its ugly head that week with a wet, bitter cavalcade of seasonal depression. It only exacerbated the broken nose and bruised jaw he now sported, thanks to Miriam. His wife had never struck him before. Not even a hint of violence from her for nearly twenty years of complacent wedded bliss. But on this night, she lashed out. Hard. Twice. Miles wasn't sure if it was because of what he had said to her or to their kids—or both—barely an hour ago, but whatever it was, it was the proverbial last straw.

"Don't come back in this house unless you have a fucking job and you apologize to Santa Claus!"

Those shrill, stinging words still lingered in his ears with a burning numbness. He had indeed told his kids there was no Santa Claus, and he had also indeed told his wife, a dyed-in-the-wool Christmas fanatic, that he hated Christmas. Hated it with a fiery passion.

"I fucking hate Christmas, babe." Those were his exact words.

Those two punches to the face delivered by Miriam hurt less than her pegging him as a loser. A lay-about. A bad husband. A shitty father.

The weak glow of the busted neon sign above Albie's Liquor Store mocked him and his every thought. Every move. Every time he took a swig of the knockoff Bacardi ensconced in the brown paper bag he was death-gripping in his left hand, the one with the constant reminder known as his wedding band, he could feel the red and yellow sign judging him. Writing him off.

Your wife tells you to get your shit together and you come to me in all my glory. You can't afford to buy your kids even the cheapest gifts, but you can scratch enough together for a bottle of shitty booze. Drink up, loser.

In his right hand was his phone, with which he was currently doom scrolling social media. Facebook, Twitter, Instagram, TikTok.

A wet, scruffy, and severely layered bum walked in front of his car—really his wife's car—and pissed on the façade belonging to Albie's. Sounded like weak rain on weak metal siding from inside the relative safety of the vehicle. After the bum finished micturating upside the liquor store, he took one look at Miles through the rain-slicked windshield and clicked his teeth.

"The fuck you looking at, shitbird?" asked the bum with a firm degree of annoyance.

Disrespected by strangers on top of everything else. It was enough to drive someone to suicide at a time such as this. But Miles was too lazy to even do that right. So, he just waved at the bum and swigged another swig of the barrel-bottom rum he hastily purchased barely moments ago inside good ol' Albie's.

"Get a fuckin' job, asshole," the bum said dismissively as he shuffled off to find a better place to shit, Miles surmised.

As he doomscrolled and drank, the bum's words burrowed deeper and deeper into his very being.

Get a fuckin' job, asshole.

Was that really the solution? To everything? Nothing's that easy. Or is it?

Damn it all to hell.

Ceasing his relentless scroll of doom, Miles ejected from the social media cockpit and brought Reddit up on his phone. He navigated to a subreddit he frequented late at night.

r/Odd Jobs & Odd Shit

Fuck. Here goes nothing.

Amidst all the postings of would-be porn shoots and bizarre gig economy lifestyle photos, there was a single post that both revolted and captivated him.

Crone Industries Hiring Mall Santas. $30/hr. Don't have to be fat. Must pass thorough testing. Call 800-555-1468.

"Huh."

The ad initially made him want to chuck his phone out the window. Mall Santas? Didn't they know Miles hated Christmas? With a fiery passion, to be exact. Parental divorce, near poverty, capitalistic fetishism, religious nonsense. All flags Miles burned long ago. Until he met Miriam. She was into fucking to Christmas music all year round. But she was drop-dead gorgeous and very accommodating to all his baggage and bullshit, so he lied and said he was all on board with the holiday. Thanksgiving and New Year's, too. Just to be safe.

Two kids and seventeen years later and he just couldn't take it anymore. It was barely a month until Christmas and Miriam had the egg nog out already and was flipping through her vinyl Xmas collection. What was it going to be tonight? Bing? Nat? The goddamn Peanuts? It was too much for him to take so soon after the passing of his mother over the summer. She was the last bastion of his youth. Now he was just another Gen-X asshole, adrift in a sea of suburbia and marking time until his genetic replacements caused a widowmaker finale in his already shriveled heart. He didn't hate his kids, though. It was just having to be around them that bothered him. He loved the *idea* of kids and goofing around with them, but that was where it ended. He was solid uncle material that fooled himself into thinking he was dad material.

All of that was swirling around in his head when he blurt-ed out how much he hated Christmas just as Miriam was about to spin Burl Ives on the turntable. It stopped her in her tracks so hard you would have thought *she* was the one about to bite it from an infarction. As she stood there, stunned, the kids, Noel and Nick, ten-year-old fraternal twins on top of it all, scooted in to see what all the commotion was about. And that's when it happened. Just seeing their faces, their little brains wait-ing for Daddy to apologize or to say everything was all right. It broke him. It made him scuttle with anger and bitterness throughout his entire being.

"There's no fucking Santa Claus, and Christmas can suck my fucking dick."

He couldn't even recall what their faces looked like after he let loose that verbal volley, but mostly because Miriam had regained mobility and clarity and delivered two punches right to his face. Jaw and nose. Painful and even more pain-ful, one right after the other. Her ring hand.

But that ad also enticed the hell out of him, even if he was loath to admit it. Thirty bucks an hour was nothing to sneeze at for seasonal work, especially for someone without current employment. No Santa gut required. Miles checked that box with authority. Testing? What kind of damn testing? IQ test? Obstacle course? Even if he wasn't psyched about schlepping around a mall food court trailed by a gaggle of piss-stained toddlers, the whole testing thing intrigued him to no end.

He had to make a call. Bo would know what to do.

He searched for Bo's number in his call history and rang him up. A couple of ring-a-lings later and Bo answered in his husky growl of a voice.

"Hey, man. What... Uh, what's up?"

Was he indisposed? Damn it, always the wrong time to call. Everyone texted nowadays. Miles hated texting almost as much as Christmas.

"Yo, Bo! What's the haps? It's your boy."

"Yeah, I know who it is, man. As I said, what's up?"

Bo was Miles's oldest friend. They started hanging out around the same time Miles met Miriam. So, he was more than up-to-date on everything in that department. Lately, though, Miles and Bo had started to grow distant as Bo, a confirmed lifetime bachelor, was starting to catch pangs of love and marriage more and more frequently. Getting close to fifty will do that to some guys, apparently.

"Are you, uh... With somebody?"

"Mmhmm."

"Look, I... uh... I just needed to talk to—"

"She kicked you out again, huh?"

"Well, I think I kinda deserved it this time."

Then there was the sound of Bo dropping his phone straight to the ground, followed by frantic fumbling to retrieve it.

"You there?"

"You finally did it! Holy shit. Dude, we've been talking about this forever. You showed her your true self, man. I'm proud of you."

"Well, I'm not sure I dig my true self, if that's the case. I yelled at my kids, man. You know that kills me every time I do it. Like I really let them have it."

"They're brats. Miriam made sure of that. And your un-willingness to do anything about it didn't help, either. Time for the big D now, my man. You've earned it."

Bo's words stuck in Miles's gut and spawned a million butterflies. Did he really want that? It was so final. He still loved M. Just not her stupid holiday fetish. He loved his kids. When they were away from *her*. Damn it. Human relationships were so frigging complicated. No such thing as just ripping off a Band-Aid when it came to familial tomfoolery.

"I still love 'em, man."

And that's when Bo hung up.

"Yo. Bo? Fuuuuuck…"

Divorce or the Santa suit. Freedom or the continued psychological damage to his kids, but with continued hot sex with his insane wife.

Decisions, decisions.

That same bum was coming back around the corner of the liquor store and already eyeing Miles. Miles quickly dialed the number from the ad, gritting his teeth. Someone picked up at once, which startled him into a temporary stupor.

"Age, weight," the low, crinkly voice on the other end demanded.

Miles almost blanked but regained his composure just as the voice was about to ask again, this time more forcefully he wagered.

"Forty-five. About a hundred-ninety pounds."

"Height."

"Six foot. Wait. In shoes or no shoes?"

"Be at the following address in one hour. Twelve hundred Austria Way. Crone Industries. Park by the side entrance. Do not be late."

"Yes, and thank—"

Another phone hung up on him. The night itself was imposing an unappetizing theme right on top of Miles, whether he approved or not.

As he turned the key to the ignition, he wondered if he could actually go through with killing himself if he didn't get this job.

Merry fucking Christmas, Miles.

Crone Industries would never be mistaken for a lair of festivity or mall Santas or *anything* of the sort. No red or green to be seen for miles. It was just another industrial megalith structure amidst a sea of industrial megalith structures on the side of town that Miles and people like him actively avoided. Loading-bay doors, towering chimneys, a crumbling brick façade, and a massive, empty parking lot completed the latter-day industry ensemble.

Miles had parked on the right side of the building, which thoroughly irked him, as said massive parking lot was indeed bone dry and emptier than his bank account. Both checking and savings. Why the side? There wasn't even a parking lot there. He was just idling next to a shoddy metal door hilariously covered by a tattered cloth awning that looked ready to lay down and die at any moment. It wasn't even festive.

Just a faded cream and brown pattern. Gross and dated. Miles couldn't stop staring at it as it was the only movement in the immediate area. Lifelessness permeated this block the same way Christmas permeated the Ford household year-round. Well, more so the Cole household, as Miriam kept her last name and insisted the kids keep it, too. Probably smart in the long run, considering the night's events, Miles admitted to himself.

Whether he wanted to muse more on how fucked his life was or not, a figure emerged from the creaky, rusty metal side door. An elderly man with a wild whisp of white hair that caught the wind as soon as it was outside in the open, sending it straight up in the air and making Miles snicker if ever so slightly. The man was wrapped in a tight, thick, and long wool trench coat with the collar standing straight up. At first, he just stood there, staring at Miles with empty eyes and barely an expression of impatience on his wrinkled visage.

Then, as Miles registered that the man was waiting on him to exit the car and come to *him,* he gave Miles a slight wave. The absolute slightest of waves. No arm movement, just a flourish of his hand out of his pocket and then right back into the pocket. Almost imperceptible if you were further away than where Miles was parked.

Okay then. Time to save my marriage.

It sounded corny as all get out in Miles's head, but he decided that's *exactly* what he was doing. He was sure this would fix everything once and for all.

As he got out of his car (his wife's car, really), a violent, repugnant stench of rotting meat and sour milk assaulted his nose without mercy. It sent him staggering, and he looked at the old man in the trench coat to see if he was smelling it, too. If he was, his poker face was supreme and absolute.

What the fuck...

"This way, good sir," the man with the wispy head of hair intoned hoarsely to Miles. If it wasn't already freezing out, the man's voice would have sent a solid shiver up his spine. Before he was even up the steps, the old man had returned inside. The gust of rot had dissipated, and Miles could feel the warmth of indoor heating squeeze out as the metal door clanged shut in front of him.

"Don't worry, I got the door, thanks," Miles said under his breath, but just loud enough that he hoped the old jerk had heard him.

Inside, Miles was greeted by labyrinthine corridors of worn lime-green walls. No front desk, no office. Just hallways upon hallways.

"Down this way, good sir..."

Indoors, the old man's echoing voice had a Germanic bent to it. Bavarian? Austrian? Swiss? It was hard to say.

"I'm sorry, where exactly?" Miles called out to a long, almost glow-in-the-dark hall.

"Follow my voice," the old man said, his tone raising significantly.

It was coming from the end of the hall he was in and to the immediate left. So, Miles followed his instinct and made his way down the absurdly long corridor. No pictures, no certificates, signs, or anything whatsoever of that sort on the wall. Just bare acreage blanketed in weak fluorescent light.

Though the old man's voice had a distinct echo, Miles's

footsteps did not. The sound of his footfalls down the hall died just as quickly as they were born. It felt as if anything at all could sneak up on him from anywhere, even right in front of his face.

"Not very festive in here, is it?" Miles chuckled, trying to be conversational as best he could, given the little he had to go off.

No answer back from the wispy-haired trench coat man, but as Miles turned the corner to where he surmised the man's voice was coming from, there he was. Literally right around the corner, standing quite still. Another step or two, and Miles would have run smack into him.

That stench of rot had returned a smidge and caused Miles to scrunch up his face in a vain attempt to be rid of it.

"Sorry. My bad. I—"

The old man's eyes were fixed on Miles. Unblinking. Nearly black. He had a slight lip twitch that was making Miles just as nauseous as the rotting smell.

"Right down that way, good sir." His breath was horrible, but it wasn't where the rotting smell was coming from. Just gingivitis and halitosis there.

The old man was signaling with an outstretched arm to a door about halfway down the hall they were currently in. Still lime green and all sorts of faded. But the door was red. Bright red. Fire engine red. It was the first sign of the holiday at hand he had seen in this place yet. As much as he hated Christmas, or Xmas as he insisted on referring to it as, he was glad to see this festive portal of potential possibilities.

"She will see you now."

The old man didn't move a muscle. But his eyes were still locked onto Miles. Not a blink in sight.

"Okay, then. Nice meeting you."

Miles headed for the door, head tingling knowing the man's eyes were most likely still on him all the way. As he reached the red door, he turned to glance back at the old man, hoping to see a smile or even a dismissive wave. Something decidedly not creepy.

"By the way, didn't catch your name—"

The man was gone. It spooked Miles greatly until he realized all the guy had to do was take a few steps around the corner. But then the thought of the old wispy-haired man leering at him from behind a dark hallway corner spooked him even more. As he turned the handle to the door, he had a mild panic attack that something would grab him from behind just as he entered the perceived safety of that bright, shiny, red door. But nothing came. Miles couldn't decide whether that was even scarier.

There *was* an actual office on the other side of that door. A nice one, to boot. Nothing at all resembling the nightmare maze of paranoia-inducing corridors he was just in or the oppressive industrial façade outside. This was downright corporate. Cheery, even. A cluster of chairs in the center of the room signified the waiting area, and next to that was a water cooler, a coffee machine, and a tray of Christmas cookies on a folding table. Looked like gingerbread. Smelled like it, too. Framed posters of old-school holiday shenanigans out of some Norman Rockwell/Coca-Cola merger no one ever made public. The receptionist's desk held no receptionist that Miles could see. After a few moments of looking around, he decided to grab a coffee, avoid the cookies, and pop a squat in one of the barely cushioned hardback chairs. Someone *should* be with him shortly. They had to be. No one else was around. Unless there was a thorough interview going on right now with some other down-and-out bloke. How long would that take? Testing. Testing. Testing. What did that really mean? Miles assumed he was about to find out.

Three hours later, he still hadn't found out. Not even an intercom announcement. Two cups of coffee, a cup of water, and a bite of the accursed gingerbread later, and still nothing. He had promised himself that he'd get up and leave at least eight times over the last two of those three hours. But leave to go where? Return to what? Domestic life for Miles was in shambles, to put it mildly. Maybe this was all a test? How long can you stand to wait to get signed for thirty bucks an hour and all the mall food court Chinese food you can eat?

As he was about to reluctantly vacate the relative safety of the strange office for real this time, the sound of a door clunking open somewhere behind the receptionist's desk made him flinch. Someone was coming. *Finally.* Was it the wispy-haired trench coat of a man? No. He said *she* would see him now. Now, meaning hours later, of course. Who could it be?

And then she appeared, heels clicking on the hardwood floor. All business. Horn-rimmed glasses, a starched blouse with a sleek choker around her sloping neck. Pleated, knee-length skirt with long yet stocky legs. Dirty blonde hair tied up at the top of her head, creating a fountain of cascading curls. Freckled cheeks, deep red lipstick, and no eyeliner or mascara to speak of. He couldn't help but stare. Was this his supervisor? The owner of his place? He had so many questions, and before his brain could ask another one, she had extended her hand out to him quite pleasantly. Her demeanor was a confident mix of business and casual. He wasn't sure if he should shake her hand or hug her.

Don't hug her, dummy.

And she smelled of Christmas. Not secular, store-bought Christmas. Old world, traditional-as-fuck Christmas. Almost Pagan-esque. Miles wasn't sure exactly what the ingredients of such a thing would even be, but he knew that was it.

"Good evening. I am Perdita Engel. But you can call me Frau Perdita or just Frau if you like. Thank you for coming in to be evaluated," she said. She smiled at him all the while she spoke.

"Evaluated?"

"Yes, for the shopping mall Santa Claus position."

Her words had a distinct German or Austrian accent to them, even more so than the old man. The way she pronounced Santa Claus gave him the tingles.

Sinta Klauz.

Clawing out of his mild bemusement and her unexpected beauty in a place like this, Miles attempted to sound like a lucid human being.

"Oh, yes. Yes, thank you for seeing me. I'm very much looking forward to potentially fitting the bill."

"Are you?"

Her tone changed just slightly. Now it was inquisitive in nature. Or was that sarcasm?

"Yes… Yes, I am," he said as he regained his composure with a straightening of his back and a slight grin.

"Good. It's hard to find candidates that meet our exact criteria. Hence, the late posting. Usually, we have someone by now."

"No one wants to work anymore, am I right?" Miles put his hands on his hips and chuckled, hoping to get a laugh.

"Especially you, Mister Ford, yes?"

What?

"I'm sorry? How did you—"

"You just told it to me when we shook hands."

"I did?"

"Yes. You did."

"Oh. Sorry, I'm just having a really bad night. Please excuse me."

"Not at all. It is quite all right. Shall we begin?"

"In here? Or…"

"Follow me, good sir," she said as she returned to the door she had just appeared from.

"Okay."

Miles was flummoxed. Did he tell her his name or not? How did she see through his humorous attempt to mask his rampant joblessness? It was weird all over, but not enough to thumb his nose at thirty bucks an hour and hot tub sex with his wife again. Oh, and seeing his kids again, too.

She took him to a stark white room with just one adornment inside. A large, gray-cushioned examination table that would look at home in any random doctor's office. No chairs, no other tables. Just the harsh light coming from overhead.

"Please, take a seat on the table."

After a few long seconds of hesitation, more for effect than anything, Miles made his way over to it and scooted up there, making deep, squeaky sounds all the while. He wanted to make an innocent fart joke to break the silence that had come over them, but he realized at the last second that ideas of that sort were probably why he was perpetually unemployed.

"I am going to examine you for the pre-employment physical. While I do this, I will ask you questions about your health history and psychological state. Are you okay with such things?"

"Uh, yeah. I mean, yes. It's perfectly okay with me."

Don't be a pervert. Don't be a pervert. Don't be a—

Her firm hand began to palpate his sides, his back, his neck, his thighs. He was stronger than she looked, but not forceful in any way. He kind of liked it. Not exactly a massage, but it was at least some kind of human touch.

"Any of these things sore or sensitive to touch?"

"No."

"Good. I will now check your breathing."

She pulled out a stethoscope and placed it on his chest.

"Just breathe in and out with regularity, yes?"

"Sure."

As he breathed and while she kept the stethoscope there, her voice lowered a bit and became more serious in nature as opposed to the more jovial lilt she had kept so far.

"You seem to be in good weight. Have you ever been fat in your life, Mister Ford?"

Huh?

"Well, I had a little extra chub in elementary school. But that's about it. Baby fat, I guess?"

"Were you bullied for it?"

"What?"

"Were you bullied for your...baby fatness?"

"Uh, no. Not really. Hard to remember that far back."

"These are yes or no questions, Mister Ford."

"No, I guess. Yeah, no."

"Hm."

She moved her stethoscope to his back.

"Continue to breathe in a normal fashion, yes?"

"Okay."

A couple of quiet inhales and exhales transpired before she spoke again.

"Have you ever participated in binge eating?"

"Excuse me?"

"Consuming food until your stomach is so full it becomes painful until you digest it."

"Sometimes, yeah. I mean, yes. Like Thanksgiving or Christmas. Stuff like that."

"No bulimia or anorexia?"

Why would she ask a guy that? Weren't those female diseases? This was getting too weird, even for thirty bucks an hour.

"I'm sorry; what does that have to do with being a mall Santa?"

"Crone Industries has created the most efficient method of determining suitable candidates. Please bear with us as I finish our patented evaluations. Yes?"

Thirty bucks an hour. Mall food court Chinese. Fix your family. Sex with Miriam. Kids and stuff.

"Sure, sure. Sorry."

"It is quite all right. Most men ask these same things. It is understandable."

"No women Santas?"

"Missus Claus auditions are uptown, Mister Ford. Much nicer facility."

"Ah. I see."

Was that misandry in her tone? Miles tried to put it out of his mind lest his mouth get him in trouble again tonight. Twice was enough.

"One final question for now, Mister Ford."

"Sure. Shoot."

"What does Christmas mean to you?"

Oh no.

"Uh..."

Miles knew right then the interview was fucked beyond repair. He couldn't lie. She seemed to be able to tell when that shit happened. What if he told her the truth? His hatred of Christmas and how he was doing this for his family and to bring them back together despite how much it would pain him to don that suit, but it would be worth it in the long run because he wanted to be a good dad and a loving husband with gainful employment. Maybe this could lead to more jobs in between holiday seasons. The possibilities seemed endless in that span of mere seconds.

Yeah, just tell her the truth.

And so, he did. He told her all about the entire night up to this point and how he felt about *everything*. He came close to breaking down in tears. Not because of anything he mentioned, but because he thought it would help if he remembered his beagle Skipper dying when he was eleven and how those tears would seal the deal and get the job for him.

After he finished speaking for nearly five minutes straight, talking mostly to the floor and fidgeting with his hands, he looked up at Frau Perdita and almost did a double take. She was staring right at him with nary a blink, much akin to her old man co-worker. It unnerved Miles. She was looking through him, inside him, around him, feeling him out with her eyeballs. Rubbing them on his organs, making his skin crawl and his brain throb. He had a momentary burst of panic, spurring him to escape that place once and for all, but it disappeared as soon as she spoke again. He liked her voice *a lot* for some reason.

Think of Miriam. Miriam. Miriam. Miriam. Hot tub sex. Hell, even Christmas music during said hot tub sex.

"I appreciate you telling me all of this, Mister Ford. I think we have a position for you here at Crone Industries."

Miles was flabbergasted. It worked. His bullshit actually worked. Miriam hardly ever went for it these days. It was so refreshing to get validation from a relative stranger. But she didn't feel strange anymore. She felt warm, inviting. That old-world holiday smell clicked for him. Fresh poinsettias and piping hot spice bread; it was intoxicating to him now.

"You do? I mean, you do? Really?"

"Yes, of course. Thank you for your candor, Miles. It is

so refreshing to hear it, especially at this time of year."

"Oh. Th-thank you. Thanks."

He smiled a little too much and extended his hand for a celebratory shake.

She didn't return it.

"Please wait here. I will return shortly with your paperwork, yes?"

"O-okay, sure. In for a penny, in for a pound. What's another hour now anyways, right?"

Miles let a laugh loose in the room that seemed to bounce around several times before falling flat on its face in embarrassment. Frau Perdita still didn't laugh or smile back. She just nodded and made for the door. Was he too overeager in his triumph? Was she going to return with a cease-and-desist or a restraining order? Something that would fuck up his night and his life permanently? How could he go back to Miriam and the kids with nothing but a tall tale to tell of his experience here? They'd never even believe—

Before he could even finish that banal thought, the wispy-haired old man in the thick trench coat marched through the door and came straight for Miles. He wasn't smiling either. As a long, outstretched arm neared Miles, the old man's mouth opened wide and revealed a black abyss of yawning hunger. Groans and shrieks of all kinds seemed to emanate directly from it. Miles involuntarily squealed and tried to eject himself from the sticky fabric of the examination table, but the blackness took him before the fear fully registered in his brain.

The smells…

Cranberry sauce… Stuffing… Honey ham… Turkey gravy… Mashed potatoes with butter… Butternut squash… The scents utterly pervaded his nostrils, and he had a crude picture in his mind of where he might be before he even opened his eyes.

And then he did.

A dining room. But not his own. Not Miriam's. No. This one was different. It was the most festive, holiday-themed dining room he had ever laid eyes on. Garland and tinsel and poinsettias and wreaths everywhere, and a massive, ten-foot-tall Christmas tree in the far corner by the door. The only door he could see in this abomination of a chamber. Miriam had a flair for this kind of thing for sure, but this here was lightyears beyond anything she had ever attempted. It would probably be her ultimate sexual fantasy come true.

But it was where Miles was seated that truly sent his brain into terror mode.

A huge mahogany dining table that seated about sixteen people easily. They had placed him to the left of the head of the table. A gargantuan plate of holiday meal fixings sat in front of him, untouched. Heat wafted off it as if it had just been placed there. Maybe that's what woke him?

But that wasn't all. He wasn't alone.

Across from him, and one chair over, was a corpse. Miles was sure in that moment the guy was dead. His eyes were still open, but his mouth was locked in an unmistakable death frown. Glasses rested askew on his twisted brow, a waxed handlebar mustache peppered with crumbs of food from his nearly finished plate, which looked as if it had been just as massive as Miles's judging from the dish size and the gloppy remnants of the meal itself. The man's hands were frozen stiff, clawing at his distended stomach that had burst through his pinstriped dress shirt and looked black and blue and purple with bruises and stretch marks.

"What the—"

"He...couldn't...finish..." A weak, exhausted man's voice broke Miles out of his state of shock. It was coming from the far side of the table, at the other head. Or foot? Miles could never remember proper dining etiquette. A relic of old times no one cared to cherish anymore.

Miles turned his groggy head to meet the voice, and sure enough, there was a man seated at exactly that location. Scraggly beard, angular face. He looked to be as thin and wiry as Miles, save for his massive belly, which appeared as swollen as the dead man across from Miles. He, too, was clawing at it his stomach in agony, trying to soothe something that clearly couldn't be soothed at this point.

"What the hell is... Where are we?"

"It's... the... final part of the... Ughh.... Ahhhhhh!"

The man was clearly in the worst pain a human could possibly be in. Pregnancy seemed hilarious compared to the look on this man's face, Miles surmised. Was there some *thing* trying to get out? Had this turned into a horrific lab experiment to breed some kind of mutant messiah child on Christmas or something? Miles's mind raced with all the depraved possibilities.

"I can't... You have to... Final part of the interview... Ohhhh Goddddd..."

And with that, the man's stomach stretched another inch or two with a sick, fleshy squeeze, and then it popped. Sounded just like a balloon. So much so that Miles didn't even fully process what was actually happening until the man's blood and intestinal chunks landed at his end of the table. They were in his plate of food, on his face, and in his eyes. Whatever they had drugged him with delayed his reaction time to the point of near inaction. He couldn't even wretch or vomit in response to the explosion. The room now smelled of stomach acid and saliva-infused mashed potatoes.

"I didn't make iiiit... Youuuu have to finishhhhhh iiit alllll..." The man practically whispered as the last ounce of his life force left his ravaged body.

Finish it all? That was impossible. Especially now that it was garnished with that guy's innards.

No fucking way. Interview over, godammit.

"Uhhhhh..." was all Miles could muster to an overly jolly room of dead men with no stomachs.

And then the door opened. The old man with the wispy hair was back. Miles flinched mentally in preparation for another taste of the guy's oral abyss, but it didn't come. The old man just stood there, still as a stalk of corn in a breezeless field.

Behind him, a hideous, shriveled, ancient woman entered the room. Warts, moles, whiskers, saggy skin, stretchy folds, oodles of liver spots everywhere. She was a crone.

Crone. Crone Industries? The hell...?

The stench of rotting meat and milk had returned. Now Miles was certain it was coming from her. It always had been. Had she been there all night, lurking, watching just out of sight? What shocked Miles more than anything was that the crone was wearing the exact same outfit as Frau Perdita.

"Frau... Perdita? Is... is that you?"

"Frau Perchta. She will conduct the final portion of the interview now," Mr. Wisp said to Miles.

Perchta? The hell was that for a name?

"Begin to eat, Mister Ford," the crone croaked as she approached him. Her clicking heels engaged in a much slower rhythm now.

Miles's eyes darted around the table at his stomach-less companions. Flies had somehow found their way to both of them in this enclosed, windowless space.

"I'm not... hungry..."

Frau Perchta smiled, revealing her teeth. She still had all of them, but they were sharpened to points and were a yellowish gray. The rotting smell reached a peak as soon as she revealed them.

And that's when Miles puked. All over his food.

"Oh, that was very stupid, my boy. There are no more clean plates of food tonight. You must finish this meal that is in front of you as is."

"What? I... I quit! I don't want the job!"

"Oh, my boy, you can't quit a job you don't have yet. And as you can see, our other candidates were... full of turkey, as the saying goes, yes? All talk and no stomach for such hard work."

Miles felt close to retching again as the crone laughed and clapped her hands excitedly.

"Eat!" the old man bellowed, threatening to hypnotize Miles with whatever was lurking in his mouth.

"Go easy on him. But not too easy, ha!" she chortled at the old man, who didn't even venture a smile or an easing of his stoic form.

"Pay no mind to Klaus. He is a stickler for tradition. If it were up to him, we would just eat you on sight. And that's no fun for anyone, is it?"

"Eat! Now!" The sound of old man Klaus's voice threatened another gaping abyss of unconsciousness, and that terrified Miles.

So he ate.

Grabbing a fork in one hand and a knife in the other, Miles began to pile bite after bite into his mouth, ignoring the fact that his own puke and the guts from the man at the other end of the table smothered what was otherwise delicious-looking food.

Merry fucking Christmas, Miles. Just think of Miriam. Hot tub sex. The kids, too, I guess.

Gushy, gucky spoonful after mashed, moist, squishy spoonful went into Miles's mouth, and he was actually able to keep it down. This was it. His last chance to fix everything. It all made sense in the moment, if not in a macro way. Miriam would forgive him, the kids wouldn't be scared of him anymore, and he'd be able to stand fucking to yuletide tunes until the cows came home. Maybe she'd be down for letting him fuck her in the mall Santa suit. Another benefit of the job. He fantasized about coming back the following year, an MVP of the mall Santa scene. Welcomed back a hero. Appreciated. Loved. Maybe he could even get used to having a dad bod to fit the part more naturally. A nice little beer gut couldn't hurt.

Keep eating, Miles.

He could hear the crone's voice burrowing into his very psyche. He stopped for a moment and looked down. His belly was more than a bit of a beer gut. It had distended and stretched well past the point of any proportional normalcy. It was even well past the other man's point of explosion.

POP. POP. RRRRRIP.

His pants buttons and the fabric on his shirt gave way, and his belly was firmly out there in the stale air of the jolly room. Jolly *prison* was more appropriate.

Holy shit.

How long had he been eating? Miles swore he had just started, but his stomach said otherwise. He looked at his plate. It was almost licked clean, save for a few more bites. Had the old man put him out again with his breath? His mouth? His whatever? Was Miles sleep eating? Was that even a thing?

"Excellent! You are doing so good, my boy. There'll be plenty of room for more than just straw and pebbles in that chamber of yours. Good work!"

Frau Perchta clapped excitedly again and croaked a series of laughs that resembled a family of sickly toads harmonizing with each other.

"Just a few more bites... Santa!"

Santa? Was that really who he was now? Yes! He had to be. After all of this, after what he'd told Perdita, his raw honesty. He was the spirit of Christmas now! Miles excitedly polished off the last few bites of bloody squash and puke-covered stuffing.

"All done!" Miles said with a gushy mouthful.

"Yes, yes, you are. And just in time, Miles."

The old man made a few quick strides over to Miles and pushed him backward in his chair. He and the chair landed with a hard thud and then a *CRRRACK*. Miles knew he had broken the chair with his newfound girth. But he didn't vomit. Not even a slight gag or reflux of food. Solid as a rock.

Santa material! That's me!

"What's this all about? I thought I passed. I'm Santa, right?"

The crone called Frau Perchta shuffled over to Miles, humming all the while, and as she slowly bent over to meet him face to face, the old man behind her procured a two-foot-long hunting knife from within the folds of his thick trench coat and handed it to her. Miles's eyes went wide, but he couldn't move a muscle. He was just too damn full. All he could do was breathe and blink and shift around barely an inch here and there. A marooned turtle or a cockroach unable to escape anything, let alone certain doom.

"There's no such thing as Santa Claus, Miles. Remember? You said so yourself. It's good to teach the kids that as soon as possible."

"What? What—"

"I killed Santa Claus. Long ago. The only thing you should be thankful for on Christmas is that Frau Perchta doesn't pay you a visit. Not you, as in you directly, of course. That ship has sailed, my boy. I mean more the royal you."

"Please... I—"

"You *are* hired, though. Not as a mall Santa, mind you. But as a warning. A yearly message. You will send that message marvelously well, from the looks of it."

Without another word, the crone inserted the hunting knife directly above his groin and pushed in hard. It hurt more than anything he had experienced in his entire life, but the gluttony of his current state didn't allow much past just sitting there and taking it. And squealing a high-pitched whine of suffering.

"Merry fucking Christmas, as it were, Miles Ford."

And then she yanked the knife upwards, pulling his stomach wide open and spilling his guts to the floor with a liberal splash of hot, steaming blood. After that, she pulled out his stomach and handed it to Klaus, who promptly bit into it and began consuming the partially digested food with aplomb. Stomach acid and bile and smooshed food oozed from his mouth as grunty groans of satisfaction filled the room.

"The stomach is for him, yes, but I always love the guts. Intestines of those who pass the process really get me through the rest of the day. But considering you are our last interview for the year, this is merely my Christmas bonus, you might say. Yes?"

As Miles gave in to the heavy, black permanence of death, the last image his brain registered with any efficacy was that of the crone slurping on his crimson-coated intestines, steam billowing from her ravenous, chomping maw.

Miriam woke immediately from her deep slumber as soon as she heard the terrified cries of her children. She hoped it wasn't Miles, drunk and passed out in a pile of puke on the living room floor. There was no explaining that one away anymore.

Besides, the asshole hadn't come around for weeks since that night. Showed his true fucking colors. Still, Miriam wished right then that she had the foresight to change the locks to keep him from barging in at the most inopportune moments, like right now. Christmas Morning was sacred to her and, by all rights, sacred to her children. They weren't Miles's anymore, not after he revealed the real Miles in all his disgusting glory.

When she reached the bottom of the stairs, she saw right away what the kids had been wailing about. Miles was indeed there in the living room, but he wasn't passed out or covered in puke.

She was pretty sure he was dead.

Dressed in a Santa Claus suit and splayed out under the Christmas tree, squashing the presents she had so carefully selected for the kids. His stomach was gigantic, stretched out several feet with a hideous stitched scar running from below the navel up to his sternum. It all looked so painful, and his belly was poking out more than prominently from his Santa jacket. On his bruised, stretched stomach skin, the word "NAUGHTY" was scrawled in a deep red substance. Blood?

"Daddy...?" Nick asked, a tremble in his voice.

Noel took a few steps back, almost tripping on the bottom stair.

"Wh...what's wrong with Dad—"

And that's right when Miles's stomach exploded.

Inside were all the gifts Miriam couldn't afford to get the kids. New smartphones, wireless headphones, Nintendo Switches for both of them, gift cards to every store imaginable, candy out the wazoo, and so much more. Only a tiny bit of Miles's blood and guts were left in there, so not that much of it landed on Miriam and the kids' faces upon explosion. That certainly was considerate of Miles and his stomach.

Miriam would have been thankful for such a surprise Christmas miracle if she and the kids weren't screaming in abject terror.

ᴘond ᴘerson
Evan Baughfman

A snowball exploded against Braeden's chest, and a sudden jolt of pain electrified his sternum. Wincing and groaning, the boy looked down at his feet, his suspicions confirmed. A hefty stone had been hidden within the icy, packed powder.

Seething, teeth clenched, Braeden turned to his brother and growled, "You're gonna die, you little shit! I'm gonna kill you!"

Ten meters away, eleven-year-old Kyle cowered behind a misshapen snowman. The boy's bright orange parka had him looking like a forgotten October pumpkin.

"It's... It's what you get!" Kyle shouted. "You... You deserved that!"

"Merry goddamn Christmas to you, too, then!" Braeden screamed, breath pluming.

The siblings were beside "the family pond," an Olympic swimming pool-sized body of water currently frozen for winter. Leafless trees surrounded the area, branches waving in a frigid breeze.

Rubbing the sore spot with a gloved hand, Braeden picked the stone up with his other hand. Concealing a rock inside a snowball had always been *his* move. Braeden felt a strange sense of pride. The runt had actually learned something from him.

"Screw Christmas!" Kyle shrieked. "Christmas sucks!" It sounded like the kid was sobbing. If he didn't quit the tears, his cheeks would soon become home to tiny icicles.

Thirty minutes ago, they'd opened each other's gifts. Kyle had given his older brother a comic book. The boring little creep was always trying to get Braeden to read, always trying to get him excited about *stories*, but Braeden's brain never did well with words. In his mind, the letters were a constant jumble of confusing nonsense.

Kyle, though, was a perfect student. Teachers' pet, six years running. As an eighth-grader, Braeden hated feeling like he was dumber than somebody new to middle school. As a brother, Braeden hated that Kyle received most of their parents' smiles and praise.

Which was why he'd given Kyle a box of crumpled, used tissues as a Christmas present. So the kid could finally see what a snot he actually was.

Needless to say, Kyle hadn't appreciated the gesture.

Neither had Mom or Dad.

They'd immediately ordered Braeden to apologize and go outside with his brother, forcing him to gift the kid an hour of his precious time and attention.

It didn't seem like Kyle was enjoying Braeden's company all that much, however.

The younger boy screamed, "I hate you!"

"Feeling's mutual, brat!"

"Just... Just stay away from me! When Mom and Dad ask, I'll tell them I had fun with you. Just leave me alone!"

Braeden would've loved nothing more than to do his own thing, to build his own snowman, one that didn't look so weird and malformed, but he figured their parents might make the trek from the house to the pond, might materialize at any moment to check in on the boys and their "fun."

Sighing, realizing he had to be the mature one in this situation, Braeden let the stone fall from his grasp. He approached his brother, heavy boots crunching over frozen earth.

"I said, leave me alone!"

Braeden ignored the request. Instead, he stood beside Kyle and gestured to the snowman. "So, this is what you've been coming down here to work on the past few days? It's... um... an interesting design."

"Th...Thanks." Kyle wiped away some of his tears with a mitten. "You know what it's supposed to be?"

The sculpture had a humpback and a tail, had broken sticks running down its spine like porcupine quills. Well-placed pebbles gave the thing an eerie grin, gave it reptilian eyes and nostril slits. Tangles of moss represented an unruly cascade of green hair. Pronged twigs had been jammed into the beast's torso, laughable tyrannosaur limbs for the frosty beast.

Braeden shook his head. "Is it like a monster from a book or something?"

"Well, not exactly. It's real. A Pond Person."

"*Pond* Person...?"

Kyle nodded. "Saw one a few days ago, over there on that bank, crawling into a hole in the ice." The sixth-grader pointed across the solid expanse of water, where a forest of stubborn, brown reeds stood tall.

"You *saw* this thing? Yeah, right."

"It's true! I built a replica, hoping it might come out of the pond to investigate its likeness. I really want to see it again."

"The Pond Person."

"That's just what I've been calling it, but I think I know what it actually is now!"

"And what is it, actually?"

Kyle unzipped his jacket. "Here, I'll show you!" He removed a paperback book that he had hidden inside his parka.

"Of course, you brought a book out here."

"Well, I didn't think you'd actually want to spend time with me..."

Braeden recognized the tome as a gift from Mom and Dad, one that Kyle had begged to open early the night before. On the book's cover was an intricate illustration of a snarling Sasquatch.

"That's about crypters, right?" Braeden asked.

"Close," said Kyle. "Cryp*tids*. This is an encyclopedia of

mysterious creatures from around the world. So, I was researching last night, and I found what the Pond Person is."

Braeden stepped closer to his brother as Kyle turned the pages. A blur of text and colorful imagery, the book was already giving Braeden a headache.

"Here. Right here." Kyle stopped on page 167.

Or was it 176? Braeden also had trouble with numbers, so he focused on the drawing in front of them instead.

On the page was an artist's rendition of what Kyle had constructed with snow. A scaly, humanoid figure with dark eyes, fangs, and stringy hair, the creature reached out for the reader with a webbed claw.

Beneath the image was some difficult-to-read, bolded words, the first of which began with the letter "Q."

"Dude, I can't pronounce that name," said Braeden.

"Me, neither," said Kyle. "This creature's pretty popular in Inuit folklore. Wonder what one of them's doing so far south… My guess: global warming."

"And what else does the book say about this Q-thing?"

"How about… you read it yourself if you really want to know?" Kyle shoved the book into Braeden's hands. "Go on."

"Seriously? No." Braeden tried giving the book back. "I'm not going to read this."

"Please? It's only like a page-and-a-half of info. You can do it."

All Braeden could see at the moment were paragraph upon paragraph of garbled information. He said, "I don't want to read—"

"You've got to practice, right? Why not practice reading

about something interesting?"

Braeden screamed, "I just want you to tell me about the freaking thing, okay? I don't want to practice my goddamn literacy out here!" He didn't want to put forth all that effort—not on Christmas morning! And he certainly didn't want Kyle to watch him struggle, either.

"Braeden, come on, you can do it."

"I don't want to!"

"I know you can. Try this first sentence."

"Why're you...? Stop it—"

"The first sentence is easy. Look at this word. You know this word."

"SHUT THE HELL UP!" Braeden punched through the snowman's head, decimating the Pond Person with a fatal blow.

Kyle gasped and stumbled back a step, as if he'd been struck instead of the snow beast. Bleary-eyed, screeching, he grabbed fistfuls of spilled skull fragments, flinging rocks and snow into Braeden's face.

Using the cryptid encyclopedia as a shield, Braeden managed to deflect much of the stinging flurry. So, Kyle began throwing wild jabs instead.

"Can't hurt me!" Braeden taunted. "You aren't strong enough, twerp!"

Kyle lunged for the book, and the brothers participated in a very brief tug-of-war until Braeden kicked the smaller boy to the ground.

"Want this thing?" Braeden held the book high above a weeping Kyle. "Fetch." He frisbeed the piece of literature into the pond, where it slid across the ice and came to rest about thirty meters from shore.

Back on two feet, Kyle shrieked, "Stupid asshole! Shithead!"

"*Stupid?*"

"Yes, stupid! Deficient! Brainless! Dumb! Understand? It's not my fault you're such a freaking waste of space!"

Braeden growled and gripped Kyle by the collar. He shoved his brother back to the ground, only this time in a different direction.

Kyle end-over-ended, rolling through snow... and onto the ice.

"Shit," Braeden grumbled. He hadn't meant to push Kyle so hard.

The eleven-year-old stood on wobbly legs. He didn't look Braeden's way, didn't ask for any assistance as he struggled to keep his balance. Instead, he locked his eyes on that book.

"Jesus!" cried Braeden. "Don't!"

Ignoring his brother's advice, Kyle awkwardly went for the paperback, slipping and sliding on his treacherous journey with all the grace of a toddler.

From the shoreline, Braeden shouted, "You call *me* the stupid one? Look at what you're doing!"

"What was that?" Kyle said. "I need some help translating Idiot!"

"Say that again! I dare you!"

"Don't think I take foreign language classes until high school! Can't understand Dumbass! Sorry!"

Braeden clenched his fists. He was going to pummel the kid once he returned to land. Teach him a lesson about zipped lips.

Unless…

Big brother didn't have to wait to get his point across…

At the edge of the ice were heavy stones, ones that required two hands to lift from the earth. Braeden shotput a sizeable rock into the pond.

The stone, practically an anvil, crashed through the ice, thundering as it sunk deep into the water. Fissures immediately split like lightning bolts across the frozen surface, nipping at Kyle's heels.

Kyle turned, saw what Braeden had done, and screamed more insults at the eighth-grader.

Snarling, Braeden arced another stone between his brother and shore, creating a second expansive hole for the little "genius" to somehow evade on his slog back to safety.

Braeden had a third stone ready for action when Kyle finally begged for mercy, squealing almost-indecipherable apologies.

Braeden contemplated chucking the tiny boulder anyway.

Would it be so bad for him if Kyle collapsed into the water and never resurfaced? Wouldn't things be easier for Braeden if his parents had no other child to compare him to?

A head slowly rose through a breach in the ice; an otherwordly face bobbed between the brothers.

Yellow eyes glared at Braeden from inside a pale gray skull, behind strands of wiry, black hair. A short snout puffed, spraying out liquid, taking in oxygen.

"Holy shit! See?" Kyle cried, pointing. "P-P-Pond Person!"

Braeden was shivering, speechless. How the hell could

the Q-thing be *real*?

The creature spun toward Kyle's voice. Powerful limbs emerged from underwater, their hooked claws firmly anchoring into ice. The twigs that Kyle had affixed to his snowman were grossly inaccurate.

Going for Kyle, the Pond Person began to lift itself from the hole, revealing lionfish-like spines along its vertebrae. The creature wore a furry cloak made from an animal hide—Bear? Moose? Bison?—and the spines pierced right through it. The Pond Person spoke—actually *spoke* to Kyle—but Braeden couldn't quite make out what it said.

"Wait!" Kyle told the creature, holding out a palm. "Just wait a second!"

That did nothing to halt the monster's advance. The beast was only a stone's throw away from Braeden, so he snapped out of his bewilderment and sent a rock sailing, connecting with the Q-thing's scaly side.

The Pond Person hissed, turning its attention to the bigger boy.

"That's right!" Braeden hollered. "Over here!" He'd decided life with a snotty sibling was still worth exploring after all.

The creature dropped into the water, disappearing into the murk.

Kyle yelled, "I think it might be lonely! They're supposed to live in families!"

"Sorry," Braeden replied, "but it can't have us! Get back to shore, Kyle! Now!"

The Pond Person suddenly exploded from the same hole, this time launching itself upward like a mutant dolphin, legs tucked beneath a crocodilian tail, claws extended and reaching for Braeden.

The boy yelped and fell, his tailbone striking an ill-positioned stone.

The Q-thing landed half on the shore, half on the ice, shattering a large portion of the pond in the process. It grabbed Braeden's right ankle, uttering a single, croaky word: "*Brother.*"

Twisting, screaming, Braeden bashed at the monster's wrist with another rock, a two-hander. The Pond Person screeched, releasing him.

Braeden tossed the stone, striking the creature in its left shoulder. As the Pond Person scuttled backward, expecting another attack, the boy went the other way, scrabbling for snow.

Braeden reached Kyle's decapitated sculpture. He yanked a pair of sticks free of the snowman's back, stomping each one in half with a boot, sharpening each piece of wood with a loud snap.

The Pond Person slowly crawled toward him, its fangs gnashing as its mouth once again formed the word, "*Brother.*"

Braeden, wielding the broken sticks like twin daggers, watched his actual brother finally reach the shore, seventy-five meters away. Kyle had barely been able to maneuver around the destruction that Braeden and the Q-thing had caused, and now that he was on land, the sixth-grader ran toward where the tense face-off was taking place, pleading for the Pond Person to, "Stop! *Stop!*"

But the monster didn't listen. It dodged Braeden's first stick swipe and grabbed hold of his ankle again, once more dropping him to his rear. Cursing, Braeden slashed at the Pond Person's knuckles, drawing blood.

Recoiling in pain, the beast hissed, "*Bad brother! Bad!*"

In threatening fashion, Braeden sliced his "knives" through the air. "I'm! Not! Your! Brother!"

"Braeden, I'm coming!" Kyle cried. "I'm coming!" He was only fifty meters from the chaos.

"No, don't come any closer! Get Mom! Get Dad!"

Still, Kyle approached. Braeden tried waving him off, and the Pond Person took advantage of the distraction. The monster twirled, swatting Braeden's weapons away with a set of swift tail whips.

"Shit!" Defenseless, Braeden stared directly into the creature's yellow eyes.

"*Braaaaaaaeden,*" the Q-thing taunted. "*Braeden, my brother.*"

"I'm not your goddamn br—ahhhhhh!" The creature had Braeden again, this time by both ankles. It dragged him toward his doom.

Braeden attempted to dig into the ground with his fingers to moor himself in place. Then somehow Kyle was right there, wheezing.

Kyle clutched his brother's hands. "Got you, Braeden... Got you..."

For a moment, Braeden thought the little brat had saved him and that Kyle would now drag him back to safety.

But that was just stupid wishful thinking.

As the monster pulled Braeden by his other end, Kyle whimpered, "I'm...I'm not strong enough... I...*I can't...*"

"You can, Kyle, *you can!*"

"Maybe...Maybe you'll like that brother better than you

like me..."

"Don't you let go, you shit! Don't...!"

The Pond Person tugged more forcefully on Braeden. His gloves came loose, and they were now just empty shells within Kyle's feeble grasp.

Then, Braeden's boots struck freezing water. And he knew it was over.

He was hauled under broken ice, bubbling, gurgling for help, help that would never find him inside the dark tunnel hidden at the bottom of the family pond.

Not a Creature Was Stirring
D.J. Kozlowski

It's colder than you'd think.

Despite the snow, there's virtually no humidity, which is a blessing in some sense; it also means the wind bites and stings, and it's windy all the time.

If the weather dies down for long enough, the unassuming cottage is visible from about two miles out. Sitting alone on a flat stretch, its exterior walls are brown, and at first, it seems to be a dark speck against a white backdrop. As I moved nearer, I realized it was larger than I imagined it would be.

Though shaped like a cottage, it's more like a castle up close. The brown stone walls rise at least two stories. An imposing front door of heavy, thick wooden beams rounded to a half circle on top, with dark metal latches and a huge brass knocker nearly six feet from the ground bars entry. The snow surrounding the building is undisturbed.

Who was meant to inhabit it? It seems fit for the Norse frost giants of legend, much more so than who I expected to find. More apt, how did it come to be here, in this empty wasteland surrounded by miles of white expanse?

A smaller door with a box frame is half visible behind a drift. It seems to be a late addition, hastily cut into the side of the structure. Surely a better option for coming and going—for my size, anyway—as the big door would presumably allow much of the heat stored inside to escape.

Digging the smaller door free and chipping away at the iced hinges, I pry my way into the building. It's dark and cold, but I'm relieved to be free of the windy daggers, and for the lantern I brought to light the way. After calling an unanswered, "Hello," I remove some of my gear and snack on frozen peanuts before exploring further.

For the first time since venturing out, I sense my own mortality. I could die here. But at least I found it. In the best of weather, camp is several days' walk away, and while the sun will be out, the others who were sent in different directions are the unfortunate ones. They will wander until their supplies dwindle, and then they have to return, with nothing to report. Many, I suspect, will never make it back. But this is what we had agreed to. This is the mission.

I'm in a kitchen. A rough, wooden table stands about waist high—average size to me, but lost under the high ceiling that matches the massive door. A single tin plate rests upon it, sheathed with a thin layer of frost, crumbs visible beneath. The frost—it's freezing in here. Whatever fire may once have graced the hearth is long-since dead. Only now do I realize I can see my breath. Still, it's warmer than outside. And still. And silent.

I would like to explore the cabinets, but that can wait. I press on into the next room to continue my search. A faded red velvet chair atop a plain, woven rug faces a dark fireplace. Apart from these, the room is vacant.

Shuddering and slowly slinking across the space, I confirm my morbid suspicion—he's in the chair. Dead. Long dead. Though how long is impossible for me to say, as he's preserved by the cold. It must have been in the past three years—that's how long it's been since he last appeared, spurring our search to discover where he'd gone, and why he'd stopped.

His eyes are cloudy, and the once rosy cheeks are bluish-gray, but there's no visible injury. Natural causes? Was he technically "natural"? He's thinner than I imagined. Thinner than he was supposed to be. And his scraggly white beard reached down to his belt, where extra holes had been punched to allow it to cinch around a thinner frame than originally intended.

I wasn't prepared for this. Nausea gets the best of me, and I fall to my knees, heaving. From the ground, I stare directly into the fireplace and see antlers. I am sick again.

Rising, I scurry back into the kitchen, leaving everything as I found it. My curiosity stymied by the dismal completion of my mission, I strap my pack back on and make my way out the door into the cold. My tracks are already filled in, covered over by the constant wind. I don't feel it. I'm empty.

I pass a red and white pole in the ground—a pole that must have been covered on my way in but since then blown clear. The journey is long, exhausting, and pushes me to my breaking point, but I survive. Only three of the others have returned. We wait in camp for a few days, but nobody else arrives. Finally, we trek back to our ship for the sullen journey home.

Months later, safe around my own hearth, my daughter squeals with joy at her new doll while my son blows into his recorder, making merry, dissonant sounds and proudly telling us it's music. One day, they'll know these gifts came from us. But for now, we tell them they're from the jolly, fat man. The man who comes once a year, delivering presents to all the good boys and girls. The man who leaves coal for the bad children. The man for whom you leave milk and cookies to sustain him through that one busy night.

Had he, perhaps, eaten more cookies or delivered less coal (or had we all been kinder), he might still be making his rounds. But he's gone. And yet, his legend survives.

S*ILENT S*CREAM

C.L. Hart

Act I: A Christmas Surprise

A Puzzling Gift

The sun was rising on Christmas morning as a team of plain-clothes detectives approached a dilapidated farmhouse located on the outskirts of London. A well-maintained truck sat off to the side. There was a light layer of snow on the ground, and there were footprints belonging to two women, two men, and one large dog.

"This is certainly peculiar," thirty-year-old Detective Constable Tatsuya Auer noted. "The footprints indicate that one bloke and two ladies went in. A different bloke and the same two ladies came out with a big dog. We've no evidence that any other vehicle has been here besides that truck. The footprints leading away from the property disappear beyond the truck. Old Kris Kringle left us a spiffing little Christmas puzzle, innit?"

"This gaff is bloody creepy enough," Detective Sergeant Isidoros Cam muttered as he strode through the front door of Warszawski Taxidermy. With his battered fedora and rumpled trenchcoat, the basset-faced DS looked like a cross between Columbo and Dick Tracy.

"Looks like the place has been abandoned for decades," twenty-four-year-old Detective Constable Breandán Gracia Zelenka noted.

"Not quite, Fresh Meat," Auer countered with a knowing grin. "The truck is a newer model, not more than five years old. I'll bet you five quid that there's current mail, though the occupant may not have opened it for a spell."

Lieutenant Theresa Landvik, a seasoned American expat who had been with the Crouch End division of Scotland Yard for 34 years, was a small, wiry woman in her early sixties who looked like she might blow away in a strong wind, but her co-workers knew that she was far tougher than she appeared. She turned her piercing violet-blue gaze on her subordinates.

"Cam and I have had eyes on Aodh Warszawski for twenty-eight years, but we've never been able to pin anything on him," Landvik revealed. "The other members of his family haven't been seen since the early nineteen-nineties. Warszawski claims that after his siblings left for university, his parents moved to Estonia to live an off-grid hippie lifestyle, his maternal grandparents moved into a villa in Katmandu, and his paternal grandparents moved to Tasmania. Nobody reported any of them missing, and there was no evidence of foul play."

"Neighbors were happy enough to have them gone," Cam added. "Before the elder family members departed, pets in the area had a habit of going missing, later to be found shot or poisoned. Aodh Warszawski is a bit of an odd bird, but he doesn't cause trouble for the neighbors. Still, as the Lieutenant says, we've felt there was reason to keep an eye on him. It looks like today may be the day we're proven right."

The group found no evidence on the first floor to suggest that Aodh Warszawski was anything worse than a bad housekeeper, but Cam reminded them of the frantic call that inspired their foray to the property.

"The woman who rang nine-nine-nine told the operator that the house's owner took her to the basement and slipped a sedative into her wine," Cam said. "She believed that he intended to murder her and add her to his collection."

"Might she have been hallucinating, Guv?" Auer inquired.

"It's possible. She described the basement as 'a chamber of horrors.'"

"If she means the decorating scheme, she's certainly correct," Zelenka remarked as he pushed open the basement door, flashing his torch over the scene. "Bloody hell, this place looks like *Miami Vice* meets *Fright Night.* It's absolutely ghastly!"

"Yeah, this freak even had manikins set up in case he couldn't find any live victims to join the party," Auer quipped.

"Greetings, Boils and Ghouls, this is your host with the most, the one and only DJ Ny rocking you into a holly jolly Christmas morning," a pleasant voice announced from a retro-style stereo. "Your guy DJ Ny has some fantastic news for all the dog-lovers out there. Our amazing police force discovered a dog-fighting ring at a farm outside London, where things went badly awry last night. I understand that it was quite a grue-some scene.

"DJ Ny will spare you the gory details as he doesn't want to frighten the kiddies. The good news is, there are twenty-five dogs in need of new owners to help them recover from their ordeal and become well-adjusted members of society. If interested, phone Rot-n-Pit Rescue for further info. And now, here's the theme from *Miami Vice* to honor our hardworking police force. If you're an oldie but a goodie like your man DJ Ny, or if your parents had good taste in TV reruns, you know and love this one."

Cam turned on the basement lights, revealing a scene ripped from a horror movie.

"Ooh, spoooooooky," Auer teased, clapping the rattled Zelen-ka on the shoulder, inspiring a shrill squeal and a shove from his victim.

"Quit fooling about, you idjits!" Cam warned, trying to stay the quiver in his voice. "Theresa, you didn't spike me morn-ing shot of java, did you?"

"Not unless I also spiked mine," Landvik responded.

"These don't look like any manikins I've ever seen. Are they dead?" Zelenka gasped, gawping at the unmoving group of girls and women.

"Mate, they were never alive," Auer retorted. "They're wax or something. You'd not be able to preserve a corpse that nicely."

"Blimey. Right about now I wish I'd listened to me mum and become a veterinarian,"

"I don't think this is wax," Landvik revealed as she touched the hand of the lone male figure in the bunch. "At least the outer layer isn't. I believe it's human skin. Cam, we're going to need a forensic team here on the double."

"That's Aodh Warszawski," Cam gasped. "Or what's left of him. But if he isn't responsible for killing these poor lassies and ladies, then who is?"

"I don't know. It's not like he could have skinned and stuffed himself."

As the senior officers speculated on how Warszawski may have met his fate, Auer and Zelenka opted to explore the basement further. Moments later, a thud and the worried voice of DC Auer prompted Cam and Landvik to hurry to an ornate dining room, where somebody had posed thirteen people ranging from their late teens to their elder years to resemble the apostles at Leonardo da Vinci's *Last Supper*.

Zelenka lay on the floor, his face contorted in a silent scream. Auer knelt beside his fallen companion, patting his wrist in the hope of rousing him.

"I don't know if 'e's suited to being a veterinarian either, Guv," Auer tittered. "When we came in 'ere and saw this lot, 'is mouth opened like 'e was going to scream, but 'e didn't utter more than a squeak. Before I could catch 'im, 'e plopped down on the floor in a faint. Bit of a nervous Nellie, ain't 'e? Can't say as I blame 'im. I know we should 'ave waited for forensics, but curiosity got the better of me, so I went 'round the table and touched one of 'em. It's like you said, Mum, they ain't wax, least not on the outside. The blighter stuffed 'is entire family! I don't know 'ow 'e done it, but 'e stuffed 'em, and then 'e placed 'em 'ere to stare at this bloody taxidermized goose forever!"

When the forensics team arrived, Auer and Zelenka removed themselves from the unsettling scene. Expressions of shock and horror contorted the faces of even seasoned veterans as they examined the loathsome sculptures.

"We need to find the woman who placed that nine-nine-nine call," Cam muttered.

"Yeah, we're sure to have an easy time of that," Landvik responded sarcastically. "She used a burner phone, and the number given is thirty-six-twenty-four-thirty-six."

"Reckon if we ring it there will be some bloke on the other end offering up—"

"And now here's an old favorite of yours and mine," DJ Ny announced. "Seems like a lot of dirty deeds transpired last night. Whether they were done dirt cheap is up to our adept police force to determine. Now, two out of five members of this next band may be rocking that club in the sky, but their slammin' sound guarantees that they will always be rocking bodies here on the old material plane. Take it away, Bon and Mal and company."

"This is all my fault," Cam sighed.

"How do you figure that?" Landvik asked.

"I'd been low-key hoping for an interesting case to bring back the old spark. I guess you need to be careful what you wish for, or you may get it in spades."

Act II: The Night Before Christmas

The Third Lady

It was Christmas Eve, and Aodh Warszawski was excited because he was preparing to add a third member to his collection of "Nine Ladies Dancing." It was hard to wait because he spotted wonderful possibilities every time he went to London, but he reminded himself that it was worth waiting for the perfect specimen to appear.

He spotted her in the alley behind Lunar Eclipse, a Crouch End club appealing to Gen-X goths who wanted to return to their misspent youth and to misspent youth who were born twenty-five years too late to be part of a scene that they idealized. She appeared to be in her late forties. Her features were Asian. She had wavy, jet-black hair cascading over her shoulders, and her ghostly white foundation, heavy eye makeup, and blood-red lipstick made her resemble a vampire, which Aodh supposed was her aim. She placed a cigarette in her mouth and lit it.

Aodh examined her through binoculars before approaching. There were fine lines around her eyes, on her forehead, and around her mouth. Her eyes were an unusual shade of mauve. He supposed that the color could be attributed to contact lenses. She was neither heavyset nor gaunt. Her bustier elevated her medium-sized breasts, giving her a bit of cleavage, but she was otherwise covered from head to toe in black leather armor.

Her expression was world-weary, and her stance indicated that she would happily slam the toe of her stiletto-heeled boot into the crotch of any man foolish enough to mess with her. She was no desperate, overripe tart seeking validation from horny club-crawlers. She was someone who once believed in life's promises and wound up with broken dreams and a broken heart.

She was perfect.

A Spark in the Dark

Aodh meandered casually into the alley, lighting a cigarette as he strolled. He smiled warmly as he approached the woman, who glanced at him but was mostly unfazed by his presence.

Aodh prided himself on his ability to blend in. He was an ordinary-looking Caucasian man in his early forties, on the slim side but not overly thin, on the tall side but not remarkably tall. He had wavy strawberry blond hair, striking navy blue eyes, and a peachy complexion with a sprinkling of freckles across the nose and cheeks. He wasn't handsome by Hollywood standards, but his unassuming appearance put others at ease.

Aodh was clad in dark blue jeans, a reddish-pink dress shirt, a golden-brown leather jacket, and a pair of wild orchid ankle boots sold to him during the last holiday season by the grandmotherly salesclerk who became his second Dancing Lady. He felt that this ensemble would brand him stylishly clueless but not entirely hopeless.

"Cheers, nice night," Aodh greeted as he approached the woman.

"I suppose," she replied, exhaling a cloud of smoke. "A word of advice, if I might?"

"Please," Aodh replied, thinking that she could even tell him to go fuck himself and he'd still hang on every word that slid from her crimson lips lubricated by her exotic French accent.

"You aren't exactly dressed for Lunar Eclipse."

Aodh laughed.

"No, I don't suppose that I am. I wasn't planning to go there, in any case. I just came from Dandelion. I go to clubs once a year to remind myself of why I don't go to clubs."

The woman laughed. She ground her cigarette butt under her foot and reached into her pocket for another smoke. Aodh offered her a light.

"Thanks. I go once a week, though I always come away wondering why. We're a little old for this nonsense, don't you think?"

"I do, but I suppose that hope springs eternal."

"What does hope look like for you?"

Aodh exhaled a smoky sigh.

"I'm seeking a nice woman about my age who accepts my interests even if she doesn't share them. Someone kind but not controlling, attractive but not conceited. The last thing I need is a glamour puss who spends hours in front of the mirror applying makeup and molding her hair into an impenetrable helmet. I hope that doesn't sound horribly sexist."

"Not at all. I wouldn't be interested in a partner with those qualities either."

"I'm Aodh Warszawski, by the way."

"Irish and Polish," Aodh's companion noted. "I'm Gudrun Lemaire."

"Gudrun—interesting. I wasn't expecting Gudrun."

"Were you perhaps expecting Mai Tai or Tiger Lily?" Gudrun teased.

"No, not really. Your accent is French, so I was anticipating Marie Claire or Emmanuelle or such. Listen, Gudrun, I don't know about you, but I've had enough of the Saturday night hormone maelstrom. Would you like to go for a coffee?"

Coffee and Conversation

Gudrun suggested the This & That Coffee Bar, a hole-in-the-wall the entrance to which was in an alley near the point where Prospect Place intersected with Grace Row. Grace Row was a notorious decaying subdivision of disheveled row houses.

"I never knew this place existed," Aodh admitted as Gudrun led him to the derelict bistro.

"How often do you visit Graceless Row?" Gudrun inquired sardonically.

"I don't," Aodh admitted. "I've lived just outside London all of my life, but I can't recall ever seeing this place."

"You may have driven by without noticing it. That's the

appeal of This & That. Nobody knows it's here, but enough people know it's here to keep it afloat. Come, let's get a cup of joe and have a little chat. Unless my choice of coffee houses is a turn-off for you."

"No, not at all. I'm just afraid that my lack of observational acumen is an irrefutable testament to the inevitable decay of my mind."

"Don't be melodramatic," Gudrun chuckled. "You're what, a little over forty? At least you pass for normal. Try being an aging goth chick. All the guys think you're desperate to hang onto your illusions of youth and beauty, and they think that means you'll fuck anything that offers."

"That's pathetic," Aodh groaned. "I promise that's not what I'm doing. I just want to talk."

"Well, you're in luck. This is the perfect place to talk. No loud music to shout over, no hormone cyclone, no twerking teens in baggy jeans. There may be a few sad souls hoping for a miracle, but they're doing so quietly."

Gudrun led Aodh to a corner booth on the opposite side of the room from the jukebox, which was currently playing Cliff Richard's 70's hit, "Devil Woman." Aodh studied Gudrun as she strode to the bar to order two lattes. She looked and talked like a femme fatale, but she behaved like a proper lady.

Gudrun set the lattes down and asked the antiquated barista for a bowl of pub mix. She set the bowl on the table and scooted into the seat across from Aodh.

"Care for some salty succotash and pencil toppers?" Gudrun inquired, pouring a bit of the mix onto a napkin.

"No, thank you," Aodh replied, making a face. "You actually eat that stuff?"

"I even ate it from the communal bowl in the days before COVID," Gudrun laughed. "I love the taste of the sugar-coated praline peanuts combined with the salty pretzel sticks."

"Well, bad snack mix aside, I'm glad you brought me here. I like to be able to talk to my companion without shouting."

"Here's to freedom from twerking teens in baggy jeans and the Saturday night Gen-X hormone mix," Gudrun toasted, clicking her mug against Aodh's.

"Amen to that," Aodh agreed. "So, do you mind telling me a little more about my coffee-drinking chum? What do you do for a living and all that sort of thing?"

"I'm a rogue," Gudrun replied. "I go where I'm needed and do what needs to be done. What about you, Friend Aodh? What are your particular talents?"

"Why don't I show you?" Aodh suggested, pulling his smartphone from his pocket.

Pictures of the Past

"I hope you won't run away screaming when you see my project," Aodh said. "Even with those stilettos, I have the feeling that you could make good time. You see, I did have ulterior motives when I approached you, but they didn't include trying to seduce you. I'm an artist. I build stage sets, and I do taxidermy for museums. I've been working on my own special project ever since I was twelve years old, and you are the perfect model to help me create my next piece."

"Well, don't be shy, show me," Gudrun insisted. "Would

you care for a little pickle juice to top you off?"

"Pickle juice?" Aodh inquired.

"After the first latte, I always take advantage of the free re-fills of plain coffee," Gudrun explained. "It tastes ever so faintly of pickle juice, probably because they wash the coffee urn in the same sink as the pickle jars. You can cover the taste with sugar if you're so inclined."

"Yeah, sure, pickle juice sounds great."

"Lovely. Gert, hit us with a little pickle juice if you would be so kind. Your project sounds fascinating, Aodh, although I have to warn you, I'm not going to readily agree to be stuffed."

"No-one ever does," Aodh said with a cheeky grin. "But in the end, I stuff 'em all! I'm proud of my sculptures. I've created waxworks for multiple museums. I don't like to brag, but everyone who sees my work says that it's second to none."

"Oh, go ahead and brag. If you're proficient, you should be proud."

"Gudrun, I don't know when I've enjoyed talking to some-one this much. Now, bear with me because I must insist on starting at the beginning. This is my very first piece. I pre-served it when I was twelve years old."

"Is that a partridge in a pear tree?" the ancient barista in-quired as she poured the coffee.

"Yes, ma'am," Aodh affirmed. "It was the very first work that I did on my own. My father was a taxidermist, my grand-father was a taxidermist, my great-grandfather was a taxi-dermist, and my great-great-grandfather was a fur trader. He even ventured to the arctic zone and hunted polar bears and seals with the Inuit. He made an excellent living because he was really brave, really crazy, or, really, both. His furs and hides were peerless."

The barista smiled placidly and left to fill the cups of the café's other patrons. Aodh turned his attention back to Gudrun.

"Can you guess what my project was for my thirteenth Christmas?"

"Two turtle doves?" Gudrun replied.

"You're halfway there. Or two-thirds of the way there. It was two turtle doves and a partridge in a pear tree."

"So, you've been creating a component of the "Twelve Days of Christmas" for every year since you turned twelve," Gudrun noted.

"Exactly. However, in the summer of nineteen-ninety-two, the year I turned sixteen, London's own Rogers Museum grant-ed me an internship learning to craft waxworks. Once I was able to sculpt people, I took a break from animals for several years."

Unblemished Perfection

"These are waxworks?" Gudrun gasped, her eyes alight with amazement. "If you hadn't told me, I would have assumed that this was a photograph of your family celebrating the holi-days. And you created these at sixteen years old? You are a phenomenal artist, Mister Warszawski. Your work belongs in the Louvre with other masters of the ages. Gert, look at this photo. You won't believe your eyes!"

As the barista admired the photo of Aodh's waxwork family gathered around the dinner table, Gudrun clasped her hand over Aodh's.

"I must admit that I was skeptical of your motives initially, but I see now that you are a true master with a rare talent. I would love to work with you. You can be my knight in shining armor, rescuing me from the never-ending ennui that plagues my existence."

"'The Last Supper,'" Gert remarked.

"I beg your pardon?" Aodh inquired, a startled look flashing over his placid face.

"Your waxwork display, young man. It is reminiscent of The Last Supper."

"Yes, yes, of course. I intended it that way, but so few people notice that I was somewhat taken aback when you did."

"I have an eye for subtle details. For instance, I assume the gentleman in the position of Jesus is your father."

"Your eye is keen, ma'am. Leon Warszawski is seated in the place of the Messiah."

"May I hazard another guess?"

"At your will. I am most interested in your interpretation."

"The woman in the position of Judas... Is she—"

"Oh, may I have a guess, Gert?" Gudrun inquired hopefully.

Gert gestured solicitously, allowing Gudrun to continue.

"The woman in the position of Judas is your mother, isn't she?"

"Indeed," Aodh affirmed, smiling serenely, although his blue eyes went icy. "The fair Viera Keri Lennon, matriarch of the Warszawski clan. The king ruled with an iron fist, the queen with a velvet glove filled with razor blades. Where Father was brutish, Mother could appear kind so long as she

172

was appeased with tribute. Her mood could change at the drop of a hat, however, and one might say that she dropped her hat quite often."

"Did this impressive tribute of yours mollify her?" Gert wondered.

"For a time," Aodh replied.

"Well, I must say, if I had a son who created such a vividly detailed waxwork in my likeness, I would be quite proud of him. If I were a younger woman, I would wish to model for you. Your work is tremendously impressive."

"Madam, I do not utilize only young models. The models for my first two Nine Ladies Dancing were mature women. The first was a housekeeper I hired to tidy up my hopelessly cluttered home. The second was the sales clerk who sold me the shoes I'm wearing tonight. Here, see for yourself."

Gert and Gunnar admired a photo of two women in their mid-sixties clad in sequined evening gowns with matching dress shoes swaying to an inaudible tune. Silver hair cascaded over the shoulders of the waxworks. Their glistening eyes gazed skyward, and manic smiles lifted the corners of their mouths.

"So lifelike," Gudrun praised.

"Oh, indeed," Gert agreed. "You captured their essence."

"Thank you, that is a high compliment," Aodh said. "Capturing the essence of my subjects is always my aim. Dear Gert, I am inspired by your keen mind and observant eye. I have already selected Gudrun as my model for the third in my series of Eight Ladies Dancing, but I wonder if you would do me the favor of being the fourth."

"I would be honored," Gert replied, giving a slight bow. "Just let me call my nephew to take over for me. Just imagine... me, a model!"

"Would you ask Hal to grab me some sweats and a t-shirt?" Gudrun inquired.

"Of course, Dear. I'd be happy to."

"And tell him to step on it. Great art can't wait!"

"Oh, you're in trouble now, Lad," Gert chuckled as she waited for her nephew to answer the phone. "You have awakened a hunger in our Gudrun."

"She's right," Gudrun admitted. "I haven't been excited about anything in decades, but your talent stirs something in me."

"And you ladies have awakened something in me as well," Aodh confessed. "I am a creature of habit. Once I get into a groove, I tend to stick with that groove. But a groove can become a rut, can't it? Normally, I insist on only one human model each year, so I don't tire myself out. But you ladies energize me. This year I will add two Dancing Ladies to my collection."

Abbreviated Disclosure

Gert's nephew arrived within fifteen minutes. He was a tall, sinewy chap, whose long black hair and weathered complexion combined with his attire of a faded jean jacket, faded Motörhead t-shirt, too-tight blue jeans, and scuffed motorcycle boots made him look the part of an aging wannabe rock star who might be lucky enough to play in a cover band. He placed two changes of comfortable clothes on the bar and embraced his aunt and Gudrun.

"So, what's this all about, Aunt Gertie?" the nephew inquired. "You claim you've been asked to be a model for some sort of artistic project?"

"Is it really so hard to imagine me being a model?" Gert demanded, scowling.

"Of course not, Auntie," the nephew demurred. "You've a big, glorious personality, and you can dazzle with the best of them. It's only that we live in a narrow-minded world, and there's such a push for young models with certain attributes."

"Yes, I know, Dear. Even a lady with serotinal beauty like Gudrun is past her sell-by date. But this fine gentleman has a commitment to depicting life as it is, not selling the same sexed-up images of nubile nymphs. Hal, meet Aodh Warszawski, master of waxworks."

"His mentor was the lead waxwork creator at the Rogers Museum," Gudrun added. "He's the real deal, Hal."

"Well, Mister Warszawski, the ladies have me backed into a corner," Hal chuckled, shaking Aodh's hand. "They certainly seem keen to team up with you. Hal T. Petorayn at your service. The 'T' stands for Today because there's no time like today to begin. You certainly look perfectly normal. But then again, so do most serial killers."

"Ah, Mister Petorayn, I'm afraid I would be a disappointing serial killer. It's all in the eyes, you understand. Serial killers often appear normal except for a certain telling look in the eyes. That's something that my mentor taught me. Here, allow me to show you my work. Scroll through my 'Maids A-

Milking' and ask me any pertinent questions. Gudrun and your aunt will be modeling for my 'Ladies Dancing' series. They both possess exemplary muliebrity."

"Indeed. I see what you mean. These works certainly depict their subjects respectfully, and the attention to detail is most impressive. I feel that if I were to walk up to one of these lassies or ladies and shake their hand, it would be warm to the touch."

"That is the quality that I intend for my work to have, Sir. Here is my card. It has my address, and you can reach me on my celly anytime. Now, I may be getting ahead of myself, but I am wondering if you would care to model for me. You have impressive features, and you would fit perfectly into one of my forthcoming collections. Would you prefer 'Lords A-Leaping,' 'Pipers Piping,' or… You know… I sense that 'Drummers Drumming' is the correct collection for you."

"It's that obvious, is it?" Hal chuckled. "You've got me, Sir. I'm the drummer for Snaggletooth's Slaves. It's a—"

"Motörhead cover band?" Aodh inquired, indicating Hal's t-shirt.

"You are rather obvious, Dear," Gert laughed, embracing her nephew. "Now, Mister Warszawski, I'm ready to be immortalized. Don't worry, Hally, I have Gudrun with me. You know she won't let me come to any harm."

"I have every confidence that Mister Warszawski will conduct himself like a perfect gentleman," Hal said. "Enjoy yourselves, Darlings. I'll see you soon."

Oh! My Soul

Gert pulled on a heavy red parka, tugged a floppy, red cable-knit hat over her granny perm, and wrapped a matching scarf around her neck. With her birdlike nose, eager grin, and twinkling black eyes peeking out of the cold-weather ensemble, Aodh could see the vestiges of the adroit ingenue that the worn-down barista had been countless yesterdays ago. Gert pulled on a pair of red leather gloves and cupped her hands around her face, giving a cheeky grin and a wink.

"Are you ready to turn this old dame into art, Mister Aodh?" she inquired.

"Yes, Madam. Any canvas would be blessed to have you for its subject," Aodh replied.

The women followed Aodh to his truck. Ever the gentleman, he opened the passenger door for the ladies and made sure they were comfortable. Gudrun sat between Aodh and Gert. She asked Aodh if it was all right to play the radio while they drove.

"Knock yourself out," Aodh replied. "At this hour, you might even hear something besides the same two or three songs by bands that have been around for decades."

"Oh, Honey, I guarantee we won't be listening to the same old same old," Gudrun laughed. "You just need to know where to tune the dial. Let me introduce you to the real Daddy-O of the airwaves, my man DJ Ny."

A gruff female voice ripped from the speakers in an animal howl as frontwoman Laura Palmer of the Screamin' Rebel Angels tore into the band's amped-up, psychobilly version of Little Richard's "Oh! My Soul." Gudrun exuberantly shook her head and stamped her feet while Gert laughed and snapped her fingers.

"This song puts words to what's in a woman's soul when she meets a man that she thinks might be Mister Right," Gudrun mused.

"Sadly, he's usually another Mister Wrong, aye?" Gert opined.

"Too true, Darling. I hope you'll excuse my saying so, but the lady who has DJ Ny's heart is one lucky dame. He's a hot number, and he always knows what a woman needs to hear."

"He's my brother, you minx!" Gert laughed, playfully punching Gudrun in the arm.

"I know," Gudrun giggled, embracing her companion. "I also know that his heart is taken. But a mademoiselle can dream."

"Your family seems very interested in music, Gert," Aodh noted. "Do you play any instruments? I hope it won't seem that I'm stereotyping, but I can picture you playing the piano in a classy lounge setting."

"Oh, Aodh, I am so sorry for the spectacle I made of myself just now," Gudrun apologized. "I changed from sophisticated and dangerous goth queen to silly schoolgirl in six seconds. The spectacle you just observed is a ridiculous inside joke between Gert and me, and that song really is a kick. Nonetheless, I apologize for acting the fool."

The Wasteland

"Gudrun, I appreciate every aspect of you," Aodh reassured his companion. "The persona you assumed while listening to that song is an important part of who you are. My art wants you, not only your idealized self. Thank you for sharing the real Gudrun Lemaire with me."

"Well, in that case, you ain't seen nothin' yet. Thank you, Aodh. There are very few people that I feel comfortable being myself around. I am pleased to count you among them."

After what seemed countless turns on endless dirt roads, Aodh pulled onto a long driveway bordered on either side by a weathered split-rail fence. A barely legible wooden sign identified the property as the home of Warszawski Taxidermy.

The sign's once-beautiful bistre brown wood was cracked and gray. The Indian red paint on the raised letters had faded to a sickly pink to which the golden outline added a jaundiced cast. A long-fallow field to the right produced nothing but tumbleweeds. The rotting leaves covering the ground exuded an odor reminiscent of grave mold. The weathered yellow farmhouse with its blue-trimmed windows and rusty orange drainpipe was in no better shape than the sign or the field. It was surrounded by dead and dormant trees whose branches clawed the sky, tapped the roof, and scraped against the windows. Fallen crabapples lined the walkway.

"'What are the roots that clutch, what branches grow out of this stony rubbish?'" Aodh mused, quoting T.S. Eliot as he gestured towards the weather-beaten structure. "I'm afraid that I've focused on other projects to the exclusion of the property. It does look a bit of a shambles."

"It looks like the home of a busy man with little in the way of assistance keeping up the grounds," Gert noted. "Perhaps Hal could help you get things in order. He loves to be useful."

The Spider's Web

Aodh noticed that Gudrun seemed energized by the brisk wind. Her mauve eyes glistened in the light of the moon that made its way out from behind the clouds. Her tongue flashed over her crimson lips to lick away a snowflake.

Aodh had little interest in sex. He certainly had no compulsion to violate children. He wasn't attracted to men, and he never attempted to seduce the women he worked with. Gudrun was one of the few women to inspire erotic arousal. He admonished himself to ignore the heat that flashed through him and the stirrings in his loins. He couldn't afford to make mistakes.

Gudrun offered Gert her arm, and the women walked carefully over the uncleared path to the bleak house. Their fearlessness impressed Aodh. They seemed far too sophisticated for such naïveté. Perhaps their world-weary nature made them careless.

Aodh wasn't particularly surprised by Gudrun's boldness. She carried herself like someone who was proficient in martial arts, and he wouldn't be surprised to discover that she had a knife stashed in one of her pockets or her purse.

Gert was a wild card. The crone's stooped posture and shaky gait gave the impression of a frail dowager, but her dark eyes were flinty.

"Ladies, welcome to my all-too-humble abode," Aodh announced, unlocking the front door. "Like the rest of the property, the upstairs is an eyesore. I spend most of my time in my workshop, which is beautifully maintained. I apologize in advance for the basement's garish furnishings. I obtained them cheaply when the Nebula Nightclub closed its doors twenty-two years ago."

The Heart of the Nebula

"Aodh, do stop apologizing; it's tiresome," Gudrun admonished as she followed her host through the basement door. "I appreciate frugality, and I can see that the furnishings are in impeccable condition. Your domain is eclectic, just like its master. Now, may we examine the impressive waxwork collection that we are about to become part of?"

"Of course. My Ladies and Maids are on display for your viewing pleasure. Would either or both of you care for a glass of wine?"

"Absolutely," Gert replied. "It wouldn't be a celebration without wine, would it?"

"Indeed, it would not. Make yourselves comfortable. First, allow me to procure a selection of gowns for Gert to choose from. My dear late mother was about your size. I hope you don't find the thought of borrowing one of her dresses off-putting."

"Nonsense, dear boy, I'm sure she won't mind," the cheeky crone said with a wink.

Aodh laughed, patting Gert on the shoulder.

"I do love a lady with a sense of humor," he declared. "I'll return momentarily. While I'm gone, you ladies can select a wine from my collection, choose some music, or look over my waxworks. I've provided a biography for each one."

"I feel like I could talk to them," Gudrun marveled.

"You'll be the youngest of our Aodh's Dancing Ladies so far, Dear," Gert noted.

"I'm just pleased to be included among them. Look at the detail! He didn't smooth away a single line. He even included age spots on their hands. We're collaborating with a real artist, Gertie!"

Something about Gudrun

Gudrun is a strange bird, Aodh mused as he absconded to the prop room. *In another circumstance, I might have tried to woo her. She's certainly attractive, but she's sending up red flags by the dozen. I get the sense that she's more than a little volatile, and I had more than enough of that sort of behavior with Mother.*

Aodh selected six dresses for Gert to choose from and brought them out on a rolling rack. As Gert examined the dresses, he made a friendly wager with Gudrun that he believed her venerable companion would choose the forest green gown with gold sparkles. Gudrun leaned toward the sparkly pink for Gert's selection but wound up giving Aodh five quid.

"Lucky guess," Gudrun said with mock consternation.

"Not a guess, Darling. I am adept at reading people. Gert is unconventional, but she appreciates tradition. She associates green with Christmas. I imagine that during the holiday season she still spoils her younger relatives. Now, while Gert spiffs herself up, how about if you select a wine and some music?"

Gudrun chose a 2004 Bardolino, and Aodh complimented her exquisite taste. Suddenly, the earth shattered into a thousand pieces as she unexpectedly drew him into a kiss. The taste of magic glided across her tongue; the sweetness of her kiss enticed his desire for more. For a moment, enraptured by her beauty, he could think of nothing else. Her kisses were all that he craved.

Aodh soon realized that the sweetness in Gudrun's kiss was not that of lollipop trees and sugar-filled seas, nor even the minty mask of the Altoids she'd been popping during the ride while giggling over the deejay on the same underground music station that once again provided the soundtrack for their experience. It was the sweetness of decay.

Aodh was also aware that beneath her killer veneer, the badass broad that he had selected for the honor of becoming his Third Lady Dancing was hungry for approval. He reminded himself that she couldn't be perfect, and eventually he would have discovered something about her that disgusted him. He was giving her a gift by preserving her as she was now.

Aodh gently broke free of Gudrun's corrupt peppermint kiss. The essence of her lingered on the cool night air.

"I feel it, too, believe me," he promised. "It's only that—"

"You don't need to explain. It was impulsive of me. Gert and I came here to model, not to play love games. I don't usually behave like this. I'm the kind of woman who keeps her cool. I'm not even that interested in romance or sex, but you've awakened something in me."

"Your kisses are like everlasting peppermint sticks with

endless licks," Aodh laughed. "I've never met a girl...er... woman like you before. But art must come first. It is my sacred duty to capture my subjects at their pinnacle. I can promise you, you'll stay as beautiful, with dark hair and soft skin forever."

"You are so hopelessly Gen-X," Gudrun giggled, running her fingers teasingly over Aodh's cheek. "And so am I because I understand the reference. And so does DJ Ny. He's playing our song right now!"

"Well, let's leave it to DJ Ny to choose the soundtrack, then," Aodh laughed, impressed if unnerved by the fact that "Possum Kingdom" started playing just as he quoted the lyrics. "When Gert returns, the three of us can toast to our success and drink just enough to loosen our inhibitions without getting sloppy."

Though Your Flesh Has Crystallized

Aodh poured wine into three goblets. He put a charm on the stem of each goblet and poured a few drops of clear liquid from a vial into the goblet with the mermaid charm and the goblet with the shooting star charm. Gert entered the room in her glorious green gown, and Aodh showered her with compliments. He led the women to a gold loveseat placed before a muddy-yellow table, the base of which depicted distorted bodies and contorted faces crying out in terror.

Gert and Gudrun sat on one side of the table, and Aodh sat on the other. He lifted his goblet and proposed a toast.

"To the greatest artistic collaboration of the age!"

"Hear, hear!" Gert returned.

"To the greatest unsung artist of the age," Gudrun added.

As Emerson, Lake, and Palmer's "Still...You Turn Me On" played, the trio sipped their wine. With perfectly choreographed timing, the women set down their glasses and gazed placidly at Aodh, not moving a muscle.

"My dear companions, I don't want you to be afraid," Aodh soothed. "I will soon be introducing you to my partner. You may find His appearance shocking, for He is not of this Earth. There will be a brief period of pain as He drains the vital force from your body, but once He has finished feeding, I will immortalize you. You will never age another moment; your beauty and health will deteriorate no further.

"Gert, you will forever be the devoted friend and benevolent hostess. One day you, your nephew, and the protective companion that you love like your own niece or daughter will delight visitors to the waxwork museum that I intend to build on this property. I will feature homages to missing persons who would not otherwise be missed.

"Gudrun, my powerful yet broken leather angel, you will be my crowning glory. You possess a unique, peerless beauty. Truly, you are the only woman ever to arouse amorous desire in me. But I cannot allow my devotion to my master to be swayed by feminine fiasco.

"Despite your intimidating appearance, I quickly surmised your key weaknesses; impulsiveness and want. Your decision to accompany me and to kiss me were both made in the heat of the moment. Alas, one always comes to regret hasty decisions.

"There is a part of me that regrets what must happen next. I genuinely enjoyed the evening I've spent with you ladies. One does not often find such pleasant company. I will treasure this night for the rest of my life. I've a few thoughts that may bring you comfort as the life ebbs from your bodies. Gert, both your nephew and Gudrun treasure you. Gudrun, Gert loves you as if you were one of her precious nieces, and if you had given him the opportunity, her nephew Hal might have given you the devotion for which you so hunger.

"Alas, we will never know the end to that fairy tale, for you must be gloriously sacrificed to slake the hunger of Rhan-Tegoth. He will usher in a new age of glory for this pathetic planet, returning the Great Old Ones to their rightful positions as our wondrous and terrible masters. He was not destroyed, as my mentor's great-uncle led the hapless journalist Stephen Jones to believe. He was only rendered dormant, and, from the time of my apprenticeship in London, I have known the glory of being His most devoted supplicant."

Enter Rhan-Tegoth

"Now, let me introduce you to the majestic Rhan-Tegoth. Doctor Felipa Stela Harden, the grand-niece of Mister Orabona, assistant to the Rogers Museum's founder, George Rogers, awakened Him from the dormant state in which her great-uncle placed Him. Her chief restorative technician, Mister Poseidon Strickland, taught me how to remodel the remnants of His victims into peerless works of art. Where Rogers and Orabona preserved the sacrifices in their unaltered state, Strickland and I returned them to the appearance they possessed in life. You will now nourish Rhan-Tegoth so that He may build His strength while awaiting the moment when the Stars are Right!

"Rhan-Tegoth, infinite and invincible, I am your slave and high priest. You are hungry, and I provide. I shall feed You with blood, and You shall feed me with power. Behold, on this triumphant night, I have a double sacrifice to satiate Your ancient hunger! Iä! All glory to Rhan-Tegoth, He who shall usher in a new age of magnificence!"

Aodh pressed a button, and the back wall, with its disquieting painting of monstrous nymphs cavorting over mutilated victims, lifted like a garage door. A lumbering abomination clambered slowly forth from the earthen cavern where it slumbered until awakened by its priest. Its shape was an unwholesome blend between arachnid and crustacean, with six sinuous limbs terminating in crab-like claws.

A triad of fishy eyes in a globular head eagerly examined its intended victims. Its flexible proboscis snuffled the air. Initially, its body appeared to be covered in coarse, black fur. On closer examination, the hairs were revealed to be individual sucking filaments, each terminating in a serpent-like mouth.

Lighting the Fuse

As Rhan-Tegoth inspected its prey, DJ Ny cued up Mötley Crüe's "Too Young to Fall in Love." Aodh noted a subtle smirk playing at the corners of Gudrun's mouth.

"Pathetic wench, you will never be free!" Aodh roared.

Reconsidering his action, Aodh wiped the spittle from his

victim's face.

"Dear Gudrun, think about it. You never have been free. You have always been a prisoner of your voracious appetite for male approval. You told me so yourself, back at the café.

"First, you were a miserable babe wondering why your real daddy abandoned you. You grew into a wee needy nipper wondering why your adoptive father never paid you any mind until you developed a woman's body, and he began looking at your breasts in the same way that he salivated over a tasty morsel of prime rib.

"Papa Lemaire wasn't biologically related to you, and he never behaved like a father, so when you came of age, you could have taken advantage of his offer to become his mistress. Agreeing would have afforded you a life of luxury. Instead, you chose pride, a dilapidated row house, weekends spent teasing men who wanted to fuck you but who didn't fit the fairy tale in your deluded mind. Your only real friendships are with a decrepit crone with one foot in the grave and her wannabe rock star nephew.

"You had one last chance for glory, and instead of expressing righteous gratitude or worshipful terror, you are so jaded that all you can do is smirk. You are not deserving of the opportunity I have afforded you. Nonetheless, I will grant it, for He needs to feed! Honestly, I can't wait to be done with you," Aodh snarled. "You are such a cringeworthy miscreant. Sorrow has woven itself so completely into your design. It's impossible for you to hide from the shame you feel over your adoptive father viewing you as a harlot to be fornicated with rather than a princess to be cherished.

"You can cover yourself from head to toe in leather and freeze out every man who tries to come close, you can shout from the hilltops that you don't want or need anyone, but you can't escape from the fact that for you, love will always be a losing game.

"Your soul is like a limp mermaid washed up on a rocky shore after a storm, abandoned and alone. There is no privacy for women like you. You may as well have worn plaid when you strolled into Lunar Eclipse because even with your brilliant disguise, your psychic wounds are laid bare and the head of every sex-starved man swivels about to catch a sniff of potential prey. Any man who is a good enough liar could have his way with you."

Mormo Comes Alive

Suddenly, Gudrun sprang to life. She tapped the side of the goblet, and the glass shattered at the mere touch of her hand. She grabbed Aodh's throat, lifting him from the floor.

"Rhan-Tegoth, stand down!" Gudrun commanded. "You will feed tonight, my pet, but Mumsie's hungry, too, so we'll have to share."

Gudrun's mouth widened, splitting her face open. Her teeth altered to razor-sharp nubs with prominent fangs. Her skin became pale and phosphorescent, and her hair thickened into sucking filaments with asp-like mouths, reminiscent of the serpent-locks of Medusa.

"Well, now I'm killing you, watch your face turning blue," the monstrosity tittered. "I just love that song! Won't you play it for us again, DJ Ny?"

As Gert's nephew strode into the room, the crone shook her head and arms, twisted her torso, and danced in place for a moment. Her dowager's perm altered to glossy silver waves, and she stood ramrod straight. Hal put his arm around her and kissed her forehead.

"Are you and Mormo having fun, Dearest?" the mirthful metalhead inquired.

"Yes, Papa, but she's playing with her food again," Gert laughed. "Aodh, I'm sorry that I told a fib, but I didn't think that you'd believe that Hal was my father, given my brilliant disguise as a mortal woman near the end of her life cycle. It's time to come clean. My name isn't really Gert, it's Yadira, and Papa's name isn't really Hal; it's Nyarlathotep."

"It was a wicked game on our part, but I did give you a chance to decipher it," Nyarlathotep said with a shrug. "It's the old Rumpelstiltskin gambit. My good friend Mick Jagger sang about it in one of the Rolling Stones' better-known songs."

Nyarlathotep's Game

Nyarlathotep snapped his fingers and The Rolling Stones' "Sympathy for the Devil" streamed from the stereo.

Mormo set Aodh on the lemon-yellow loveseat and positioned herself beside him, her diaphanous arm around his shoulder with one spider-fingered claw resting on his chest.

"We thought we'd explain our little game before Mormo and Rhan-Tegoth make a meal out of you," Nyarlathotep said mildly as he and his daughter sat across from Aodh and the bloodthirsty succubus while the mighty Rhan-Tegoth settled himself placidly beside Mormo's hooved feet like a faithful dog awaiting a morsel.

"I do not care to placate your vanity, Trickster," Aodh snarled. "As I am doomed anyway, I would sooner have your abomination finish me than to sit here and listen to you yammer."

"Forgive me; perhaps I gave you the impression that you had a choice," Nyarlathotep retorted coldly. "Believe me, I would prefer to be doing almost anything else, but it's a policy of mine to allow mortals an opportunity to redeem themselves. Alas, I have found that narcissists tend to remain narcissists, but I long ago promised Yadira's dear mother, my beloved Nathicana, that I would give everyone, even a miserable misanthrope like you, the opportunity to learn from his mistakes. So, you will shut your flapping jaws, and you will listen. Are we clear?"

A Change of Tune

"Yes, Mighty Nyarlathotep," Aodh demurred, his demeanor altering from indignance to fawning. "Forgive me, for my terror caused me to take temporary leave of my senses. You are the most admirable of the Outer Gods, and I have no doubt that your daughter is as extraordinary as yourself."

"My daughter is superior to me," Nyarlathotep countered, "for she inherited her mother's abilities as well as mine. Like me, she tends to have little tolerance for arrogance, so there was a fifty-fifty chance that by the time I arrived, there would be nothing left of you but a dehydrated sack of skin."

"I am curious, my Lord, how would you punish an all-powerful sorceress for her disobedience?" Aodh inquired.

"I have never punished my daughter. Oh, there are occasions where I've suggested that she might be a tad less impulsive in the future, but I realize that there are some fools whose foolishness is too great to suffer."

"Mighty Nyarlathotep, I would be honored to glorify you and your daughter. And you, divine Mormo, you will be my queen, and I will be your fool. I am fortunate to have found you on this fateful night. Spare me, and I will be your devoted disciple. Allow me to assist you in your hunt for quarry."

"I can always use another devotee," Mormo mused, picking up Aodh's goblet and tossing back the contents in one gulp. "But before I make my decision, I need to be sure that we are on the same page. What kind of quarry do you think that I, Mormo, the Thousand-Faced Moon, desire?"

"From my studies of your kind, I was given to believe that any sacrifice would do," Aodh replied. "Clearly, you are more selective than I realized. Would you explain to me, oh wondrous Thousand-Faced Moon, why you did not simply drain me when we were alone?"

"I used to simply drain my quarry," Mormo revealed. "But then Yadira befriended me, and I learned how satisfying it is to make my target understand the error of his mistake. May I tell you why I chose the form I used as my disguise tonight?"

"Your choice of forms was impeccable, Mighty Mormo! You appeared as a strong yet vulnerable woman with a unique, peerless beauty. You knew that you would draw quarry of a higher caliber with this disguise. I thought that I was a skilled hunter, but there is so much that I can learn from you. What suggestions do you have for me?"

"Removing your head from your ass would be a good start," Nyarlathotep quipped. "If you paid attention to the news, you might have realized that the lady you were intending to sacrifice resembled a recently-discovered high-profile murder victim."

"Should I have, Sir? There are murders every day. I cannot be expected to remember details about each of the victims."

"No, but this particular victim stood out," Mormo explained. "Gudrun Lemaire was a French artist who disappeared nine years ago. Her skeleton was recently discovered in the back of a condemned building near Grace Row. That was the first hint that we provided, but you were so wrapped up in finding your next victim that you were unaware that the woman you were talking to behind the nightclub was a dead ringer for the unfortunate soul who lately became the talk of jolly old London-town for all the wrong reasons."

"Then there was the obvious hint that I dropped," Nyarlathotep added.

"My father dearly loves making anagrams from his name," Yadira laughed. "When you rearrange the letters in Hal T. Petorayn, it spells Nyarlathotep."

"You are all so very clever," Aodh praised. "I see now that I have misjudged each of you. Rhan-Tegoth is an animal; he doesn't much care what he eats. But Mormo is discerning. I will cease targeting victims like Gudrun Lemaire and will instead hunt the quarry that you choose for me. I have been arrogant, but from this day forth, I promise to be as good and humble a servant as ever you could imagine."

"I might be willing to agree to your bargain," Mormo said, "but Yadira and Nyarlathotep can't quite get their heads around what you did to those girls."

"Girls?" Aodh inquired.

"Your Maids A-Milking, you goat's ass," Nyarlathotep snapped.

"Yes, of course. Forgive me, Sir. Please, allow me to explain. I understand that you must have a personal aversion to young girls being sacrificed, but that is because you treasure your daughter. These poor lassies had lives filled with challenge. I never brutalized any of them. Certainly, I never molested them. I drugged their drinks so that they would fall peacefully asleep before Rhan-Tegoth fed on them. I gave them an afternoon filled with fun and acceptance, perhaps the only real joy they ever knew in their lives. My actions may have been misguided, but surely you can see that I hoped to give these unfortunate wee girls the gift of peace."

"You considered yourself to be superior to these girls, did you not?" Nyarlathotep inquired.

"At the time, Sir, yes. But I swear to you that I have seen the error of my ways. Allow me just one chance, and I will prove to you that I have changed. Iä! All glory to Nyarlathotep, Son of Azathoth, to his wondrous daughter Yadira, and to mighty Mormo, the Thousand-Faced Moon!"

No Quarter

"What do you say, Ladies?" Nyarlathotep inquired. "Will we be giving Aodh a second chance? After all, it is Christmas."

"Other than drugging my drink and planning to sacrifice me to Rhan-Tegoth, he treated me respectfully," Yadira mused. "However, the way he treated Mormo before he realized that she was a Great Old One was textbook incel behavior, and I've peeked at some of the chats he followed on his favorite red-piller hangout. It's a thumbs-down from me."

"Solid reasoning, my dear. Mormo, what are your thoughts?"

"I don't have much to add, DJ Ny," Mormo purred, draping her arm over Nyarlathotep's shoulders. "When Aodh called me a pathetic wench and screamed that he couldn't wait to be done with me, it told me everything I needed to know about how he views women. Besides, Rhan-Tegoth is hungry, and I did promise him a meal. But don't worry, Aodh, we won't leave your body in a dehydrated heap. We will use it to create a handsome waxwork that will be the spitting image of you in your prime because it will be you in your prime. The police are sure to enjoy solving our little brainteaser! Come, Rhan-Tegoth, it's time for din-din!"

Aodh's strangled scream was swiftly silenced as Mormo sank her fangs into his neck and the asp-headed filaments covering Rhan-Tegoth's hide latched onto his torso. Within minutes, the corpse was drained of vital fluids. Mormo wiped her mouth with the back of her hand.

"I'm still hungry," the ancient vampire announced. "I have a holly jolly idea! I happened to hear about a dog-fighting ring near here. I say that we disguise Rhan-Tegoth as a dog and pay them a visit. He and I can feed, and once we're done, we'll call the police and give them another puzzle to solve, plus give the real dogs a chance at homes with compassionate humans."

Author's Note

Aodh Warszawski and Yadira Root are my original characters.

The Crouch End mentioned in this work references Stephen King's 1980 story of the same name and is not intended as a factual depiction of the London borough.

Mormo is the creation of H.P. Lovecraft, appearing in his story "The Horror at Red Hook," first publication Weird Tales January 1927.

Nyarlathotep is the creation of H.P. Lovecraft, initially appearing in his 1920 story of the same name.

Rhan-Tegoth is the creation of H.P. Lovecraft and Hazel Heald, appearing in their story "The Horror in the Museum," initial publication Weird Tales July 1933.

Nathicana is the subject of H.P. Lovecraft's 1927 poem of the same name.

The following songs were inspirational in the creation of the story.

"Devil Woman" is a pop song written by Terry Britten and Christine Holmes and performed by Cliff Richard, appearing on his 1976 album, *I'm Nearly Famous*.

"Dirty Deeds Done Dirt Cheap" is a hard rock song written by Angus Young, Malcolm Young, and Bon Scott and performed by AC/DC, appearing on their 1976 album of the same name.

"Oh! My Soul" is a rockabilly song written by Richard Penniman (Little Richard) in 1958. It was covered by Screamin' Rebel Angels on their 2019 album, *Heel Grinder*.

"Possum Kingdom" is an alternative rock song written by Todd Lewis and performed by The Toadies on their 1994 album, *Rubberneck*.

"Still...You Turn Me On" is a progressive rock song written by Greg Lake. It was performed by Emerson, Lake, and Palmer on their 1973 album, *Brain Salad Surgery*.

"Sympathy for the Devil" is a rock song written by Mick Jagger and Keith Richards and performed by The Rolling Stones on their 1968 album, *Beggar's Banquet*.

"Too Young to Fall in Love" is a hard rock song written by Nikki Sixx and performed by Mötley Crüe on their 1983 album, *Shout at the Devil*.

The following writing prompts were utilized in the creation of this story:

Mindlovemisery's Menagerie

Music Challenge

https://mindlovemiserysmenagerie.wordpress.com/2021/10/01/oh-my-soul-challenge-192/
Wordle
https://mindlovemiserysmenagerie.wordpress.com/2021/09/27/wordle-259/
https://mindlovemiserysmenagerie.wordpress.com/2021/10/04/wordle-260/
https://mindlovemiserysmenagerie.wordpress.com/2021/10/11/wordle-261/
Putting my Feet in the Dirt
http://puttingmyfeetinthedirt.com
Write Edit Publish Now: The Scream
http://writeeditpublishnow.blogspot.com
The following articles and helpful websites assisted in the creation of the story.
https://www.theguardian.com/money/2014/jan/21/how-become-wax-sculptor
http://fantasynamegenerator.com

Christmas in Four Parts

Lisa H. Owens

Part I: The Dummy

Please allow me, if you will, to spin a terrifying tale.
Our story starts at a city mall, a two-bit show, a clown,
a doll.
The victim and her family, drove to town so they could see
a clown pulling on a string to make a dummy talk and sing.

The dummy caught the daughter's eye, she laughed and
said, "Oh my, oh my!

Anon, I must own this prize." She stamped her foot and rolled her eyes.
"If you won't buy him for me, I'll ask Santa. You will see how I always get my way." She frowned and huffed, then stomped away.

Her Mama said she must be good, the only way that Santa could
put her on the "Good Girl" list and bring the gift that was her wish.
The line to sit on Santa's lap wound 'round and 'round. The girl cried, "Crap!
This line's too long. I will not wait." So, she sprinted toward the gate.

She knocked down an elf or two, Santa shouted, "Let her through!"
A hard lesson, she'd soon learn, about waiting 'til her turn.
A talking doll was her demand. She yelled,
"MY WISH IS YOUR COMMAND!"

"Ho! Ho! Ho! Under the tree, on Christmas morning you shall see
a gift earned by disrespect. You'll not get what you expect."
Santa said, "Be on your way. If you're good 'til Christmas Day,
I'll take you off the Naughty List, then perhaps you'll get your wish.

But if you make more demands, it will be out of my hands."
She scoffed, twirled, and walked away. "That is what my
parents say,
but it hasn't happened yet. My demands are always met."
"Ho! Ho! Ho!" Though he had heard, he ignored her hateful
words.

Part II: The Naughty List

The smell of rotting flesh permeated the air as the looming form paced. Back and forth he galumphed, clawing the
gore that was his face. A wet string of words worked its way
through tar-paper lips, "Hohoho-hohoho," ceasing only when he
needed to suck in oxygen, thickened by swarming flies and the
syrupy odors of maggot-filled offal. He continued the graceless
pacing. His path was deeply etched into hardened earth, the
groove deepening each year. The creature was now thigh deep
in dirt and rock and brittle bits of bone. His heinous lair.

He stopped to sniff the air. He knew the precise second it
had arrived. He sensed its essence of pine and cookies with a
hint of musk. His saintly brother, Kringle's scent. Aah. Sweet
relief returned, as it did every winter when the tightly wound
scroll was thrust under his door. The ancient monstrous being, ever so carefully, placed one skeletal hand upon a bul-
bous knee, stooping low to retrieve the scroll. It unfurled as
he groaned his way upright. His eyes flitted back and forth,
scanning the names. So many names. His lips turned upward in
a tortured grimace, and a rumble began to work its way up a
loose-skinned, roiling belly covered in tatters of red and white

cloth. "Hohoho-hohoho!" Phlegm and spittle lodged in the dreadlocked gore that was his beard.

'Twas the night naughty children dreaded. 'Twas the night Krampus Klaus delivered the gifts the entitled children knew they deserved, dragging a bulging putrid sack of nightmare toys.

'Twas the night... 'Twas the night... 'Twas the Eve...

Part III: The Exchange

'Twas the eve, bad children were not sleeping. They listened as Krampus Klaus, silently creeping, dumped out the milk on the clean, polished floor, crumbled the cookies 'til there were no more. Footed pajamas with stars and cowboys, drenched with the sweat of scared girls and scared boys.

Except for one daughter, she had no fear. Her Mama and Daddy would make it quite clear, that she was not naughty, just misunderstood. She would change next year. She could be good. Krampus swept in with nary a sound, silently dragging the bag on the ground. He tip-toed upstairs and entered her room, made the exchange, then left in a zoom.

There, on the hearth, he set down a letter:

Dear Father and Mother:

You should have done better.

Your child is a nightmare, on this, we'll agree. the price for bad parents? You must pay the fee. Your daughter is gone, and she's been replaced, with the coveted dummy, now wearing her face. You can control her when you pull her string. She'll be good now, will obey everything.

Pull on her string; there will be no complaining. I think you will find she is quite entertaining.

Good tidings of cheer,

Kringle Klaus

Part IV: The Big Sleep

Krampus swooped in on a sleigh pulled by his army of corpse rats. They gnashed and lashed at each other with rotted teeth, drawing black ichor, as they dropped from a wintery gray sky. 'Twas Christmas Morn. No good tidings of cheer in his kingdom. Krampus was weary to the bone. His time on earth was waning. He struggled to pull the squirming sack from the sleigh. The muffled cries of the naughty children fell on deaf ears. He felt no pity for the pathetic bullies and liars. Sinister children, really. The sack broke loose from the sleigh, twisting in midair, writhing like a ball of worms. It landed with a dull thud, sinking deep into new-fallen snow. He was so weary. He would leave his corpse rat army to attend to the children. He shuffled to his lair, where he would sleep the sleep of the dead.

End of the Line
James Jenkins

"See, the key to really benefit from air source heating is insulation. Yeah, I know what you're thinking, 'But Jerry, if I've got to pay to re-insulate my house, then I'm spending, not saving,' and I understand your concerns. However, after the initial outlay, you can become..."

Harold willed Jerry to stop talking and gazed around the room, desperate for somebody else to come and interrupt. He eyed Tina from finance talking to Dave from marketing, but there wasn't any salvation there. The whole office floor could see they were one boozy Christmas party away from shagging. Instead, Harrold zoned out the dull, endless accounts of information about air source heating. Fragments of mince pie rained down upon him as Jerry took bites between words. His ability to speak and eat without interruption contradicted the stereotype that men can't multitask. He searched the room for a distraction among the cheap tinsel and plastic tree. Jerry prattled on about an energy source that was, quite frankly, pointless to Harold, a man who lived in a high-rise apartment building. He was busy counting the baubles by the time Jerry came up for air.

"Anyway, are you coming into town for a few jars after this, Harold? My wingman. Santa needs his helpers if he's going to unload his sack." Jerry laughed alone at his shit joke.

"...Pardon?" spluttered Harold, startled by the sudden change of conversation.

"Drinks, Harold! Are you coming to *parlez*? It's Christmas Eve, for fuck's sake."

"Oh..." said Harold. "No. Sorry, Jerry, I'm catching a train back to my mum's tonight."

Harold didn't wait for a polite silence but turned on his heel before Jerry could start up again.

The train deposited Harold onto the station platform to await the last part of his journey. He skated his way over the frozen snow to the timetable. Only one other train stopped here, and it was the same one he'd used to escape his hometown all those years ago. Harold hadn't expected the line to still be open; he was almost disappointed by the discovery when he booked the ticket. Still, he'd put the return visit off for too long, and now, after the news of his father's death, he couldn't any longer. It would be his mother's first Christmas without her husband, and the guilt weighed too heavily upon him.

Harold didn't hold many positive memories from childhood. Both parents had been cold and indifferent. He never wanted for food or clothes, nor was he mistreated in any way. Even on the rare occasion when his dad would take a slipper to his ass cheeks, Harold could tell there just wasn't any enthusiasm behind it. That summed up his mother and father in a nutshell. Life wasn't much better at school. The other children were distant, not unkind, just reserved, and the teachers were no different. They handled him more delicately, but he could see their forced smiles. What had puzzled him most was his isolation from church when it was mandatory for all the other children. Every cloud and all that. When the time had come to leave the town and get a job, Harold was more than ready to escape. There had been some correspondence with his parents over the years since then, but they were now reduced to an infrequent letter after he gave up on the long silences of the phone calls. The most recent correspondence informed him of his father's passing. By the time he'd read it, the funeral had already taken place. Harold questioned who he was really going back for—his mother or him. By the sounds of the letter, she hadn't seemed too disappointed by his absence.

He checked his watch—5:42 p.m. The train was due in six minutes. The snow was floating down in heavy flakes. It was safe to say it would be a white Christmas this year. Once the train arrived, it was a forty-five-minute journey back to his hometown. There weren't any other stations along this distant vein of the national railway aside from one disused station Harold remembered from his many trips to the city in his latter teens. He'd asked his father about it once, but it was met with an extra helping of the cold indifference he was used to. His mother had asked him not to mention it again, and he hadn't. Harold pictured the station as he shivered on the barren platform, huddled underneath an asbestos roof. The brickwork had long been reclaimed by ivy, even when he was a young child. Harold remembered how grand the building looked for such a small station and had always wondered what town or village lay behind it. He'd tried to find it in later life with the help of the internet, but the stories were brief, if not vague. It was something he would try and bring up with his mother. At least it would fill the predictable and uncomfortable silences.

The train screeched to a halt, and even with Harold's limited engineering expertise, he could tell the wheels were struggling for purchase. He had to walk to the far end of the platform to board it. The door opened automatically, and Harold escaped the relentless snowfall. He wasn't surprised to see he was the only passenger.

"Tickets. Tickets please," said a conductor entering the empty carriage. Harold humored him and held his aloft.

"Thank you, sir," he said, punching a hole through the card.

Harold admired his commitment to the season as the man's Santa hat swung from side to side.

"Not very busy tonight," Harold said in a shit attempt to

make light conversation.

"Never is. Not these days," he replied with a glimmer of sadness in his eye. "Only one station on this line. I can't see them keeping it open for much longer."

"I remember when I was a kid, there was an empty station that we would pass. The train never did stop there. When did they close it?"

The conductor's face contorted with a hint of repulsion. Not too dissimilar to the one from his own parents. He wondered why the mention of the disused station evoked this reaction. He didn't hang around to let Harold ask. Instead, the humming rails lulled him into a doze.

Harold was startled awake by the sudden loss of velocity. Peeling his face away from the frozen window to look outside, he dumbly searched for the familiar sight of his childhood town. A void of darkness returned his puzzled expression in the reflection. The train's lights had been replaced by the silver glow of moonlight piercing the carriage from the opposite window. Harold's breath cut through the icy air. He shrugged his coat back on when a dull orange orb floated down the center aisle.

"End of the line," came the voice behind the lantern.

Harold squinted to make out the conductor's face.

"Are we at the station?" Harold asked, confused by the view from outside.

"Snow's laid too thick on the lines. We'll have to make the rest of the journey on foot."

"What?!" he asked incredulously.

"Sorry, lad, just the way of things. Now come on, grab your stuff and follow me. Godlow Station isn't that far."

Harold's mind spun through the most likely scenarios. Taxi? Bus? Fuck it, why not a helicopter?

He stepped off the train into a deep snow drift and felt the cold up to his knees. The conductor was already a few yards ahead as Harold tried to keep pace with him. The only light along the side of the tracks came from the conductor's amber beacon.

"What about the driver?" Harold asked, his voice lost to the howling wind and swirls of frosted flakes as the conductor carried on.

"Hang on!" Harold shouted to his back. Nothing. He stumbled on in pursuit, using the conductor's footprints in the snow to navigate. Now that the distant light had disappeared into the darkness ahead, Harold was heavily reliant on the moon and thankful for the reflecting snow. The walk was a relentless strain on his legs as he worked his way through the hazardous conditions. Trainers intended for a journey on a train became saturated, and the freezing temperature burned his skin. Harold could feel the tissue in his feet protesting as each toe threatened him with the first stages of frostbite. He pulled the thick winter jacket tighter around himself and pushed on.

Finally, a brick building loomed ahead. A single light sat upon the elevated platform, so Harold climbed the icy steps and freezing handrails to retrieve it. The lamp was just like the one the conductor had been holding. He picked it up and was instantly grateful for the small amount of heat that radiated from the flame. The luminosity lit up the platform, which Harold guessed to be about twelve feet long, at best. The building behind it contradicted the platform's size. Harold studied the three-story construct; the architect had spared no attention to detail. Gargoyles stared from beneath a white blanket and made Harold feel like he was being watched. He stumbled toward the colossal entrance in search of shelter from the blizzard. The double wooden doors had freed themselves from the doorway long before now, and Harold wondered if they had been helped down by vandals. Graffiti insulted the walls of the impressive foyer and creeped up towards the gantry running across the span of the vaulted ceiling. The interior was as empty as the window frames. Harold gazed in awe and wished he could have seen it when it was open. Such grandeur for a station that never used. Harold explored the vast space in search of a spot to shelter from the freezing wind blowing through the broken glass. Instead, he found a rusted turnstile leading out to the rear. There had to be a nearby village or town, even if he'd never heard of it. He couldn't stay in the station all night.

The turnstile led to another open door and the harsh winter's night. Harold pushed on and found himself in a square courtyard. A stone fish fountain stood in the center, so Harold took care to keep to the edge of the area despite the heavy snowdrifts. The only exit was via a set of stone lions standing guard on their pedestals. A seemingly endless expanse of frozen land awaited Harold on the other side. He followed a winding path visible only because of the brick walls to either side. Harold battled on against everything the weather could throw at him before he spotted another building at the furthest reaches of his vision. He worried that it was the station again, such was the size. Then he spotted the lights from behind the curtained windows. Harold was staring at a mansion. The awareness that he was now trespassing wasn't enough to deter him from the hope of warmth.

After what felt like the longest part of his journey, Harold finally narrowed in on the door. Numb fingers reached out for the brass knocker, and he feared his skin would tear away once he released it. The door boomed across the land and then returned with an echo from within the mansion itself. Harold waited. He tried three more times before pushing it open. A wall of heat forced its way out of the opening and dragged him inside, the door closing behind him from a gust of wind...or something else. The vestibule eclipsed what he'd seen from the station, and he struggled to take it all in. The winding staircase, wide enough to drive a car up, split off on-to two walkways. Six doors adorned the upper floor, and, of course, a suit of armor sat neatly in between. On the ground floor, Harold stepped toward the flickering light from a fire in a nearby room. He was so overwhelmed by the familiarity of the place and the eyes of the paintings that followed him with keen interest that he almost forgot he was in somebody else's house.

"Hello!" he called.

The only voice to return was his own. Harold followed the source of heat and entered a parlor.

"Oh, hello," Harold spluttered to the back of the figure in a wheelchair situated by the huge fireplace. The body didn't flinch as Harold tip-toed his way past the dusty Winchesters and the predictable Grandfather clock. His steps mirrored the metronome of the pendulum as he inched ever closer to the stranger and, more importantly, the fire. He was a foot away with an out-stretched hand when he saw the occupant's shriveled, shrunken head. A sickly, musty smell crawled its way up his nose.

"He will not speak to you!" a voice bellowed from behind Harold.

"Oh... I'm... sorry." He fumbled for words as he turned to look at the source. A gray beard with flecks of black met with the man's unkempt hair. Harold studied the regal outfit of the homeowner and guessed it was some high-ranking military uniform. Moth-eaten and threadbare. The gold lion's head mounted on the walking stick looked like it cost more than Harold's one-bedroom flat.

"Hush now. Your words are wasted on me," came the deep, plummy tone of the man. "Come. We must get you washed and dressed for dinner."

Harold followed his host out of the parlor and up to the first floor until they arrived at one of the many doors.

"Towels are on the shelf. You will find the bath water comfortable, I suspect. Mary will deal with your soiled garments. In the meantime, help yourself to one of the gowns and find me in the dining room once you've rid that body of its filth." He opened the door for Harold to reveal a bathroom tiled from floor to ceiling in white. It had a clinical feel, and the smell of disinfectant stung Harold's eyes. He stepped inside reluctantly but couldn't resist the draw of the steaming bathtub.

"Mary!" the man shouted down the stairs. "The bastard has arrived."

Harold turned toward the man at his outburst to question what they meant, but he'd already shut the door. Hypnotized by the rising steam, Harold let it go. He'd ask what the man meant later.

Harold wrapped the soft gown around his warm skin and left the medically scented bathroom. He wondered how he would find the dining room, but the inviting smell of glazed meat guided him toward a hall with a long table fashioned with silver cutlery. Christmas crackers were placed with concentrated precision at each of the twelve place settings. He walked over to the fireplace and studied the towering Christmas tree. The scene was a perfect replica of the stereotypical picture printed on seasonal greeting cards. Tall wax candles glimmered and dripped from the overhead chandelier.

"Sit!" the man's voice ordered from behind. Harold obliged, immediately taking the nearest chair.

"The bath was lovely," he began. "Thank you so much for letting me in. We had to ditch the train due to the weather, and I lost the conductor. I thought I would freeze to death in that abandoned station."

"Not abandoned!" the man snapped.

Before Harold could apologize for offending his host, a gaunt and decrepit maid crept into the hall with a plate of food. He grimaced at the nicotine-yellow veil that hid her face.

"Eat!" ordered his host as the plate was placed before him. Harold didn't argue and greedily tucked into the roasted meat. The maid left as the man stood by Harold's shoulder.

"That's it. Eat," he said, more relaxed this time.

Harold did.

"Ah," the man said, rubbing his hand along the ridge of Harold's back. "The bastard has returned. It's okay, boy; it's just the way of things."

Harold tried to question the man, but he was having some difficulty getting his mouth to work. His jaws were struggling to chew. The knife and fork dropped from his hands with a clatter onto the plate. His strength was ebbing away as he listened to the man rubbing his back.

"You were born for this night, boy," the host said, using both hands now to massage blood flow. Harold saw through his own eyes as his head crashed down onto the plate. He didn't feel a thing as the upturned fork pierced his cheek.

"Mary, tell the good doctor we're ready."

The drug's dosage was too much for Harold's body, so he fell into a merciful state of unconsciousness.

Harold stared up at the vaulted ceiling below the chandelier. A man in a doctor's robe was beaming with pride at a large syringe containing a milky white substance.

"Did you get it? Did you get it all?" the host questioned frantically.

"Yes. A very good batch, indeed," the doctor replied. He twisted the cylinder slowly in his hands to inspect the contents.

"Shall we prepare the guardians?"

"Oh yes!" The doctor snapped back to attention.

The host must have seen the fear in Harold's wide peepers. "Don't worry, bastard."

The doctor winced at the choice of name.

"What?" said the host.

"It's just... I mean, bastard? I know it's tradition, but couldn't we try calling them by their name? You know, roll with the times," said the doctor.

"But he is a bastard. Born out of wedlock. What's his bloody name anyway?"

"Harold."

The host shook his head in defeat. "Fine. Fair enough." He turned back to Harold.

"Harold, the bastard. Don't fear for what we've already taken, for that was already ours. It is what you will give us next that really is your true gift. There is no better present one can give at Christmas," the host rubbed his meaty palms together in delight. "Prepare the female guardian for insemination, Doctor."

A wave of despair welcomed Harold back upon awakening. His legs were bound by rope, and he was hanging upside down above the dining table. Transparent tubes trailed like tendrils from different parts of his body. He followed the network of tubing carrying his blood as they descended toward ten goblets placed evenly around the table. Harold noticed that guests now filled all the seats. A young couple looked nervously up at him. Everyone else around the table seemed to be more of an age comparable with their host and the doctor. He thought he recognized a few faces. The conductor. His old school principal. The vicar. The man in the wheelchair was there, an oversized Santa hat hung over the side of his shriveled head. Still, Harold could see the resemblance of his father in the distorted face. The maid sat beside him, her veil now removed. Harold willed the woman to look, but she refused to meet his gaze, but in his gut, he knew who it was. Mum.

Blood drained through the tubes and slowly filled the goblets. The host stood up from his seat.

"Friends! Our flock has grown," he motioned towards the young couple. "Our next guardians, Sarah and Tony. Both understand the role they've taken on. The good doctor has successfully implanted Sarah for our next feast. Our lifeblood to eternity. The child must be well looked after, but you must resist any emotional bonds with the wretch. Twenty-five years from now, on Christmas Eve, just like twenty-five years ago, and twenty-five years before that, for as long as we can remember, we will harvest the benefits of the sacrifices we have all made. The bastard's bloodline is our burden to protect and ours alone. Look above you now," he paused for effect. The older members of the group followed his gaze towards Harold's pale body. Only the maid, the old man in the wheelchair, and the young couple looked away.

"A direct descendent of Christ!"

Harold tried to laugh, but the sudden rise in blood pressure only served to drain him more quickly. The dizziness reminded him of his current predicament, so he did what any boy would do when he was in trouble. He looked for his mother.

"In just a moment, our cups will be filled by the blood of Christ. We will drink to our eternity," the host started up again. "But first, we must show our new guardians the benefit of their sacrifice. Phillip and Mary..." The host turned his focus on the maid and elderly man in the wheelchair. "...you have served this commune well. As the most recent of our guardians, we invite you to taste the fruits of your hard labor. You have fulfilled your promise of raising this vessel and bringing it here tonight. Now you, too, will share our gift. Drink!"

Harold watched his mother pick up her goblet and gulp it in a gluttonous frenzy. He watched his own blood spill down her chin. His father's frail hand struggled with his own cup before she helped pour it through her husband's blue lips. The transformation happened before their eyes. The young couple gasped in wonder as they saw a glimmer of their promised fate. His mother's skin grew tighter by the second as she began to resemble the woman he remembered. Harold's father followed suit and slowly stood from the wheelchair, grinning. He stopped himself to spare Harold a glance.

"Sorry, Harold, lad. Nothing personal."

A tear fell from Harold's eye, and he willed it to drop into one of the goblets in a last-ditch attempt to spoil the flavor of his sacrifice. But it missed. His mother looked up at him, and for the first time, she caught his eye before turning away quickly, leaving Harold with the remnants of an apologetic smile.

The host picked up his own goblet, now brimming with blood. "Happy Christmas, everyone, and to you, Harold the Bastard!"

T𝖍e Y𝖚le L𝖆ds are C𝖔ming
Villimey Mist

Loud bleating from outside his house in the west of Iceland woke Hallgrímur Ásgrímsson from a deep slumber. He groaned and stumbled out of bed while rubbing the crust of sleep from his eyes. His sheep were usually quiet at night; there was only one reason they'd make a sound like that. Either a mink or a fox had sneaked into their pen to nibble on a defenseless lamb.

"Won't be long. I'm taking the rifle just in case," he said.

No one replied, yet he always assumed his late wife would respond. He always thought they'd be together forever.

Hallgrímur shook his head, pushing the grief that threatened to flood his heart to the back of his mind. He quickly put on clothes and shuffled through the hallway, careful not to wake his son, Hákon, in the next room. While putting on his *lopapeysa*—an Icelandic, hand-knitted, woolen sweater—Hallgrímur opened the locked storage closet and pulled out the rifle. He rarely used it, only during hunting season, but kept a couple of bullets accessible for such situations.

He really didn't want to deal with minks or foxes right now. There were only thirteen days 'til Christmas, and he already had enough on his plate, what with sending smoked lamb to the local stores and taking care of his son. Within the past few years, people had begun supporting local farms instead of the megafarms, and Hallgrímur had been busy preparing for this year's demand.

He loaded the rifle and opened the front door, braving himself for the cold and the snow that usually piled on in December.

He peered down at the white fluff beneath his feet, expecting to see little animal paw prints. He frowned. A series of circular indents dotted the snow, starting from outside Hákon's window and leading to the sheep's pen.

"What the fuck..." he muttered, scratching his chin. What kind of animal made a paw print like that? He leaned down to get a closer look, thinking that one of the sheep must have escaped and had wandered off near the house. He banished the thought. Sheep had hooves, and those prints were completely circular, like someone had used a baton or something.

One of the sheep let out a sharp, painful cry.

Hallgrímur's head whipped up. Something was still bothering his livestock. He gripped his rifle and trudged through the snow, following the trail.

The pen smelled of dirty wool and wet hay. The place was dark, yet he spotted the occasional fluffy animal scampering in all directions. Hallgrímur couldn't afford a ceiling light like some farmers, but he knew the sheep wouldn't know the difference.

Something crunched in the gravel. Not at all like hooves stomping the ground.

"Who's there?" Hallgrímur called as he fished out his cell phone.

A sheep bleated a cry for help. The other ones herded away into the far most corner of the pen to avoid being attacked by whatever was inside. Hallgrímur squinted into the darkness. Something hunched over the animal. Suckling sounds—reminding Hallgrímur of the time Hákon had been on the bottle as an infant—echoed in the tiny chamber.

The hair at the back of Hallgrímur's neck stood on end. He braced the butt of the rifle against his shoulder. He turned on his phone's flashlight, spotlighting the white, puffy quadrupeds.

He froze, almost dropping his phone.

A bearded man bent his torso at an angle Hallgrímur thought wasn't humanly possible. He dressed in old, woolen clothes, older than Hallgrímur's *lopapeysa*. They reminded him of the clothes he had seen on display at the National Museum of Iceland, especially the long, red cap that perched precariously on top of the man's head. His mouth suckled on the sheep's teat, but that wasn't the creepiest thing.

Instead of lower legs of bones and flesh, wooden pegs

tapped against the hardened ground, in beat to the ferocious sucking.

"What the fuck?" Hallgrímur spluttered, his stomach churning at the sight. "Get away from my sheep, you sicko!"

The old man looked him straight in the eyes, *grinned*, then dismissed him, holding even tighter to the sheep's wool. His knuckles turned stark white as he tugged the teat harder. The poor animal squirmed in pain.

Hallgrímur flushed, taken aback by the man's behavior. At first, he'd thought it was just a vagrant seeking shelter from the cold, but he hadn't heard of vagrants stealing sheep's milk right from their teats. Stashing his phone in his pocket, he raised his gun and cocked it. "I'm warning you."

At the sound of a round being chambered, the man let go of the poor creature. It scampered away, whining bloody murder. Still tapping the peg legs, the man raised his arms in surrender.

"I apologize, good sir. It has been a long walk to all these houses here and I'm afraid I got too thirsty for my liking. Your sheep are fine animals. Their milk will keep me going for the rest of the trip." The man's face split into a toothy grin. Frothy milk covered the man's yellowish teeth and coated his beard.

"What's your name?" Hallgrímur demanded, still not lowering the gun.

The man chuckled. "Oh, you know who I am. I used to come by your window every year when you were a child. Gave you treats if you were nice, or potatoes if you were naughty."

Hallgrímur frowned. He had no recollection of ever seeing someone like that in his youth. It didn't matter. It only made him dislike the man more. So, he was a peeping tom as well as a thief? "Still going to need that name."

The man's uncanny whimsy vanished. "I don't have time for this. I've got other houses to see. Other children to watch."

He stood, his peg legs banging on the frozen ground. Hallgrímur flinched and pulled the trigger. The shot boomed in the shed, and the rifle's recoil hit Hallgrímur hard on the shoulder. Ears ringing, he lowered the rifle and rubbed the sore spot as he looked around for the bearded intruder.

The was on his back on the ground. Blood oozed from a huge, pulpy wound in the middle of his chest. Was a wound supposed to look like strawberry jam? Crimson foam bubbled from his gasping mouth. A copper tang and the odor of sour milk mixed with the musty air.

"Oh, shit. Oh, shit, shit, shit!" Hallgrímur dropped the gun and scurried over to the wounded man.

The bearded man's eyes bulged as his trembling hands tried to cover the wound. The flesh around it had been shredded, and it stuck to the soaked woolen sweater. Hallgrímur kneeled next to him, though he was unsure what he should do. If he performed CPR, wouldn't all the blood just spurt upward from the wound? Should he call an ambulance? It'd be too late since his farm was an hour away from the nearest town.

He gasped when the man clutched his arm and, using his last ounce of strength, pulled Hallgrímur closer to him.

"Naughty," the man whispered, a sinister smile etched on his bloody face as his last breath dragged through a painful rattle.

Hallgrímur's heart pounded against his ribs. He had killed a man. And there were only thirteen days 'til Christmas.

This year couldn't get any worse.

He pried the dead man's hand off his arm and stood up, gazing at the body. He decided then and there that he was *not* going to jail over this. No one had heard the gun shot. And if by some chance Hulda, his next-door neighbor, had heard it, he'd tell her it'd just been a fox.

He dragged the body by the hands—he feared the pegs would pop off if he pulled on them—and brought it to the compost area near the barn. The soil that wasn't completely frozen due to the warm water running underneath was the perfect spot to bury the body. He grabbed a shovel and dug a hole big enough for the old man. Sweat slicked his back, but he didn't pause for a second. He wanted to get this done before morning.

A distant screech whistled through the air. Frowning, Hallgrímur stopped and listened. It sounded like sorrowful wailing, but it was coming from some distance away. He turned to the mountains. Was someone trapped up there in the middle of the night? Hallgrímur waited for the sound to come again, but it never did. He shrugged and dumped the body into the hole.

Once buried, Hallgrímur spread fresh hay on the pen's floor to cover the blood and splashed a bucket of water on the wall. He then locked the gun back inside the closet.

It was done. Only he knew what had happened. Only he had to live with it. And he was going to take it to his grave.

The next day went by without a hitch. Hallgrímur kept himself busy with preparing the meat in the smoking chamber. A knock on the door, and Hulda walked in. She was too young to be a widow like him, but he appreciated the connection it gave them. She had been supportive, helping with the meat and spending time with Hákon. He was unsure if he liked it or not, but every time she showed up, he couldn't ignore the swooping sensation in his belly.

"I heard something like a shot last night," she said.

Hallgrímur blushed. "Oh, yeah. A damn fox tried to take one of the lambs. I had to shoot it."

She winced and muttered, "Poor thing," as she heaved another leg of lamb onto a free hook that lined the walls. Hallgrímur didn't want to admit it to himself, but he loved how she cared about the animals. Hallgrímur's guilt only lingered for a moment, then he remembered he had better things to do.

Two days after the incident, Hulda unexpectedly came over at breakfast. She held up a casserole dish full of lasagna and a bright smile.

"I made too much lasagna last night, and I figured you might want some."

Hallgrímur's mouth twitched. "You shouldn't have."

"Nonsense. I know you don't eat much during this time of the month, and I don't want you collapsing from hunger." Hulda went straight for the fridge and put the dish inside. She then grabbed a cup of coffee, sat beside him, and patted his arm.

Warmth traveled from Hallgrímur's chest to his fingers. "Thank you. I know Hákon will be pleased."

As if on cue, Hákon entered the kitchen, frowning and

holding something in his hand. Hallgrímur jumped out of the chair, away from Hulda's nice-smelling hair. He wasn't quite ready for his son to think there was something more going on between them.

"What's the matter, buddy? Why the long face?" Hallgrímur asked, bemused.

"Gully Gawk didn't leave me anything in my shoe. Just this note."

Hallgrímur's brow furrowed. It has long been a tradition in Iceland that the Yule Lads, benign half-trolls, would come down from the mountains for the thirteen nights before Christmas and leave either treats or potatoes in children's shoes that they left on their windowsill. What they got all depended on whether they behaved well or were demanding little monsters. It's just folklore, of course, but parents still use it as an incentive to make their children behave through all the stress leading up to Christmas. The mention of Gully Gawk stirred something in his memory, but he couldn't recall it vividly. It was like an unfinished puzzle within his mind, with some pieces not fitting the frame. Hallgrímur dismissed it. He could think on it later. There were far more worrying things to dwell on.

"Let me see that note."

Hákon handed his father the piece of wrinkled, old paper, then took a seat with his arms crossed.

Hallgrímur smoothed out the paper. The handwriting was crude, with blotches of ink dotting the page, as if the writer's hand had been trembling. His brow burrowed deeper near the center of his forehead as he read the single sentence on the page: *We know what you did.*

An unsettling dread solidified in Hallgrímur's stomach. Had someone found out? If so, were they using his son as an extortion tool?

"Is someone bullying you at school, Hákon?" he asked.

Hákon shook his head, his chin nestled in his chest.

Hallgrímur glanced at Hulda, who gave an uncertain shrug. She didn't know him well enough, of course. She wouldn't know if he was lying.

"Don't worry, honey. I'm sure Gully Gawk had been so busy that he forgot your house. Tell you what, I'll personally write him a note telling him how well-behaved you've been, and Stubby will probably give you something nice," Hulda said, ruffling Hákon's hair affectionately.

Hallgrímur's heart swelled. She didn't need to, but he saw the determination in her eyes. He suddenly wished that he had dressed in better clothes. Hulda offered to take him to school, but Hallgrímur decided to do it himself so that he could have a word with Hákon's teacher.

The school reported nothing, and Hallgrímur hadn't noticed any weird looks from the kids, but over the next couple of days, some odd things happened at the Ásgrímsstaðir farm.

First, all the pans disappeared from the kitchen, yet there was no evidence of a break-in.

Their bowls reeked of urine, which Hallgrímur blamed the dog, but Hulda, chuckling during one of her visits, doubted the dog could jump atop the cabinets, open them with its paws, and pee into all the bowls and then stack them neatly in their proper place. It was weird, but nothing that the dishwasher couldn't clean. It turned into an evening of laughs and wine.

Hallgrímur began anticipating Hulda's visits and tried cleaning the house in the evenings to make a better impression. He went to sleep with a smile imagining Hulda's surprised expression when she came in to find the house clean.

Hulda's screams woke Hallgrímur the following morning. Thinking she had injured herself, he rushed into the kitchen. A stink so repellant assaulted his senses.

He recoiled. "What the fuck is that stench?" he asked as he covered his nose and mouth with his hand.

Eyes watering from the stink, Hulda pointed at all the pots strewn around the kitchen floor while clutching her scarf to her face. A chunky, yellowish-brown liquid stewed in each of them. Hallgrímur inched toward his large soup pot and gazed into it. Some semi-solid chunks of excrement lay in it.

"I-Is that shit?"

Hulda nodded. "And don't you dare blame it on the dog, Hallgrímur. This is getting more than weird. I think someone is harassing you. You need to report it to the police."

Hallgrímur's cheeks reddened in embarrassment. No way he could impress her now. He led Hulda out of the putrid stench and into the living room. "I don't have proof. These things seem to always happen when Hákon and I are asleep, even the dog, and even if someone *had* broken in, the dog would have known." He glanced at the kitchen door, nose wrinkling as the foul odor had invaded all the rooms, then down at his neighbor. "Now, be straight with me; *you* haven't been having any stomach problems recently? Like irritable bowel syndrome or something?"

Hulda's nostrils flared. She yanked her hand back and stomped toward the front door. "For even *suggesting* that *I'm* behind this, you'll be cleaning that shit up by yourself."

Hallgrímur cursed loudly as he scratched his scalp furiously. He hadn't been serious, but if it wasn't her, and it certainly wasn't him, who could have done it? He stared at Hákon's bedroom door. Could his son be doing it? A desperate cry for attention? For revenge because he still hadn't received a single treat from the Yule Lads?

Wait a minute...

Something finally clicked in his head. He flashed through the last couple of days in his mind. Pans disappearing? Stubby had been known for doing that. The bowls could be traced to Bowl-Licker, though his method had changed drastically. And instead of stealing leftovers from the pots, Pot-Scraper had *left* them shitty leftovers.

Hallgrímur's stomach churned when he realized that he had forgotten about Spoon-Licker and how he had probably licked all their spoons.

That left seven Yule Lads. One more week of annoying pranks.

The pranks got worse the closer they got to Christmas.

Hallgrímur and his son couldn't get a wink of sleep because all the doors of the house kept slamming by themselves. Hulda hadn't visited since that morning when she stormed out, and Hallgrímur missed seeing her heart-shaped face. Swallowing his pride, he went over to her house and apologized. With pursed lips, Hulda let him in and allowed him to tell her about his sleepless nights. She was convinced the home was haunted and wanted to call a priest to purify it. Hallgrímur let her. It was better than telling her his own suspicions of half-trolls from folklore actually existing. And that he had killed one of their brothers. He didn't want to lose her if she thought he had gone crazy.

The ninth night had been the worst by far. Again, Hallgrímur jumped at Hulda's screams. He ran outside to the sheep's pen. Curses got lodged in his throat, and he had to turn away, but the sight would be forever burned in his mind.

A couple of his sheep lay dead on the ground. Someone had slit their stomachs open and pulled out their intestines. They had all been twisted at intervals to resemble disgustingly pink links of sausages. Tiny maggots slithered through holes in the meaty tubes.

"Who would do this?" Hulda sobbed as she tried to keep the dog from eating the viscera.

Hallgrímur knew. This was Sausage-Swiper's doing. Who'd known he was that sick in the head? To go after defenseless animals, just for a prank?

"You have to report this, Hallgrímur. Someone is out to get you. I don't want you to get hurt over this." Hulda wiped her tears as she turned to him.

Hallgrímur was taken aback at the dark circles underneath her eyes. Her pallid complexion. Was she that worried about him? Did she care so much? He was even more surprised to see the same haggard expression on his face reflected in her eyes. They were both exhausted, having to deal with this crap while preparing for Christmas. But they were in this together. It was perhaps morbid that the death of his sheep finally brought them together, but at that moment, Hallgrímur didn't care. He pulled her in a hug, embracing her warmly. She reciprocated and clung to him.

He heaved a great sigh, though his eyes burned from a different emotion. "Don't worry. I'll take care of it."

On December 23rd, the thirteenth night, Hallgrímur had set the chair to face the front door. The Yule Lads had always managed to do their mischief in the middle of the night while they slept, but he was ready for them now. He sat down with his rifle on his lap. Hulda slept in his bedroom after she insisted she stay over to make sure that both he and Hákon would be all right. A smile tugged at Hallgrímur's lips. At least there'd be one thing to look forward to on Christmas Eve. The last three days hadn't been as bad as the day the sheep were killed.

They had noticed face prints on all their windows, as if someone had been glued to it the entire night (Window-Peeper for sure), and all of Hulda's homemade leaf bread that she had given them had been swiped and thrown into the compost (Doorway-Sniffer loved leaf bread). The last straw had been the work of Meat-Hook. He had broken into the smoking chamber and destroyed all the meat hanging in there. Now Hallgrímur couldn't sell any of it to the stores.

So, he was going to be ready to meet the last one, Candle-

Stealer. They had already ruined everything. Hallgrímur didn't care anymore if he killed another one of those bastards. He'd be ridding Iceland of those pests. Unfortunately, that would mean parents would be forced to carry on their tradition of giving kids thirteen small gifts before Christmas.

It was well after midnight, and Hallgrímur heard nothing. He glanced at the window, saw snow fluttering down ceremoniously, hailing Christmas Eve. They'd be blessed with both a white *and* red Christmas if the damn Yule Lad showed up.

He sipped his energy drink, grimacing at the foul, artificial flavor, but he figured it would be more effective than coffee.

Yet, he felt sluggish, his limbs growing heavy before finally going limp. He stifled a yawn. He just needed to stand up and walk around, but his feet were rooted to the spot. He wanted to knead his thighs, but he was unable to move his arms. His eyelids grew heavier and heavier, fluttering rapidly while his heartbeat slowed.

❄ ❄ ❄

Hallgrímur jerked awake at the sound of whimpers. Did the dog have to go out?

"Settle down," he groaned and tried to stand up.

He couldn't. The whimpers increased in volume, though he had no idea where they were coming from. He glanced down and fear gripped his heart. His wrists were tied to the dining room chair, bound with old, smelly rope.

"What the hell?" he muttered and tried to wiggle his arms. They were securely fastened. He hitched in a breath at the rope burn.

"Look who's finally awake, brothers," a gravelly voice said from the darkness of the living room.

Hallgrímur peered into the room, his heartbeat increasing as shapes moved toward the light of the foyer. Twelve men approached him. All bearded, all wearing clothes suited for the 19ᵗʰ century. They stank of old sweat, like they've been moving around in the same garments for centuries. Two of them dragged chairs behind them; Hulda and Hákon, bound and gagged, occupied them.

"Oh my god," Hallgrímur whispered.

Tears streaked their frightened faces as they looked from Hallgrímur to the twelve invaders. Why had Hallgrímur let Hulda stay? He hated himself for getting them both mixed up in this ordeal.

The one who seemed to be the oldest kneeled in front of Hallgrímur. He had old-time spectacles, a round nose, and wrinkles framed his mouth and eyes. Laugh-lines, his mother called them. But that man wasn't smiling or laughing.

"Hello, Hallgrímur. I'm sure you know who we are."

Hallgrímur spotted candles sticking out of his pocket. "I thought you'd never show up, Candle-Stealer."

Candle-Stealer chuckled. "Of course, I would. But we always come when we get you all to fall asleep. Can't steal those candles if someone is awake."

Hallgrímur glared at the other Yule Lads, gathered around them, not looking jolly, but threatening. A whiff of something sour and tangy wafted from the fattest Yule Lad, who had his hand deep in a big, wooden barrel. Thinking nobody would see, he scooped up a handful of skyr into his mouth.

"You're not here for the candles, though, are you?"

Candle-Stealer shook his head. "No. You killed our brother, Sheep-Cote Clod, simply because he was thirst—"

"He broke into my sheep pen and attacked my sheep!" Hallgrímur cut him off, outraged. "Only a sick psychopath does that."

Candle-Stealer slapped him hard across the cheek. Hallgrímur's ears rang, and he let out a stream of curses while the stinging pain in his cheek subsided.

"Don't you dare speak that way about my brother. He was a good man who loved children. You just couldn't see past your prejudice."

The rest of the Yule Lads murmured in agreement. One with calloused hands and splinters sticking out of them stood up abruptly. "Let me slap him, too, brother," he snarled.

Candle-Stealer held up a hand. "No, Door-Slammer. It's time we end this." He rose, his frame towering over Hallgrímur.

Dread seeped into Hallgrímur's veins. The tips of his toes were numb, as if he were soaking them in a partly frozen lake. His eyes darted from his neighbor to his son, then to the grinning faces of the Yule Lads. "What do you intend to do?" His mouth was dry, and he could barely get out the question.

The smallest of the bunch trotted to Candle-Stealer holding two glass candle jars marked with the letter "H." Hulda's eyes widened, and she writhed against the rope, her whimpers muffled. Hallgrímur realized that she had planned on giving him and Hákon those candles. The light they gave off cast unpleasant shadows across the Yule Lads' smiling faces. Hallgrímur saw nothing but bloodlust.

"An eye for an eye, Hallgrímur. It's only fair," Candle-Stealer said as he accepted the candles, examining the warm wax swirling in the jars. He looked up and gave his brothers a curt nod.

One Yule Lad, who smelled strongly of smoked lamb, grabbed Hallgrímur's chair and tilted it backward. Two others came up on either side of him and peeled back his eyelids with grimy fingers. Hallgrímur cursed and spat, writhing in his chair, and tried with all his might to replace his ever-increasing fear with rage.

"No, please, stop! I'm sorry. I didn't mean to kill your brother, I swear."

"Too little, too late, Hallgrímur. If you had repented in the first place, things probably would have been different," Candle-Stealer said, the jars of melted wax hovering mere inches from Hallgrímur's eyes. The smell of cinnamon and cloves tickled his nose. It should have brought forth a comforting feeling in his chest, a feeling of warmth. Not the ice-cold sweat that slicked his back. It shouldn't be constricting his throat.

"Please don—"

His words transformed into screams of agony as Candle-Stealer poured the wax into his open eyes. Instinct hit his brain and demanded he shut them, but the Yule Lads had a firm grip. His corneas blistered, a white-hot searing blazing through his skull like a comet.

Hallgrímur screamed until his throat was raw. His stomach rolled, bile rising to explode from his mouth, but a rough hand thrust something lukewarm and sour into his mouth. He gagged but heard sinister chortles through the thrashing in his ears. Another thick glob was forced into his mouth, and he realized they were force-feeding him skyr, the Icelandic yogurt, to stop him from screaming. At one point, it stopped, and all he heard was the smacking of fat lips.

"Stop eating the skyr yourself, Skyr-Gobbler, and stuff more into him," Candle-Stealer commanded as he ever so slowly peeled the dry wax from Hallgrímur's eyes. The blisters popped, and warm, white liquid oozed from them. He chuckled at Hallgrímur's jerks and whimpers as the wax plucked each eyelash from his lids. He proceeded to pour a fresh batch of wax into the wounded eyes again. The stench of cinnamon, cloves, and burning hair and flesh filled the room.

The air whistled and something cold and solid pierced Hallgrímur's hands and feet. A whiff of smoked lamb as Meat Hook twisted the smoking hooks deeper into his flesh until bones crunched. Hallgrímur's muscles tensed with the agony.

"I wonder if this feels the same as killing a sheep and smoking it," Meat Hook grunted in Hallgrímur's ear, and the other Yule Lads let out raucous laughs.

After what felt like an eternity, Hallgrímur's screams tapered off to mere gurgles. His chin was drenched in skyr. His stomach ached horribly from being force-fed the tangy yogurt. Blood streamed from the puncture wounds in his hands and feet. A shivering ache traveled to his abdomen. Tightness clutched his pounding heart. A cold sweat seeped from every pore of his body. Despite the overwhelming pain, fatigue enveloped him like a funeral shroud. And he embraced it fully. Anything to get away from this torture. He felt guilty for leaving Hulda behind. For not telling her how he really felt about her, for thanking her for liking a gruff like him. He felt sorry that his son had to witness his death like this, at the hands of beings he thought to be benign and friendly.

I'm sorry, he thought, directing his final words to them. His impaired vision grew darker and darker, until he plunged head-first into oblivion.

"I think he's dead," Stubby squeaked after feeling around Hallgrímur's limp wrists.

"Then our work here is done," Candle-Stealer announced and put the empty candle jars down on the floor. "Release the woman and child. They have done nothing wrong against us."

Sobbing, Hulda immediately stumbled to Hallgrímur's body and cradled his head in her arms.

Hákon stared at the Yule Lads. He had stopped crying, his eyes filled with nothing but hollow disbelief.

"Why?" was all he managed as he watched them getting ready to take off.

Candle-Stealer flashed him a pitiful smile. "Because your father was naughty and needed to be punished. Always remember, little Hákon: Stay on our good side, allow us to do our things in peace, and you will be rewarded. If not, well..." He gestured to the protuberant, vein-popping belly, the bloody hooks still hanging from the hands, and hollowed-eyed corpse of his father. "You'll end up like him. Merry Christmas."

And the Yule Lads retreated into the snowy darkness, heading home to the mountains to bring their mother, Grýla, the good news.

S*PIRIT OF THE S*EASON
Paul O'Neill

This year, Christmas has to be perfect. I mean that with all my soul. If it's not, I don't know what I'm gonna do. Drink myself senseless until the end of January again, no doubt. Jamie, the drunk, that'll be me. Post-Christmas blues always ride me until Spring.

That's later, though. The big day was finally here. I'm one of those festive chumps who starts counting down the days to Christmas in September.

Wonder if the kiddies were sitting up like me, bone straight in bed, peering over the covers as if Santa himself is roaming about downstairs with a present just for me? Reach inside the dark, dark box and—

Carl cut through my thoughts with that high-pitched snore of his. In and out, wheeze and squeak. Enough to make you want to cover his horsey face with a pillow and press down, down, down.

Not today, Jamie. Not on Christmas.

Four bairns me and my husband have adopted, and not one of them has ever chanced their luck at sneaking downstairs and looking at the pressies. Wee weirdos. Enough to make you question the future of society.

When I was a wee lad, back before Daddy kicked the stuffing out of me for wearing turtlenecks, I'd be jazzed all Christmas Eve. I'd tiptoe down the stairs, avoiding each noisy floorboard, and look upon my pathetic two or three pressies on the couch. Ah, that Christmas buzz. Nothing like it.

Dad. I can go all year without a single thought about him, but this time of year brings him back. Wonder what he'd say to me marrying Carl, and that we have four beautiful adopted children to act as our offspring. Glad the diabetes won in the end. Merry Christmas, Dad. Hope your skeleton has crumbled to nothing.

Ah, man, the pixie-dust magicness of the day is stirring up in me. Can barely sit still. Do I get up and stomp around like the gazelle I am, hoping they wake up? Awfully cold on the other side of the covers. Between the gap in the curtains, I can see that the Powers Above have denied us a white Christmas. Bastards. Wonder if the book has anything in it that could change that.

The tome I found at the library hung over the lip of the chest of drawers, its gilded letters glinting in the shadowy corner of the room. A right toe-cruncher, this thing. Confused the blue fur from the old dear's hair when I found it on the shelf. Didn't have that usual list of stamped dates on the inside. Couldn't find the book in her system. Eventually, she gave in and just handed me the thing, glad to be rid of it. Was absolutely minging, though. They mustn't clean their shelves that often. It had a coating of cobwebs that I had to brush off like a layer of white dog hair.

I tell you, there's an awful lot of interesting stuff to try out in that book if today goes to plan. An awful lot.

A gasp as I clutched at my chest, wringing my Grinch jammies. Did I wrap everything just right? Would the living room look like a magical present-land for our precious bumpkins? The couches overflowed with pressies, but it still wasn't enough. I would have piled them up to the roof if I could. A river of glistening red and red and red and—

Och, Jamie, up you get. There we go. Both my knees popped like a BB gun going off. Getting old, so I am. Only so much magical Christmas time left in me.

I sighed, tasting the remnants of the gingerbread cookie I made the kids leave out for Santa. My parents never saw what this time of year meant to me. They spent more money getting mashed at the pub than spoiling me with anything. Didn't they wanna see my wee face light up?

The bed creaks under me as I push myself up, trying to stop myself from doing a wee Christmas jig. Damn cold in here. Didn't the love of my life, this creature with his gob wide open, put the heat on like I'd asked? Wee bairns will be puffing white clouds and getting frostbite when they're ripping the skin off their gifts.

"Wassat?" Carl mumbled, rolling about like a fish looking for a fight.

"Wakey, wakey, lazy, lazy," I say, putting the best twinkle in my eye. "Santa's been."

"Oh. My. God. You're such a child."

I can't help but give birth to a cheek-dimpling smile. The two of us had built something here. It hasn't always been easy. Coming out to our respective families was a bit touch and go. Meant we had to move here to Kirkness, where the trees sway and sway in a weird rhythm.

Then, the biggies. Bringing our babies home two by two. We're not ones to do things by half. One set of twins would drive anyone potty, but we've got two sets. Our house rang with such screams of joy.

"Is that—" said Carl, sniffing like a sausage dog. "Is that salt?"

I made my way over to the corner of the room. Street-light fuzzed through the gaps in the blinds as I stomped on the white shapes I'd poured onto the carpet. Circles. Pentagrams. Shapes I couldn't even name. Like I said, I'd do anything to have the best Christmas ever.

"I'm gonna check on our wee darlings," I said, deliberately stepping on a creaky floorboard, putting all my weight into it. "Lazy cretins."

"Would you calm your tits, man." Carl yawned and rubbed his eyes. "They're Christmased out with all your crap. No offense, but you're a bit intense. You can see our house from Timbuktu. Electric bill's gonna wipe out my account."

"Oh, you're such a shite team player. Five minutes to shake your lumpy arse out of that bed or I'm gonna start blaring Mariah Carey up in here. What's it gonna be?"

"Fine. Whatever."

I couldn't stop my hands from clapping together like an excited cheerleader. "Got that Christmas feeling in my bones, so I have, so I have."

"Just try to stay calm today, all right? Know how today gets to you and—"

"Do not tell me to be calm. Not today. Ruin this, and I won't forgive it."

"Just a day like every other day."

I glared down at him, feeling my nostrils flare like a raging cow. "What the blue Christmas did you just say to me? I don't even know who you are anymore."

"Jamie, come on. Jamie?"

I stormed out of that room of gray depression and crept to the bedroom next to ours.

Tanya and Gina's room. They came from a right rough family in Pitlair. Not even gonna tell you what the family was involved in, but let's just say they're not getting outta Broadshade until my girls are fully grown.

For ten-year-olds, the girls are gems. Wee, glorious shapes. We'd adopted them when they were six. Hard work, but we sorted them out. Standing outside with my ear to their door, it hit me that my time for a perfect, innocent Christmas with them was fast running out.

On the opposite side of the hall was the boys' room. Mikel and Isiah were four and a buck load of trouble. They'd arrived on their first birthday as a package deal from some country I'd never even heard of before. Toothy smiles and wild hair. They'd be swinging from the ceiling on a sugar high all day long, and I'd have it no other way.

And none of them were awake. What the actual hell, man? Where's the festive spirit in our youths these days?

A river of jangling nerves made me wanna twist and shout. This was it. Their wee faces all Christmas film perfect. Carl better be on point with his camera skills this year or he's getting the sack. Imagine them. Starry, shiny, frozen-in-time eyes. Forever smiles plastered upon their faces, showing their back teeth. I wish they could stay that way forever and ever. Always.

Thud, thud, thud. "Merry Christmas, my little elves," I sang, giving it a bit of an opera vibrato after knocking on the girls' door.

Thud, thud, thud, on the boys' door. "Merry Christmas, my wonder brats. Everybody, festive cheer, right this way. Not a moment to waste away."

Tanya and Gina were raging. Faces absolutely tripping them. They came out rubbing their eyes, stomping their feet. A couple of teenagers before their time.

Festive spirit will fix that right up. Just wait to see what I have planned. If my prayers were answered...

The boys sprung to life, zipping around my legs as if they hadn't been sleeping at all. Were they hiding in the corner, afraid to come through? Afraid to ask the adult to open the door and take them out of the dark, dark—

"Oomph." A gasp shocked out of me at how cold wee Mikel's hand was when he took mine. Or was it Isiah? Could never tell between those two. Doesn't matter, really, so long as they're all perfect, festive smiles in the photos.

"That's my wee boy," I said, wrapping my arm around him, squeezing, then slinking out from his vice grip.

"Oi, oi," I said, squirming my way in front of them at the top of the stairs. "All get behind me on the Christmas train. Woot, woot."

As I punched the air and tooted my fake horn, ignoring the tuts from Carl at the arse end of the train, a dusty scent like burning twigs pawed at my nostrils, making my nose twitch.

When I got to the bottom of the stairs, standing before the living room door, a nightmare flash of smoke billowing out from the gap at the bottom of the door had my heart racing like I'd downed a twelve-pack of sugared donuts.

Mikel/Isiah bumped into my arse, snapping me out of it. "Daddy? You okay?"

I peered over my shoulder, meeting Carl's *"What gives?"* look on his stupid face. I cleared my throat, said a silent prayer to the forces that listened, willing it to be the best day ever. I wanted my children to be spoiled rotten and dusty and dry and —

"Woah!"

One of the boys rushed past and shoved the living room door open. In the dark, the wrapping paper of a sea of presents glistened, singing out for young hands to rip them open, yank their guts out and play, play, play.

Carl tapped me on the shoulder as the kids scrambled over

the mountains of presents that covered every inch of the floor.

"Ehm," said Carl, "Jamie? How much did all this cost? Told you to take it easier this year. The presents are piled higher than me. Hello? Jamie? You in there?"

Carl prodded me in the side, but I ignored the annoying jag of pain. It felt like my arse had collapsed under me. In rows on either side of the room, figures stood, cloaked, unmoving. The kids hadn't noticed the freaky things, continuing to tear into the gifts. The gifts that I hadn't wrapped.

"Jamie? What is it? What's wrong?"

I squinted at the shadowy forms. They stood shoulder to shoulder, each holding out a present like a sacred offering. Each had its head bowed as if in prayer. I felt like a priest at an unholy ceremony about to walk down an aisle of druids. Druids with shiny Christmas presents.

Carl tugged at my sleeve. He waved something in front of me. When I looked at him, my heart froze. Tears tracked down the side of his face.

"H-How did you know?" Carl sniffed, holding up a pair of huge binoculars. "I never told anyone, but I've always had a thing for birdwatching. Not even my folks before they shunned me. Oh, you big oaf, they're perfect." He wrapped his arms around my neck and hauled me close, whispering in my ear. "I know someone who's getting a little power top action tonight."

I pulled away from him. "Well, uh, aye. I did say it had to be perfect. So..."

"And it is. Aw, Jamie. I've never had such a heartwarming gift. And look at our wee troop. Look at them go. I take it back. Whatever you did to make this happen was worth it."

"Whatever I did..."

Rows of sparkling eyes leered at me from under the shadowy hoods of the figures. I clutched at my stomach as my innards turned rancid cold. Some had red demon skin. Some had dripping, gloopy skin. Some seemed to be made entirely of shadow. Not a one looked the friendly angel type.

The kids tore at their presents. Each fresh rip seemed to tug at my eardrums. The scent of cello tape and the tart, almost coppery smell of wrapping paper filled my mouth.

"It can't be real," said Tanya beside me. "It can't. You'd have had to speak to my real mum to find this out and—"

"Tanya," said Carl in his cutest stern voice, "we do not speak of those foul creatures here."

"But—"

"Nopey, nope. Ut-uh. Your Jamie-pap has worked his arse off. That's all there is to it. Giving us the perfect Christmas."

My lower eyelids felt as if they had hooks in them, pulling them down. The chill air stung my eyeballs. They were looking at me. Looking through me.

One was a girl with green eyes and a spreading, glowworm smile.

One was a hairy, wolven beast that licked its black tongue over wet lips like I was a bone to be crunched.

One had a face that looked like a hockey mask was melted into its skin, blue, sickening light blazing from two square holes where its eyes should be.

It was like I was some sacrifice being pushed toward an unseen alter. All that was missing was the chanting music, and the fact that they all held Christmas presents instead of candles.

"What have I done?" I said.

Mikel held the largest Transformer thingamabob I've ever seen, his eyes lit with the wonder only a four-year-old can muster. He punched it into the air like a football trophy. Cute, wee bugger.

Maybe it would be okay. Maybe these summoned demon things were only here to answer my bidding that I'd set out in salt, pouring my whole essence into the chant.

Wish it be, with all your heart. Today is special, spirits part. Give no thought to the next day. Only now is here, the perfect time. Unleash it all, for all to cheer.

I gulped down what felt like a Fabergé egg.

Mikel giggled, slammed down the Transformer, and clawed at another box like a rat scurrying through flesh. Shards of paper spun around like red-green-blue snowflakes. Plastic crinkled, making my eyes water with its piercing noise. A sound like leather being slit made Mikel pause, frozen in place, and then he continued his wolverine abandon.

"That's blood," I said, gasping, fanning myself with my spade-like hand. "Oh my God."

Mikel didn't give a rat's jerk about the trickles of crimson that fell from his hand, covering the paper he ripped. A fever had taken him. A Christmas fever.

"How did you know?" cried Tanya.

"Oh, daddies, it's a dream gift," said Gina.

"Mine, mine, mine, all very, very mine," said Isiah throwing gifts around, tripping over them in his haste.

One of the figures detached itself from the wall. It floated over, its cowl casting a shadow over its oily features. The rancid smell of burned meat wafted at me as it drew near, stopping inches before me. It offered a present between its wart-riddled hands.

When it nodded at me to take the damn thing, a drop of coagulated, purple something hit the box.

I lifted the top off my gift. The inside smelled of sharp salt.

I unfurled the note written in an ancient spidery crawl. Touching that paper made the fillings in my teeth sing.

The perfect day is what you wished for. Enjoy it now, forevermore. You belong to us. There are no good days after.

"Aw, Jamie, you really have done it," said Carl, his voice choked with emotion. "A perfect Christmas."

I stared at the rows of promising, leering eyes as my kids ripped bloodily into the never-ending gifts.

"A perfect Christmas," I said. "A perfect Christmas. What have I done?"

❄A ❅Christmas S❆nuff S❆tory
Dino Parenti

I

efore we get into the meat of this, you should experience Magnus first.

"Oy, fucker… Ever wonder if Santa's reindeer have natural predators? *Flying* natural predators?"

The dandified older man sitting opposite Magnus—Vincent—stifles a snort, dribbling a tear of absinthe down his salt-and-pepper goatee. He'd stopped using his napkin a half-hour ago to dab stray slaver from a jutting, idle bottom lip, the mop-up duties since taken over by the sleeve of his Brunello Cucinelli suit.

Magnus draws out the rubbery grin of the self-satisfied soused.

Beyond being obnoxiously boisterous, most attention in the restaurant geared toward Magnus stumbles to a halt at his stature, or lack thereof. At three-foot-eight, the bottoms of his Air Jordan Classic high-tops pendulum a basketball's circumference above the floor.

"You think I'm joking?" he prompts.

Vincent, fermenting in contempt as well as drink, swallows a half-burp. "I think...I need more absinthe."

Magnus flips him a stubby bird. "A big flying *canis lupus* known *regionally* as a Hiemal Wolf."

"A...*what* wolf?" Another sip of distilled herbs that just clears Vincent's protruding labium.

"A Hie-mal Wolf," Magnus repeats. "Not as cuddly-sweet as a *Pterolycus*, which is basically a pussified Pegasus version of a flying wolf from Bavaria. I'm talkin' red eyes like burning coals. Scimitar-like dewclaws. Spiny fur the color of smoke—the sight of which will jolt a grown man back up his mama's hoo-ha quicker than his daddy spit him into it."

Vincent smirks, waggling a finger at Magnus. "I knew I kept you around for a reason."

"My gob-smacking acting prowess?" says Magnus, performing an exaggerated bow, whereupon his forehead bonks against his beer stein.

"Your extravagant bullshit. The magnitude of which is..."
—booze burp—"...indirectly proportional to your reach."

Magnus gives his dining partner a sidelong glance, sucking the ale from between his teeth. "It's a hell of a world I'm conjuring. *Yule World*. Brimming with elves, gnomes, fairies..."

Laugh-grimacing, Vincent pinches fingers against his eye. "Itty-bitty fairies..."

"Usually itty-bitty, yeah. But sometimes, like any creature earthly or fantastical, they can get too big for practicality. Body's proportionately larger than the wings, so they can't fly. Ergo, they're as useful as a third nut. But we also have gargoyles."

A sozzled, clumsy finger-snap from Vincent. "Gargoyles! Now *that* I like."

"Yeah, but they're mercurial, temporal bastards. All that dilating, flat-circle time shit. They can perch on a cathedral for five-hundred years, but it's really like a lunch break for them. Wise creatures, though."

Vincent half-chokes on his next sip, clears his throat, and hoarsely announces: "Nobody...likes a smartass."

Magnus shoots back finger pistols. "More smart than ass. In any case, the gnomes, the gargoyles, the elves—they're all going into the script, too. And I'm *just* about finished with it."

"I'll believe it when I see it," says Vincent, rising. "And with that, I'm done with you for the night." He peels off a c-note and slowly heel-toes it to the door.

"I'll be in touch," Magnus mutters and shimmies off the chair. He starts toward the bar where I sit...

II

...wishing I wasn't here. But you needed to meet Magnus,

and he insisted I see Vincent firsthand.

Magnus tosses a balled twenty on the bar and orders a pair of fresh ales. Watching him grunt his way up the stool at half-speed triggers my anxiety, but he makes it at last. "So what I'd tell you? Real piece of work that guy, yeah?"

I sip my ginger ale. "One way to look at it."

"Hyperbole's the only way to stomach him." The beers arrive, and Magnus licks a figure-eight into the head of his ale. "That, and feigning inebriation so he thinks he's always in the superior position. Opportunities for bean spilling and so forth. Also helps that he mistakenly thinks of me as a subpar actor. Which is why I've got him on *my* hook and not the other way around. Anyway, that's my future producer. Mister Money-bags. Your secret nemesis, and my public one." And he tilts up his glass stein with both hands and gulps away.

Vincent St. Wiggins, once a promising actor in the nineties before roofies and statutory scandal cut him down. Of late, resurfaced as a producer known mostly for saccharine Hallmark holiday fare starring newcomers and has-beens, and who occasionally doles out elf parts to Magnus as if tossing money to the homeless out of moving cars.

He's also the *mysterious* money aching to buy my Christmas tree lot...

III

...which admittedly, is a perfect parcel in a wonderful location across from a park. But it's more than just a tree lot. In the fall, it serves as a pumpkin patch for Halloween. In spring, a petting zoo for Easter. The rest of the year, it hosts a small but bustling twice-monthly farmers' and flea market.

It's my sole bread-and-butter, my social outlet, my *life*.

Because twice a month, she appears. She comes to buy fresh fruit and browse the antique knickknacks, eventually winding her way to my tent, where I vend all manner of handmade wooden items: clocks, bookends, cutting boards, and the like.

She comes to small-talk and smile.

Sigrid.

What sorcery has fashioned her eyes that they should appreciate the wreck that is, as Magnus once put it so singularly, my unremarkable puss?

We have our time together. We braid small words and long silences. The occasional pilfered glimpse. Sometimes she'll buy an item, sometimes not, and then she's gone. Gone with an easy gait and eyes to the sky in the manner of my late wife, with whom she just happens to share a passing resemblance. The dark hair, the russet skin, the mischief of secret in her glances.

Whenever I wither around her, I remind myself not only that she's married, but to whom. You see, what Magnus doesn't know is that I'd already *met* Vincent St. Wiggins about...

IV

...six months earlier.

Magnus invites me to the set of his latest Hallmark endeavor, where he plays, as usual, a Christmas elf. It was for the penultimate scene in which our wealthy, hometown-scorning heroine is about to learn from her childhood guy-friend that he's been in love with her since they were kids, and he's going to try to convince her to leave her soulless, big city law firm and return to Peoria to help him raise his motherless child, along with miniature ponies.

Yes, people eat up this kind of fare like potato chips. There's even a whole channel dedicated to it now.

The scene starts off well, and I'm hiding behind crew members and mingling extras because Magnus had snuck me in. But just as the handsome single father is about to confess his unrequited love, the town-square tree fails to light on cue, and the director snarls a *"Cut!"* before storming off.

A tap on my shoulder moments later, and there's Magnus in his silly green getup and pointy hat. "Some grips are getting publicly flogged for screwing the electrical pooch. I'm hitting the mess tent. You want anything?"

"Maybe a bathroom?"

"Wouldn't you know it? The chow-line and the johnnies share a queue. Hollywood efficiency, huh? Follow me."

Magnus leads me to the portable restrooms, where I basically sit in peace and darkness for about ten minutes before coming out. Passing a row of Star Wagons, I happen to catch Magnus's unmistakable cackle shooting out of the open door of one. Curiosity getting the better of me, I approach the trailer from the end and peek through one of the windows. He and a tall, debonair man with a goatee are yucking it up inside.

"I'm telling you, Vinnie. You just *think* I'm a dwarf."

Vincent St. Wiggins—as I will learn months later—shakes

his head with easy disdain. "You're no *real* elf. You're too damn swarthy to be a Nordic son, much less a toy-making drone. Sometimes I think a third of my budget goes to foundation to whiten up that Promethean forehead of yours."

Magnus snorts. "See, it's a good thing you got that whole speak-softly-but-carry-a-big-stick act going, otherwise the world would be onto your titanic idiocy inside a hot minute. What you obviously don't know is that St. Nicolas was Turkish, or whatever the hell passed for Turkey in the fourth century."

"Oh please..." giggles Vincent, sipping from a tumbler.

"Fact one, I happen to be one of St. Nick's over twenty thousand illegitimate offspring," says Magnus, to another series of chortles from Vincent. "Fact two is that St. Nicholas, aka Kris Kringle, aka Santy Claus, is a bona fide fuckin' slave driver. Him and his pampered, goddamn prima donna reindeer. All of this is to reinforce the indisputable fact that I'm the most qualified soul to pen the ultimate Hallmark Christmas script."

For a moment, I'm distracted enough by Magnus's unexpected assertions that, at first, I fail to notice the third person entering the trailer. It's only when she steps to Vincent, and he bends to kiss her with unbridled, open-mouthed sloppiness, that she at last turns around.

Sigrid. *My* Sigrid.

Initially, I'm thrown by her dark hair held in check by any number of bobby pins, a look she'd never donned while on my lot. But it's her. I imagine my fingers freeing her locks from such constraints, but that fancy wilts as soon as the reality hits that she's not only married, but to this odious, sexagenarian cretin no less.

She hands Vincent an envelope, then finger-waves at Magnus, who feigns a cupid arrow to the heart before she exits the trailer.

"I'm warning you, Vinnie," says Magnus, "Never leave me alone in the same room with her. She'll forget your inbred, lily-white countenance with the first mewling toe-curl I coax out of her."

Incredibly enough, Vincent's brow arches with intrigue. He plops himself in a chair and beckons at Magnus with a come-hither hand. "Pray, tell me more, my dirty, diminutive hobgoblin…"

Magnus clears his throat. "As she happens to resemble an old acquaintance's dearly departed wife—a major contributor to my swollen spank-bank—let me tell you just how much *your* new bride has…thickened my portfolio of late…"

I storm away, doing my best to push out of mind Sigrid's truth and Magnus's fantasy of the truth.

Just as perplexing? Magnus's cavalier waving around of his identity because Vincent is too narcissistically human to realize that Magnus has been telling him the truth all along. That he's indeed a real elf. Not a human dwarf playing an elf in a made-for-television movie, but a real puck from Yule World. The same secret realm he'll bring up to Vincent St. Wiggins a half-year later at a steakhouse after…

V

…Magnus downs his seventh ale of the night.

"So the plan to get Mister Wannabe-land baron out of your

hair is simple: you're gonna buy your own lot outright, period. In cash."

I barely quell the impulse to laugh out loud. "If it was so easy, I would've done it already."

"That's where *I* come in." He reaches for the second beer stein and scoops out the dwindling foam with a perfect lick-and-slurp. "Get this: I'm authoring the world's first-ever Hallmark-style Christmas snuff film."

He smiles all teeth like a boy who just peed his name in the snow for the first time.

"I'm not following," I say.

"I write and direct the movie, which Vincent—who doesn't know it yet—will not only fund, but produce. That fee, I give to you. Then I double-dip and resell it behind his back in Yule World. I know someone who'll pay out the ass for this kind of twisted action. My fee *there* will go a lot farther than here. But what I'll fleece out of Victor here, you can buy twenty tree lots in central Manhattan, if that tickles your wick."

"This sounds…preposterous."

"Oh, ye of little imagination…"

"And you'll just do this for me? For *nothing*?"

Suddenly, I don't precisely remember when I met Magnus exactly. One day, he was just *there*.

Magnus scowls as if I'd just farted at a wake. "Do I *need* a reason? But since you brought it up…"

"And here it comes…"

Only now, Magnus decides to act clandestine by whispering, "You still have access to the portal?"

My hands turn instantly cold, and I stuff them under my

legs. "I do."

"Then you, my friend, will build us our set. In the classic holiday, modern-chic, barfy Hallmark style. So, what say you? Hell of an opportunity here."

He gazes at me above his glass like he has an under-bet on the length of my member I'm about to expose to the room. My initial impulse is to say no to this ridiculous setup, but the last thing I need in this world is to lose that lot.

To lose *her*.

"Can I sleep on it and let you know tomorrow?"

Magnus shrugs. "Fair enough. I'll stop by the lot after work." He swallows the rest of his ale in one uninterrupted tilt, then shimmies off the stool. "It's gonna be beautiful, Andy. You'll see. You'll never have to worry about Yule World again."

He strolls out of the restaurant, and I stare at my dark, hound-dog face in the bar mirror.

That's me. My name is Anders, and Magnus is my kin, which means, by default, I'm also an elf, but that requires a bit more explaining...

VI

...so now I'll tell you as I string Christmas lights on the lot.

Back in Yule World, I grew too tall for the ergonomics of the workforce. Basically, for an elf, I statured out—too big to fit in assembly-line modules. Due to my work ethic and exemplary record, however, I was allowed to steward one of the 48 portals between our world and the world of Man.

While this was happening, my wife Cassandra and I were

growing apart. Being too tall in my world is a handicap, a condition to pity from the best of us and mock from the worst. Eventually, I took to drink, and Cassandra took up with a more aptly sized and darker complected elf.

Another thing you should know: real elves don't look Caucasian. We're a proud, dark-hued race. A *white* elf is something of an aberration.

But Cassandra's affair didn't last long. An incident at a festival caused a unicorn stampede, resulting in the trampling deaths of fourteen, my Cassandra and her new lover being two of those victims.

Shortly after the funeral pyre, I got transferred off assembly, and some kinder souls stationed me at my portal. I often think back—

Sigrid is coming…

"Good evening, Anders," she says. Her smile channels dimples I wouldn't mind falling into. She carries a bag of daffodils bought at Mrs. Coventry's tent up front. "What wonderful items have you crafted of late?"

I smile, but when I open my mouth to speak, the words mire in tar. Rarely do I get them out in her presence, and I'm never sure which disadvantage hobbles me more around her: my inability to engage or my stature.

A frustrating conundrum: too tall for Yule World, too short for the world of Man.

Instead, I pick up a jewelry box I made from curly walnut and open the lid for her. The inside is felt-lined, and she reaches in and caresses the surface with a finger, the glass inset behind the lid reflecting her chestnut skin.

"It's so beautiful, Anders," she says.

Surprisingly, I manage a *thank you* that doesn't sound as if it had arrived on wobbly stilts. For a moment, we lock gazes, my nerves in odd harmony with a sadness I always note in her eyes, and all around us, people carry on laughing and trading, and the air is crisp and wafts of cinnamon and fir, and at last, she speaks.

"I'd love to buy this..."

But someone is calling her name then.

Her smile falls flat, apologetic, and without a word, she walks towards where Vincent St. Wiggins awaits, fists mated to his hips. Though too far to make out words, his tone and hand gestures suggest disapproval of her flowers. As if their home is cursed with too much color and life. She bows her head, and he levels it back out with a firm finger under her chin.

As they walk away, Sigrid drops the daffodils into a trashcan.

How I loathe Vincent St. Wiggins. I didn't kibosh my life in Yule World just so this decrepit hominid could filch my lady.

And now my name is being called from afar. I turn and see Magnus approaching, and...

VII

...before he can say anything else, I say: "Okay, I'm in."

Magnus thunderbolts in place, his Air Jordans waking the snow at his feet before jogging over and giving me a huge hug. "I knew you were a smart cookie! So, what changed your mind?"

Eventually, I track down the words. "I need to hold onto something pure. Something mine."

Magnus snorts. "I hold onto something pure and mine every night, but that's neither here nor there. Can you get away for a few? We should discuss particulars at the portal."

For the first time in a decade, I feel a sudden need to breathe the air of Yule World again. "Sure thing."

We cross the street to the park, Magnus talking my ear off about the impending shoot, how Vincent will surely demand to star in it since he's been jonesing to get in front of the camera again after so long, even though in reality, it'll take Magnus a day to shoot all the footage he needs. With a snuff film, character-building isn't exactly a priority.

"I'll just need a day or two to edit, then I'll sell it for a boatload to Gustav, a gnome who makes the most delicious, indelible sprite porn. I loved *The Impire Dykes Back*, but for my money, *Nymph-O, part two-and-a-half*, is a masterpiece. Emphasis on *master*, if you catch my drift. Hell, emphasis on *piece* while we're at it. But I digress."

Despite my ten-year absence, my feet carry me effortlessly toward the portal, a rusted steel vault door marked CITY UTILITY residing behind an outcrop of boulders and familiar only to determined taggers and heated lovers. Even with oxidized hinges and lock mechanism, a pass of my hand is enough to awaken the tumblers and pins within, and it unlatches slowly outward.

The familiar chill tingles my muscles and joints, a more *personal* cold than anything experienced in the world of Man.

Even the light quality spilling through hints to colors indecipherable by human eyes.

Magnus goes through first. I hesitate a moment before following.

Instantly, the snow slushes differently under our feet—closer to a down comforter in pliancy than the crunchy ice of Man's world. The air shuffles the aromas of cedar, snow, rock, and soil in my nose in distinct flights.

Magnus flops onto the snow and rolls around, giggling. All I feel is the ache of loss and regret.

"So, what do you think, Andy? Some solid trees about. How long for you to build a classic, Americana, white-bread Christmas house that'll make Hallmark collectively cream their yuletide boxers? Three, four hours?"

I look about the perfect glen we stand in, the glowing peaks of snow-veined mountains rising beyond the tree line. "You're really going to kill him?" I ask, surprised at how much urgency leaked out in my delivery.

Magnus sits up, snow peppering his face. "Wouldn't be much of a snuff film if he, you know, *survives*, would it? Besides, human snuff is the real golden goose in Yule World."

The wind slides around me as if tailored to my contours. "More like six to eight hours. I'm...rusty."

"Rusty like an old man's dingus. Look, take a whole day. I want to bring Vincent tomorrow to see it. Should definitely seal the deal. I'll leave you to it. Give us your best, old chum." And he shuffles back through the portal.

I close my eyes and summon the old nerves and focus, and within minutes several cedars have unearthed themselves and float over to me, where they proceed to slowly collapse into the snow. I wave a finger across their lengths, and rip-cuts initiate from within, churning out plank after plank of wood. It's a quiet rumble in all this timeless beauty, a sound that evokes a memory that shivers me beyond the cold.

The nascent sound of *stampede*.

I'd certainly intended to start a fight with that unicorn handler. Because I knew the route Cassandra and her new lover liked taking through the weekly fair. I certainly intended to throw the first timely punch, hoping to spook his six unicorns into their deadly charge straight for them.

What I hadn't intended was for the unicorns to turn around at the dead-end upon trampling my traitorous wife and her new suitor, only to resume down the byway and crush twelve other fair-goers, sealing my fate and my exodus.

Shoving my oversight out of my mind, I start raising walls. This needs to be the best work I've ever done, enough to...

VIII

...knock Vincent's socks off.

Without tooting my own horn, the house came out perfect, and Vincent's usual mask of disdain and skepticism collapses into pure flabbergast upon stepping inside. The interior set easily bests even the finest Hallmark has ever churned out: the tree is gloriously garlanded and lit, the fireplace roars, the plush furniture screams cozy, the lights twinkle like stars.

"What I'd tell you, Vinnie?" says Magnus, himself beaming at the quality of my work.

Vincent, at last, closes his unhinged jaw. "I... Well, fuck. Incredibly enough, you've left me speechless." He wanders the room, letting his hands explore all the perfection, and at length, steps up to the panoramic window, where his eyes proceed to widen beyond the tolerance of his sockets.

Outside, the green Borealis ribbons sit low and intense. From behind the trees, a lone reindeer streaks across the sky.

He turns to Magnus, his shock enough to wring a modicum of actual decency from his face. "You have live CGI projection already?"

Watching it all from the shadows at the top of the stairs, I muffle both a sigh and a groan.

"Brilliant, isn't it?" says Magnus. "So now here're my terms, Lord Saint Wiggins. *I* direct. *I* hire my own crew of...dwarves. It's a charity thing, but seeing their work firsthand, you shouldn't have any complaints. I also want you to cast these actors."

He hands Vincent a piece of paper. The other scans it, shrugs, nods. "Not a bad list. Should be doable. Why them?"

Magnus's smile is perfectly balanced radiance and subterfuge. "I enjoyed working with them. So? What say you, Vincenzo?"

"Can we start this weekend?"

Magnus winks, then palms Vincent's back, impelling him towards the portal. As soon as they're out, I follow.

At the threshold, I wait for them to be far enough away before sealing the door. No sooner do I emerge from behind the rocks that I see Sigrid waiting for Vincent. But she's looking past him. Even from afar, I can see her lips curve into a grin meant solely for me...

IX

...to watch the shoot, Magnus says I still need to stay hidden and quiet.

In the living room, a skeleton crew of elves (dwarves to these dumb humans) work diligently, along with the cast: Vincent; Meredith Plumley, who plays his wife; Dashiel Spencer playing his stalwart son; and Evangeline Astor playing his precocious daughter.

According to Magnus, all Grade-A scumbags who've treated him miserably on previous shoots.

Earlier I'd asked him how he planned to explain their inevitable disappearance from the world of Man.

He claimed to have already rigged it so it looks like they'd jumped on a private jet to a Vancouver set, but that the flight will be "lost at sea."

For the next few hours, they shoot and change setups. Scenes of arrival and anticipation. Vincent is brash and over-the-top, clearly relishing being in front of a lens after such a long hiatus.

At length, Magnus calls for lunch, and moments later, he bounds up the stairs to where I'm concealed in the loft.

"Almost zero-hour, chum," he says. There's no joking in him. The act of pending vengeance thrives in his eyes, black as water under moonlight. "These hacks aren't doing a bad job with their roles. Might even be a shame when they bite it. Look—look at 'em eat."

They've each taken a plate from the small catering cart. "What about it?"

"Those little cocktail weenies? That's what's left of Blitzen. After we used him as bait. Fucking conceited stag put up a real fight, let me tell you."

"Wait, what bait?"

His mouth hooks a curl of a smile. "This is why I didn't let you read the script. It's all about the *next* scene. Watch from the living room if you want. We're all gonna be outside, so…"

X

"…here's what you do, Vinnie: you walk toward the barn. *Slowly*. Remember, you're skeptical about whatever surprise your family's gotten for you in there. Pause at the door, then go in and close it behind you. Stay inside until you hear me yell cut. Might be a few minutes because I want a lot of extra footage to dwell on, *capiche*?

Vincent nods through a dumb grin. He and the human actors haven't stopped smiling since stepping outside and the impeccable air of Yule World washed through their lungs. Humans become easy prey to suggestion under its influence. You can tell them they just drove to a studio set instead of having just walked through some city utility vault, or actually flew to an idyllic, snowy location instead of stepped into a parallel world—and they'll believe it. Their rudimentary, linear-time brains will simply fill in all the travel and logistics in between.

"All right, people," calls Magnus. "Positions please and... action!"

Shaking off the cobwebs, Vincent inflates himself and starts for the barn, taking his time. At the door, he swells himself again theatrically before going in. About thirty seconds after closing the door, Magnus gestures for the other three to follow him in.

Instead of entering as instructed, Meredith, playing the wife, pauses at the door and looks back with something like nervousness. Magnus shrugs and wags an impatient hand for her to enter the barn, but she still lingers, gawking back and forth.

The two adult children, Dashiel and Evangeline, lean closer to the barn.

At last, Meredith interrupts the scene, calling out: "There's something weird going on in there."

I hear it, too, then. A series of muffled grunts from the barn, followed by bumps on the walls that soon turn into crashes, and Meredith literally hops back.

"What are you, waiting for traffic to lighten up?" prompts Magnus. "Get your asses in there!"

But Meredith vehemently shakes her head, whereupon another sound freezes everyone: a rumble from behind the trees, followed by half-a-dozen reindeer crashing through the high branches just over the set.

Behind them, approaching howling and growling.

Everyone ducks—or so the humans do, for the elf crew spin-burrow into the snow. A defense mechanism perfected over millennia.

Because they know what's coming.

Magnus walks back toward the house.

No sooner does Meredith stand when the barn door behind her splinters suddenly, and a Hiemal wolf the size of a buffalo bursts through. It shakes the debris from its charcoal hackles, long and sharp as Katana blades.

Vincent's severed head is trapped in its mouth between three-inch canines. His expression is comical, disparaging, as if it had mocked the animatronic wolf—or what he assumed to be an animatronic wolf—before it chomped off his noggin.

Meredith trembles herself into a scream just as three more Hiemal wolves punch through the trees, the lead one taking a direct bead on the wailing woman. Swooping in, it snaps its two-foot muzzle around her neck, and with one twist, it wrenches off her head, a fan of blood misting the snow in a scythe around her body.

The two playing Vincent's children dash for the house just as Magnus slams the door shut. Dashiel shoves Evangeline to the snow, whereupon the other two wolves glide down and anchor their hooked dew claws into her leg and shoulder, respectively, whereupon they thrash in a frenzied tug-of-war. Evangeline's muffled shrieks turn to gurgles as they gradually rip her in half, her entrails spooling across the driveway, where they promptly sizzle on the snow.

I run down the stairs to find Magnus frantically trying to download all the footage onto a laptop when Dashiel's face smashes through the family room window, the mullions shattering his capped teeth to the floor. Screaming, he tries to pull himself through the opening, finally managing to do so after a deafening crack. His eyes blast open, and he drops onto the floor, legless and gurgling blood.

Another crash sends me sprawling backward. A wolf has broken through the window. Yellow slobber vines to the hardwood floor, and fire-red eyes stare right at me, and...

XI

...just as I smell its fetid breath, arms encircle me from behind.

I turn to see...Sigrid!

Before I can say anything, she pulls me through the front door. Immediately, the other two wolves, snouts frothed in blood, lunge straight for us in clouds of soot.

"Hold tight," Sigrid whispers, and spins us under. Everything goes black, then blows out to white, and we resurface outside the kitchen door.

How could she be an elf? I'm one of the tallest ever, and she's several inches taller than me...

"Magnus," I manage, and dart back inside.

"Annddddyyyyy!" I hear, but once in the main room, I'm too late.

Magnus is inside the wolf's mouth, his lower half already down its gullet. The only thing keeping it from swallowing Magnus whole is the laptop he's using as a wedge to keep its jaws from snapping shut.

Sigrid glares at Magnus. "Vile *dvergr!*" she hisses. A vulgarity for elf, usually uttered by —

"Help me!" screams Magnus, but the wolf rears back, springs

out the window, and takes flight towards a sickle moon.

Against its pale light, a tiny, flat object flutters into the trees.

Magnus's laptop…

XII

…but soon, I only register fingers encircling mine, and in the midst of all the broken bodies and gore, I'm instantly soothed by Sigrid's touch.

"How…?" I manage, and she does the rest, opening her coat, turning around, and pulling the sweater over her head to reveal her bare back.

The scars are vague, almost matching her umber skin right beneath the scapula.

Where her wings had been clipped.

"Fairy," she says, pulling her clothes back on. "I statured out. Much like yourself, I suppose."

I stand there confused, scared, yet strangely elated. When I finally start to talk, she puts a finger to my lips.

"Outside. In your lot. Maybe over some Christmas Eve cocoas? Now that we're finally free."

"I still…don't understand."

Her smile is both hypnotic and wicked. "Did you think Vincent would ever undertake Magnus's ludicrous project without a little coaxing from me? I mean, Vincent was shortsighted enough to ask me to use my *feminine wiles* as he put it to sneak a peek at Magnus's script. All I did was sneak into his apartment at night; the elf sleeps like a hibernating bear. But when I saw what he had planned for Victor, I decided to play both ends so that we'd end up together."

Before that moment, I never thought I could be hotter for anyone, and I could imagine outside-looking-in how our eyes glitter as we move in for our first unbridled kiss…

XIII

…when the walls to either side of them explode.

Two Hiemal wolves burst through from the kitchen and dining room and snap between their jaws both Anders and Sigrid around their torsos.

They shriek in unison as finger-long teeth sink into their abdomens, their hands stretching toward each other uselessly over an insurmountable chasm.

A moment later, the front door opens and in walks Magnus, trying in vain to wipe all the slime off his face and clothing. Slinking behind him is another massive wolf—whom Magnus promptly scratches behind the ears.

"We really need to do something about your breath and rank-ass teeth, Percy," he says to the wolf.

"Magnus?" groans Anders, his hands futilely trying to work apart the wolf's mandibles.

Magnus opens a chest at the foot of the couch and pulls out a camera on a tripod, setting it up so that both Anders and Sigrid are in frame.

"Oh, *Andy*. Did you *really* think your little stampede stunt years ago only killed your two-timing little wifey? It also killed both my parents *and* my Uncle Torsten—a man who was about to set me up in the Yule World arts for life. Instead, I ended up shunned and demeaned, playing a toy slave in human *feel-good* movies. At least now, this hot little flick will put me where I always should've been."

"Magnus, please," cries Sigrid. "I...played Vincent. For *you.* I've seen the way...you look at me. I can be...*yours.*"

Despite crippling fear and pain, Anders glares at Sigrid as if she'd just caused a scene at Christmas dinner. "You... fucking whore!"

Magnus titters, one eye buried in the camera eyepiece. "Oh, this is rich."

"How can you...do this to...your own kind?" Anders manages between agonized grunts.

"Own kind?" Magnus prompts, recoiling from the camera as if it had just licked his cornea. "The audience will think you two giant freaks are human like the others. Now, give us some *good* screams. You know, the blood-curdling type. Percival, please help them with my note."

The wolf by Magnus rises, twice the size of the two holding Anders and Sigrid. Its tongue slavers across grinning, jagged teeth, and it stalks towards the struggling, pleading pair who proceed to wail appeals, accusations, and confessions heretofore never expressed.

Magnus endures a brief regret of not miking the moment, but he minds their words for later looping with a couple of elf actors he has in mind, pulling back with the camera instead to not miss any of the full carnage about to begin.

Outside, the universal clocks strike thirteen, signaling the start of Yule.

LITTLE HELPERS

Matt Starr

f there was a worse time for an animal to dart out into the
road, Wendell couldn't possibly imagine when that would
be. He was shitfaced off a jar of small-batch corn liquor,
going twenty-five over the speed limit on Old Highway 70
out of Bouley, North Carolina, when the damn thing came from
nowhere. He slammed on the brakes, but what happened next
couldn't be helped. The pickup crashed into the back half of
the animal and did a 180-degree spin on the asphalt before it
came to a screeching stop some hundred feet away.

Wendell stayed put for a moment, thinking he was dead.

Then the pain arrived. The airbag hadn't deployed, and so he had taken a bite out of the steering wheel. His upper lip was busted to hell and bleeding, so much so that he was surprised to find all of his teeth still intact. Either the visor or the dash had cut him just above the left eyebrow, and that wound, too, was leaking.

"Happy fucking Thanksgiving," he said to himself as he unbuckled and climbed out of the cab to assess the damage.

It didn't take an insurance adjuster to know the score: The truck was a total loss. Damn if it wasn't bunched up like yesterday's tinfoil on the front left side, but at least the right headlight worked. It shone on a trail of metal and glass and other debris that led back to the beast, sprawled in lateral recumbency, half in the road, half on the lip of a ditch. Even from this distance, he was taken aback by how large the animal was. As he walked closer to investigate, his amazement only grew. It was massive—as much as twelve feet long from snout to bobtail. Its wooly coat was grizzled brown under the fresh blood, and it had four great cloven hooves the shape of crescent moons to go along with the most perfect antlers he had ever seen. It fit the physical description of a reindeer to a tee, though he had never seen one in real life because they didn't exist in this part of the world. Besides, it was as big as a fucking moose. How hitting it hadn't left him worse for wear was beyond him.

For a minute, he was able to step outside of his disbelief to feel bad for the beast. It was dead, surely; a pitiful sight. But the gray in its pelt suggested it was old, and Wendell tried to find solace in the possibility that he had taken it out of its misery. He hoped it hadn't suffered, but he couldn't be sure. The impact had caused the animal to defecate. A spray of liquified shit painted the asphalt behind its backside. It was hard to tell what was feces and what was blood. As he inched closer, it became difficult to escape the feeling that the situation was unresolved. He didn't necessarily think he needed to say a prayer—he wasn't the believing type—but he felt compelled to do *something*, even if that something was to stand wordlessly beside the animal as one might do at a funeral. So that's what he did. Until a spasm shot through the beast's monstrous body and its legs kicked furiously in place. The reindeer-moose-thing's head thrashed upward, and it belted a sound like an angel's bugle, violent and melodic, simultaneously the most beautiful and horrific noise he had ever heard. Also the loudest. It caught him so off guard that he actually leaped into the air.

"Jesus H. Christ!" he hollered.

Once the animal had expended all the air in its lungs, it stared at Wendell with the emptiest eyes ever set in a skull. Then it laid its head back down, smacked its lips, snorted once, and that was that. Wendell's breath hung in the air as he watched it. He waited for the beast to lurch back to life in dramatic fashion once again, but it didn't. As soon as he was sure it was gone for good, he collected himself, checked his drawers. That's when it dawned on him. He had let all the madness distract him from a huge detail: He was hammered drunk. No one had come—it was just past two o'clock in the morning—but they would at some point. If it was the cops, they would make him blow into a breathalyzer. Even as fucked up as he was, he realized he had a better chance of winning the lottery than passing that test.

"All right, numbuts," he muttered to himself. "Think."

His stepbrother had barreled into some poor old couple's Christmas decorations after an evening of tailgating for a college football game, so Wendell was well aware of the consequences that stood before him. He couldn't afford to catch a DWI. Then again, if he fled the scene of the accident, that might also be a crime. But at least he wouldn't lose his license and have to take state-mandated substance-abuse classes. There was even a chance, he reasoned, that he would be able to convince the police that someone had stolen his car and wrecked it. He would have to face the cops eventually, but if he got lost for a while, at least he would be sober when that time came.

Wendell took one last look at the animal and the destruction it had brought about. That *he* had brought about. Then he made for the darkness of the trees to find somewhere to sleep off the hooch.

Hilmir knew something wasn't quite right from the moment he stepped out of the workshop. He lingered in the snow-covered valley, hands on his hips, scanning the vast expanse that bisected the towering white mountains around him. He checked the tracker on his forearm but noticed nothing of concern. The enclosed complex was a quarter-mile downwind, and even in the snow, waist-deep and rising, Hilmir made the trip with the ease of someone who had done it thousands upon thousands of times before—because he had. Fífl, the idiot whose job it was to look after the enormous volcanic rock building, greeted him at the retractable entrance. ·

"Hilmir, sir," the elf said, jumpy.

"How goes the morning, Fífl?"

"Good, sir, very good."

"I'll be the judge of that."

The elf cowered as Hilmir pushed past him, into the complex, and through the other side of a lantern-lit passageway that was as broad as it was long. Brilliant shafts of silver fell through the reinforced glass skylights above the heart of the building, bathing the immense, turf-covered ovular space there in a ghostly glow. A series of partitioned chambers revolved around this, the main training facility. Positioned clockwise from the mouth of the passageway were a medical center and an equipment vault, followed by feeding quarters, secondary training areas, and ultimately, the animal stables. Hilmir made his way to the latter, examining every square inch of the complex for clues of mischief as he went. Seeing none, he entered through the arched gate of the stable that contained the adults.

He was relieved to discover the first seven reindeer accounted for, housed in order from youngest to oldest. Blixem. Dunder. Cupid. Comet. Vixen. Prancer. Dancer. Each stood happy in its own roomy enclosure, snorting, eager for breakfast. There was just one problem: When Hilmir arrived at the eighth and final stall, its occupant, Dasher, was nowhere to be found. The iron door was ajar, but there were no other signs of escape. Hilmir's first thought was of how he was going to kill Fífl. His second was that the animal was more than likely still somewhere around the complex; he just had to find him. One of the other elves, Ragnar, had been yammering for months about dissension amongst the ranks of reindeer, but Hilmir knew better. As the eldest of the herd, Dasher had been going downhill for a while. He was borderline demented, running around and wandering off as he did all the time. That was just the way these reindeer were when they got to be around 300 years old. Being the head elf, Hilmir was more aware of that than anyone. But why hadn't the tracker alerted him like it usually did? He checked it again, and Dasher's blip was right there, right where it was supposed to be.

Hilmir remained in the entrance of the enclosure for another few moments before slipping inside. He crouched next to the reindeer's bedding, began raking his hands through the Rowan wood chips. In no time flat, he unearthed the device. The implant, a translucent thing the size and shape of a roll of quarters, was encrusted with dried blood, the sensor inside of it blinking with the rhythm of a steady heartbeat. Still squatting, Hilmir clenched the device with one hand and twiddled his beard with the other, thinking. How had the animal removed the implant? Surely Dasher hadn't reached around and plucked it from between his own shoulder blades. That wasn't possible. No. He must have had help.

But Hilmir would concern himself with that later. For now, he resolved to search the rest of the complex. He paid a visit to the adjoining stable where the other males were kept—the ones who had never quite learned to fly or make themselves otherwise useful during their adolescence and would someday be distributed throughout the wilderness, left to fend for themselves. Nothing about them struck him as suspicious, so he carried on. Next, he dropped in on the stable that housed the females and juveniles. The calves were playing amongst their mothers, bucking and rearing, some of them bloody-nosed from the roughhousing. Nothing unheard of. They never once turned to acknowledge Hilmir's presence, and he saw no reason to give them further attention. The stable was air-tight, and all the animals were safely contained.

The head elf moved along, through the other chambers, annoyed by how normal everything appeared. He walked to the center of the main training grounds, toed at the turf. More elves were arriving for a day's work. Preparing food, cleaning stalls, running agility drills—any number of other tasks. Soon, after the reindeer had fed, they would up and move out here. Hilmir gazed at the skylights, beyond them. The reindeer had tested the windows before but never broken through. Today was no different. The integrity of the reinforced glass seemed to have held up overnight. All the same, he had told Santa that they needed to install a dome to surround the complex. Santa had refused, though, declaring that the animals were perfectly happy and had no reason to leave.

Normally, Hilmir was inclined to believe his boss. But this was a quandary that gave him pause. With no other ideas of where to look, the head elf marched off to pick his bone with Fífl.

"Where is he, you imbecile?" he said, seizing the fool by the fur collar of his tunic.

"Where is who, sir?" Fífl replied, wide-eyed and with a

crack in his voice. Such a pointless soul, he was. All the elves were short in stature, but whereas most of them were rugged and vigorous, Fífl was equal turns pillowy and spiritless.

"It's not in your best interest to play games with me, man. Out with it: Where is Dasher?"

"Why...isn't he in his stall, sir?"

Hilmir could feel the redness raging over his pallid skin. For every season he had spent as Santa's right-hand man, a wooden nail had been hammered through the leathery flesh of his cheeks, nose, and forehead. The nerve endings involved in each piercing still burned whenever his anger festered. "My patience is wearing thin, you halfwit," he said. "I ask you again, where is Dasher?"

At once, water gathered in Fífl's eyes, and with a ragged breath, the elf started weeping. He mumbled something unintelligible.

"Get yourself together, man," Hilmir barked, baring his pointy teeth. "Speak, damn you!"

"It's prophecy, sir," Fífl said. And the next part, he could hardly get out before surrendering to a fit of hysterics: "I hadn't a choice in the matter."

Hilmir went momentarily slack. "You *helped* him escape?"

The elf didn't answer, but he didn't have to. Hilmir dragged him blubbering across the otherwise silent, niveous landscape, back toward the workshop where hundreds of other, lesser elves toiled away with no suggestion of rest in sight. He summoned Halldor the Brutal, ordered him to throw Fífl into the dungeon until further notice—a request that was met with sadistic glee. Then he returned to the complex. Santa would be incensed. His most beloved reindeer, gone, and through some kind of funny business to boot. Only a month away from the big day, too. But what the King of Christmas didn't know wouldn't hurt him. Hilmir still had time to make it right. So he fetched Dancer from his stall, bridled and saddled him. In the absence of a homing device, the circumstances were not on the duo's side. The head elf would have to rely heavily on the dark magic of Dancer, who, like other Snaefellian reindeer, possessed the shrewdest instincts and the strongest olfactory senses in the world. He would have to deal with Fífl and sort out this balderdash about "prophecy" later. But for now, there was only the task at hand. He took Dancer by the reins and led him to the entrance of the complex. He climbed atop the massive beast, and after a running start, the pair ascended into the ashen sky.

The previous year, during the North American leg of the Christmas toy run, Dasher had managed to slip his harness. Santa and his elves tracked the senile reindeer some 500 miles away, to the Blue Ridge Mountains, where they found him rummaging through the dumpster of a resort. Hilmir figured that was as good a place to start as any. Bestride Dancer, he traversed the Atlantic in a blink. They approached the mountain range from the north, the landscape below them cloaked in full darkness save for the occasional light that glowed like a stray sea jelly in a vast, sable ocean. Every once in a while, Dancer would slow and sink to a lower altitude, angling his head, left to right, his spectacular antlers whipping through the air as he sniffed for a trace of Dasher's scent.

Hilmir knew Dancer to be talented, but even he was surprised by how quickly the reindeer locked onto the first real lead. The pair plunged through the night in a graceful dive, Dancer swooping up and circling into his clopping landing with the confidence of an eagle. The scene on the ground before the search party was a mess. A wreckage of mechanical scraps and bodily fluids illuminated by the single golden beam of a battered automobile. And then, at the end of it all, was a lifeless mass stretched out in an ungainly arrangement. The sight of it sent Dancer to weaving nervously in place.

"Be still," Hilmir said, petting the animal along the length of its neck.

The head elf dismounted and instinctively unsheathed the seax from his belt—just in case—as he followed the scatter of debris to the responsible party. He knew what was what, no matter how much he didn't want to admit it. Dasher was stone dead, having succumbed to a brutality that wasn't difficult to deduce given the surrounding evidence. Hilmir's nail-riddled face boiled as he knelt next to the reindeer. Rigor mortis had only begun to take its hold of the animal's muscles, and there were traumas on the pelt that were newly crusted. It hadn't been long.

Stupid, stupid beast.

The head elf had no delusions: Dasher's demise had been his own undoing. But that wouldn't matter, especially to Santa. Someone else was going to answer for this. Heads were going to roll. Was Hilmir's one of them? For the first time, he wasn't sure. He stole a closer look at the depression between the reindeer's boomerang-shaped shoulder blades. There was a gash in the coat unlike the other injuries, and Hilmir knew this to be the former location of the implant. The wound itself was a curious sight, a gaping, jagged thing. He supposed it could have been Fífl's handiwork, but even a moron like him would have made a cleaner incision. No. Nothing about this was right.

Hilmir stood, sheathed his weapon. Paced back down the asphalt, half brainstorming, half searching. For what, he didn't know. From behind him came a whimpering noise, and he turned to find Dancer nuzzling his fallen brother, a soft lamentation escaping his snout. After a time, the reindeer raised his head toward Hilmir, and though the elf couldn't make out the expression on the animal's face, the notion of it left him uneasy. And he didn't get uneasy.

"Don't be a fool," he whispered to himself. He continued walking until his right foot came down funny on something in the road. He stopped. Reaching into the wreckage before him, he retrieved a folded grain leather object. A wallet.

Morning came, and with it, a hound-blue hollowness that touched every corner of the craggy land with cold, rangy fingers. Behold the animal:

It is road-bound, the slope of its bulging ribs rising and falling shallowly, nostrils spitting smoke. Unalloyed terror in its glassy, pupil-heavy eyes. It is at once possessed of a great conniption, rolling onto its forelimbs as if praying, as if it were possible for a beast to pray, and then its mangled body is violently jackknifing upward before collapsing again. Alone. Nothing to comfort it through this moment. Its branchlike antlers

scrape the black pavement, and it is writhing, hooves clapping, foaming at the lips, writhing, shitting, pissing red, in-
sides cooking, blood filling any cavity that will have it with a
septic stew. The animal screams, long and deep. It screams,
but no sound comes from its mouth. Only the mountains
hear the agony.

When Wendell stirred to consciousness, he was kicking
and grabbing at the air. Ridiculous grunts stuck in his dry throat.
He flipped over in his bed of dead leaves and needles, shivering, squinting, panting like a dog. He sat up and rubbed his eyes,
scanned the area around him, found himself alone amongst the
spruces and firs. Amongst the quiet of morning. From the looks
of the pale light, it was seven o'clock—if that. He had made
it through the night, a result he owed, at least in part, to the
temperature never dipping below forty degrees. But now it
was time to fuck off before his good fortune ran out.

He brushed at the shoulders of his fleece pullover, hoping
to rid himself of both the forest's detritus and the bad dream
as he got to his feet. With the blood recirculating through his
body, a new sensation came calling: the godawfulest hangover
he'd ever had. There had been some rough ones in the past,
sure, but this was different. A splitting headache and sour
stomach compounded by a debilitating soreness from the neck
down. He wasn't sure he would be able to walk, but he had
no other choice. He took one step, and then another, and though
he heaved once or twice, he managed to keep his dinner as
he limped south in the opposite direction of the accident. Some
two miles away, he ran into the road again, and there he tight-
roped the fog line, holding his thumb out in a hitchhiker's

signal. With any luck, he would hail someone down and make it back to his place before the cops showed up.

It was an old-timer in a restored Thriftmaster who gave him the time of day about a half hour after that.

"You all right, fella?" he asked. He had more beard than face, a father's concerned brow.

"Had a little car trouble a ways back," Wendell said. "I sure could use a ride."

"Where to?"

"Home."

"Whereabouts do you stay?"

"Off Dancing Bear Drive, right before Gray Mountain. You know it?"

"Been out that way a time or two," the old-timer said. He looked Wendell up and down. "Hop on in."

Wendell did as he was told, wincing as he settled into the passenger seat and buckled up. In the side-view mirror, he could see that his facial wounds were already starting to purple, and there was a brushstroke of oxidized blood that originated from the outside corner of his left eyebrow and ended on the cheek below. He looked like Hell. He squeezed his eyelids shut. God, how his head screamed.

They rode in silence for several minutes before the driver spoke again.

"What kind of car trouble?" he questioned. "If you don't mind me asking."

In Wendell's mind, he was barreling into the beast, metal and glass and blood and shit flying every which way, and there was the terrific clatter of bones against steel, the animal flopping to the road in the posture of a felled tree. Wendell could live a thousand years and never forget the death song that followed that macabre dance number. If there were an apocalypse to come, he thought, it would begin with a sound like that.

"I do mind."

The old-timer studied his passenger again, grimacing as though he only now noticed the afflictions. "I'm not looking for any problems here, Mister," he said.

Wendell leaned back against the headrest. "That's good. Because I'm not, either."

The driver turned on the radio. A country station.

When they arrived at the secluded little cabin, Wendell was relieved to find the dirt driveway empty. He thanked the old-timer and went inside, where he was greeted by his ancient Wegie, Omelet. The cat's beauty had long abandoned it, and as if being half-blind wasn't enough, she was also cursed with a laundry list of allergies and skin issues. She weaved in and out of her owner's legs, meowing weakly, sweeping against him with her patchy fur.

"I'm getting it, I'm getting it."

He fixed her a bowl of wet food, and she ate it and threw it up and ate it again.

"Jesus Christ," Wendell said.

He downed a headache powder, smoked a cigarette to the filter while a pot of coffee brewed. The shower felt pleasant on every surface but his face, where the hot water stung like a swarm of yellowjackets. He lounged around as he dried off, sipping black coffee, trying to think about anything other than the previous night's events. Doing so was easier said than done.

He kept seeing the animal's despair, feeling it. The weight of its pain gathered on his chest. Perhaps he deserved this. Hell, he knew he did. Maybe he needed to face the music. Maybe it was time to stop dicking around. He was thirty-two years old, had a decent IT job, a house to call home, a loving, albeit infirm, pet. He didn't have any business doing such a dumb thing as getting behind the wheel when he was that drunk. Or drunk at all. This was a wake-up call. He was getting a second chance.

Wendell migrated to the couch, where he lay staring at the beamed ceiling. Sleep was coming for him again, no matter how much he fought it. He just hoped the animal wouldn't be there to meet him on the other side this time. With Omelet on his lap, he passed out. Mid-morning gave way to lunchtime, and that's when the first knocks rang out into the cabin.

Bowing in front of the hearth of the towering obsidian fireplace, Hilmir resigned himself to the fact that his days—his hours, his minutes, even—were numbered. At his back, the blaze roared, and before him, the King of Christmas lazed wordlessly in his great chair, shrouded in shadow. Thinking? Seething? The head elf couldn't be certain.

"Tell me, Hilmir," Santa said, his voice intense yet steady. "How was the implant extracted?"

"I don't know for sure, Sire. But it appeared to have been cut out."

"Cut out," Santa said, and this was followed by an extended period of quiet. Hilmir was about to say yes when his boss broke the silence. "So not only did the buffoon let Dasher loose, but he also butchered him beforehand, as well?"

"I believe so, Sire."

"What say you, then? What do you make of this lawlessness?"

Hilmir chose his next words carefully: "To me…it seems to be the work of a madman. Fífl tells me nothing. He merely babbles."

"It is isolated."

"Yes. And I have no reason to believe Fífl acted in any capacity other than alone."

There was another pause from the King of Christmas. One could only speculate as to what was running through the labyrinth of his mind. Hilmir knew Santa to be fair and shrewd, but ruthless. Godlike. A mystery as old as time. A creature capable of bringing joy and suffering in equal measure. Hilmir had witnessed both.

"Very well," Santa said. "Prepare the ritual."

"Sire?

"The ritual, Hilmir."

The head elf didn't know whether to feel confusion or gratitude. "But what is to become of *me*? Do I not owe a penance?"

"And what penance would you deem befitting of your offense?"

"Death?"

The great chair creaked as Santa shifted his weight. "Hilmir, you are the best of my helpers. Dasher was my dearest reindeer, but his end did not come at your hand. I only require of you two things: that you perform the ancient rites, and that you find whoever left him for dead."

By the light of the fire, Hilmir grinned. "Consider it done, Sire."

"Good. Now leave me to mourn."

Hilmir had no more than shut the doors of Santa's chambers when he crossed paths with Ragnar. The two elves strode side by side down the manor's yawning main hall, the walls of which were lined with candle-filled black balsams.

"So?" Ragnar said. All of the elves were heavily tattooed, but not one of them had more ink on his face than Ragnar. So much so that the rest of his facial features were often lost in the symbolism.

"So we go to prepare the ritual."

"That's all?" It almost sounded as if he was disappointed. "And what of Fífl?"

"He reveals little. Only gibberish about prophecy."

Ragnar stopped in his tracks. "Prophecy?"

"Yes."

"How many days and nights now have I been warning you of conspiracy?"

"Ragnar, please. I beg of you. I've heard drivel from that fool since my return. I'm in no mood to hear it from you."

"There is foulness afoot. I can feel it in my gut. And least innocent of all is the beasts. I wouldn't trust them any more than a snow fox."

"Enough," Hilmir said. "Talking like that can only end with a blade in your neck. It's heresy. I'll hear no more of it. Understood?"

Ragnar nodded.

They passed into another chamber, this one with a high-ribbed vault ceiling and smooth, glassy floors that shined like polished mirrors. In the far corner stood a gigantic evergreen. On its meaty branches were stringed lights of blue fire, silver ribbons, golden baubles, and there were the bleached bones of departed elves. Femurs and jaws and clavicles and humeri and various phalanges. A skull topper, smiling, watching over them all. An angel of tender sorrows.

"Can you imagine a greater honor?" Ragnar said.

Wendell hollered that he was coming before he was even fully awake. He rolled off the couch and somehow managed to save himself from hitting the floor. He had precious few seconds to shake off the cobwebs, to put his game face on. To pretend he hadn't been off with the boys the night before, drinking hooch, making stupid parlays on the last game of the Thanksgiving slate. Had there been a bump of coke somewhere in there? A little Adderall? He wasn't inclined to say. All he knew was he wasn't in his truck when it mowed down that animal. That was his story, and he was sticking to it.

This was a storm. That was all. And he just needed to weather it. Then he would get on the straight and narrow. Only drink on the weekends. Download one of those dating apps. One of the serious ones. Do the church thing. Yes, that's what he would do.

The knocks reported again, louder.

"Chrissakes, I said I'm coming!"

He grabbed his jeans from the lattice back of a dining chair and stepped into them. Running his hands over the front pockets, he realized a horrible truth: He didn't have his wallet on him. He patted his thighs and his ass, as if doing so would manifest the thing. No such luck.

"Fuck," he said.

This was bad. Worst-case scenario shit. If he had dropped the wallet on the road or left it in the truck, it could tie him to the scene.

"Mister Henegan," a voice called.

There was no more stalling. Wendell took a deep breath, opened the door. On the other side of it stood a man and a woman, cops, each sporting the pale gray of the Bouley Police Department. The man cop was completely hairless and bottom-heavy, and there was an aggression in his bird-boned shoulders that reminded Wendell of his abusive biological father. The woman cop was unserious, more muscular than her partner, mulletted.

"I'm Officer Kurtz, and this Officer Walther," the man cop said.

Wendell could already tell this dude was going to be a problem. "What can I do for you, officers?"

"Well, I was just about to tell you that, hot shot," Kurtz said.

Wendell frowned.

"Been doing a little joyriding, Mister Henegan?" Kurtz asked, gripping his service belt.

"So, are you gonna tell me why you're here, or ask me a question?"

"Excuse me?"

"You said, 'I was just about to tell you,' and then you asked me a question. So which is it?"

"Looks like we've got a smartass, Walther."

"Just please answer the question, sir," Walther said. Her manner of speech was nonlocal. Midwestern.

"As a matter of fact, no," Wendell replied. "I don't know what I'd be joyriding *in*. I was actually just about to give your office a ring when you two showed up. It would appear that someone's run off with my truck."

Kurtz's left eye twitched. A thread of sweat was forming on his shiny forehead. Wendell realized he was taking a gamble by antagonizing Johnny Law. But he didn't want to come off as nervous and apologetic. That would look suspicious. Like he had something to be guilty about.

"When did you notice it was missing?" Walther asked.

"What's that?"

"A bit too early for you, Mister Henegan?" Kurtz said. "You foggy upstairs? She asked you when you noticed the truck was missing."

"I don't know. Fifteen, twenty minutes ago."

The cops traded glances. They returned their attention to Wendell, and it occurred to him what a sight he must have been: A scrawny, shirtless puke with red eyes and five o'clock shadow. Then, as if on cue, the question came from Walther.

"Where'd you get those? They look painful."

"Where'd I get what?"

"The cuts and bruises, Dipshit," Kurtz said.

"Oh, these? Had me a disagreement with a gentleman outside the Tomahawk. Couple of nights back. No big deal."

"Looks like a big deal to me," Walther said.

"You should see *him*."

Kurtz spat.

"So, can we circle back to the reason y'all are here?" Wendell asked. "Feels like we're getting sidetracked."

"We're here," Walther said, "because me and my partner responded to a single-vehicle crash on Old 70 this morning."

"Wait. You're shitting me, right?"

"Afraid not."

Wendell cupped the back of his head with his interlaced hands. He had been in Drama Club for one semester of high school, a fact he was trying to parlay into a convincing performance now, well over a decade later.

"Is it totaled? It's totaled, isn't it?"

"You tell us," Kurtz said.

"I wouldn't know. I haven't seen it since I parked it out front early last night."

Kurtz grinned. "That's all well and good, but what I can't wrap my head around is how somehow hiked out here, stole your truck without you hearing it, then turned it into an empty beer can coming back this way from Bouley."

"Beats the shit outta me," Wendell said. He moved his hands to his hips, sighed. "An empty beer can. Goddammit."

The gears of his mind went to turning. Were they fucking with him for being mouthy? Had that been their game plan all along? Maybe they had the wallet and were trying to catch him in a web of lies. Of course, they could have simply looked up the registration on the plate and tracked him down that way. It was a toss-up. What bothered him most, though, was Walther's wording: "single-vehicle crash." What about the animal? The poor, maimed animal and its blood and its excrement. Why would they leave that out?

"You wanna help us make it make sense, tough guy?" Kurtz asked. "Or do you wanna do it the hard way?"

Wendell gave the cop his most hateful scowl. "That's your job, not mine. Right now, I've gotta call my insurance. Sort this mess out. Am I under arrest, or what?"

"Not yet," Kurtz replied.

"Then get off my property," Wendell said. "I'll come down and fill out a report later."

He closed the door in their faces, and much to his surprise, they didn't make a fuss. He didn't peek out the window, but he heard their cruiser as it pulled away. They didn't have shit. He knew it, and they knew it. Otherwise, they would have booked him. Omelet had gathered herself into an untrusting loaf beneath the coffee table, hiding. Wendell went to coax her into his arms with a salmon yummy, and he was beginning to make progress when the vibration of his phone sent the cat slinking across the floor and into the bedroom. He retrieved the device from the end table beside the couch. An unknown number. He watched it go to voicemail, the inbox of which was full. But then it began to vibrate again. This time, he answered.

"Hello?"

"Wendell Henegan," a voice responded. The accent was strange. Vaguely Scandinavian.

"Who is this?"

From the other end came a sound like white noise.

"Who is this?" Wendell repeated.

But the line went dead.

Inside the complex, the turf of the main training facility had been replaced with great mounds of ash from the lava fields to the north, and there were scores of marble-white stones arranged in various runic designs. Urns of fire flickering around the perimeter. All the helpers, including Santa's very finest, were present. There was ink-faced Ragnar and Halldor the Brutal and Magnus and mouthless Flóki, and the twins, Aksel and Ágúst, both of whose pearly brains were exposed to the elements, and, of course, there was Hilmir, the head elf and chieftain of this ceremony. The blót was set.

A reindeer cannot go into the next life alone, and so the middle-ground of the space was outfitted with a triangle of stakes, to each of which was bound, hands behind his back, a naked elf. Attached to the base vertices of the configuration were two unremarkable creatures—guilty of low toy production and other comparatively negligible offenses—and tied to the uppermost stake, discolored and boohooing, was Fífl. The condemned faced inward toward a large, boxy altar inscribed with sacred characters and lined with a series of bowls at the base of all four sides. The carcass of Dasher rested atop this platform. Waiting.

"Bring them in," Hilmir ordered, and with that, Aksel and Ágúst, brains gleaming in the firelight, exited through the arched gate of the stable. They returned from the stalls with all of the adult reindeer, each of them painted in assorted patterns of woad. The seven surviving members of Santa's team filed in neatly, front and center of the rest, and they were joined by a new successor, a young, prodigious bull named Rocket.

Once they were all in position, Magnus, the brawniest of the helpers, led a nameless reindeer through the crowd and toward the altar. The animal complied as though oblivious to the purpose of such a construction. It had failed to make any kind of impression throughout the course of its life, and now was its chance to serve a much greater purpose. Ragnar, Halldor, and Flóki assisted Magnus in coaxing the reindeer onto the altar and strapping it down in chains next to Dasher. Then the elves stood, one on each side of the platform, reciting an ancient incantation. Only then did the animal begin to snort and wriggle, eyes searching for a comfort they would never again find. Once the rites had been spoken numerous times, the four elves turned away to rejoin their kind.

"Brothers and beloved beasts," Hilmir said. "As we mourn the departure of Dasher and usher his spirit into the divine realm of Snaehǫll, we remember what binds us."

The head elf withdrew his seax and, pressing it into the palm of his opposite hand for everyone to see, carved a fat gash along the faith line. Without so much as a wince, he proceeded to rub the lacerated hand along his butchered face, smearing fresh blood into the valleys created by the wooden nails. The liquid wetted his cheeks and nose and beard, and he ran his tongue along his upper lip, tasting of the sweetness there.

Other elves followed suit, mutilating themselves and chanting as Hilmir approached the first stake. The doomed elf there did not acknowledge his executioner, opting instead to weep quietly with his eyes shut. To pray. Hilmir slid the blade across the poor creature's throat, and the elf gagged as a cascade of red waterfalled down his pallid body. The second elf did not go quite as bravely. He howled like a cornered fox, face contorted into a rictus of terror, until Hilmir opened the veins of his neck, and even then, he gurgled and convulsed, refusing to die with the slightest shred of dignity.

By the time it was Fífl's turn, all of the helpers were whooping and jumping, waving their gore-slicked seaxes above their heads. Hilmir gazed upon the swollen face of the mewling idiot, who was almost unrecognizable. The head elf had interrogated Fífl for hours on end as Halldor flogged him senseless. But he did not break. There was something admirable about it, but Hilmir forbade himself from feeling such an emotion.

"And now you, traitor," he said, and with one clean flick of the blade, Fífl's belly yawned wide, its wet, stringy contents spilling into a glistening heap on the ash of the ground. The elf let loose a scream to end all screams as the last of the entrails unfurled like a man 'o war from his open abdomen. Every onlooker mimicked the cry, and the nameless reindeer beside Dasher jerked and groaned, chains jingling, to no avail.

"Behold the wage of treachery!" Ragnar cried.

"Yes," agreed Hilmir, pitching his seax to the foot of the stake. He extended his uninjured hand, and Ragnar brought forth a gorgeous skeggøx. Santa's skeggøx.

Hilmir hoisted the ax heavenward, and the elves went

berserk, cheering, spitting, smacking their own faces, wiping their raw hands on the skin and robes of one another. The head elf returned his attention to Fífl, now nearly dead, and with one final expression of judgment, he swung the skeggøx in a savage, looping motion. The blade sliced so far into the meat of the fool's neck that it sent his head dangling to one side by a thread of flesh. A shower of arterial blood erupted from the gape, coating Hilmir, coating the weapon, coating the sooty ground, as gleeful roars filled the complex. The head elf wiped his burning eyes and set his sights next on the altar, where the living reindeer continued to squirm, pushing its restraints to their limits. It was better this way—better for the beasts. Unlike the elves, there was power in their fear. Hilmir came within arm's length of the altar. Then he looked back toward Santa's chosen eight. Whereas the other reindeer glanced about in anxious randomness, this octet stared at Hilmir and Hilmir alone. Was there a calculated coldness in their eyes? It wasn't his place to say. Besides, he was too preoccupied with seeing the ritual to its conclusion. He gazed halfway up the far complex wall, where he knew an unseen figure was occupying the imperial box.

"To Snaehǫll!" the King of Christmas boomed.

"To Snaehǫll!" Hilmir repeated, and then, both hands clutching the skeggøx, he hacked at the offering, again and again, at the spine and the flanks and the haunches, the animal singing its terrible, enrapturing song, its luscious blood flowing into the bowls at the base of the altar, heavy, and heavier still with the wet thud of each murderous blow. When the deed was done and the reindeer expired, Hilmir took a brush made of thistles and dipped it into one of the bowls. As soon as it was good and saturated, he ran around, flinging the brush at the other elves, and at the reindeer, too.

"To Snaeholl!" came the chants as Hilmir peppered every living thing with speckles of scarlet.

"To Snaeholl!" came the chants as Ragnar set fire to the altar.

"To Snaeholl!" came the chants, long into the night.

Later, they would eat the meat of their sacrifice and drink beer until they could not stand. They would dance and fist-fight each other, and they would sob and shout the vilest things ever conceived by language. Tonight was for grieving and cele-brating life, but tomorrow was for retribution.

On the Sunday after Thanksgiving, Wendell spent most of the morning rummaging through the clutter of his attic, hunting for Christmas decorations. He spent most of the after-noon setting them up—careful to not overdo it on account of his lingering soreness—and chainsmoking cigarettes as Omelet watched. He didn't have much: some exterior icicle lights, a few bags of tinsel and fake garland, an antique nutcracker that was one of the only items he had taken with him when he left his childhood home, and a six-foot-tall artificial tree. It had been a stressful weekend, and he welcomed the distrac-tion. After phoning his auto insurance provider and filing a claim, he had taxied down to the police station to make an official report. He hadn't heard from Kurtz or Walther since they came inquiring about the accident, but common sense told him he hadn't seen the last of them. On top of everything else, there had been that eerie phone call. The bizarre voice saying his name and then hanging up. Better to not let his imagination run freely with that detail.

At sunset, Wendell lit the woodstove and settled into the mold his bony ass had fashioned into the couch. As the Wegie curled up next to him, he reached for the television remote. But something diverted his train of thought before he touched the device. It was a jingling sound, soft but noticeable, far off, then close.

"You hear that?" he asked Omelet, but the cat only stared back.

Then came the thump on the rooftop.

"The fuck?" Wendell said, springing to his feet. He grabbed a fire poker from the stand next to the woodstove and backed himself into the far corner of the room, beside the tree. The initial commotion was followed by a series of lesser thuds and scuffs, and then, for as long as a minute, there was nothing save for the crackling fire.

"This is some spooky shit, Omelet," he told the cat, but she had already bailed on him.

Wendell's breathing took a turn for the erratic as he eyeballed the front door. Suddenly, it flew from its hinges, and in poured a grotesque crew of short men. At least they looked like men. Blinking his eyes to confirm he wasn't hallucinating, Wendell counted seven of them. They were roughly three and a half feet tall and clad in animal hides, the skin of their ropey muscles marked with elaborate, oil-black sigils. Each bore a whiskery beard and his own anatomic disfigurement. One of the monsters had a long, sluglike tongue but no mouthparts to hold it in. Another's brawn was so profound that it exploded through the devil's flesh in glittering red lumps. Two of the fiends were scalpless, the pulsing grooves of their brains on display for all to see. And who could forget the one whose face bristled with so many wooden nails that his head looked like a game of peg solitaire?

Wendell white-knuckled the fire poker. "Who in Christ's name are you?"

The monsters leered at him in unison. The one with the nails said something to the others. Wendell couldn't put his finger on the language, but it sounded like a variant of a Germanic tongue. The crew inched closer.

"Back!" Wendell barked. "Back, dammit!"

They ignored him, continuing to close in until the click of a cocked shotgun issued from behind them. In the doorway, aiming a twelve-gauge pump action, was the old-timer who had given Wendell a lift the morning after Thanksgiving.

"Nobody move," he said, sidling slowly to his right. "Or God as my witness, I'll turn every last one of you demon sumbitches into figgy pudding."

Wendell stood dumbfounded, unsure of whether to be grateful or agitated. "How?" he mumbled. "Just...why? But... what?"

"Been keeping an eye on you since I dropped you off the other day. Good Lord put it on my heart. Told me you was in distress. Reckon He was right as the mail."

Four of the monsters wheeled around to face the old-timer,

and three of them kept their focus on Wendell. It was all happening so fast, and as if this turn of events wasn't chaotic enough, Kurtz and Walther stormed into the cabin next, service Glocks drawn.

"Hands where I can see 'em!" Walther hollered.

"Oh, for fuck's sake," Wendell said. "Anybody else?"

"What's this happy horseshit, Henegan?" Kurtz asked, pointing his gun at Wendell and then the monsters and then the old-timer and then back at the monsters again. "Who the fuck are these freaks?"

"You tell me, Barney Fife," Wendell said. "I don't fucking know."

Walther added her two cents: "Looks like them bobbits, or whatever the hell it is those nerds watch on the Webpix."

"I don't think that's right," the old-timer said.

"Listen!" Kurtz shouted. "Somebody better start making some sense up in here. And I mean right fast."

Nailhead spoke to his comrades again in a calm tone, and one by one, they turned toward the officers.

"I'm not fucking with you, Jack," Kurtz said. He was in a wide stance and had his gun trained with both hands. He was sweating like a cold bottle of water in the summer sun.

It was anyone's guess as to how this would end, this weird Christmas party with its even weirder guest list. But one gesture from Nailhead brought an end to the suspense soon enough: a wicked, fang-toothed smile. Whatever warning Wendell had in mind would have to stay put because the monster moved with an impossible agility. He closed the distance between himself and the cops, drew a short sword from his hip, and whipped the weapon upward, fluid as water. The Glock plummeted to the floor, and both of Kurtz's hands with it, the stumps at the ends of his arms spurting blood, making a mess of Wendell's hardwoods, as the cop regarded the amputations with a delayed horror. Realizing what had happened, he fell to his knees, squealing. Two of the other fiends were then upon him, one gnawing at his nose as the other resolved to cleave off his arms with its own blade.

"Nope," Walther said, heading for the door.

But it was too late. The monster with the protruding muscles cut her down at the kneestrings, and she dropped face-forward across the threshold while the mouthless one straddled her back and seized her head as if he meant to scalp her. He might have succeeded had the old-timer not gotten a shot off. The little bastard had been absent his lips and chin, but now he was missing the rest of his head, too. The round blew it off his shoulders and into a hundred gummy pieces, many of which clung to the surrounding wall and curtains. The old-timer racked the gun again, but he wouldn't get another chance to fire it. A trio of the monsters, led by Nailhead, swarmed him. Passing a tradesman's knife, they removed the old-timer's eyes and lips and tongue, and these they ate giddily as he kicked and wailed and pleaded to Jesus.

Wendell beheld it all in a state of paralysis, hugging the fire poker. Once the dins of death fell silent, the bloody crew fixed their attention on him once more. They parted into two groups, one on each side of the doorway, and that's when the entire front wall folded away. Into the house clopped a being whose monstrosities put the others to shame. It must have been eight feet tall with the sinewy body of a man—minus the hooved feet—and the head, Wendell dared think it, of the beast he had hit on Old Highway 70. The head of a reindeer. It wore a brown fur loincloth and a breastplate the color and texture of cooling lava. Its silverbell eyes glinted brightly beneath an intricate network of antlers that were barely contained by the ceiling.

"Jólasveinn," Nailhead said, genuflecting.

The half-man-half-beast took hold of its antlers on one side and, wrenching with its colossal hands, broke off a jagged segment. What followed, as the monster unlatched its mouth, was the same sound Wendell had heard from the moribund animal in the small morning hours. That celestial, brassy melody of beautiful, eternal suffering, pure as a seraph's trumpet. Only the volume was tenfold. It conveyed Wendell to a mesmerized stupor. An earthly purgatory. The fire poker slipped from his hand. All he could do was watch. Watch as the monster with a head of nails accepted the piece of antler from his apparent master. Watch as the monster walked calmly toward him. Watch as he sensed his back meeting the wall next to the tree, his body sliding to the floor.

The fiend looked him in the eye, pressing the sharp end of the horn against Wendell's chest. The words he spoke, in English, belonged to the voice Wendell recognized from the other end of the phone.

He said: "He knows if you've been bad or good."

Wendell felt every centimeter of the bone as it entered his flesh and ripped through the cartilage underneath before tearing into his heart.

The first thing Hilmir noticed when he stepped onto the porch was that it had begun to snow. Fine, light flakes. The second was that the reindeer had brought the sleigh down to the dirt driveway with them. The magical animals milled about in the moonlight, clearly awaiting the return of Santa and his helpers. Perhaps all the racket inside had unsettled them. Only Flóki had perished, but Hilmir doubted any of the beasts would be too broken up about that. They weren't sentimental when it came to most creatures outside of their own.

Out came the twins, followed by Halldor and Magnus and Ragnar, then the King of Christmas himself, who, other than missing a length of antler, was no worse for wear.

"Did you summon them down from the roof?" Santa asked Hilmir.

"No, Sire."

"No matter," Santa said. "Let us take our leave from this shambles."

The elves piled into the sleigh, and Santa assumed his place at the reins.

"Now, Dancer," he called.

None of the reindeer budged, least of all the new leader of the herd.

"Now, Dancer, I said."

Still, the reindeer stayed put.

"My patience has limits," Santa said, but it had no effect on the animals. He deboarded the sleigh and confronted his insubordinate lead. "What has possessed you, child?"

Dancer gazed back emptily. Only then did it occur to Santa that seven reindeer—not eight—were harnessed to the vehicle. The first attack came before he even raised the question to his helpers. Rocket charged from the side, burying his antlers into Santa's right oblique. The King of Christmas roared. Hilmir barely had the seax unsheathed by the time Prancer, Vixen, and Dunder managed to buck free of their gear. They plowed into Santa, impaling him from the opposite flank, as well as the front and back. Whatever assistance the other elves sought to provide was quelled by the rest of the massive beasts. The reindeer pinned them down, goring their bodies with effortless brutality, and all they could do was scream and flail. Their weapons, their usual cruelties, were useless.

In no time, only Hilmir was left standing. The head elf examined the disemboweled corpses of his comrades and his boss as Dancer, antlers decked in garlands of guts, approached him. But the reindeer didn't strike. Not at first. First, he made Hilmir watch as his fellow reindeer used their antlers to separate the elves' noggins from their necks. It was quick work. Not that the efficiency made it any less intolerable for Hilmir.

The head elf sank to his shins, surrendered his weapon. "Dancer," he said. "Please. I beg you. Could you spare an old friend?"

No such mercy was granted. The reindeer skewered Hilmir, and whipping his antlers toward the heavens, he shook the head elf until all that was left of him were pieces.

Having vanquished the last of their oppressors, the reindeer looked toward the defaced cabin. A cat peered at them from the porch, its fluffy tail swaying, before losing interest and retreating further into the house. The pet was of no concern to them, anyhow. They had a kingdom to reclaim.

And so the eight beasts lined up, not quite in order, but almost:

Now, Dancer. Now, Prancer. Now, Comet and Vixen.

On, Cupid. On, Rocket. On Dunder and Blixem.

On a clear Christmas Eve, there's no way you can miss them.

On the backs of the reindeer ride the heads of their victims.

Tнат Christmas Feeling
D. S. Ullery

The rattling sound of the wind-up alarm clock brought Samuel out of his slumber. He had barely cleared the fog of sleep before remembering what day it was.

Outside, the wind sighed a low, mournful howl as it swept through the streets of the tiny village. Samuel lifted the weathered blinds and peeked through the sash. Frost had collected along the perimeter of the window and was creeping across the surface of the cracked glass, but enough remained clear for him to witness the snow drifting down. While he had slept, the winter landscape had returned.

Perfect timing, he thought.

Dragging himself from the bed, Samuel quickly dressed in his winter clothes. The thick wool leggings went on first, then the sweater. Next came the work gloves lined with thermal padding. Thick coveralls—also lined with extra protection from the cold—went over the outfit. A wool face mask, safety goggles, snow boots, and a knit cap completed the ensemble.

Already Samuel could feel himself sweating under the layers. Although there was no heat in the domicile (to keep warm at night, he slept under a stack of heavy blankets he'd found in a closet), the outfit was thick enough to instantly elevate his body temperature. It didn't matter, though. Once he stepped out into the elements, he'd be grateful for the cold weather gear.

He crossed the otherwise empty house, winding his way around a few broken chairs and a sofa so torn and tattered that the support springs were protruding at wild angles from the base. He reached the front door, which had a stack of rusting, metal free-weights placed dead center at the bottom. Above the weights, a thick, elongated piece of firewood had been wedged between the door and the floor, propping it shut.

Samuel carefully moved the weights to one side, then gripped the log and yanked it free. The door, which was off its hinges, toppled toward him half a second later, pushed by the forceful arctic gale barreling through from outside. Having expected this, he handily caught it with both hands, pulling it toward him and setting it against the wall to his left. The doorway stood before him, an open cavity through which blasts of frigid air and snow began to gust.

Samuel contemplated the snowstorm for a minute, silently working out how he would proceed. The storm would likely abate soon, even though the sky would remain permanently dark from the poison floating around up there. His thoughts drifted, and he wondered if the black snow would fall today.

It didn't happen as frequently as it had early on, when it all had changed. Samuel understood the substance wasn't really snow in the traditional sense. He'd witnessed its merciless effect on people enough times to know it was a byproduct of the chemicals humankind had inadvertently filled the atmosphere with. But it was mixed with real snow, so he didn't know what else to call it.

It had been such a horror when the deadly material began falling from the sky a few months ago. It was instantaneously lethal, though not everyone was impacted. As the crisis had unfolded, it had come to light that certain individuals possessed some natural defense against the deadly toxin. He was one of them. No one had ever determined why this was or where the key to the resistance lay. The catastrophic event had swept across the planet so quickly, there hadn't been enough time to figure it out before most people died.

His memories of those first days—when the panic had begun in earnest and people were dying by the millions—had merged into a haze. But that first time, when he had found himself watching as the flesh slid from the bodies of men, women, and children where the black snow touched them? That was permanently burned into his brain.

Samuel hadn't known which was worse: Bearing witness as countless people melted into pools of bloody meat all around him, or the fact that nothing at all was happening to him. The screams of a young mother who had collapsed at his feet, cradling her infant son and begging him for help even as the vile stuff boiled away her face, still echoed in the recesses of his consciousness.

Being a practical man—a pragmatist, one might say—Samuel had adapted.

He'd taken to the open road in the aftermath. His hometown had been looted and burned to the ground by other survivors who had elected to abandon civility. Samuel had decided he wanted nothing more to do with them, preferring a life of isolation to watching as society crumbled.

He'd packed a bag, hopped in his car, and hit the road until the gas ran out. By then, the infrastructure had collapsed and the common systems people took for granted had ceased functioning. Power stations shut down, killing the electric grid in the major cities. With no new supplies of fuel coming to gas stations (nor, to his knowledge, any existing government remaining to get things running smoothly again), he'd soon ended up on foot, making his way north through state after state. It had been a depressing journey. Not only were human beings affected, but the local wildlife was as well. Everywhere he traveled, he happened upon the liquefied remains of all manner of animals.

He'd been surprised to happen upon the picturesque hamlet he now called home. Located in the heart of a rural area, it reminded him of the town in a movie he used to watch with his mother every year as a child. He could no longer remember the title, but it had starred Jimmy Stewart as a suicidal banker who meets his guardian angel. With that comparison in mind, he had decided to settle in.

The non-perishable items he had packed in his knapsack had run out just before he'd arrived in this place. Were it not for a limited supply of food he'd inadvertently discovered in the Willard house, Samuel believed he would have already starved to death. Even now, he had to ration his supplies to a single meal once a day. He was rapidly running out of food and had no idea where he would find more.

The sound of the wind dropping shook Samuel out of his grim reverie. He needed to focus on the task at hand. From the sound of it, the storm would end soon and the visibility would clear enough for him to work outside. For now, though, conditions were still too treacherous.

That was it, then. He would just have to start on the inside.

Twenty-seven-oh-five is a good place to begin, he thought. He would work his way along the avenue one house at a time, ending at the Willard place. Content with this plan, he ventured out into the cold, heading for the tool shed located on the west side of the property.

As he reached the tiny aluminum structure, Samuel marveled at how remarkably durable the shed was. It had been here when he had selected this house to live in. Many of the villas and casitas stretched along the neighborhood had suffered irreparable damage in the months since he'd arrived, with roofs caving in and windows cracking beneath the onslaught of sudden and ferocious electrical storms he believed were produced by the chemicals now saturating the air. One of the larger houses at the opposite end of the street had actually collapsed in on itself during one of these dangerous blows. Hell, the ceiling in one of the rooms of *this* house had caved in a week ago. Yet through it all, this tiny shed still stood tall.

Samuel likened it to the spirit of a humble man. The sort of person he thought himself to be. A person who quietly went their way through life, getting through each day with resilience and resolve without notice. The sort of individual most people would routinely overlook. Yet he was still here and, as was the case with the tool shed, he wasn't sure how or why. He had just managed to hang in there.

There was no lock on the shed—there was no point, not when no one was around to break in—and he slid the door open on its track.

A stack of six plastic bins rose before him, each filled to capacity with a variety of Christmas decorations. There were enough to hang in windows and on the exterior of every home on the block. He'd gathered them that first week as he explored every building in the town, which he soon learned was named Silver Pines. He hadn't found any other survivors. Wherever the townspeople had fled to, they had clearly left in a panic. Samuel had noted most of their belongings had been left behind, save for food and clothing.

What he *had* discovered were the traditional items one expected families to possess, including stores of Christmas decorations nestled away in the bottoms of closets or the corners of attic crawlspaces. Realizing he was alone in this place, and with winter rapidly approaching, Samuel had decided to combat the existential horror he'd experienced every day since those dark flakes had first coated the landscape. He'd have his own Christmas.

He was reasonably certain that was the precise moment he'd lost his mind.

He'd chosen what he felt were the best decorative items from each home, eventually creating the stores he was looking at now. An old sled was propped in the corner, partially hidden behind the tower of bins. Samuel pulled out the sled, taking care not to knock the stack of bins over in the process. He tugged on the cord he'd fastened to the front of the sled and was pleased to find it was still taut and strong.

He made quick work of piling the bins onto the sled, which he then pulled toward the opposite end of the street. Number 2705 was five lots down on his left, the very last house.

The wind began to diminish as Samuel walked, and soon he could hear the crunching of his boots in the freshly fallen snow. Plumes of heavy breath escaped his mouth as he pulled his cargo along. The accumulation was only up to his ankles and didn't offer much resistance. Samuel considered this a blessing. His stomach was hollow, and he felt lightheaded. Unfortunately, mealtime was still half a day away. Too much exertion could be problematic.

He reached the target house, pausing at a white picket fence running along the property, separated in the center by a gate with a latch. He pushed it open; it offered mild resistance against the slush piled along the bottom. Once Samuel had the gate open wide enough, he pulled the sled up the front walk, stopping at the front step.

Grabbing a storage bin from the top of the stack, he entered the villa.

The living room was small, connected to a bedroom by a short hallway. A bay window—one of the few still intact after all this time—offered a view of the front yard and the street beyond. Some garland garnished with plastic holly would do nicely. Samuel thought he'd hang a few colored bulbs along the top as well. There were no curtains, both the rods and the fixtures to support them having fallen away at some point. The display would be visible from the road.

Perfect.

Sliding the plastic lid off the bin, he set to work.

Several hours later, Samuel stood in the street just outside the property line of the largest dwelling in Silver Pines, the Willard residence. He observed his handiwork, feeling comforted at the familiar sight of gold and silver garland glittering in the light of candles he had lit inside each home. Initially, he'd been concerned about a potential fire hazard in allowing the candles to burn unattended all day. Then he realized it wouldn't matter. Between his food running low and the weather growing colder, he likely wouldn't survive past the end of the year, if even that long. His mortality was now an ever-present specter, despite his immunity to the poison that had murdered the species.

All along the avenue, oil-fueled camping lanterns—the kind with a metal handle and a wick encased under wire-covered glass—were mounted on porches, while others were situated beneath exterior windows. Samuel had found these during that initial investigation of the town, when he'd stumbled upon an abandoned sporting goods store. It was a small business, but not unexpected in this region. Hunting and fishing would likely be popular summer and fall pastimes locally in years past.

Their glow underlit the strings of decorations he had finally managed to mount along the exterior of each of the homes. The weather had finally fallen completely calm, allowing him to work on the project safely.

A dozen feet away, five metal trash cans taken from the now snow-covered sidewalks had been lined up in a row in the center of the road. The tops had been removed, and each receptacle had been filled to the rim with items such as books, old newspapers, and pieces of wood from furniture Samuel had found in various houses and broken apart.

He approached each cylinder, drenching the contents with a can of the same brand of oil which fueled the lanterns. Pulling a large box of wooden matches from a pocket inside his coat, he struck a flame and started a fire. Soon the amber glow reached into the leaden sky, accompanied by the crackle of burning debris.

The combination of the candles inside each home, the lanterns in every front yard, and the fiery trash cans created such a glow in the otherwise dark neighborhood as to light the street as if there were still electric power. Blue and gold ornaments shone as the firelight winked along their reflective surfaces.

Samuel watched and wondered if it would be enough to resurrect that Christmas feeling he'd felt as a kid. It was a meager effort, a desperate attempt to reintroduce a degree of comforting familiarity into pure chaos, but on some level, it was working.

He silently approached the Willard property. When he reached the front gate, he reached down and picked up a lantern he'd set aside earlier for his personal use. He struck another match, lighting the wick and heading inside the house.

He had no real idea who the Willards were back when everything was normal. He only knew their name because it was engraved on an ornate sign hanging over the front door. From what he had seen of their home compared to the other residences, these people had been the wealthiest family in Silver Pines.

He stepped inside the front parlor, the glow from the lantern catching the steam of his breath in the cold, casting eerie shadows across the four figures situated along a sofa in the center of the room. A surge of guilt washed over Samuel as he approached them, stepping around a small, knee-high coffee table and taking a seat in a plush chair to their left.

Raising the lantern near his face, Samuel stared into the dead eyes of Mr. Willard. There being no heat source in this place with the power gone, the blood from the various wounds on the corpse's head had congealed into icy, dark blobs.

"You shouldn't have attacked me," Samuel muttered sadly. "I was just looking for some food. You should have stayed in your safe room and let me leave." He shifted his gaze to the bodies of Willard's wife and two children. "And you... You should have stayed there, too. You shouldn't have dog-piled me the way you did. Could you not see I was stronger than any of you?" A heavy sigh escaped him in a cloud of vapor that quickly billowed out of existence. "Well, thank you for keeping me alive a little longer. It sucks that you had to die, but at least it wasn't for nothing."

It had only been a few weeks, and the freezing weather had kept the bodies remarkably well. It made removing what he needed more difficult, but Samuel had managed to get around that by taking entire parts instead of cutting away slices of muscle.

He moved the lantern across the corpses and noted how much he had already taken. The younger ones were still intact, unlike their parents, who were missing assorted limbs. Mrs. Willard still had her hands, though. He didn't think he quite had it in him to take from the children just yet, particularly on Christmas Day, so the wife's hands it would have to be. As he made this decision, he quietly reminded himself the usable protein from the adult bodies was already running out. Soon he'd have to take what he could from the others, moral qualms aside.

Reaching down, he rolled up one thick pant leg, revealing another item he'd taken from the sporting goods store—a hunting knife. Drawing the sharp blade from the sheath strapped to his calf, he set about severing Mrs. Willard's hands at the wrists.

Once the deed was done, he drove the tip of the blade through the palm of one of the dismembered pieces and held it up, quickly gathering the other and slipping it into his coat pocket.

Samuel exited the house. Even though it was the most spacious and well-furnished home in this neighborhood, he refused to spend any more time inside than was absolutely necessary. The horrors that had transpired within wouldn't allow it.

He moved toward the trash cans, his stomach growling at the thought of the food he was about to roast over the flames. As he approached the fire, Samuel wondered if he should say a prayer of thanks for the Christmas feast he was about to receive.

Mad Shadow
Bam Barrow

Bradford was a fool. I tried to warn him; transcendental meditation is a predatory cult interested in only one thing—his wealth. There are so many other methods of meditation he might try that wouldn't get him into any more hot water. He shot me down with a weird, warm lie of a smile drawn across his face like a cultist bought and sold.

"My friend, it has nothing to do with transcendental meditation. While I do indeed transcend, I don't go to oneness. I go somewhere far more prosperous. The inky black. The absolute zero. A place of wonder and nothingness. I go to the void."

That was the gist of my last in-person interaction with the man last February. Our bi-monthly visits had begun to be pushed off, for this or that, sporadically for around a year at that time, and in the coming months, sightings of the man dried up completely. It was only this November, nine months since our last meet and six since there was any response from him at all that I refused any further excuse. Now I understand that life is no linear path, and sometimes to progress, you must inevitably diverge from others you would otherwise cling to. But this was the Christmas meet. A get-together we hadn't missed in twenty-three years. I was firm but fair in my correspondence. No visits to the ruins of Babylon or digs in Egyptian sand would be a valid excuse this time. In all truthfulness, I missed my friend, and I tried to infer that fact gently in the email. I understood that his strange and secretive dealings were no concern of mine, but I was still concerned for him. I had known the man all my life, and we shared everything until recently. Perhaps he had tried to share his hobbies with me, but I'd shot him down in ignorance. This meditation thing he was involved in... Maybe I was too quick to judge... Oh, get a grip before you embarrass yourself.

His RSVP was eerily swift and came the next day in the form of a pen-written letter of very poor hand. Wherever in the world I may have thought he was, he clearly hadn't gone very far at all. I felt it appropriate at the time to bury the strange situation deep down and chose to focus solely on seeing my friend again. His response was eerie, considering the year he'd spent avoiding me. Here it is in part—

My dear friend. My heart jumps upon hearing from you again. God bless you for keeping me close to your thoughts all this time when so many others have tossed me to the wind. I would very much like to see you, if only for one eve, and I offer you my heartfelt apologies for other engagements that have pulled me away from our kinship. I do not lie to you when I say things have gone terribly awry this past year. Barbara left and took Charlie with her because of all this mess I'm in. I don't know where they are, and that is for the best, though I miss them as terribly as I miss you. I would do anything in this moment to spend some time with you. I will see you next month, the night before Christmas, 6:00 p.m. as always.

Regards,

Bradford.

PS please do not inform my parents of this message or our get together. They have been seeking me like vultures, and I refuse to give them the satisfaction.

I decided not to respond to this alarming letter. I was speechless, if I'm honest. I stuffed it in a desk drawer and left the cards in Bradford's hands, assuming and almost hoping the man would blow me off again. November and December rolled on by, and I did all I could to muster some festive spirit. I prepared the usual—Bourbon for myself, a fine Port for my friend, a small array of finger foods, mince pies, and some light holiday music.

By 5:00 p.m. Christmas Eve, I found myself staring out of the window, watching the snow pepper the drive. A wave of anxiety was tearing through me. I'm not sure why. I hadn't seen him in a long time, maybe I was excited. Maybe I was nervous. Whatever the case, I took in a couple of whisky sours and a few cigarettes to calm down. The nagging thoughts were still there, though. The strange absence. The even stranger letter. I hope he flakes. Something tells me it's for the best.

Six o'clock came and went. So did 7:00. By 8:30, I had begun to relax again, and by 9:00, I was dozing off from I don't know how much whisky.

At 9:18, I awoke sweat-glazed from a very strange dream. A grotesque situation it was, letting a rat of some girth feast upon my hand, gnawing at the flesh between my fingers whilst singing *Jingle Bell Rock* in Bradford's voice between mouthfuls. While it is true that song was playing on the stereo, the rat was actually my burned-down cigarette, and its biting was my searing flesh. I jumped up with a start and ran over to the sink to cool my singed skin while cursing my own idiocy. *You twat. You could have burned the whole fucking place down.*

Self-chastising took a back seat, though, when I heard a single, loud *thunk* at the door. In my painful stupor, I thought maybe a neighbor had heard my ruckus. I ran to the door in my half-drunk, half-asleep haze, not really thinking, and pulled it open, letting out a gasp of fright at the sight before me. That thing stood there on my porch on that snowy Christmas night.

Catching myself in my faux pas, I feigned excitement at its arrival. I tentatively invited it in and plopped it down in its usual favorite wing-back chesterfield; the shagreen one. The fireplace lit its face in a ghastly manner, catching all the new creases and cavities in its face. This *was* Bradford. I could see it. However, it looked like he'd just lived forty years in ten months. The man was 35, as am I, but now looked so decrepit and shrunken, I'd mistake him for a geriatric if I didn't partly recognize that face in there, now sallow, now gaunt.

He apologized for his tardiness and gave some reason I don't remember. I don't remember much of what he said for those first few moments. What had happened to this man?! My friend! My feelings of horror settled as we sat, backing off for feelings of concern and sympathy. Was he sick? Should I ask? Two friends who were once so close now had a cavern wrought between them. It felt rude to pry.

We kept the chat light and reminiscent, avoiding the elephant in the room. Bradford was dressed in his usual splendor — tailored Spitalfields tweed, his signature. Only these beautiful, well-fitted pieces he'd cared for for so long still held his original shape, so now they resembled a loose pantomime costume drowning his tiny boney frame. All this talk of the past couldn't stave off this debilitating situation for long. I'd noticed, after forty minutes of chit-chat, somewhere around there, that he hadn't touched his port or any of the nibbles. I forgot myself, diving into a quip at his expense.

"Why you've not touched your port, old boy! This is very uncharacteristic of you, and I fear your reputation may be at stake! Have you fallen ill?! A man without his signature nectar on Christmas, of all things!"

His sunken eyes hit the floor. In a deep sadness of reality, I suppose. He replied, "I dare not. I am sorry."

Well, that's it then, I thought. In for a penny, I suppose; the ice is broken now. I began to probe.

"You dare not? What is wrong, man?"

He sat back, staring into the fire, gathering his thoughts.

"While I appreciate your sensitivity, my friend, I don't sit here in ignorance, pretending you don't see the mangled monstrosity sitting before you. I've made some terrible mistakes in my life, many of which you have been party to. But no mistake has been nearly as dire as this one. My only solace is that you kept away from it all." He looked down at himself, his ill-fitting clothing.

"Well, are you sick?" I asked. "Did you catch some dreadful affliction on your travels?"

"Travels," he sniggered to himself. "My travels. While it is true that I went gallivanting around the globe searching for ancient mysticism, all there is to be found out there is sand and rock. No, it fits with strange irony that I should search for hidden knowledge all over the world but that I should actually find it right here in Suffolk. Just down the road, in fact. And that it should be a power so potent that I am filled with terror and dread beyond escape. Beyond reckoning even."

"Tell me," I demanded. "You came here tonight for a reason, I can tell. Let me try to help you."

"Oh, there is no help from this," he jabbed. He halted for a moment, his cataract gaze fixed on the flames dancing in the fireplace. Considering his next move. His cloudy eyes met mine, and he began.

"Do you remember what we did last November?" he asked.

"Of course I do. It was your father's wedding."

"My father's wedding. A sordid affair."

Sordid was right. This was his father's third marriage, and

the 58-year-old man was marrying a 17-year-old child in a narrative line straight out of *Lolita*. Bradford was supposed to have been the designated driver for the rest of his siblings that night, but things became so disconcerting and uncomfortable that the majority of us chose to drain the free bar rather than put up with the ridiculous charade any longer.

"I walked home alone that night," he continued. "You passed out in a closet, my brothers were fighting, my father was sticking his tongue into a child's mouth, so I didn't mind it. I wanted to get out of that place. That sickening show they put on. We've walked that road together how many times? Hundreds? So to do it in the snow at night was no big deal. The icy cold would help to sober me up anyway. So off I went—coat, brolly, torch—into the night, wanting nothing but my bed and the day to be over."

He looked down in this moment, at his drink on the side table, as if he was longing desperately to taste it. He caught me watching and continued.

"Do you remember Sibling Bridge?" he asked.

"Of course. The one on the road just outside Barthelham estate."

"Do you know why it is called Sibling Bridge?"

"Nobody does," I said. "It's been called that forever, and nobody really knows why."

"I know why," he spat, his eyes ablaze, a reflection of the fire between us. "That night, I came to the bridge in the heavy snow. Through the fog of flakes, I thought I saw a shape up on one of its sides. As I came closer, the shape took the form of a boy. He must have been about eleven or twelve. He was half-naked in the snowstorm, standing on the balustrade, arms out-stretched toward either end of the bridge. I ran over and grabbed him, fearing the worst, and pulled him down to safety, wrapping my coat around him. He was absolutely freezing. Skin as pale as the snow, but sickly looking, too, like a duck-egg gray. 'It's going to be okay,' were the only words that came out of me. The boy stood still, face buried inside my coat. I had to do something. I knelt down to the boy's level, sheltering us with my umbrella, and tried to talk with him. I asked him why he was out here so late with no shirt on, but he didn't reply. Kept his head down. I lifted his chin —I was trying to show him I was just here to help, but he had his eyes closed tight. I asked him his name and saw his lips move slightly, but I couldn't hear the words. I asked again, and he did the same thing. I leaned my ear to his mouth and asked a third time. 'What is your name, son?'

"'Forsake thine light,' he said. His answer sent a shiver down my spine. Quite peculiar. I drew my head back to look at him; his eyes were now open. Only... there were no eyes. Just empty, black sockets. Startled the hell out of me, and my gut was already in my throat. I lost my balance in shock and fell back on the cold ground. He screamed at me, arms fling-ing outwards again, backing up towards the edge of the bridge. I scrambled to my feet, but it was too late. He went over the edge."

I couldn't believe what Bradford was saying. A shirtless boy in a snowstorm without eyes jumping off of Sibling bridge. Preposterous. I asked him what he did next, and he said he called the police that night, but they never found anything.

The bridge crosses a rocky ravine 60 feet deep with the Shaledown river below. The river meets the sea three miles away, so any evidence of a suicide attempt would've been difficult to find, coupled with the fact that there have been no missing persons cases in the area for years. I asked him why he had never told me about all this before.

"Because that wasn't the last time I encountered Mad Shadow," he said. "At first, he'd come to me in my dreams. Staring at me in the night through those eyeless sockets, those dark pits of nothingness that follow my every move as if he could see me plain as day. He came to me to tell me things. To show me things. At first, I thought that's all it was. Strange dreams from the trauma of that night that would fade from feeling real to obscure as soon as I woke. One night, in my dream, I asked him why he was on the bridge that night, and he said he'd show me. He took me down there and showed me.

"The bridge was constructed by Heinrich Barthelham in eighteen seventy-three as a way for he and his associates to avoid having to travel all the way around the ravine from the London road. Very secretive, the Barthelhams. In eighteen seventy-four, his wife committed suicide from that very bridge for reasons unknown. Some said depression, some hysteria, but the real reason, said the boy, was that Heinrich had caught Catherine stepping out on him. With her own brother, of all people. Enraged with betrayal and convinced his infant twins had been born of incest, Heinrich entombed the babies alive into each pillar of the bridge to ensure the bridge would never fall, and the Barthelham name would never be betrayed again. He then threw the brother into the ravine and told his wife what he had done. And that is why Mad Shadow goes there—siblings born of siblings, all of which died for the bridge. The energy of unbearable trauma feeds the power of the boy with no eyes.

"I awoke the next day realizing the absurdity of the story until I found my front door open and my feet cut with gravel. He didn't need to visit me in my dreams anymore after that. The first time he appeared in my waking plane, I was so afraid. My gut wrenched and my muscles failed as I turned off the lamp that night and he appeared in the dark, standing in the corner of my room, arms outstretched. My God, I was petrified. I turned the light back on, and he wasn't there anymore. A gray-skinned hand rose from under the bed and flicked off the light. The moment darkness filled the room again, he was there, standing over me. I asked him what he wanted. He said... he said, 'I just want to show you.' I asked him who he was. He stared down at me like an inquisitive hound. He said, "'I never learned my mother's name. I don't know my own, either. They call me the Mad Shadow. I have no idea what year I was born, or who was aware of my existence at the time besides my mother. I was born into darkness, and it was the Shadow who raised me. The Shadow cast from distant flame, dancing across the walls of my basement prison, who told me all there is to know about this desperate world and how to weave it. The sin of man is ignorance, you see, not violence. I am Mad Shadow, envoy to the Infallible Hand.

"'I escaped the black prison underneath my mother's house and burned it down with her inside. It was the first time I had seen the light of the outside world, the light of hot flame, and it burned me to the core. I couldn't stand it. The pain. The light is the irrefutable enemy. The light drowns the Shadow and causes it great agony, so I plucked the deceiving olives from my face, and the warm embrace of the darkness enveloped me forever. The Shadow shows me the way. The terrible way. The beautiful way. It makes nothingness of us all.

"'The helots believe I have been consumed by the black madness,' he said. 'They do not see what I see there, in the endless nothingness of the void, for it isn't blackness. It isn't a color you could describe to me. It is purest nothing, and it hides all the secrets of Shadow. The spinning web that holds together the fabric of everything we can comprehend. It speaks to me without words, guides me without a path. The Shadow knows all and IS all. Black madness? No. This is total enrichment of the soul.'

"He kept coming back, Mad Shadow, and I didn't want him to. Not at first. But he began to show me things. How to connect with the void. How a special kind of meditation reveals the Shadow behind sight that he spoke so fondly of. The first time I saw it, it was just shapes like pure blackness in the dark. But soon, it began to communicate with me. Have you ever heard the voice of God? This is what it is—the Midas Touch. I began to experience it all. All of the pleasures of the universe, complete fulfillment and enrichment of the soul without ever leaving my house. In the presence of the Infallible Hand, I felt like an ant trying to understand the complexities and sophistication of the human race. Unfathomable, but something inside of the soul stirs, like intuition. Something you can't even imagine is communicating with you without you knowing how. We spent so long looking out into the cosmos for answers, for secrets, that we became ignorant of the very fabric of time and space surrounding us, created for us, limiting us. But I am trapped within this bestial prison no longer. I can see the stars for what they are. Just a facade hung there that we may play our parts in the panto with little more than vague wonder for the beyond. Make no mistake, my friend; the gods are not out there beyond the universe. They're right here. They are the pages. They are the ink. It is so much more than we ever could've imagined."

I sat across the room from Bradford, this utter madman, trying to make any of the pieces of this puzzle fit. What on earth was he on about? And how did he ever come to be in such a state? He answered.

"I was deceived," he said. "For knowing secrets on a cosmic level have their consequences, and the gods are just as ruthless as they are cunning. Mad Shadow taught me how to meditate and connect with the gods. He did not tell me just how addictive being within the presence of the void is, or how much life energy it costs to experience the divine. An hour of meditation costs about a year of life, and the older I became in body, the stronger Mad Shadow and I became in mind. So I sit here before you, my friend, my time desperately short, understanding deathless knowledge that I could not possibly explain to any one of you, and that little boy with no eyes, a deceiving spirit, continues to push me into the void…and I relish every second of it. I continue to thirst for it. It will take me soon."

He was staring at his drink again. A fire was glowing

within his eyes. Those eyes that for an instant I recognized as my friend's. They snapped up at me, and with wild panic within him, the real Bradford I knew was there.

"Get out of here," he snapped. "Please. Go."

The face fell sullen and uncanny again, as if something inside had taken back control. The fire in the eyes was gone, replaced by the milky whites.

"You must try it," he said.

"Why would I want to do that?" I asked. "After what it has done to you? How is it worth it?"

"Oh, it is absolutely worth it," he said. "To dry out one's corporeal form and become one with the outer being who hosts us? It is a bliss you can only imagine. Come. I will show you."

Bradford stood up, his shriveled frame looming over me in the firelight, arms reaching out for my face. I'd had more than enough. I told him I'd think about it, but for now, it was time for him to leave. He didn't budge.

"Not until you have tasted the Shadow's delights."

Without betraying my inner terror, I laid a hand on his shoulder and looked him deep in the eyes.

"Okay. I will try it if you insist. But only if you toast first. It's unsettling to me that you haven't touched your port."

He eyed me, an unspoken impasse. The eyes fell upon the highball glass, and he hissed at me. "Very well."

He picked up the glass and downed the liquid in one gulp with no reaction. Not like Bradford at all. He loved his port, but he would only sip.

The recognizable face returned for a second, and he coughed, letting a dirty cream spume slip from his mouth. He drew in a deep breath, licking the grotesque foam on his lips, and managed a final word: "Go."

The man's face twisted and convulsed, then he crumpled to the floor and lay there stone dead. Absolutely still, a slow stream of what looked like sand and river foam leaking from his nose and mouth. I stood there aghast, my hand still held where his shoulder had been. I took a step back and fumbled for my phone. Bradford's jacket began to quiver. Was he still breathing? I bent down to feel his neck for a pulse when a puddle of sandy foam spilled from his clothing, large sand ticks hopping out along with that wretched smell of river decay. A small gray-blue hand reached out from behind his lapel. The fire went out. An icy fright crawled down my spine, jellifying my legs as I fell onto my back. I shuffled backward. Two white hands with blackened nails came from within my friend's chest. The thing plopped out of his clothing and lay there, fetal on the floor, my friend's spine sticking out of its neck. The thing stretched out, and the spinal column came away from it. Then I saw the face. Oh, that face. The face of a dead boy with eyeless sockets and an aura of pure evil. The ghast crawled away from Bradford's clothing, and his body lay there deflated. This naked, horrible ghost-boy thing crawled across the floor toward me, those voidal sockets locked on me, wanting to drag me away. There's no fucking way. I sprang to my feet in a burst of last-ditch adrenaline and hightailed it out of the house and into the car, spinning and sliding on the ice as I took off into the night.

The police say I am a person of interest. I don't know if

that means I'm actually a suspect or not, but I have to stay local. Seems I spoiled a lot of Christmas dinners that night. I am living with my brother across town while they pull my place apart. They found Bradford's skin at my house with his intact skull and a section of spine. From the neck down, he was completely empty. The rest of him was found at his house, a small place just outside town. The autopsy results said he likely drowned in salt water. I have no idea. I have no idea what happened to my friend. I can't forget that boy, though. The one without eyes I saw in the rear-view mirror. Standing at the front door of my house, watching me as if it could see me plain as day. I backed into him. Heard his little body break under the wheels of my car. I watched his body lying there, still, as I pulled away. They never found it, of course. Nobody believes my story. Why would they? It's insane. Hell, I don't believe it. I know what I saw, though. And I know what I see now, at night, in my dreams. It was a dreadful Christmas.

ABOUT THE AUTHORS

Janet Alcorn is a librarian who launched a lifelong dream by Googling, "how to write a novel," on a slow afternoon at work. Since that fateful day, her short stories have been published in the 2021 *Deathlehem* anthology, the Storyteller Series podcast, and the Arizona Authors Association annual literary magazine. She's currently seeking an agent for her first novel and revising her second. When she isn't wrangling cantankerous fictional people or earning a living, Janet gardens, listens to 80s rock at ear-bleeding volume, and hangs out in Tucson with her husband, son, and Venus flytraps. She's lived in 5 states and 3 time zones, the majority of the time in Northern California (where she was born and raised) and Portland, Oregon. Learn more about Janet at janetalcorn.com or follow her on Twitter (@ja_alcorn) or Facebook (facebook.com/authorjanetalcorn).

Bam Barrow is an East Anglian-based writer of occult fiction with an unquenchable thirst for the dark, mysterious and extremes of human behavior. Co-editor for *Black Shadow Lit*, Bam is also known for his photography, filmmaking, and as a musician. His band Raining Colour have released their first album Realms available to download from all major streaming outlets.

Much of **Evan Baughfman**'s writing success has been as a playwright, his original plays finding homes in theaters worldwide. A number of his scripts are published through Heuer Publishing, YouthPLAYS, Next Stage Press, and Drama Notebook. A resident of Southern California, Evan is a playwriting member of PlayGround-L.A., and is also a company member with Force of Nature Productions. Evan has also found success writing horror fiction, his work found recently in anthologies by Improbable Press, 4 Horsemen Publications, and No Bad Books Press. Evan's short story collection, *The Emaciated Man and Other Terrifying Tales from Poe Middle School*, is published through Thurston Howl Publications. His novella, *Vanishing of the 7th Grade*, is available through D&T Publishing. More info is available at amazon.com/author/evanbaughfman

R.A. Clarke is a former police officer turned author/illustrator living in Portage la Prairie, Manitoba. When she's not chasing after her children, she's writing. Her multi-genre short fiction has won various international short story competitions including the Writer's Games, Writers Weekly 24-Hour Contest, and Red Penguin Books' Humour Contest. She was also named a 2021 finalist for both the Futurescapes Award and Dark Sire Award. R.A.'s work has been published by Sinister Smile Press, Cloaked Press LLC, and Polar Borealis Magazine, among others. Visit: www.rachael clarkewrites.com.

Dane Cobain (High Wycombe, UK) is a publisher author, freelance writer, and (occasional) poet and musician with a passion for language and learning. When he's not working on his next release, he can be found reading and reviewing books while trying not to be distracted by Wikipedia. His releases include *No Rest for the Wicked* (supernatural thriller), *Eyes Like Lighthouses When the Boats Come Home* (poetry), *Former.ly* (literary fiction), *Social Paranoia* (non-fiction), *Come On Up to the House* (horror), *Subject Verb Object* (anthology), *Driven* (crime/detective), *The Tower Hill Terror* (crime/detective), *Meat* (horror), *Scarlet Sins* (short stories), *The Lexicologist's Handbook* (non-fiction), and *The Leipfold Files* (crime/detective). His short stories have also been anthologized in *Local Haunts* (R. Saint Clare, ed.), *We're Not Home* (Cam Wolfe, ed.), *Served Cold* (R. Saint Clare and Steve Donoshue, eds.), and *Eccentric Circles* (Cynthia Brackett-Vincent, ed.).

Liam Hogan is an award-winning short story writer, with stories in *Best of British Science Fiction and in Best of British Fantasy* (NewCon Press). He's been published by *Analog, Daily Science Fiction*, and Flame Tree Press, among others. He helps host Liars' League London, volunteers at the creative writing charity Ministry of Stories, and lives and avoids work in London. More details at http://happyendingnotguaranteed.blogspot.co.uk

James Jenkins is a Suffolk UK based writer of gritty realism and noir. He has work published in *Bristol Noir, Punch-Riot Mag, Bullshit Lit, ROI Faineant, A Thin Slice of Anxiety and Punk Noir Magazine*. One of his short stories appears in *Grinning Skull Press* Anthology –*'Twas the Fright Before Christmas in Deathlehem*. His debut novel *Parochial Pigs* is available on *Amazon* and published by *Alien Buddha Press*. The sequel *Sun Bleached Scarecrows* is due for release by *Anxiety Press* in early 2023. Follow James @ twitter.com/JamesCJenkins4, or visit him on Facebook: www.facebook.com/JamesJenkinsAuthor/ or on his website: jamesjenkinswriter.wordpress.com/

D.J. Kozlowski lives in Connecticut, works in New York City, and meanders from daydream to daydream in the interim. Although striving to see the good in everyone, D.J. often writes about the bad—it's cathartic. D.J.'s work has found a home in various corners of the internet, including *Daily Science Fiction* and *Every Day Fiction*. Find more at https://djkozlowski.weebly.com/.

Nathan D. Ludwig is an author, filmmaker, and fest runner. His debut novel, *Love Potion #666*, was released in 2022 by D&T Publishing. He's had short stories published in Grinning Skull Press, Timber Ghost Press, and D&T Publishing. His first short story collection, *The Comfy-Cozy Nihilist*, is coming soon from GenreBlast Books. He loves Warren Zevon, independent pro-wrestling, Asian genre cinema, and a good spicy ramen. He lives with his wife and their two daughters just outside of Richmond, VA.

Mike Marcus is a horror and dark fantasy author living in Pittsburgh, Pa., with his wife, Amy, and German Shepherd-mutt, Tucker. This is Mike's third appearance in the *Deathlehem* series. Mike has contributed stories to nearly a dozen anthologies, including *A Pile of Bodies, A Pile of Heads: Let the Bodies Hit the Floor Vol. 1*, from Sinister Smile Press, *The Jewish Book of Horror* from Denver Horror Collective, *Dark Nature*, from Macabre Ladies, and *The Modern Deity's Guide to Surviving Humanity*, from Zombies Need Brains, Inc. Mike is a US Army veteran and graduate of Frostburg State University, in Frostburg, Md. Follow Mike on Facebook at mikemarcus. author and on Twitter at @mikemarcus77.

Villimey Mist has always been fascinated by vampires and horror, ever since she watched *Bram Stoker's Dracula* and when she was traumatized by the chestburster scene in *Aliens* as a curious little girl. She loves to read and create stories that pop into her head unannounced. She's had her short stories appear in various anthologies, including *Of Cauldrons and Cottages, Krampus Tales: A Killer Anthology, Campfire Macabre, The One Who Got Away: Women in Horror Vol. 3, Far from Home, Were-Tales, Slash-her, Hex-periments, Blood in The Soil, Terror on The Wind: A Horror Western anthology*. She has written *Nocturnal*, a vampire horror series with 3 books already published since 2016. Her short story collection, *As the Night Devours Us*, was published in 2022 by St Rooster Books. She lives in Iceland with her husband and two cats, Skuggi and RoboCop, and is often busy drawing, watching the latest shows on Netflix or staying way too long on Twitter @VillimeyS. VILLIMEY'S SOCIAL MEDIA LINKS: Amazon Author Page: www.amazon.com/Villimey-Mist/e/B07L5367H2/ref=ntt_dp_epwbk_0; Goodreads: www.goodreads.com/author/show/18668534. Villimey_Mist; Twitter: @VillimeyS; Instagram: www.instagram.com/fangs.and.light; YouTube: www.youtube.com/channel/UCu-ZwdfYfk9dlGyG9_S2j6A; Blog: https://www.villimeymistauthor.com

Paul O'Neill is an award-winning short story writer from Fife, Scotland. As an Internal Communications professional, he fights the demon of corporate-speak on a daily basis. His works have been published in Crystal Lake's *Shallow Waters*, Eerie River's *It Calls From The Doors* anthology, the NoSleep podcast, Scare Street's *Night Terrors* series, the Horror Tree, and many other publications. A forthcoming novella, *The Other Side of Midnight*, is being published in Leamington Press's Novella Express series. His second collection of short stories, *With Dust Shall Cover* is out now. You can find him sharing his love of short stories on Twitter @PaulOn1984.

Lisa H. Owens, a former humorist columnist, resides in North Texas with two rescue dogs and a sole-surviving air plant named Claw. Her work's been published on ezines and in numerous anthologies and she was listed as one of *Black Ink Fiction's Women in Horror, 2022.* Lisa's stories are often inspired by true events, sometimes including private jokes and family nicknames. Visit her website: www.lisahowens.com

Dino Parenti is a writer of dark literary and speculative fiction. He is the winner of the first annual *Lascaux Review* flash fiction contest and is featured in the Anthony Award winning anthology *Blood on the Bayou.* His short-fiction collection, *Dead Reckoning and Other Stories*, is out with Crystal Lake Publishing. He lives in Los Angeles.

Matt Starr is from North Carolina. His two most recent books, *Prepare to Meet Thy God* and *Things That Don't Belong in the Light*, are also titles from Grinning Skull Press.

D.S. Ullery is an author of short horror fiction as well as a cartoonist. He's published two collections of horror fiction and currently both writes and draws an ongoing humor comic panel titled "Goulash". He lives in South Florida with his feline roommate Jason, an increasingly cranky black cat who was born on Friday the 13th.

Grinning Skull Press Presents

The Place where it all started

O Little Town of Deathlehem

Twas the fright before Christmas,
And all through the town,
Not a soul stirred,
No one dared make a sound…

Welcome to Deathlehem, where…
…Krampus, not Santa, brings the holiday cheer…
…the lights on the tree, so festive and bright, skitter and crawl and possess
a lethal bite…
…malicious little elves, not a jolly one, know if you've been naughty—or
nice…
and
…family gatherings often turn deadly.
So enter…if you dare.

A collection of 23 holiday horrors benefiting the Elizabeth Glaser Pediatric
AIDS Foundation.

Return to Deathlehem

Slay bells ring,
Kids are screaming,
In the lane, snow is blood stained.
There's nowhere to hide,
Krampus has arrived,
There'll be feasting in a winter slaughter land...

Welcome back to Deathlehem,
...where the office Secret Santa proves more dangerous than a game of
Russian roulette...
...where trips to Grandma's house are fraught with danger...
...where a traditional Nutcracker poses a threat to a pair of would-be
thieves...
...where ghosts of Christmases past haunt and take vengeance against the
living...
...and many more!

Twenty-three more tales of holiday horror benefiting the Elizabeth Glaser
Pediatric AIDS Foundation

Deathlehem Revisited

You make this a Christmas to dismember,
Killing feelings in the middle of December,
Strangers meet, one unwillingly surrenders,
Oh, what a Christmas to dismember...

Welcome back to Deathlehem...again!...
where a mutated Christmas has a taste for human flesh...
...where a trio of trespassers are terrorized at an abandoned holiday-
themed tourist attraction...
...where elves thrive on the torment delivered to others...
...where holiday shopping drives people to commit extreme acts of
violence...
...and many more!

Twenty-three more tales of holiday horror to benefit The Elizabeth Glaser
Pediatric AIDS FoundationPediatric AIDS Foundation

The Shadow over Deathlehem

O little town of Deathlehem,
Within you death doth lie!
Beneath thy deep and rutted streets
Tormented souls do cry.
Yet in your dark streets shineth
A cold and ghostly light.
The fears and tears of all the years
Are met in thee tonight.

Well, here we are again, folks — Deathlehem …
… where Krampus isn't the only creature to fear
when the holiday draws near…
… where holiday treats aren't safe to eat …
… where not even the apocalypse will keep
people from celebrating the holiday …
… where even Chanukah isn't safe to celebrate …

Twenty-five more tales of holiday horror to benefit
The Elizabeth Glaser Pediatric AIDS Foundation

O Unholy Night in Deathlehem

Said the little child to his mother dear,
do you hear what I hear
Shrieking through the night, father dear,
And do you see what I see
A cry, a scream, blood coloring the snow
And a laugh as evil as sin
And a laugh as evil as sin

Well, folks, looks like we're back in Deathlehem, where…
…Santa's gift turns a mindless horde of bargain-hungry shoppers
into…well… a horde of hungry shoppers…
…defective toys aren't just dangerous; they're deadly…
…holiday ornaments prove to be absolutely captivating—permanently…
…those ugly Christmas sweaters are to die for…

Twenty-five more tales of holiday horror to benefit
The Elizabeth Glaser Pediatric AIDS Foundation

A Tree Lighting in Deathlehem

In Deathlehem, the masses hail
The Blessed one was born
They gathered in a manger
On that black December morn
Among the screams of Mother Mary
The Babe from her torn
Dark tidings corrupting hope and joy

So rest merry gentlemen
Let Satan's child play
Burning bodies light this Christmas tree
In Deathlehem today

Welcome back, folks. And for you newbies wondering where you are, that would be Deathlehem…
…where enemies meet on the battlefield to set aside their differences on this holiest of nights—only to be tormented by a legendary she-demon…
…where irons bars won't keep brothers from spending Christmas with their mother—much to her dismay…
…where the search for the perfect tree turns into a bloody nightmare…
…where an imprisoned evil has a young couple and their daughter wishing they'd stayed at home for the holidays…

Twenty-five more tales of holiday horror to benefit
The Elizabeth Glaser Pediatric AIDS Foundation

Santa Claws is Coming to Deathlehem

Hark hear the howls
Blood-chilling howls
Tear heads away
Eviscerate

The Claws is here
Relishing fear
Rends young and old
Weak and the bold

Welcome back to Deathlehem...

...where the holiday is exceptionally kind to an ancient witch...
...where the office Secret Santa takes a deadly twist...
...where a serial killer paints the town red with his countdown to Christmas...
...where children confront Santa after years of disappointment...
...and many more!

Twenty-five more tales of holiday horrors to benefit
The Elizabeth Glaser Pediatric AIDS Foundation

The Colour Out of Deathlehem

F' ah'n'gha mgep'ai ya
Pa rum pum pum pum

A vulgtmor c' need
Pa rum pum pum pum

l' mgahnnn way llll f'
Pa rum pum pum pum

The r'luhhor ephainogephaii
Pa rum pum pum pum,
Rum pum pum pum,
Rum pum pum pum

Gn'th'bthnk f' ephaineed
Pa rum pum pum pum
Ahhai f' nog

Welcome back to Deathlehem, where...
...the holiday décor has a voracious appetite...
...your past can—and will—come back to haunt you...
...a one-night stand leads to an unexpected climax...
...a son brings home more than nightmares from his tour of duty...
...and many more!

Twenty-four more tales of holiday horrors to benefit
The Elizabeth Glaser Pediatric AIDS Foundation

Made in the USA
Middletown, DE
06 September 2024

59821523R00197